PENGUIN BOOKS

T0166950

Sixty SUMMERS

Amanda Hampson grew up in rural New Zealand. She spent her early twenties travelling, finally settling in Australia in 1979 where she now lives in Sydney's Northern Beaches. Writing professionally for more than 20 years, she is the author of two non-fiction books, numerous articles, and novels *Two for the Road*, *The Olive Sisters*, *The French Perfumer* and *The Yellow Villa*.

Sixty
SUMMERS

AMANDA HAMPSON

PENGUIN BOOKS

PENGUIN BOOKS

UK | USA | Canada | Ireland | Australia
India | New Zealand | South Africa | China

Penguin Books is part of the Penguin Random House group of companies
whose addresses can be found at global.penguinrandomhouse.com.

Penguin
Random House
Australia

First published by Viking, 2019
This edition published by Penguin Books, 2020

Copyright © Amanda Hampson, 2019

The moral right of the author has been asserted.

Cover design by Nikki Townsend Design
Text design by Samantha Jayaweera © Penguin Random House Australia Pty Ltd
Cover photographs: Eiffel Tower by Marcello Landolfi/Shutterstock;
bougainvillea by Christian Camus/Shutterstock; background by Slobo/Getty;
floral bouquet by Anastasia Lembrik/Shutterstock
Typeset in Adobe Garamond by Midland Typesetters, Australia

Printed and bound in Australia by Griffin Press, part of Ovato, an accredited
ISO AS/NZS 14001 Environmental Management Systems printer

A catalogue record for this
book is available from the
National Library of Australia

ISBN 978 0 14379 212 3

penguin.com.au

MIX
Paper from
responsible sources
FSC® C009448

To Bronwyn, a friend for life.

Part One

The Call

Chapter One

Oblivious to the golden morning awakening around her, the chorus of birdsong and the heckling of kookaburras in the ghost gums, Maggie swam laps of the pool. As she alternated laps of freestyle and breaststroke, beyond the pool the bay was a sheen of light, and white yachts bobbed gently at anchor. But her thoughts were focused on the day ahead. She was dreading this afternoon's meeting with her husband, Kristo, and his three brothers. There was always shouting at these meetings, and today would be worse than usual.

As Maggie pulled herself out of the pool, she looked up towards the house and noticed that her mother-in-law, Yia-yiá, was already busy sweeping the deck. She was at war with fallen leaves and couldn't understand why Kristo and Maggie wouldn't see sense and remove all the offending trees. It was a month since Yia-yiá had moved in and already it felt like years. Maggie had only half-believed Kristo when he said it would 'just be for a week or so'. Respite, he had called it. His mother had been in some sort of conflict with another resident at the retirement village, and they all needed time out. Privately, Maggie thought it was all part of Yia-yiá's master plan. She'd never wanted to live in a retirement village, and Kristo, who craved his mother's approval, didn't take much convincing to bring her home.

Maggie sat on the edge of the pool and felt the rivulets of water trickling down her arms. Lately she'd had the strangest sensation that she was living someone else's life and she couldn't quite work out how she had got here. One minute she was a laughing girl with her life ahead of her, the next thing she knew, she had hurtled through time and arrived here. She looked out across the glittering bay to the open sky beyond and wondered for the hundredth time if it was all worth it. She already knew the answer. She could barely remember a period in her life when she had been so deeply unhappy.

In the years when they were establishing the family construction business, although stressful, it was also exciting, and she hadn't questioned their direction in life. Family meetings were celebrations of new contracts won and projects completed; of money in the bank. In those days, the whole family would come together to eat and to talk. She got on well with her sisters-in-law and, within a few short years, there were cousins who played together. That was long before they lived here in Bayview in Sydney's Northern Beaches. Back then they filled a modest brick house in the inner-city suburb of Marrickville. But everyone knew that the Dimitratos family were a dynasty in the making, and Maggie believed herself to be an integral member of the team.

As the financial controller, Maggie liked to consider the business in terms of balance and buoyancy. In the beginning, it was like a rowboat with too many passengers and everyone trying to seize control. As the business flourished, the boat got bigger, more comfortable and stable. These days, she seemed to be the only one who fully understood that it could still sink. If a project the size of the one they would discuss this afternoon went under, it had the potential to take them all down with it.

Today, the only thing Maggie could look forward to was packing an overnight bag and getting into her car. She would then turn off her phone and enjoy an hour of peace while she drove to Rose's place. As they did every year, Rose and Maggie would prepare a simple meal, and Fran would join them via a video call from London. They would celebrate forty years of friendship and, for a few sweet hours, become the laughing girls they once were.

Right now, that seemed too many hours away.

She wrapped a towel around her and wandered up to the house.

On the bedside table, her phone showed four missed calls from Anthea, and three from Elena, and she felt the familiar twist in her gut. It could be something quite small, she told herself. Elena was probably calling on Anthea's behalf. It was a twin thing she had got used to; right from when they were babies, her daughters tended to wind each other up rather than calm each other down. She really wanted a shower before having to deal with whatever was going on but the phone rang again and she took the call.

'Mum! Where *were* you? I've called you a *thousand* times!' Anthea sobbed.

Now Elena was calling at the same time.

'Hold on! Just give me a second.' Maggie put on her reading glasses and messaged that she'd call Elena back. Her anxiety was diminishing by the second – they were both fine. It was just a fresh drama that would be resolved in either minutes or hours.

'Okay, what is it, darling?' Maggie asked in her kind, under-standing voice. 'Try and calm down . . . Could you blow your nose? I can't really understand you.'

Anthea spoke between shuddering sobs. 'I need to come home. I'm getting a divorce.'

Maggie wondered if there was any way that she could fob her daughter off until she'd had that shower. Unlikely. She switched to speaker and put the phone on the bed while she peeled her wet bathers off and put on a cotton robe. 'All newlyweds have their ups and downs, Thea. You just need to talk things through with Aaron, calmly and sensibly. You can work it out. Why is Elena ringing me too? What's her involvement?'

'About the divorce, obviously! Are you even listening? *Shit!*'

'Darling, this is between you and Aaron. Please don't involve your sister. He doesn't need you two ganging up on him.'

'Ganging up?' Anthea screeched. 'You haven't even *asked* what he's *done*.'

Maggie took a deep breath. 'Do I really need to know? Think about this, please. I don't really want to be involved in your mari-tal disputes. I especially don't want to know the details —'

'He filmed us having sex and put it online.' Anthea waited breathlessly for her mother's reaction.

Only a year ago Anthea was radiant in a froth of white tulle, walking up the aisle of the Holy Trinity on her father's arm. Now this. The little shit.

Maggie had never really liked Aaron, but having been treated as an interloper herself, she had made it her business to welcome him into the family. Yia-yiá always maintained that he wasn't good enough for Anthea but Maggie dismissed this dislike of outsiders as un-Australian; a throwback attitude imported from the old country. Yia-yiá referred to him as a *vlákas*: an all-purpose Greek insult that in this context translated to an idiot. She was turning out to be right. What the hell was he thinking?

The horror of her beautiful daughter's private moments being shared around the globe was overtaken by her realisation of the widening circle of affected parties. Kristo would not deal well with this – and nor should he – but his brothers would go crazy. She heard herself whispering, 'Shit . . . shit . . . shit . . .' as each new thought occurred to her. How could they get the video taken down? Was this a criminal matter? Police or lawyer? Or both? Yia-yiá would blame Maggie, always insisting she was too lenient with the girls. Kristo would blame her too. They would all blame her.

'Mum, say something! It's disgusting and the comments . . . they're so *filthy* . . .' Anthea began wailing loudly.

'Don't look at the comments. Don't tell your father. Don't do anything. Just wait a minute and let me think, for goodness sake.'

Anthea bawled, hiccupping like a child, and Maggie felt her insides being squeezed and twisted, her throat choked with tears. For twenty-seven years she had protected her girls from all the predatory males of the world. She couldn't protect them from this. She couldn't protect them from anything now they were adults.

'What will Yia-yiá say?' Anthea sobbed. 'I could die. I wish I could be swallowed up by a huge earthquake and buried underground.'

The sheer melodrama of this wish brought Maggie back to earth. 'Okay, let's deal with everything when you get here. Do you want me to come and help you? Just bring a few things; we can sort out everything later.'

'Elena's coming over now.'

'Isn't she at the salon today?' asked Maggie.

'It's a family emergency, Mum! You worry about the most stupid things!'

'Listen, darling. I need you to send me a link to the video. I'm not going to look at it but I need to contact our lawyers . . . I won't look, I promise.'

Her phone beeped. Maggie stared at the link as though it radiated danger and she knew that, sooner or later, she would be forced to look at it.

'I'll be here waiting, Thea. We'll get it taken down. Don't worry about it for the moment. Just drive carefully and stay off your phone in the car, *please*. Where's Aaron now?'

'He's gone to his mother's place. I was looking for something on his laptop and found it in the history.'

'Why were you looking in his history? What were you looking for?'

'*Argghhh*, do I have to answer all these questions?' Anthea paused and came to terms with the fact that she did. 'I wanted to see what sort of porn he was watching; that it wasn't anything . . . you know . . . *weird* . . .'

'What? What do you mean by *weird*? Actually, I really don't want to know —'

'Mum, I just need you to fix it. I'm not the criminal.'

'Okay, okay . . . just pack a few things and come over.'

'Fine,' said Anthea and she was gone.

Maggie lay down on the bed. She was cold from the pool and not drying herself properly. She reached over and pulled the bedcover over her for a moment of comfort. Possibly the last today.

Yia-yiá appeared in the doorway. 'Why you lie down? Swim. Lie down. You sick? The boys come today. We cook now. *Páme!*'

Páme – let's go – was one of Yia-yiá's favourite expressions, as if everything could be solved by moving. Maggie didn't want to move, and she especially didn't want to start cooking. Yia-yiá accepted that Maggie had an important role in the company, but didn't see that role as superseding the vital task of feeding her sons. It was assumed Maggie would fulfil both obligations equally. Yia-yiá adored her boys, and they were inordinately proud of her. At eighty-two years old, she could barely read or write but had all her own teeth, sonar-like hearing and twenty-twenty vision. She didn't miss a thing.

More than with all her other grandchildren, Yia-yiá was besotted with the twins. They were the first born, and having twins was special and almost magical to her. It would completely break her heart if she found out what had happened.

Maggie would have to cancel on Rose and Fran this evening – there was no way out of it. Tears of self-pity stung her eyes. Her friends asked nothing of her apart from this one time together, once a year. One time when she could relax and be herself, not be in charge, and not be making everyone else feel okay. The idea of letting her friends down was devastating. Rose's husband, Peter, had gone away for the weekend so the two women could have the house to themselves. And Fran looked forward to this so much.

The family meeting was set for four o'clock. Maggie made a mental note to check there was plenty of beer in the downstairs fridge. Maybe she could present her case for cancelling next week's concrete pour, then leave them to argue it out and be on the road to Rose's by five. She'd have to be absolutely uncompromising

9

about escaping. Right now, all she felt was a crushing grief at the public exposure of her daughter's intimate moments.

'Okay, Yia-yiá, *mia stigmí* – one moment.' Maggie only had a few Greek phrases and used them routinely to reassure Yia-yiá that, even though she wasn't the preferred Greek daughter-in-law, she was still a good daughter-in-law. She closed her eyes and felt the old woman's breath on her face.

'You look sick, *paidí mou*.'

Maggie always felt a softening towards her mother-in-law when she called her *paidí mou* – my child. She could be a brittle, unforgiving, stubborn and demanding old witch, but then she got to you when you least expected it.

'I'm fine. I'll have a shower and be down in a moment.' Maggie rolled over towards the wall and pulled the bedcover with her. She felt so cold. She sensed Yia-yiá was still there and waited for her to realise she was dismissed.

'I calls Kristaki *mou* now.'

'No, Yia-yiá, please – he's busy. Just leave it. I'm fine.' There was a moment of silence followed by a shriek and a torrent of Greek. Maggie rolled over to see Yia-yiá staring at her mobile phone screen, her face distorted with horror.

'Yia-yiá! No! Oh, God!' Maggie leapt off the bed, caught her foot in the covers and fell heavily on her knees. Yia-yiá let the phone slip from her fingers to the floor. She looked down at Maggie, her eyes full of tears, her mouth forming words that never came out before she rushed from the room. Maggie could hear her ragged sobs all the way down the hall until the door of her room slammed shut.

Not bothering to get off her knees, Maggie picked up the phone. What she could see, even without her glasses, was that

Anthea, astride Aaron, was looking towards the camera, which was set to one side. Puzzled, Maggie grabbed her glasses from the bedside table, slipped them on and saw in sharp focus that Anthea was not only looking at the camera but pouting like a sassy porn star. After a moment's consideration, Maggie deleted the message. There was no point in going to their lawyers with this. It was a timely reminder of how little she understood her daughters, let alone their relationships with men.

Maggie had first set eyes on Kristo in the summer of 1982. She was dancing with Rose at Selina's in Coogee. Michael Hutchence cavorted about onstage, sighing more than singing, 'I need you tonight . . .' At a gesture from Rose, Maggie had turned to see Kristo standing in the crowd watching her. For years afterwards, when she heard that song, she would feel the same soft falling away in the pit of her stomach. She and Rose used to joke that it was her uterus firing up. She was blindsided by his wide smile, soft eyes and olive skin. He was only just taller than her, thickset with wide shoulders and a gentle masculinity. They danced together, silent and self-conscious. They sat on the beach and talked until sunrise. She was in the second year of her commerce degree, on her way to becoming an accountant. He was in his final year of construction engineering. He told her about his parents, how hard they had worked all these years running a fish shop seven days a week. Kristo had bigger plans for the family and would soon put his education to good use. He joked that they would be a perfect partnership; he planned to build an empire and she could cook the books.

Maggie had gone home and called her then boyfriend to break up with him; he'd become redundant overnight. She knew enough Greek and Italian girls to realise that she would present a dilemma for Kristo because of his family. His mother would never approve of her but Maggie wasn't willing to be simply a conquest. She made him work for her, and she made him wait. She'd never suffered from a lack of suitors but she knew that Kristo was the man for her.

Back then, Yia-yiá was Mrs Dimitratos, all four boys still lived at home and Kristo's father was in charge of everything. But once Kristo set his mind on something, things happened quickly and within a year they were engaged. Kristo was the eldest son and somehow managed to persuade his mother that Maggie's qualifications, to some extent, compensated for the fact that she wasn't Greek, and she was grudgingly accepted into the fold.

In the early days, his extended family had seemed like a dream come true for Maggie. Two years earlier, her own small family had splintered when her parents split up. Her father had recently remarried, and family occasions were increasingly fraught; relationships more fragile.

Kristo's family life was more robust; there was food and more food, sometimes singing and often dancing. They seemed to enjoy nothing more than all being in the same room together. Their family life was like an out-of-control party that never stopped and Maggie was swept along with it all. The engagement party was a riot. The wedding was a year in the planning with extended family coming from around the world to celebrate the first marriage in the Dimitratos family.

Maggie's mother, Celia, although relieved of any financial responsibility for the celebration, found it all quite overwhelming. 'I never imagined anything quite like this for you,' she told Maggie. 'I thought you'd be married barefoot on the beach with a few close friends. It's as though you've signed up for a new religion.'

She wasn't far off the mark. In the first years of marriage, Maggie became a born-again Greek, embracing the culture with the fervour of a convert. She learned to prepare dolmades and moussaka, and her baklava was highly praised. She attempted to learn the language and pushed for them to visit Kythera so that Kristo could get to know his ancestral home. Kristo was bemused by her enthusiasm. Growing up Greek, as the eldest of the four, had been a burden. He thought of himself as Australian – Greek culture was the underpinning of his life and he'd never known anything different. He felt no need to explore or embrace it.

Kristo did his best with Celia, offering to fix this or that and generally being a good son-in-law. Celia liked him but she became reluctant to be involved in the frequent family events that the Dimitratoses insisted she must attend. She later admitted finding these occasions exhausting and intense. Maggie suspected her mother's move to Queensland was, in part, to put some distance between herself and the in-laws, and couldn't blame her.

By the time Anthea and Elena were born, Kristo's younger brothers had finished their trade apprenticeships and were all partners in Dimitratos Constructions. The projects grew increasingly ambitious, with a team of contractors: carpenters, renderers, plasterers, painters, bricklayers, plumbers and electricians. Some Greeks, but many Italians and Eastern Europeans. Fiery arguments, sackings and even brawls were commonplace on construction sites in those days.

Kristo ran the projects while Maggie was in charge of the administration, accounting and payroll. Work was like a religion for the Dimitratoses – children had to fit around it. There was an assumption that Maggie would hand the twins over to Yia-yiá and carry on working. But she resisted. She wanted to be a proper mother, as she saw it. And she and Yia-yiá had conflicting ideas about what was right for babies.

The company was growing so fast, the strain of managing the accounts with its uncertain cashflow and lines of credit was relentless. Maggie had welcomed the advent of computerisation, but never seemed to have enough time to make it truly efficient. She increasingly felt as though the entire Dimitratos empire rested on her shoulders. Kristo's parents had slaved for years over a hot fat fryer and the boys had grown up out the back of the fish shop. Every cent they had accumulated from that enterprise had been invested in this family business.

Her most vivid memory of that period was trying to close off the accounts for the end of financial year; writing the final cheques, figures blurring before her eyes as she battled with the new spreadsheet technology. It must have been 1991, the twins were still babies and waking constantly with colic, day and night. She remembered weeping involuntarily with fatigue. One breast throbbed with mastitis and her hair was coming out in handfuls. She felt utterly alone with her responsibilities. Earlier in the year, they had won their biggest project yet – an industrial estate in Emu Plains. During the week, Kristo and the boys lived in a caravan onsite, and Maggie spent her time calculating the hours until he walked through that door.

There was one night when she felt an overwhelming urge to simply run from the house, desperate to escape the wailing babies. She called Rose and sobbed on the phone. Half an hour later, Rose turned up wearing a coat over her pyjamas and bearing strawberries and chocolate. Peter was at an overseas conference, so Rose had to bring Elliot and Max with her. She tucked the boys into the spare bed, then she and Maggie worked in tandem to calm the fretful babies, only managing an hour or two of sleep before dawn.

Maggie would have liked to take some time off when the twins were babies, but the Dimitratoses were adamant that only a family member could handle the finances. The tax accountant they used was not a blood relative but he was Kytherian, which was the next best thing.

Kristo had wanted his parents to retire and rest but his father, Pappoú, insisted on being involved. He wanted a full report from Maggie at the end of every month but his experience was limited to single-entry bookkeeping. They had never hired contract staff and had always paid workers cash from the till. Having to explain everything to him added to her workload but, as a result, he gained a grudging respect for her business acumen.

Kristo did try to be understanding but his own job was mind-bendingly stressful. These days the company had multiple jobs going, there was hardly a day when something didn't go wrong and he would come in the front door with sparks flying off him. He would take Maggie in his arms and edge her towards the bedroom. Afterwards, he would be calm and loving, his sense of order restored. He would nuzzle her neck and squeeze the excess flesh of her belly and whisper that she was eating too many *bougatses* – which she didn't appreciate. But it was better than the shouting. At his absolute worst, he was capable of ranting for an hour at full volume about some slip-up on a job that would cost them money and venting his frustration at the increasingly large amount of paperwork and legislation and worksite safety. When he was in those moods, she kept her head down and her mouth shut.

It was only when Pappoú became ill and Yia-yiá was busy caring for him that Maggie started to gain some power back. She and Kristo built the house in Bayview; she had a cleaner and a gardener, the girls were at school, the business was more stable and she had more freedom to do a few things that she wanted to do.

When Pappoú finally died, it was clear to Maggie that Yia-yiá had set her sights on living with them at Bayview. She was constantly on the phone or having one of the brothers drive her up for the day, but never seemed to arrange transport home. Maggie was convinced that this problem at the retirement village was Yia-yiá's latest attempt to make Bayview her permanent home.

Maggie walked down the hall and knocked on Yia-yiá's door. There was no response and she opened it slowly. 'Yia-yiá? Are you all right?'

The old woman sat on the bed fingering her prayer beads. She looked up and pointed a gnarled finger at Maggie. 'You faults.'

'I know. I know. *Syngnómi* – I'm sorry,' said Maggie, bowing her head in false contrition. Everything the girls did was her fault. The tight short skirts, obsessive use of their phones, unreliability, tardiness, and even the brief foray into veganism. It was all the fault of the mother – everyone knew it and there was no point denying it.

'Okay, Maggie *mou*. Now you make for fixing. Kristaki – he's can never know. Never. Never.' She shook her head in disbelief. 'That boy – this *vlákas* – he fixing it. You say to him.' She flicked a finger in Maggie's direction to indicate she should do that now.

Maggie scrolled through her contacts and pressed Aaron's number. The call went to voicemail, as she knew it would. She spoke in an even, calm voice. 'Aaron. This is Maggie. If that video is not taken down by the time Kristo gets home, he will be coming to see you. Do it now, please, immediately and —'

Yia-yiá, her mouth a knot of contempt, beckoned for the phone. She held it in front of her between finger and thumb, as if pinching its cheeks – something she inflicted on her sons as required. She let rip with a long and detailed string of invective that would be lost on Aaron since he didn't speak a word of Greek, but he would no doubt get the idea. Maggie wanted to caution her not to threaten him, especially when it was being recorded – they'd had legal problems over the years with the boys behaving in this way. But it was too late for that.

For the rest of the day, Maggie waited for the girls with growing agitation. She often imagined that her life was like an extreme game show where she had to struggle over slippery obstacles and wobbly bridges, cling to moving props and, when the end was in sight, she would be blindsided and thrown into a muddy pool. There were no prizes or cheering crowds at the end, because there was no end. She wanted nothing more than peace and quiet, something that was always just beyond reach.

The twins were only an hour away but the entire day was punctuated by update texts. They were getting a coffee to calm themselves down. Now they were having their nails done for the weekend. Now they were having lunch. She wondered why they sent all this detail. She would prefer a definite arrival time. They still hadn't turned up by the time Kristo and Nico, George and Jerry arrived. Yia-yiá had been cooking all afternoon and the kitchen was in chaos.

In her role as financial controller, Maggie had heard a lot of excuses from property developers over the years and she was convinced there was trouble ahead with Mr Lau, who was currently one of their biggest clients. Years ago they had mainly dealt with Greek, Italian or Yugoslav developers who were tough and volatile but Kristo and his brothers were also tough and volatile and it worked itself out. The Chinese developers were different – more strategic and controlled, and harder to read. Maggie had information from another developer that Mr Lau had fallen out of favour with his backers in China and her intuition told her that he was avoiding meeting with her until after the concrete pour. He probably figured that Dimitratos Constructions was solid enough financially to carry his project while he refinanced and once the pour took place, they would be in too deep to stop work.

Maggie's challenge this afternoon was to convince the directors to cancel Monday's pour and insist on a meeting before proceeding. It wouldn't be easy. The brothers were the builders, managing the projects onsite, and they were driven by unforgiving construction deadlines. When she told them to back off on a project because of a money problem, it was catastrophic. It went against everything they believed in: scheduling and deadlines and the complex interlocking of one trade with another. This afternoon she would present her case. There would be shouting. She felt exhausted thinking about it. She couldn't decide whether to ring Rose now and cancel or try to soldier through. She had her overnight bag packed and, if there was an opportunity, she would slip away.

The meeting went exactly as she envisaged. George blamed her for not having pinned Mr Lau down earlier. Nico defended her. Kristo reminded Nico that it was *his* job to defend his wife.

Maggie attempted to stick to the business at hand and distributed a spreadsheet detailing the impact of three possible timing solutions; this stop-work might go on for weeks if Mr Lau had to find an entirely new financier. They were deep in discussion when Anthea's car pulled into the driveway. Maggie excused herself and went out to meet the girls.

Anthea accepted her mother's embrace. 'Did you talk to the lawyers?' she asked.

'I'm not sure there's any point in talking to them. I've told Aaron to take it down,' said Maggie. 'Come inside, we'll talk about it.'

'What do you mean, there's no point?' demanded Elena, dragging a suitcase out of the car.

'Have you seen it, Elena?' asked Maggie.

'Of course she has. What are you going on about?' said Anthea.

Maggie glanced over her shoulder at the house; she could see Yia-yiá's shadow hovering behind the upstairs louvres.

'Let's just go inside and discuss it privately,' said Maggie, picking up one of three large suitcases. Why, she wondered, were there so many suitcases? 'Elena, you're not moving home as well, are you? Seriously? Why?'

Ignoring the question, Elena dumped her suitcase on the ground as if she were dropping anchor. 'Are you saying there's nothing we can do?'

'All we can do is get it taken down. I understand that you didn't want it put online, Thea, but the way you're playing up to the camera, you clearly knew you were being filmed —'

'You looked at it? You promised! How could you?' Anthea shouted, while Elena shook her head in furious disbelief.

'Doesn't matter,' said Elena. 'Thea didn't know he was going to put it online —'

'I don't get why you felt the need to film yourself in the first place . . . look, let's discuss —'

'So you didn't even call the lawyers,' said Elena.

Maggie took calming breaths through pursed lips. 'It's going to be very difficult to prove . . . I'm just not sure that we want to spend a lot of money and risk bringing it to the attention of the media.'

The girls exchanged looks of wide-eyed outrage. 'It's always about the money with you, isn't it, Mum?' said Elena. She put her arm around Anthea's shoulders in a show of solidarity that Maggie had witnessed too many times over the years.

The unfairness of the accusation stung Maggie to the core. It was Anthea's word against Aaron's. The girls had no idea of the tens of thousands that would be eaten up by lawyers with no result at the end of it. 'You should also know that Yia-yiá has seen it too,' she said.

All colour drained from Anthea's face. She collapsed, sobbing, in Elena's arms.

'You *showed* her?' Elena asked.

'Of course not. She saw it on my phone. It wasn't intentional, I promise.'

'I've *told* you so many times to lock your phone! You're so hopeless. She picks up anyone's phone and just presses random things. Oh my God!' said Elena.

Anthea, her face puffy from crying, lifted her gaze and stared past Maggie, the corners of her mouth tugged down like a two-year-old's. 'Dad!' she sobbed and ran towards Kristo, who stood on the front step wearing an expression of bewilderment as she flung herself into his arms.

Chapter Two

Fran often woke before dawn these days. If there was the faintest glimmer of light in the sky, she felt triumphant, as though she had slept heroically. Today, she was relieved to hear the soft rumble of London traffic, reassuring her that daylight wasn't far away.

She hadn't heard Louis leave. In earlier times, he would make her tea and blow a lingering kiss from the door, as though he could hardly bear to be parted from her. Lately, she had begun to suspect that he slipped away as soon as she fell asleep. He had recently taken to tucking the covers in neatly on his side of the bed, as if to imply that he was never there at all. That was most unlike him. He was a man who left a trail of disorder in his wake. Perhaps he wanted her to get used to the idea that, at some point, the other side of the bed would remain flat and neat indefinitely. That the smell of cigarettes and sweat, the red-wine taste of his mouth, and the comfort of his presence would no longer be part of the fabric of her life. She didn't mind going to sleep alone. It was waking up alone she hated – the dawning realisation of her aloneness . . .

'I don't like upsetting people,' he always told her as an oblique explanation for his lack of commitment. She took this comment to mean that, at some future point in their relationship, there would likely be an upset if she asked too much of him. It seemed to her like a cowardly excuse for not being honest, although she had a particular dislike of people who, under the guise of being honest, were insensitive and disagreeable. Ironically, that description fitted Rose perfectly, and she was one of the people whom Fran loved most in the world.

She wondered where on earth Louis was disappearing to in the night. It made no sense for him to go back to his bleak flat with its empty fridge and unmade bed. It used to be that he would turn up, hook his jacket on the chair and flop onto her sofa, as though he had looked forward to this moment all day. She would pour him a glass of wine (Australian reds were his favourite) and he would tilt his glass in her direction and breathe a great sigh of contentment. 'Home is where the heart is,' he would say. 'And my heart is here, darlin'.' Every time, the same creaky old cliché, like a line from a cheesy country and western song. In five years he'd never actually said he loved her, but she was convinced that this was his way of expressing it and she warmed herself on that tiny flame.

He would unlace his shoes and, tossing his damp socks to one side, rest his soft white feet on the coffee table and tell her about his day while she stirred the pasta or grilled some chops and tossed a salad together. He worked in an insurance office assessing claims and sometimes had amusing stories about outlandish claims and devious claimants. Other times, when he was frustrated, he would describe, in painful detail, his interactions with his knuckled-headed colleagues, and she would wonder how he kept his job at all. Even in his version, he sounded uncompromising and aggressive – particularly for someone who supposedly didn't like upsetting people. According to him, he was one of the company's most valuable assets, having saved them millions of pounds by ferreting out spurious claims. His experience counted for something and he would be there until his retirement.

At some indefinable point, he stopped saying his heart was at home with her and she couldn't help but wonder if it had found a new one. It seemed an extraordinary effort for a man in his mid-sixties, his prime a distant memory – long before she had met him – to go out looking for a new relationship when there was nothing wrong with this one. He wasn't a great catch. He was the exact opposite of a single man in possession of a good fortune. He had never got around to divorcing his wife, Barbara, didn't own his home and would be dependent on his State Pension when he retired. But London was full of older single women who couldn't afford to be fussy if they wanted some company and a warm body in the bed; hair was an optional extra and he did have plenty of that going for him.

These days, when she woke, she seemed to take longer to come into her body. It was as though she was suffering an accumulative fatigue that had gathered momentum. Leaning against the bench, she watched the teabag seep wearily into the boiling water and the milk reluctantly stain the mix. She squeezed the teabag and tossed it in the sink among the unwashed dishes from the evening before. She put the empty wine bottle in the container under the sink to eliminate all reminders of Louis. He always left a shadow of sadness in his wake, the flip side of the brightness she felt when he was coming over. On those days, she smiled at customers in the shop, answering their questions about obscure books and dead authors as brightly as if she had never been asked before. On those days, she would catch sight of her reflection and be struck by her youthful radiance. She could pass for fifty in that frame of mind. If only she could stay in that frame of mind. If only it wasn't dependent on Louis.

She stood at the living-room window and watched a grey dawn emerge from the darkness. She sipped her tea from the mug that had been her favourite for a decade, bought at the V&A Museum on the occasion of an exhibition long since forgotten. It was bone china with a smooth, fine lip and decorated with an elaborate William Morris design. In those years, she had looked over its rim at a few different lovers, all of whom offered potential at the time. It had graced four different addresses. The mug was the constant. But now she saw it had a hairline crack. Louis. He always rinsed out the cups in a slapdash way, sloshing water around in an effort to draw attention to his helpfulness. She felt a pang that this would be her last cup of tea from this mug. If he didn't want to upset people, he shouldn't be so careless.

The big drawback with this flat was its proximity to the main road, although that was the only reason she could afford the rent in this location. Originally a grand Victorian house, it had been hacked up into a dozen flats in the seventies and every flat was a different shape and size, depending on the original rooms. Fran's was a large high-ceilinged drawing room on the first floor with a tiny kitchen off the living room, and a bedroom built into one corner. It was quaint and antiquated, with floorboards that creaked, sash windows that rattled and an odd smell, close and intimate, like the inside of a shoe. The escalating rents meant she had been forced to move further out every few years. It was hard to know where the next downgrade might land her but hopefully somewhere quieter, more peaceful. Somewhere she could open the windows without feeling the traffic was driving right through her living room. She longed to look onto trees or a garden.

In the meantime, she had her indoor garden. Every surface spilled with pots of plants. Some she had grown from cuttings, like the begonias, African violets and baby's tears. She grew sage, mint, parsley, coriander and thyme in old tins on the windowsill. In the larger pots were plants she'd had for years: *Zamioculcas*, *Peperomia*, palms, yukkas and orchids. She made containers from found objects and rescued plants wherever she could, but Louis often commented that her obsession with plants was a drain on her finances. He had a point. She was infatuated with the idea that she could make something grow. These plants satisfied her desire to nurture, they rewarded her care with a new bloom or the unfurling of a bright-green frond, and masked the peculiar smells of this old building.

Today, as she stood at the window and sipped her tea, her view of the swarming cars surging towards the traffic lights was overlaid by a holographic reflection of someone she barely rec-ognised. The shadows cast by the silvered morning light traced vertical lines down her cheeks like delicate scratch marks. She pondered the idea of being clawed by time. She imagined her-self as one day becoming a linocut version of herself, depicted entirely in vertical and horizontal lines. Perhaps that's why Louis had left in the night lately – he couldn't bear to see her crumpled morning face. Never mind that his face was creased and worn and his whiskers bristled in every shade of grey. His hair seemed to be getting darker, so he wasn't beyond vanity. She didn't mind any of that. She loved the soft folds of his cheeks, his pliable skin, his smoky laugh and the way he teased and flirted with her sometimes. She did love him. Not the intoxicated, possessive love of youth. More a deep and forgiving affection. She'd never told him. It was impossible to know how he might react, and she didn't want to put him to the test. The accumulated knowledge acquired from other relationships had made her cautious, hesitant.

It was good that she was up early today. On the other side of the world, in Sydney, Maggie and Rose were meeting up for dinner and would be calling her soon. She would be a remote guest. They did this every year, and she always had a niggling anxiety that once they opened the wine, they might forget about her and just celebrate the anniversary of their friendship with each other. It was silly, she knew. They were the oldest and most devoted friends she had – just so far away.

Fran had met Rose in high school. They were in different classes, but she'd known Rose by sight and reputation. Tall and lanky, she was the girl who accepted dares, gave both boys and teachers cheek and hitched up her gym slip higher than anyone else.

Fran, however, lived in fear of after-school detention, regarding it with the same trepidation as arrest, while Rose had managed to set a record for her consistent attendance there. She was rough and loud, a country girl who lacked finesse and never stepped back from a fight. Fran was in awe of her.

It was Miss Gordon, the deputy headmistress, who brought the two of them together, both pulled out of assembly for chatting, and sent to sit outside her office to await her return. As they watched the hallway for Miss Gordon's lumbering approach, Fran asked Rose, 'Do you think we'll get detention?'

Rose shrugged and, to demonstrate her indifference, got up from her chair, positioned herself in the open doorway of Miss Gordon's office and farted loudly.

Fran heard the squeak of Miss Gordon's rubber-soled shoes advancing down the corridor and, almost fainting with fear, begged Rose to sit down.

A moment later Miss Gordon rounded the corner and was upon them: 'Yes, girls?'

'You sent for us, Miss,' said Rose.

Miss Gordon looked from one to the other. 'Just refresh my memory.'

Fran was about to speak up when Rose cut across her, 'We came top in the English exam. We're here for our merit certificates.'

Miss Gordon looked puzzled for a moment and Fran couldn't believe she would buy it. 'Well done, girls. You'll need to get them from the office and bring them for my signature.'

'Thanks, Miss. We'll do that,' said Rose.

The teacher nodded and dismissed them. Rose grabbed Fran by the hand and tugged her down the corridor, breaking into a run as soon as they were out of sight. Rose was laughing at the success of her ploy. Fran was laughing with relief. It remained a mystery to Fran how they then became friends, but she was eternally grateful for Rose's friendship – it had changed everything for her.

Later, in their early twenties, Fran and Rose had come over to London from Sydney together to have their 'overseas experience', as it was known before the term 'gap year' was invented. They stayed in a run-down B&B in the Hogarth Road near

Earl's Court tube, sharing a saggy bed while they searched for a flat. Both found jobs within a few days, Rose as a barmaid in a nearby pub called the Marquis of Dewberry, and Fran in the accounts office of an advertising agency.

It wasn't long before they realised that they looked like country hicks in their high-waisted flares and platform shoes. They picked up a couple of Laura Ashley floral dresses on sale and immediately felt demure and English, convinced they now fitted in. Every shop they entered was playing Blondie's 'Hanging on the Telephone'. Rose, whose hair was frizzy and untamable, threw out her straightening tongs and adopted a dishevelled Debbie Harry mop. Fran's dark hair was fine and straight and didn't lend itself to many styles other than the short bob that she still wore today.

London was a spinning blur of sights, sounds and smells, overloading their senses with exotic fragrances of spices and curries and the garlic-drenched sweat of hundreds of doner kebabs turning menacingly on the spit; a delicacy they had been warned guaranteed food poisoning and likely death. Exploring the West End, they had clutched each other every time they found themselves on a street familiar from childhood games of Monopoly. Rose even remembered the prices: 'Regent Street £300, Park Lane £350, Mayfair £400.'

Fran felt strangely at home in this cosmopolitan city where English was one of a hundred languages spoken, although sometimes it was difficult to understand their own language. Rose had a talent for mimicry and quickly built up a hilarious repertoire of British accents.

Music flooded their senses, from the eerie wailing of Kate Bush to the shrill harmonies of the Bee Gees (both preferred their old stuff) and everywhere they went they heard the throbbing pulse of steel drums and reggae music. 10cc's 'Dreadlock Holiday' became their anthem, christening anyone they took a shine to as a 'brudder from the gudder'. It was the only time in her life that Fran could remember not caring that she didn't have a boyfriend. Instead she had Rose, who was brave and forthright and decisive, and didn't take shit from anyone. Everything was sharp and vivid and funny. They wore themselves out laughing.

Fresh out of home, they were unprepared for the ordeal of flat-hunting in this huge and labyrinthine city. Every day they checked the papers and perused the handwritten notices in the window of the corner shop. In the evenings they queued up with twenty or more other hopefuls: a few Brits and Irish but mostly Pakistanis, Indians and West Indians. At the lower end of the market, landlords would give the place to the first person who could hand over cash for two weeks' rent. The rest were turned away. They soon realised they couldn't afford Earl's Court and instead moved their search to Shepherd's Bush and Acton and then in the other direction to Battersea and Clapham. It was hard to find the time to fit flat-hunting in with work. It was exhausting being constantly lost, their London A to Z directory soon crushed and creased from use.

Rose's boss, Mr Ainsworth, who was like a caricature of a British publican with glossy red cheeks, a bulbous nose and a big round belly, mentioned that he knew a Mrs Bishop with a flat to rent nearby. She didn't advertise the place because she didn't care for strangers, which was hardly encouraging. He told Rose he would give her the address and a reference, if she gave him a kiss. Rose declined, explaining that she had infectious mononucleosis (one of her proven strategies) and it could infect him through his pores, so he should be careful not to make skin contact with her at all. He must have felt sorry for her because he gave her the address anyway. Sometime later, he offered her ten pounds to kiss a customer he had a grudge against, which she did, finding an excuse to give the man a smacker on the cheek. She spent the tenner on a pair of high-heeled leather boots that concertinaed flatteringly around the ankles, and Fran felt a bit jealous, never quite sure whether she envied the boots themselves or Rose's chutzpah.

Mrs Bishop wore her hair in tight grey curls pinned flat to her head with bobby pins and further reinforced by a hair net. She looked Fran and Rose over suspiciously and stood back to allow them entry to her hallway which was dark, the air dense with the smell of pine disinfectant. She opened the door into a dark downstairs bedroom. There were twin beds covered with faded green candlewick bedspreads, a combined dressing table and wardrobe, and a small hotplate on a table. 'Share bathroom's on the landing. You can use the laundry out the back on Saturdays, otherwise there's a laundromat round the corner,' said Mrs Bishop.

'What do you think, Frances?' Rose asked, her tone artificially polite.

Fran found it difficult to believe it was such an effort to rent something so awful. They currently shared a bathroom with other guests at the B&B, so weren't as put off by this inconvenience as they might have been a few weeks earlier, but the room was so dreary.

'It's quite nice,' said Fran, concerned about offending both Mrs Bishop and Mr Ainsworth.

'There's plenty of others who'll take it in a flash,' said Mrs Bishop, nodding her head towards the imaginary queue outside her door. 'I prefer English people, but I don't mind Australians. No Jews, though. I don't take them. And no men allowed in the place. You can smoke in your room but no drunken parties. That's the problem with Australians. They're as bad as the Irish with the drink.'

Later, over a pint at the Marquis, Fran wasn't so much angry as repulsed by the thought of sharing a house, let alone a bathroom, with such an odious person.

Rose seethed with indignation. 'Is it even legal to discriminate like that, and so brazen about it too? I'm pretty sure back home you could report someone like that to . . . I don't know . . . someone. It's disgusting.'

Mr Ainsworth came over to their table, his eyes roving over Fran hungrily. 'How did you go with Mrs B?'

'No luck, I'm afraid,' said Rose. 'She didn't care for Fran's religious affiliations.'

He nodded as though this was perfectly reasonable. 'She's a character. Shame. She keeps a clean house, that one. I'll put my thinking cap back on,' he said, winking at Fran.

As he walked back to the bar, Rose murmured, 'Why doesn't he just keep his thinking cap on all the time. I mean, why take it off and act like a dickhead?'

'He makes my skin crawl. Are they X-ray vision glasses, do you think?'

Rose laughed. 'That would explain a lot. He's not very subtle. Easy to outsmart, though. His stupidity is his finest quality.'

Fran knew that she couldn't have worked for Ainsworth; Rose had a higher tolerance for bad behaviour. The people Fran worked with were more sophisticated – of a different class, as the British would say. The account managers at the advertising agency were dashing young men who wore double-breasted suits and bold neckties that flagged them as creatives types. They swaggered about as if they imagined all the females in the office worshipped them, but they didn't salivate the way creepy Ainsworth did.

The novelty of the Hogarth Road B&B was wearing off. The house was tall and narrow with six rooms rented out and people tramping noisily up and down the stairs half the night. It was run by an elusive and nervy woman who lived in some unseen room behind the kitchen. Or perhaps in the kitchen itself, since she only ever opened the door a crack to answer queries. Every morning she delivered the breakfasts on trays outside the guest rooms. Two slices of toast with jam, a boiled egg and a cup of milky tea. She would tap tentatively on their door, as if afraid to wake them, and they soon became used to cold tea and soggy toast. Rose and Fran both loved to sleep and on Sundays would sometimes doze until early afternoon and feel groggy for the rest of the day, only coming right at dinnertime. They had the same dinner every night at a pub on the Cromwell Road: sausages and mash washed down with half a pint of Guinness, which Rose insisted was nutritious.

A couple from Perth, who lived above them, invited Fran and Rose to a party at a house in Chelsea. The ratty-looking terrace house didn't seem all that big from the street, but turned out to be a large share house tenanted by nine Australian dentists, all male. They were packed in, two and three to a bedroom, with a couple of fold-out beds in the living room for new arrivals.

Despite the proliferation of men, it was Maggie who first caught Fran and Rose's attention. Wearing a loose shirt and faded jeans, she wasn't dressed to attract attention, but Fran had the sense that every man in the room was acutely aware of her. She had a tawny mane of hair, a strong profile with high cheekbones and a wide, generous smile. She wasn't just beautiful, she radiated an energy that was deeply attractive. Rose later described her as ravishing. It felt as though Maggie was the central point of that room and everyone revolved around her.

Noticing Fran and Rose, Maggie came over and introduced herself as a fellow Sydney-sider. 'I'm so relieved there's a few more girls here,' she said, glancing around. 'These guys are getting on my nerves.' She indicated one of the fold-out beds. 'That's my room, for the moment.'

'You live with all these men?' asked Rose, who obviously found the idea appealing.

'I've only been here a week. They're all dentists working for the National Health. That one's my cousin,' she said, pointing to a curly-haired fellow sculling beer from a yard-glass. 'He's got me a job as a receptionist at his practice. Now I'm looking for a place to live. I need to get out of here.'

'We're living in a poky room in a B&B in Earl's Court,' said Fran. 'At least this is a nice big house —'

'And there's no shortage of blokes,' added Rose. 'Wanna swap?'

Maggie laughed out loud and heads turned in her direction. 'These guys have all bought tax-free cars to take home to Australia – that is the *only* topic of conversation . . . oh, apart from football and cricket.' She grimaced. 'The place is an absolute tip and no one cares.'

'You wouldn't be short of a date, though,' said Rose, unconvinced by the negatives.

'Er, it's more like being harassed day in, day out. One of them, I'm not sure who, but I have my suspicions, tried to feel me up while I was asleep.'

Fran shuddered. 'Oh, how awful for you.'

Noticing Rose checking out the talent, Maggie said, 'If you're looking for a good time, Rose, there are rich pickings here. These guys are all making about four hundred quid a week.'

'Far out!' said Rose. 'That's ten times what we make!'

'And you'll be chauffeured about town in style.' Maggie pointed out various dentists around the room. 'He's got a Porsche 911. That one's got a Ferrari. The stocky, drunk guy there has a BMW. Another Porsche. Austin Healey . . . they're all desperate for a date. Take your pick!'

Fran was less than enthusiastic. 'But what if you get the bad apple?'

Maggie agreed. 'There's a house in the next street, full of Aussie veterinarians. Personally, I think they're a better bet.'

To illustrate the point, the stocky drunk, clutching a can of Fosters in each hand, shirt hanging open to his waist, wandered over, planted himself in front of Maggie and gazed longingly at her breasts. After a moment, he gathered his wits and said, 'Show us your tits, gorgeous.'

Maggie's face went blank. She looked away as though she hadn't heard him.

Rose turned to him. 'Show us your doodle, pal. We need a good laugh.'

He looked around in confusion as if he hadn't noticed Rose until that point. But before he could retaliate, Rose said, 'No? Okay, fuck off then. We're busy here.'

Looking only mildly offended, he shrugged and wandered away. Maggie snorted and thanked Rose. 'See what I have to put up with?'

'There's your bad apple,' said Fran, unamused by the exchange.

Maggie wanted to know how Rose and Fran were settling in and they regaled her with stories of their adventures with Mr Ainsworth and Mrs Bishop and the strange landlady who lived in the kitchen. By the early hours of the morning, they had agreed to team up and look for a place together. Maggie was more cashed up than they were, and she was more motivated and organised than the two of them put together. Within a week they had a two-bedroom flat on the seventeenth floor of a tower block in Battersea, looking over the Thames and half of London, for twelve pounds a week with a garage.

Maggie brought a different sensibility to the group. Rose was the reckless, impetuous one; Fran was more considered and cautious, but Maggie was entrepreneurial and had a natural authority. She made things happen. They would never have bought the Kombi and set off to explore Europe that summer without her.

When their working visas expired, Maggie and Rose went back to Australia to start the next phase of their lives: university, work, marriage and family. Fran's mother had recently remarried and Fran didn't feel she had a home to go back to any more. She had deferred her Arts degree to come with Rose – she wanted to do something creative and London offered more potential. She feared domesticity, imagining a life of romantic bohemia.

Fran had discovered an interest in live theatre and, as well as the West End, she attended performances at the nearby Battersea Arts Centre. She offered her services on the production side, painting the canvas backdrops and helping with set construction, and soon found a community within the theatre. She left the advertising agency to work in a bookshop and have more time for the theatre work but, in the mid-nineties, the shop closed and the arts centre burned down. If she was ever going to go back to Australia, she should have gone then, when she was young enough to start something new. She just didn't realise it at the time.

These days she worked in a second-hand bookshop in Kennington and, the way things were going, it would probably be her last job. The owner, Mr Elcombe, referred to it as anti-quarian, selling 'rare and fine books', but that market was dying and most of them were just old. She spent long days in the shop alone. Sometimes a bona fide customer would appear but often it was local eccentrics or homeless people. If Mr Elcombe was away, which was often, she would let them sit by the gas fire and read. The shop had a cat called Gigi, whose job it was to keep the mice under control, but sometimes Fran smuggled her home and spoiled her with chicken livers and fresh salmon. They had a special understanding and, without her, Fran's job would be almost unbearably lonely.

Her relationship with Rose and Maggie had never really changed despite how differently their lives had turned out and the physical distance between them. It was only at the ten-year mark that the trio began to take the anniversary of their friendship seriously. Back then, a ten-year friendship seemed an extraordinary length of time. Now it was almost forty years. At first they had exchanged long letters, then they recorded ram-bling cassette tapes, later it was faxes, but now they were more connected than ever through social media. These days Fran got to see more of their lives and their children's lives as well, but increasingly it was having the effect of making her feel more alone and detached from their worlds.

The three had managed to meet up a couple of times and celebrate their anniversary together. One time, by sheer luck, Rose and Maggie's travel plans intersected and they were both in London at the same time. There was a week in Lucca when they all turned fifty and Maggie had rented a villa to mark the occasion. Fran had taken her boyfriend at the time, Steven, who was quiet and aloof with Maggie and Rose's rowdy families. He kept slipping away to work on his novel in their bedroom and she felt obliged to make excuses for him, citing his shyness and dedication to his writing, but felt torn the entire time between her friends and her lover.

Maggie's husband, Kristo, was loud and energetic, directing everyone with great enthusiasm. Fran found him tiring to be around. Peter, Rose's husband, was more peaceable but, as an academic and lecturer, he had an expectation that when he spoke, a hush would fall and he would have everyone's rapt attention. He and Kristo were not ideal holiday companions but, like good husbands, they made it work.

Later this year, Rose, Maggie and Fran would all turn sixty. It seemed inconceivable. Fran wished she could afford to make the trip home so they could spend it together, but unless she had a lottery win, that was not going to happen. She wondered if Maggie would think about renting a villa again. Louis wouldn't come. She'd have to go alone.

Fran finished her tea, had a shower, brushed her hair and applied mascara and lipstick. Not so much for her own vanity as to make her friends feel less depressed about the passing of time, although both seemed to be coping with the ageing business better than she was. She put on her black skirt and jumper so she was ready to walk out the door when the call was over. The shop didn't open until 10 a.m., so there was no real rush.

She opened up her laptop and sat quietly, waiting for the familiar faces of her dearest friends in the world to magically appear. The cracked William Morris mug sat on the table. Bloody Louis. But for some reason, she couldn't bring herself to throw it out.

Chapter Three

In an old hall in Glebe, women's voices rose as one and divided into harmonies as the sopranos soared above the altos and tenors. Rose felt her spirits lift and glide overhead on a thermal of sound, her voice indistinguishable as it melded with the others. She was transformed into an instrument, only the tiny tremors of vibration throughout her body connecting her spirit with her material being.

The thought entered her head that when you feel like screaming, singing is the antidote – a harmonious release of pent-up emotions. Screaming shatters and breaks you, not to mention pissing other people off. Singing nurtured the body and fine-tuned the world around you.

The song, an African a cappella entitled 'Freedom Is Coming', felt like her own personal anthem right now. She was aware of the irony of appropriating a sentiment related to freedom from the oppression of apartheid, but she felt a growing desperation for a different sort of freedom. Rose felt as if she had been waiting her entire life to be free, and she worried that by the time it was there for her, she would be too old and afraid to grasp it. Realistically, she could never be truly free while Peter was alive. Not that she wished him dead – he was her husband and she was fond of him. But still, she had a pervasive feeling of being trapped.

When the song finished, a faint reverberation hung in the air as each voice returned to its owner and they resumed their individuality. The women gathered in a circle, held hands and made a moment of acknowledging each other. As each set of smiling eyes met hers, Rose wondered if anyone else heard that song as a siren call beckoning them away from all that was safe and comfortable.

The choir leader thanked them and confirmed the details for a performance at a cultural event the next week. On parting, the singers always hugged one another. Not an air kiss or a cursory hug, a good, solid heart-to-heart embrace. Rose loved this tradition and enjoyed sharing an embrace with someone who wanted nothing from her but human contact.

Out in the hot afternoon sun, she strapped on her bike helmet, feeling that she was being physically torn from that melodic utopia and dragged down into the hell realms of the real world. The sounds of the traffic and smells of the street were all the more offensive to her sensibilities as the high she had experienced only moments before evaporated in the wet heat of the afternoon.

Home was a ten-minute ride away and she stopped on the way to pick up the last bits and pieces for dinner, cheered by the thought of spending the evening with her two oldest friends, even if one was on the other side of the world.

As she walked up the front path to the stone and timber house that she and Peter had lived in for the past thirty-five years, she cast a critical eye over the front garden. Weeds pushed up through the paving of the front path and dandelions were taking over the two patches of lawn either side. Too late to do anything about that now. Not the sort of thing Maggie would care about anyway.

Rose chained up her bike on the covered front verandah. It could do with a sweep if she had time later. It was only occasionally, when someone was coming over, that she noticed that the house looked not exactly abandoned, but certainly neglected. At those times she would often get stuck in and mow, weed and sweep and would love how smart the place looked until it reverted to its natural state.

She hung up her helmet and walked down the wide hallway that divided the front part of the house in half, past the bedrooms on either side, to the open living room and kitchen that ran the full width of the rear. The house was silent. Was it remotely possible that Peter had already left and she had the place to herself? Yes? Yes! No. There he was in the back garden battling to separate two old fishing rods that had become entangled with each other. She went out onto the verandah. 'What are you doing, dear?'

He glanced up briefly. 'What does it look like? Do you want to give me a hand?'

She absolutely did not, but left to his own devices, he'd still be there this evening. 'You haven't used those rods in twenty years. Why not just buy a new one? You probably won't even do any fishing while you're there. You know the boys don't enjoy it.'

'Rose, I'm not going to buy some cheap nasty Chinese rods when I've got two perfectly good ones right here. Aren't you the one always telling me to reuse, recycle, repurpose?'

They could bicker about this for hours. It was a delaying tactic. Don't argue, she told herself, just untangle him and set him free. 'Have you packed your bag?' she asked, already knowing the answer.

'I don't need very much,' he said. In other words, no.

'What time are you picking the boys up?'

Peter gave his watch a long blank look. 'An hour ago.'

Rose took her phone out of her pocket. She'd set it to silent during choir practice and now a stack of messages awaited her. One from Elliot asking where his father was, a voice message from Peter asking where the overnight bag was (only the same place it had been kept for thirty-five years) and one from Max saying he didn't feel well. Every year the pattern was the same.

Rose went inside, got the overnight bag down from the wardrobe, packed Peter some underwear, socks, spare shorts, an extra T-shirt and fleece. She put it on the floor near the front door and went back out to the garden.

'Leave the rods to me, dear,' she said. 'Just get your toiletries and put them in the bag I've left by the door.'

Peter obediently let her take over and went inside. Rose laid the rods on the ground, thoroughly examined the problem and set about quickly separating them. She went indoors to get something to wrap them up in and saw Peter wandering down the hallway carrying his toiletries bag and looking lost, as though she had set him an impossible task. 'Which —?'

'Front door!' she called in a tense singsong voice.

Finally, Peter was installed in the car. Rose slung the fishing rods in the back and gave him a farewell peck on the cheek. 'Have fun, Prof.'

'You know, Rose, I've never been able to decide if that moniker is vaguely hostile or genuine affectionate teasing. In any case, at the end of the month it will become an irrelevant title and you'll have to think of something else.'

'I'll call you Professor Emeritus from then on,' Rose said kindly.

He gave her a wan smile. 'That's something to look forward to at least.' He always seemed so dejected when he talked about his retirement. She did feel sorry for him but felt so much sorrier for herself that it cancelled out all sympathy for him.

'Give my regards to Maggie,' he said. 'I'll see you late Sunday.'

'Off you go, drive carefully and please don't call unless it is a genuine emergency, in which case ring emergency services.' And then, to be absolutely sure, she added, 'Triple zero.'

He nodded and started the car, his expression one of suffering and forbearance. He loathed going away without her and she had to appreciate the effort it took to allow her this one weekend a year. Elliot was now thirty-five with his own family, and Max four years younger, but the boys continued to cooperate with this long-standing tradition, having given up trying to convince their father to try a different destination or, at the very least, a different cabin.

She watched the car disappear down the street and turn the corner onto the main road. She waited a few minutes, half expecting to see him coming back under some pretext. The street remained empty. It was safe to assume he was gone. She was alone. She walked through the house singing 'Freedom Is Coming' at the top of her voice, wheeling around, arms outstretched to embrace the rooms emptied of human habitation. She half thought of doing a cartwheel down the hall but reconsidered at the prospect of spending the rest of the day in Emergency. Her cartwheeling days were probably behind her now.

It wasn't as though Peter took up much room. He was relatively compact, but he was like those pop-up ads you couldn't seem to get rid of. One minute he needed her help to find something – he spent most of his waking hours searching for mislaid items, both virtual and real – the next he had a paper needing writing or her feedback on a lecture or her opinion on some faculty politics. There was never a moment when they were both in the house that she could settle down to a task without the fear of interruption hovering over her. Soon he would be at home all day asking where she was going and when she was coming back, and what she had planned for lunch. Her life would become intolerable.

Her phone buzzed with a message. She willed herself not to look at it, wanting to continue revelling in solitude. It buzzed again. It could be Maggie – she had better not be cancelling! The first message turned out to be from Elliot's wife, Prya, wanting to know if Rose could babysit Austin this evening since Elliot was away – seemingly having forgotten the whole point of the exercise was that this was Rose's night.

Rose constantly had to battle the urge to silently criticise or find fault with Prya, who was actually flawless, except for being a tiny bit self-absorbed. She led the sort of life that people idealise on social media – but for real. You could send a surprise drone through her house and find everything in perfect order. Beds neatly made and cushioned up. Wildflowers in interesting vintage jars dotted about. Every drawer and cupboard compliant with surgical standards. Prya and Elliot never needed to declutter because clutter never crossed their threshold. This orderly approach was the antithesis of Rose and Peter's house, which had become untidy-able; everything was clutter. It wasn't that they were hoarders, it was just an accumulation over time and the fact that, when offspring leave home, they leave their clutter behind and are touchy about anything being thrown out. There were books stacked here and there because the shelves were full, paintings that no one had ever got around to hanging leaned against the walls and a patchwork quilt that Rose had begun several years ago but hadn't completed – yet – draped over one end of the dining table. Rose could see the muddle of their house made her daughter-in-law twitchy but Prya also had beautiful manners and was far too polite to say anything.

Prya had a masters degree in pharmacology and was employed by a company that regularly allowed her to work from home and offered free yoga classes. Her exotic ancestry had bequeathed her an almost exquisite beauty: dark eyes, burnished copper skin and silky black hair. She had a knack with clothes and was always beautifully groomed. She was the financial strategist of the family – all expenses were spreadsheeted and analysed. She and Elliot owned a lovely unit in an up-and-coming suburb and employed a cleaner. On the days when Prya worked, they paid so much for childcare, it would be cheaper to book Austin into a five-star hotel with room service babyccinos.

On the days Prya was caring for Austin, who was about to have his first birthday, she would occasionally invite Rose to join them on one of their excursions. Rose enjoyed the cultural ones like the Babies Proms at the Opera House but the more athletic ones involved a toned squad of mothers in lycra with shiny hair and strollers that folded up like origami swans to fit neatly in the back of their SUVs. Surely, Rose thought, somewhere there were still mothers wandering around in a weepy daze wearing baggy-kneed, milk-stained tracksuits? Or had women actually nailed this now? Were women allowed to be this efficient and flex their organisational muscles without apology? Had women stopped apologising full stop? Or was there another tribe hidden away indoors who were not coping, crippled by self-loathing that was further exacerbated by these frisky super-mums?

Prya was the new breed of wife who had established ground rules for Elliot right from the start. Rules that he respected and adopted without question – and good on her. Peter once commented that she kept Elliot on a 'short leash' and Rose had pointed out that apart from a few notable exceptions – such as Joan of Arc and Boudicca – women had been on a short leash *en masse* since the dawn of time. It was about time that situation was reversed.

Rose didn't begrudge Prya living the feminist dream, so why did it niggle that the martyrdom had been eliminated from motherhood and marriage? It wasn't as though Rose thought suffering was a badge of honour, or even necessary. Elliot had a demanding corporate job that Rose didn't quite understand, but he never seemed to resent being left with Austin while Prya went out to her many social events and fitness classes – even the occasional 'pampering' weekend away! The longest Rose had ever left the boys with Peter was to rush to the supermarket for a last-minute item. In fact, Elliot was full of praise and admiration for his wife's talents and capabilities, which was more than Rose could ever say for Peter.

If she was honest with herself, Rose would admit to feeling slightly inadequate and unrefined, as though she needed to be on her best behaviour around Prya and appear to have her shit together as much as possible. Anyway, much as she adored her grandson, looking after him tonight would be a no.

The other message was from Fitz asking what she was up to and did she fancy coming over for a spot of conjugation sometime this weekend. There was never a time in her life when Rose thought that having a lover, let alone one ten years her junior, was an ideal situation. It was still confusing as to how she had acquired one so easily and that he had fitted so seamlessly into her life.

They had met a year ago in the language section of a city bookshop, both looking at the books of French verb drills. There was a brush of skin on skin and laughing apologies. Rose felt herself go hot and tingly all over, as if she had been hit with a straight shot of oestrogen followed by a chaser of testosterone. She imagined her hormones sitting up like meerkats, scoping out this intruder wandering into the barren terrain of her sexual life. He was so attractive she didn't think for a moment that he'd be interested in her. It had been a decade since anyone had shown her the slightest interest, even longer since her husband had. They had compared the various books available, confessed they'd both learned French on and off for years, dropping it and picking it up again without making much progress. It was an easy move across the road for coffee. After an hour of stimulating conversation, they had agreed to meet up and help each other with their verbs.

A week later she found herself rolling around naked in a strange bed in the middle of the afternoon to the sounds of AC/DC's 'Highway to Hell' at full volume and felt twenty years younger for the experience. A year later they had still not practised a single verb but had fine-tuned their rolling around to a mutually satisfactory level of expertise. She felt no guilt, no remorse. She just wished that he wouldn't text her so often in between times. It was a no for him as well. Or, perhaps a 'maybe tomorrow' after Maggie left.

Rose enjoyed a cool shower and slipped on a cotton muu-muu, which was practically all you could tolerate in this late summer humidity. She had a glass of cold rosé while she chopped the garlic for the spaghetti vongole and tossed a green salad together. She put on some Norah Jones and hummed along contentedly, planning to savour every moment of the evening with Maggie and Fran. She ignored the first call from her mother but the third time the phone rang she capitulated. 'Emergency, Mum?' she asked, already knowing that it wouldn't be.

'Can you please explain to your father that we were married in 1952. Here he is.'

'Mum, no . . . no . . . please. It doesn't *matter*.' But it was too late, she could hear her father breathing into the phone. She wondered if people still did that – breathing into phones. It used to be a thing but now seemed tame given that there were so many new, much worse, things people did with phones. 'Hi, Dad. How are you?'

'Who is this?' her father asked.

'It's Rose, Dad. Your eldest daughter.'

'What do you want? I'm busy right now.'

'Is there a lady with short dark hair near you?'

'Affirmative. Pink blouse and maroon skirt.' Rose flinched; it couldn't be anyone but her mother wearing that colour combination. 'She's quite pretty actually, although I think she's taken liberties with the hair colour,' he added in a hushed voice.

'Can you pass on a message for me?'

'Fire away,' said her father.

'Okay, this is it: My apologies, you're absolutely right.'

There was silence at the other end and Rose wondered if he had twigged to her.

'Did you get that, Dad?'

'Yes, I believe so. Just repeat it for me.'

She said it again and heard her father repeat it word for word with the same emphasis. 'She said, "thank you very much",' he reported back.

'Well done. Now you go and relax. Bye, Dad.'

Her mother came back on the phone. 'I knew he'd listen to you.'

'Listen, Mum, he's not trying to annoy you. If he's bothering you, just go home. He probably won't even notice. The staff can take care of him. Maybe you don't need to be there so often —'

'I won't be able to come at all if your sister has her way. You know she told them not to let me bring your father food, because, apparently, I am trying to poison him!'

'Yes, she sent me a long email about it. Flimsy evidence at best. You're not, are you?'

'Very funny,' said her mother. 'Can you tell her to pull her head in? I'm not putting up with it. I'm eighty-five next week; I shouldn't have to deal with this shit from my own daughter.'

Rose had to agree. She promised she would deal with it, but *not this weekend*.

'Rose, I want you to know that I do love your father. It's just I never agree with anything he says.'

'So, what you're saying, Mum, is that arguing is the foundation of your relationship.'

'I suppose so, if you put it like that,' she agreed reluctantly. 'I just wanted you to understand that.'

'If you enjoy arguing with him so much, why do you need an arbitrator? You could go on for many happy hours arguing about that one thing.'

'I just can't stand it when he gets his facts wrong, and he's so stubborn!'

Rose sighed. 'Okay, fine. Listen, I'll see you Sunday, Mum.'

As she disconnected, there was a message from Max to say that Peter had forgotten his reading glasses. She ignored it, figuring they were too far away to turn back, and also that three capable men – well, Elliot was very capable – would work something out.

As Rose resumed her preparations, her thoughts turned to the evening ahead and the friendship with Fran and Maggie. It might not have been evident to anyone at the time, but when she'd met Fran at high school, Rose had been struggling to find her place there. Her parents had recently sold their share in the family farm and bought a suburban newsagency. At fourteen, Rose was tall and awkward with freckles and hair that fought its way out of every style. Not one to be easily dismissed, she made a name for herself at high school through sheer bloody-mindedness. Looking back, some of the things she did were quite unhinged. She was all reaction, no reflection. Fran was the voice of reason and had calmed Rose down, made her less wild.

Fran was her opposite: small and anxious with dark woodland-creature eyes, almost hidden in the shadow of a heavy fringe. It took a long time to get to know her. She was guarded – not one of the popular girls; her foreignness and her reserve marked her out as different. She never brought lunch to school. Rose thought she was on a diet but later, when they became closer, Fran admitted she had almost stopped eating when she was thirteen and her oma died. Back then, anorexia was almost unknown and it was years before Rose realised it was a condition.

Fran didn't have a father around and she wasn't close to her mother but had adored her oma. For years she couldn't mention her grandmother without getting the wobbles. The not-eating nonsense went on for years too. It was only after they got to London that Fran began to relax and eat properly. Rose had made sure she got plenty of food and gallons of Guinness to build up her stamina.

What Rose had liked about Fran from the start was that she was a good audience and laughed at all Rose's jokes. Rose had been looking for a partner in crime, but somehow ended up going straight. As it turned out, there were other more productive ways to make her mark.

In their years on the farm, her family's entertainment had revolved around the radio. They sat together in the evenings and listened to serials and music. Everywhere was miles away, and long hours spent in the car were for family singalongs. Rose's mother was an Elvis fan, her father did a memorable rendition of Val Doonican's 'Walk Tall' and they sang endless rounds of Bing Crosby's 'Swinging on a Star'. With the move to Sydney, they no longer spent much time in the car. They went their separate ways and forgot about their happy times singing together. Rose never forgot. Music was her passion and singing always made her happy.

Fran had somehow missed the sixties music revolution. She was brought up on classical music and played the piano. She was dazzled by Rose's repertoire of pop music and encouraged her to use her voice. On top of that, after a lifetime of having the wrong hair, Rose now had the right hair that could be teased into an afro. The musical *Hair* had been an enormous hit and, on the crest of that wave, Rose put together a garage band. Fran quickly overcame her lack of confidence with a pitch-perfect voice, a gift of her classical training. She read music, played keyboard and taught Rose the science of singing harmonies. They found guitar-playing girls but a drummer was more difficult. In the end, they compromised with a token boy, who wasn't much of a drummer but owned a drum kit.

After endless practice, and not a few disputes, the band performed at the end-of-year concert and their rendition of 'Aquarius' had the audience on their feet and dancing in the aisles. It was a good year for both of them. Fran had discovered that as a performer she was more extroverted and could even be slightly provocative. And, by some miracle, Rose managed to get through that entire year without one detention.

When she and Fran moved into the flat with Maggie, it didn't take long to realise their new friend had hopeless taste in music. At a time when some of the best music in history was being produced by the likes of Pink Floyd, Santana, the Rolling Stones, Queen, Blondie and dozens of other legendary artists, Maggie, when pressed, elected John Denver and Glen Campbell as favourites. Rose and Fran had to completely re-educate her.

Forty years. Fran hadn't changed all that much. Rose's hair had turned silver and still defied gravity. But Maggie, the beautiful one, hadn't aged well. She still made an effort to have her nails done and her hair coloured but she was carrying too much weight. She'd come to resent her much-admired breasts, irritated by the male attention they attracted and the discomfort, and wore baggy clothes to hide them. Her signature bubbling laugh was rarely heard. Worse, she'd become more combative, as if she couldn't be stuffed with diplomacy any more.

Rose was about to pour her second glass of rosé when she heard the purr of Maggie's Audi in the driveway. Standing on the front step, Rose watched her friend get an overnight bag from the back seat. Maggie's shoulders were hunched and, as she turned from the car, her face was visibly flushed. For a moment she was almost unrecognisable – an old woman – then somehow she quickly morphed back into Maggie. Between the driveway and the lawn, she missed her step and staggered heavily. For a moment it seemed she might fall. Rose rushed to take her arm and steady her, only to see Maggie's forced smile crumple into a grimace of misery as she burst into tears.

Rose held her while she sobbed and apologised and sobbed again. Her breath came out in gasps and Rose was afraid for her. She had been worried that Maggie could drop dead of a heart attack from the stress she had been under these last few years. Anthea and Elena, whom Rose privately referred to as the evil twins, had no hesitation about putting their mother through the wringer – standard practice in that family. The stress was probably no worse than it had been, but Maggie's ability to cope with it had diminished, and she'd had problems with her blood pressure lately.

'It's all right, everything's all right. Let's get you sitting down with a drink.' Rose guided her inside and down the hall to the living room, where Maggie collapsed onto the sofa. Rose poured her a glass of wine and sat down beside her. 'What on earth's happened?'

Maggie took a gulp of wine and brushed away the tears that continued to slip down her cheeks. 'I think I'm having a nervous breakdown.'

'You've thought that before, Mags. You'll come through. You always do. What's happened this time?'

'I don't know where to start. Well, okay . . . one thing, the latest . . . Aaron put a video online of him and Anthea having sex.'

'Oh, *shit*! What? Why on earth would he do that? Poor darling. She didn't know?'

'He's a bit of a social media animal, always posting selfies of the two of them glued to each other. So, I imagine it's because he thinks they're "hot" and for some reason he thought it was okay. She knew she was being filmed . . . but she never agreed to put it online.'

'I think that's quite common . . . the filming, I mean.'

Maggie gave her a look of distaste. 'Really?'

'I mean, I wouldn't do it . . . *obviously*. But I think some people find it titillating to watch themselves going at it.'

Maggie considered this for a moment and grimaced. 'It makes me cringe, it's so . . . personal . . . and private . . . Anyway, it gets worse . . . she sent me the link and Yia-yiá saw it.'

'Far out! No wonder you're in such a state.'

'Then the girls turned up while Kristo and the brothers were there – and now everyone knows.' Maggie sculled her wine.

'*Faaark!* Have you warned Aaron? Honestly, things could get much worse if they go after him. Remember that boyfriend of Elena's —'

'Yes . . . don't remind me. No, I just grabbed my bag and left. I honestly felt I couldn't stand another minute.' Maggie's eyes brimmed. 'That family is killing me, Rose. It's like living in a nuclear reactor that's on the brink of blowing, and I'm the only one who can cool it down. What gets me is that I'm the only one who *wants* to cool it. Everyone else feels they have licence to let loose and it's up to me to sort things out.'

'I know. I'm so sorry, Mags. I think I have things tough with

my lot but yours are so much . . . louder. And a tiny bit dangerous sometimes.'

'They're tough people,' agreed Maggie quietly. 'And when
they're all riled up at once . . .'

'Do you want to put Fran off? We could do it tomorrow
instead?'

'No, she'll be all ready and I don't want to disappoint her.
Let's try and forget all that crap. I'm here. My phone is off. Let's
get pissed and talk shit and be young again for an hour or two.'

'You won't feel young in the morning,' said Rose. 'I'll just get
the pasta going. I've got the iPad set up on the table.'

'How is Fran? I actually haven't spoken to her for a couple of
months.'

Rose filled a pot with water and set it on the stove. 'I don't
know. A bit lonely, I think. She doesn't light up when she talks
about Louis any more.'

'I know we haven't actually met him but, even based on what
we know from her, I'm not sure why she would light up about
him in the first place.'

'"Last Resort Louis". I reckon he's probably just another old
bloke looking for "a nurse and a purse" – don't you reckon?'

'I don't think Fran would be a likely candidate for him,' said
Maggie. 'She's got no money. She might pop out a painkiller for
him, but I can't see her going beyond that. She's not that domes-
ticated. If he was green and leafy, she'd lavish attention on him.'

'Get him under her green thumb,' suggested Rose.

Maggie snorted and held up her empty glass for a refill. 'Do
you want me to do something?'

Rose assured her that all was in hand and they chatted about
other things while she concentrated her efforts on the food.

But as she served up the vongole, Rose realised her good spirits had evaporated and been replaced by a dark sense of time passing and things lost that could never be recaptured. Of everything changing, collapsing and disintegrating. Life was slipping through her fingers like smoke. Nothing could be grasped or held onto – in the end all would be lost. It occurred to her that Maggie might not make it through this crisis. She had become brittle, and there was always the risk that the next drama could be the one to break her.

The thought of losing Maggie brought a lump to her throat. She had to stop and try to calm herself, jolly herself back to her earlier mood. She brought the wine to the table and filled their glasses right to the rim, just like they used to, so they had to lean over them to slurp the first mouthful. Maggie gave a soft laugh.

Chapter Four

Waiting for the faces of her dearest friends to pop up, Fran felt the usual twinge of nostalgia for the humid embrace of Sydney in late summer, with its shrilling cicadas. She longed to smell the rich scent of frangipani. These days she often pondered – quite pointlessly – whether she should have gone home (she still thought of it as home) when Rose and Maggie had, or even sometime in the intervening years. Now it was too late.

When she was alone in the shop, she often daydreamed happily-ever-afters for herself, imagining a final act so glorious that it made the years of heartbreaks, betrayals and disappointments all worthwhile. She saw herself in the countryside, a cottage surrounded by gardens, rolling fields and trees beyond. Someone kind and caring, soulful, at her side. They would walk together in the evenings, perhaps with a devoted labrador. While she had always loved working with books, lately she'd become acutely aware of the thousands of voices trapped within those silent tomes, clamouring to be released. She spent too much time alone. Too much time in her head.

When Maggie and Rose had left in 1979, Fran was still infatuated with London – she felt at home as a foreigner among so many other foreigners. She was fascinated by the discovery of the many cities within the city, the mosaic of cultures. The intriguing coexistence of grime and glamour, poverty and affluence and the sense of being central to the world instead of peripheral. It was a place where anyone could belong, something that Fran had never experienced before. Her father long gone, Fran had grown up with her mother and grandmother as her entire family. They spoke only German at home (but never outside). It was their secret language, and one that was imbued with comfort.

For Oma, home was not Sydney, but Vienna before the war. She lived as someone in exile; their flat was a tiny sovereign nation within this bright city with its bleached skies and sunbaked skins. From early childhood, Fran had loved Oma's stories about the big house in Döbling and the family jewellery business, their life in Vienna before everything was taken from them, including Fran's grandfather. As a treat, Fran was sometimes allowed to look in Oma's jewellery box at the small pieces she still owned: a diamond brooch and amethyst ring, a pearl choker and some earrings with miniature screws on the back. There had been many more pieces, Oma told her with regret, all stolen or sold over the years.

Fran's mother, Lena, had begun her career as a sales assistant in a fashion shop. There, she learned enough to start her own wholesale business importing costume jewellery and accessories, scarves and handbags from Europe. She crisscrossed the country, from state to state, four times a year to show her latest products and take orders for the next season, and was often away for weeks at a time. Life at home with Oma was unchanging, with few interruptions from the outside world. In the evenings, Fran did her homework and practised piano. They often played cards together or Fran would read aloud to Oma, translating from English to German as she read. Patrick White's novels were favourites.

One afternoon, when she was thirteen, Fran had arrived home to a silent house. No Oma there to greet her with hugs and kisses. No glass of milk and slice of *apfelkuchen* with cream on the kitchen table. Oma lay on her bed, her hands clasped together. Her eyes were closed and her expression serene. Fran thought she would never get over the loss.

With Oma's death, all comfort and love and certainty vanished from Fran's life. Lena insisted there was no need to speak German at home any more, it was time to integrate. She was still often away and Fran was home alone. The flat was quiet and empty when she left for school in the morning, and even more so when she arrived home in the afternoons. Rose changed all that, and Fran never looked back.

When she moved to London, Fran had her Aunt Marie, whom Oma had often talked about. Aunt Marie had never married and she was a softer version of Fran's mother, more like Oma. Fran felt an immediate affinity with her and they soon became close. They often went out together to exhibitions, theatre and foreign language films on the South Bank.

Fran was in love with Tony, the Irishman, at that time. All that remained of him now was a hazy memory like a composite picture: the dark grey eyes, heavy brows, tousled black hair. They worked together in a bookshop on Charing Cross Road and sometimes kissed in the storeroom, although not as much as she would have liked.

Tony lived in a squat in an old school in Hammersmith that had a grubby bohemian charm. It was another city within the city, populated by fringe dwellers: junkies, communists, musicians and artists, many of them Irish and Scots. Tony was opposed to formal education. He loathed the government and the middle classes. They discussed existentialist philosophies for hours on end; he introduced her to Foucault and Sartre.

Fran's imagined bohemia involved cheap red wine, European literature and crushed velvet. But the most popular books in the squat were crime novels Tony stole from their employer, and the favoured drinks were Strongbow or Tennent's Super, neither of which were to her taste. They smoked hash and dropped acid and talked endlessly about leaving London for Ibiza or Morocco. He was determined to live without boundaries, and Fran struggled to emulate him.

Fran held a tenuous idea that this could be the making of her. She could see them living somewhere simple and primitive, like peasants, with ragged children running wild. Then she had a bad acid trip, followed by days of terrifying flashbacks, and when Tony moved on to heroin, she was too afraid to go there.

It wasn't long before he began to borrow money, forgetting to repay her and fending her off with less and less believable excuses. Finally he was arrested, found guilty of a string of burglaries and sentenced to three years in Brixton. She visited him every Saturday, but three years was an awful lot of Saturdays. More worrying was his lack of remorse. He didn't accept that he played any role in his incarceration, believing himself a victim of English prejudice.

Fran wrote to Maggie about her Irish dilemma. She didn't need to ask Rose, because she knew Rose's advice would be to

dump him. A letter came by return mail that was warm and compassionate but also firm. Forget him. Fran respected Maggie's
advice. She stopped visiting but never quite forgot the Irishman.
The one thing she did learn from him was that living without
boundaries wasn't her thing after all.

Maggie's face, when it appeared on the screen, looked tired, her
smile strained.

'Are you all right, Maggie? What's going on?' asked Fran with
concern.

'I'm not sure —' Maggie's voice sounded breathless and faint.

'She's at the end of her tether,' Rose declared. 'She's fallen off
the end, I think.'

'Oh, Maggie,' said Fran. 'I'm surprised it's taken this long for
you to get there.'

Maggie nodded. 'Let's not go into it, I just want to relax and
enjoy the evening.'

Rose turned to look at Maggie for a long moment as though
she didn't know what to do. But she accepted Maggie's request
and changed the subject, telling a story relating to her frustration with Peter and some fishing rods. Fran only half listened
as she watched Maggie silently fork pasta into her mouth without pleasure, only pausing to take a distracted gulp of wine, her
eyes distant. Her eyes were the most worrying sign. Once bright
with interest and twinkling humour, they were dull, and beneath
them were dark pockets of accumulated worry and stress. Her
long thick hair, once so envied by both Rose and Fran, had a
seam of grey pushing at the parting. It was so unlike Maggie to
let herself go. Tears of compassion welled up in Fran's eyes.

Rose interrupted herself to say, 'Oh, bloody hell! Don't you start. Why are you crying?'

Fran reached for a tissue and carefully mopped under her eyes so as not to smudge her makeup. 'Why do you think, Rose? Maggie's the stoic one. She's the rock. If she's falling apart . . .'

'I'm stoic too,' said Rose peevishly. She turned to look across at Maggie. 'But yeah, you're right. I don't know what to do. Something has to change, Maggie. How can we help you?'

Maggie put down her fork and sighed heavily. 'I feel as though I'm holding up this great boulder that just gets bigger and heavier. Not just responsible for my family and Kristo's family but also the livelihoods of employees and contractors . . .' Her mouth tugged down in an effort not to cry. 'It's crushing me. It's crushing the life out of me. Some nights I lie in bed and the only relief I get from the stress is planning how to disappear.'

Fran glanced at Rose and saw her own sense of alarm reflected in her expression.

'People disappear all the time,' said Maggie defensively, as though it were a logical choice. 'And I understand why they disappear, because there is no other way out. There's no way out for me. I find it comforting to plan it all out, detail by detail . . . where I'll park the car . . . where I can swim out without anyone seeing me . . . out beyond the breakers and then just let myself drop . . .' She gave a shuddering sob. 'The idea that there is some relief in sight is the only thing keeping me going. Otherwise it would be unbearable. I have to keep a grip on myself because I have to manage everyone's anger. When do I get to be angry?'

Rose leaned over and put her arms around Maggie. 'Oh, Maggie. I'm so sorry. I didn't know. I didn't know things were so bad.'

Maggie nodded numbly. 'Me neither. It's become normal to me. Now I'm looking at the expressions on your faces and . . . well, it's clearly not.'

Fran didn't know what to say. It was taking all her strength to hold back her tears.

'Does Kristo know you feel like this?' asked Rose. 'Or the girls?'

'Of course not. He's got enough to worry about. It would just annoy him.'

Rose frowned. 'No. I think you've got that wrong, Mag. You need to talk to him.'

'I'm just a cog in the wheel of the great Dimitratos empire. They're practical people. His parents made so many sacrifices to get the family to where they are now. They were *tireless*. For me to say I'm exhausted . . . it would become a family joke because I sit in a nice clean office and work on a computer – they are in a shit fight every day getting the "real" work done.'

'Can you get more help?' suggested Fran.

'To be honest, I don't really have much say in the scheme of things. I'm not a partner in that business, you know.'

'That's ridiculous. You've been running the whole bloody thing right from the start,' said Rose. 'They couldn't do it without you.'

Maggie shrugged resignedly. 'That's not how they see it. I'm an appendage of Kristo and it's my job to run the financial side of the business, because I can. They would have no idea of what's involved with managing the cashflow and lines of credit, payment schedules, insurances, tax. Running a business is a hundred times more complicated than it was twenty years ago, let alone forty years. Yia-yiá seems to think it's like running a fish shop, but with bigger fish.'

'I wish you were here so I could give you a hug,' said Fran.

Maggie smiled. 'I wish I was there. Anywhere but here, actually. How are you, anyway? What's happening with Louis?'

'I wish I knew. He's become rather elusive. And evasive as well . . .'

'Instead of erudite and enigmatic?' suggested Rose.

Fran laughed. 'He's never been erudite, let alone enigmatic. I've been sliding down a greasy pole of educated men, decade by decade, from that Oxford scholar in 1980 to an insurance assessor whose spelling is atrocious and who prides himself on never having read a novel.'

'What sort of a person has never read a novel?' asked Rose. 'A Neanderthal?'

'Actually, I get the impression he thinks he's too clever to waste his intellect on such a trivial medium,' said Fran.

Rose laughed out loud and Maggie squeezed out a smile.

'So what does he have going for him?' asked Maggie.

Fran had to think for a moment. 'He's kind and can be quite sweet.'

'How's his performance in the sack?' asked Rose. 'That counts for a lot.'

'Oh God, Rose. Some things never change with you,' said Maggie, refilling her glass.

'I think he used to be okay. He was loving anyway. Now he goes through the motions,' said Fran. 'It's like he's fiddling around under the bonnet trying to get the car started and thinking about what he'll have for breakfast.'

'Sure he's not tinkering with someone else's engine?' asked Rose.

'Rosie!' Maggie protested. 'Why put that idea into her head?'

'Sorry. The thought just occurred and popped out. As it does.'

'You could be right,' admitted Fran. 'He's mentioned his wife, Barbara, a few times recently, as in quoting something she said. Never divorced. I get the impression they're seeing more of each other than they used to.'

'So you think he's getting his rations with her?' asked Rose.

'Rose, do shut up, will you? You're just making things worse,' Maggie admonished.

'No, I won't, Little Miss Bossy. I'm not going to sit back and watch Fran wasting her life on some loser who's bonking his wife and popping over to Fran's when he feels like a bit of TLC. I reckon he's hedging his bets, Frannie. And when he retires, one of you will get the booby prize and be stuck with him.'

'He did tell me that Barbara's thinking of moving to Malaga.'

'Well, if he starts taking Spanish lessons, give him the old heave-ho, I reckon,' said Rose.

Maggie pushed her plate away and pulled her wine glass towards her. 'Okay, Rose, let's shine a spotlight on your life so we can give you the benefit of our advice. I've heard about five messages come through since we've been talking to Fran. Peter wanting you to drive down the coast and blow his nose for him?'

Rose laughed. 'Peter can't text, thank God! It will be Max complaining.'

'So has Peter retired yet?' asked Fran. 'How's that going to work out?'

'He's got another month to go. I'm *bloody* dreading having him home all day. I have three days teaching, but I'll have to find him a hobby or another job, otherwise it will actually be unbearable. I'll be swimming out into the harbour with Mag . . . wait, can we joke about that yet? Too soon?'

Maggie frowned. 'Let's see how we go.'

'It will lighten your workload,' said Fran. 'Not having to do his papers and whatnot. Although he might want you to ghost another book for him.'

'Not happening,' said Rose. 'You know, the advice I give young couples getting into a relationship? Start the way you mean to continue. Advice no one gave me. If I had known back then that I'd spend my life shoring up Peter's career as his "wing-woman", I would have done things very differently. Married someone else, for example. Or stayed single like the sensible Fran.'

'But you wanted him to keep his tenure,' Maggie reminded her. 'It's exactly like my situation – you pitch in and support the family, they move on and you're left holding up the building, because you're the foundation.'

Rose growled under her breath. 'You know what really gets my goat? Last month, when he got that history award, he had to get up and make a speech. He wasn't expecting it, or maybe they told him and he forgot; anyway he had nothing prepared —'

'You had nothing prepared, you mean,' interrupted Maggie.

'Exactly. He made this rambling speech thanking everyone from the cleaner up. Then, finally, his eyes fell on me and he added, "and, of course, my dear wife"– not even my name! I was so pissed off.'

'Perhaps he'd forgotten your name?' suggested Fran.

Maggie started to laugh. 'Oh, poor Peter, he's a darling in so many ways, but that vagueness is too much. You are a saint to put up with him. It's like having a large child on the loose.'

Rose suddenly looked uncomfortable. 'He's not quite that bad. He does hold a job down. And I'm definitely not a saint. Far from it.'

'So he's obviously good in bed,' said Fran with a smile.

Rose stared at the ceiling, appearing to rack her memory. 'It's been that long, I can't recall. I gave him *The Joy of Sex* to read thirty years ago. I'm pretty sure he has never even opened it.'

Fran grinned. 'Tame stuff, Rose. You should have gone for the *Kama Sutra*.'

'Yes, well, I envy you the lack of sex. I have an oversupply situation,' said Maggie.

'Difficult to get the balance right, isn't it?' said Fran. 'Life is so often all or nothing.'

Rose drained her wine with a flourish. 'You know, every year I think this is it. This is the year my life will start. Then Peter gets prostate cancer or white ants invade the house and I realise *this* is my life and it will always be like this. My time will never come. It's been and gone and these dried up bloody . . . *crumbs* are what's left behind.'

'It's not like you to be so defeatist,' said Maggie. 'You're not dead yet.'

'It just wears you down; saps your energy,' insisted Rose. 'I'm worried that I've left my run too late . . .'

'How did we end up here?' sighed Fran. 'We had such high hopes for ourselves . . .'

'And for each other,' added Maggie.

'Do we have any hopes for ourselves now that we're about to crack sixty? Now our girlhood is well and truly over?' Rose continued.

Fran laughed. 'Rose, our girlhood was over about forty years ago.'

'No, it wasn't. We were still girls when we lived in London, when we went travelling. We were beautiful innocent children, seeing everything for the first time. Nothing has ever been as fresh and glorious as it was then. Nothing has ever been so vivid and exciting.'

'It was the freedom,' agreed Maggie. 'The absolute freedom to take each day as it came, to go to somewhere we'd never been before . . . no responsibilities or obligations.'

'We'd never been *anywhere* before. We didn't really care where we were going, we just went,' said Rose. 'And figured it out when we got there.'

Fran sighed. 'We were so confident . . .'

'We were so *ripe* and *succulent*. Now we're withering on the vine,' said Rose.

'Our lives fruitless,' added Fran.

'Rotten to the core?' suggested Maggie. 'Okay, that didn't quite work.'

'I don't really even remember who I was back then,' said Rose. 'I was so unevolved and lacking any sort of self-realisation but, you know what? I reckon we were our true selves. Unfiltered.'

'In photography, the image you take is called a raw file – it's just as the camera saw it,' said Fran. 'Then it's manipulated and compressed —'

'Exactly! We were raw and unfiltered then,' said Rose. 'We've been manipulated and compressed by everyone around us. We've compromised until there's nothing left of our true selves.'

'Back then our lives felt infinite. Now we're at the other end of life —' said Maggie.

'This is the last frontier,' said Rose. 'If we don't get our shit together, we're going to arrive at the pearly gates well and truly pissed off with ourselves.'

'Is there more wine in the fridge, Rose?' asked Maggie in a weary voice.

'Yes, but you've had enough. It's just going to make you maudlin.'

Maggie cast Fran a look of wide-eyed disbelief.

'When I delve into my memories of that time,' mused Rose, 'it's like everything is in soft focus, drenched in dappled sunshine. Like an art film . . . it's almost holy for me. There's a beautiful purity about everything.'

Fran smiled. 'I doubt if London was drenched in sunshine, apart from the odd day here and there. But I know what you mean, that time has a dreamlike quality for me as well.'

'We've talked about it so much over the years, haven't we?' said Maggie. 'But it hasn't worn the memories out.'

'No, I think it's helped preserve them,' said Fran. 'Remembering the thrill of that first time walking down the Champs-Élysées —'

'Arm in arm,' interrupted Maggie, smiling at the memory. 'The laughing girls.'

Rose smiled. 'Like we'd stepped out of a movie about three gorgeous young women on a mission to see the world.'

'We didn't know we were gorgeous . . .' said Maggie.

Rose leaned over and kissed her on the cheek. 'We knew you were gorgeous, darling.'

Maggie shook her empty glass down for the last drop and sighed. 'The time in Greece is what I remember most. Sleeping on the beach in Corfu, waking up at dawn and falling into that crystal-clear water.'

'Maybe that experience predisposed you to becoming a faux Greek,' suggested Rose.

Maggie gave a dry laugh. 'I never thought of that.'

'I still remember that bitter homemade yoghurt we'd have

with a block of chocolate at the Blue Moon for breakfast,' said Fran. 'I've never tasted yoghurt like that since.'

'I'd never tried yoghurt before then.' Rose laughed. 'I thought it was something to do with vegetarians.'

Maggie had disappeared for a moment and reappeared with another bottle of white wine. She poured herself a full glass and offered it to Rose, who agreed to a 'tiny bit'.

'We were so open to everything then. We had no sense of our limitations. I know we had our anxieties . . .' Rose's eyes glazed over as though searching for that earlier time. 'But I think we were largely untroubled.'

'I think you're just forgetting the things we worried about,' said Maggie.

'We didn't worry about our futures,' argued Rose. 'We knew, absolutely *knew*, they would be glorious.'

'That's true,' said Fran. 'Mine certainly hasn't been. It's like I got stuck in a cul-de-sac and couldn't get out.'

'You were waiting for the right person to rock up in a Mustang and drive you off into a movie-style sunset,' said Rose.

Fran laughed. 'Mercedes, please. It might still happen.' She thought of Louis, who drove a twenty-year-old Lancia and, whenever they went somewhere together, would grumble about the cost of petrol until she offered to pay and then refuse to accept it. 'I'm embarrassed to say that I still feel as though I'm waiting for my life to start.'

'Oh, Fran.' Maggie sounded both sad and slightly exasperated, which Fran could quite understand.

'Remember the way the men used to look at us on that trip?' said Rose wistfully. 'Especially the Italians. As if we were God's gift in triplicate.'

Maggie shook her head. 'The last thing I want is men looking at me. That's the best part about getting old. Becoming invisible is underrated, if you ask me.'

'We should go somewhere together this year, just the three of us,' said Rose. 'Celebrate our sixty years gracing this earth.'

Fran waited hopefully for Maggie's response – perhaps the villa in Lucca? How she would love that, especially if it was just the three of them.

Maggie turned to Rose. 'What did you have in mind?'

'I don't know. I just thought of it then.'

'I haven't the energy to organise anything right now, Rose.'

'You don't have to. I'll do it all.'

Maggie hesitated. 'Maybe. Let me think about it.'

Fran could see the excitement fizzing up in Rose. 'Let's do it again!' said Rose.

'What part of "it" are you referring to?' asked Maggie. 'Let's be young again?'

'If only. Let's go back to the places we visited on that first trip.'

'The objective being . . .?' asked Maggie, frowning.

'An experiment to see if we can catch a glimpse of . . . of who we were back then. Of our true selves. We need to open our minds to possibilities.'

'So trekking all over Europe, looking for our lost hopes and dreams?' asked Fran, only half joking.

'It sounds a bit depressing to me,' said Maggie. 'But maybe that's just my current state of mind.'

'That first trip we did through Europe marked the end of the first quarter of our lives. This is the end of the third quarter. We

have to do something. Reassess. Not just plod on until we die.'
Rose looked from Fran to Maggie and back again. 'We could do
it this northern summer.'

'So, I would just buzz off and leave the business to run itself.
And Anthea to sort out her marital problems . . . and Yia-yiá,
and Kristo, and the house . . .'

Rose stared at her. 'That's got to sound appealing, right? Plus
I'm sure they would prefer you going away to the ocean-swim
option.'

'How would Peter manage without you?' asked Maggie.

'I could get a sitter for him.'

Maggie smiled. 'And what about Max?'

'He's over thirty now, he needs to sort himself out,' said Rose.
'Look, I'm not saying it's any easier for me to get away. Dad's in
care, Mum hasn't come to terms with his dementia, my sister
thinks Mum's trying to poison him, and she's going through a
bad time . . .'

'I just can't see that traipsing around Europe is going to pro-
vide any answers.'

'Maggie, I'm worried you'll drop dead in the harness and, if
that happens, life will be so much worse for us. I may seem patient
but it's an act. Deep down, there is a boiling resentment. I don't
think about drowning myself but I do think about running away.'

'Don't you think we're becoming a bit self-involved?' asked
Maggie. 'Feeling sorry for ourselves? White middle-class women
suffering affluenza?'

Rose poured herself more wine. 'Are you serious? We're not
self-involved enough! We're completely "other"' centric.'

'It's a nice idea, Rose, for when I win the pools, but right
now I have to go off to work,' said Fran. 'If I'm two minutes late

opening the shop, Mr Elcombe gets cross. Even though no one ever comes in first thing in the morning.'

'You still call him Mr Elcombe? After all these years?' asked Rose.

Fran laughed. 'It's not like we're friends. We virtually never discuss anything other than work. He's not in the shop that often these days. He spends most of his time driving all over the country buying dead people's books and going to jumble sales. I think it's a ruse to get some distance between him and Mrs Elcombe. Wherever he is – Scotland, at the moment, I think – he always calls the shop first thing to check on me.'

'Think about it, Fran,' said Rose. 'Let's walk the Champs-Élysées arm in arm again. It's not just about the places and memories. It's about the three of us making that journey together again, rediscovering ourselves.'

'I absolutely love the idea but, right now, a week in Torquay would be a stretch, let alone a European jaunt,' said Fran. 'Sorry, my darlings.'

'And it might just puncture our fantasy of that first trip. We could end up disillusioned, without even those memories to hold on to,' said Maggie.

'It's possible,' conceded Rose. 'But we'd also have some new experiences, some new connections with those gorgeous girls we once were.'

If Fran could afford it, she'd agree in flash, but it was out of the question. Maggie obviously couldn't see the point and had nothing positive to say about it, and Fran realised that their normal pattern with each other had been interrupted by Maggie's current state of mind. Rose had always been the one to come up with the crazy ideas. Fran went along for the ride but Maggie, right from the start, was in charge of the practical application. Without Maggie's energy behind Rose's idea, it was doubtful anything would happen.

After they said their goodbyes and terminated the call, Fran sat staring at the blank screen for a long minute with mixed feelings of longing and loneliness. The flat felt suddenly empty in the same way her mother's place had felt after Oma died. She looked around at her nesting efforts – her plants and books, odd bits of furniture and bric-a-brac she had picked up at markets over the years – and it seemed like a stage set, something artificial she had created to look like a home. The truth was, she could walk out and leave it all without a second thought because all she had ever wanted was a home for her heart.

Rose was right, something needed to change in each of their lives. Fran picked up the cracked mug and threw it in the bin.

Chapter Five

When Maggie left Rose's place the next morning, the idea of going away on a trip was the last thing on her mind. On the drive home, her thoughts leapt from Anthea to Yia-yiá to the business and Mr Lau, then to Kristo and his brothers, and back again. Every scenario was painful, interconnected and unstoppable, like juggling daggers. As far as she could see, none of these problems was within her power to resolve. She realised with a pang how much she missed Pappoú, his calm counsel and his control over the family.

In the early days, Kristo's father had been difficult to deal with. He was poorly educated and only learned to read as an adult, but he was intelligent and a commonsense business person. Eventually he came to have a grudging respect for Maggie's abilities across the many aspects of the business; she could lobby him for support and the boys would fall into line. Kristo had respect for her recommendations, but his brothers didn't understand the due diligence she put in behind the scenes. The truth was that, despite all the years she had put into the business, they still saw her as an outsider. One who could divorce Kristo and tear the business apart. They didn't entirely trust her.

Maggie walked back into her house half expecting to find Anthea and Elena still crying, Nico and Kristo still shouting at each other and Yia-yiá still distraught at the contents of the video. But all was quiet.

She walked through the house to the back deck. Down on the lower level of the garden, Anthea and Elena lay on the sun beds beside the pool, both wearing orange bikinis, their attention focused on their phones. Beyond the pool, the blue bay was a serene reflection of the sky, clear and bright all the way to the horizon. Maggie took a deep breath and closed her eyes for a moment, ingesting the calmness. Within seconds, there were footsteps behind her and the sense of a hovering presence. She opened her eyes to find Kristo standing beside her, his face creased with worry.

'Maggie, come into the bedroom with me.'

'What? Kris, I've just walked in the door.' She tapped her non-existent watch. 'It's not even lunchtime.'

'No, no . . . not that. I want to talk to you, alone.' He wore the beseeching expression that always irritated her. Kristo was the pick of the Dimitratos boys. He was still the most handsome of the four and had the kindest heart. Though he had thickened and weathered with age and his hair – once loose black curls – was now like a cap of grey twist-pile carpet, his emotions still showed in his eyes, and they were now bright with tears.

'Can't you be alone with me here? We're alone now.'

'Maggie, I just want to talk. I promise. Am I such a monster that you are afraid to be in the bedroom with me?' He looked pale and worried.

'What's it about? Those two, I suppose?' She nodded in the direction of the pool.

'They're fine. Anthea has talked to Aaron and he's taken the video down.'

'He's an idiot. What was he thinking?' She and Kristo watched as their daughters took shots of each other, pouting and smiling. They were too beautiful and Anthea in particular had an appetite for attention. 'And what did you decide about the pour on Monday?' Maggie asked.

'The concrete is postponed for twenty-four hours.'

'Well, you know my opinion on that. It's not long enough. You're just going to have to —'

'It's not about that,' he interrupted.

'So what else is there to discuss?' Maggie could hear how bad-tempered she sounded.

'Rose called me,' said Kristo. 'I want to talk about you.'

She felt a prickling of anger at Rose's interference. Maggie had to be very careful what she told Rose when it came to family business. Rose had a habit of interfering, thinking she was being helpful, but was oblivious to the possible repercussions. More worrying was that since revealing her true state of mind last night, Maggie had the sense of something inside her starting to unravel, exposing her nerve-endings. Her ability to pretend was slipping and now she risked putting herself in the – mostly incompetent – hands of those around her. It was a terrifying thought and she felt herself withdraw from Kristo, resenting him for involving himself, but at the same time knowing how unreasonable that was.

Kristo put his arm around her shoulders. It was a caring and gentle embrace, not like the way he would sometimes urge her to come to the bedroom as if sex were the medication for all that ailed him. Despite her resistance, she allowed him to lead her into their room and he closed the door and locked it. 'No interruptions,' he said. 'Just you and me.'

Maggie sat on the bed and he sat down beside her. He entwined his fingers in hers and kissed her on the neck. She gave an exasperated sigh. 'Okay, so what do you want to talk about? What did Rose say?' She levered him away with her elbow. 'Kristo, you don't have to sit right on top of me. Just give me some space.'

He raised his hands in mock surrender, got up and pulled over the armchair to sit opposite her. 'Rose said you were suicidal. Is that true?'

'I'm not going to *do* it. I just find it comforting to plan it. To know there is a way out. Can't I be allowed that one indulgence, at least?'

He looked as though he'd been slapped and she was surprised to realise that she didn't care. She felt like slapping him. Even though he'd done nothing, apart from take her for granted. She was afraid to plumb the depths of her anger. Fearful of unleashing it and tearing everything apart. 'Anything else? Or can I go and make lunch now?'

'Darling, why didn't you talk to me?' His face crumpled as the tears welled.

'Why are you crying? I thought this was about me. Nothing is ever really about me, it can only ever be about how my misery makes someone else unhappy.'

'Maggie, you are my life, my soul . . . you are the kindest, most loving person I know . . .' He was really crying now, as though she were already dead.

'I used to be, not any more. I'm hard and cynical – and mean. You're only crying because if I died, you'd have no one to run the business, organise the house, manage your mother, manage your children – and shag.'

He flinched. 'Maggie, that's not fair. It's nasty. I'm trying to make things easier for you. I thought Mum could help you. Do some of the cooking and help take care of the place.'

'Kristo, can you see that's like getting an extra staff member onboard? Someone has to manage that person. She's eighty-two, she needs looking after herself. She's lonely and bored . . . and interfering. I don't think you have any idea how much responsibility rests on my shoulders and the stress I'm under every single bloody day.'

'It's a stressful business. We're all under intense pressure. Out on site —'

'Are we still talking about me?' Maggie interrupted. 'Or are we back to talking about the family now?'

'You need to see a doctor,' said Kristo. 'I'll make an appointment on Monday.'

'I'm quite capable of making my own appointment, thank you.'

He leaned towards her and rested his hand awkwardly on her thigh. She knew that he wanted to make love to her, find his way back to her, to comfort her – and himself. But she wasn't having it. 'Sometimes I see an ambulance go past and long to be inside it, being whisked away to a place where I can rest and be looked after. Where no one wants anything from me.'

Kristo withdrew his hand and leaned back in the chair. 'I don't know what to do.'

'That's because it's my job to know what to do about everything,' Maggie said bitterly. After a moment she felt sorry for him.

'Look, I don't know what to do with myself. Right now it's like everything has the same level of stress for me. There is a pulse of electricity running through my body day and night. I'm on constant red alert, like a one-woman response team. My nervous system is worn out.'

'And you do a wonderful job. That's why we love you,' said Kristo, cradling her hands in his own and gazing into her eyes like an adoring puppy.

'And if I wasn't doing a wonderful job, what then?'

'What are you saying? What do you think? I'll fire you – or divorce you? I want to help you. It's not like you to be so nasty. I don't know what's changed.'

They both turned at the sound of the door handle being twisted back and forth. This was followed a moment later by Yia-yiá shouting, 'Maggie! You sick? Kristaki *mou!* Why's you hide? Open this door!' She broke into rapid Greek and Maggie quickly lost the thread, but judging by Kristo's expression and his mother's hectoring tone, it seemed some new drama was being set in motion.

'She thinks we're in here plotting to get rid of her,' said Kristo. 'I better go and calm her down.'

He kissed Maggie on the forehead and left, closing the door behind him. She was alone, and nothing had changed. She went downstairs and made a couple of ham-and-salad sandwiches and took them down to the pool for the girls.

'We're into Paleo,' said Elena. 'We've talked about this before, Mum.'

Maggie began to eat one of the sandwiches. 'That's fine but you'll have to do your own hunting and gathering. I can't cater for everyone on different diets. Look, Elena, I really think you need to stay out of this business with Aaron. There's obviously been a misunderstanding somewhere along the line. Anthea, I know it's old-school, but perhaps you could consider not filming yourself, or taking nude shots —'

'Hashtag victim blaming,' interrupted Elena.

'Elena, could I please have a moment to speak to your sister alone? There are things we need to discuss. Things that don't require hashtags, or even your opinion.'

Elena picked up the other sandwich, poked through the contents distastefully with her fingernail, and began to eat it as she walked slowly up the steps towards the house.

'I'm sorry, Mum,' said Anthea. 'I am really, *really* embarrassed.'

'I know, darling. But right now, we have to be practical. You're not going to like what I'm about to say, but it has to be said. Your father and I gave you the deposit for the flat, so you have some responsibility to us for that. You can't just walk out. You need to stay there and try to resolve things, or ask Aaron to move out.'

'I don't want to talk to him right now. Don't make me. And don't start talking about how much the wedding cost.'

'The wedding is irrelevant now. Before you do anything drastic, you need to speak to our lawyers. I'm not familiar with family law, but we need to find out how it all works.'

'Can't you and Dad handle it? Or are you going to humiliate me by making me go to the lawyers and show them?'

'Anthea, you're an adult, and have been for some time. You need to face up to the situation.' Maggie looked at the unhappy face of her daughter. 'You don't really want a divorce, do you?'

'I don't know,' she said sulkily. 'I just feel . . .'

Hearing voices, they looked up to see Elena and Kristo coming down from the house. 'Let's talk about this later,' Maggie said quickly.

'Dad,' said Anthea, as soon as he was in range. 'Mum said I have to go to the lawyers and tell them everything.'

The colour drained from Kristo's face. 'No bloody way! Everyone will know. The whole fucking Greek community —'

'Hang on, Kris . . . there's such a thing as client confidentiality.'

'Bullshit. No lawyers.' Now he was riled, there would be no reasoning with him. 'No divorce. You've only been married five minutes. You're going to embarrass the whole family!'

'She can't stay married to him, he's a —' began Elena.

'Elena, stay out of this,' pleaded Maggie. 'I asked you to go inside.'

'What am I, ten years old?! I'm the only one sticking up for Anthea!'

'We're all here for Anthea,' insisted Maggie, knowing it was futile. 'Can we please take this argument inside? So at least the neighbours don't have to know.'

Anthea began to cry. Kristo stormed off up the steps to the house and Maggie followed him. When she looked back, the twins lay side by side on a sun bed, Elena's arm outstretched taking a selfie. Hashtag sad face.

The argument didn't stop there. It raged all through dinner, giving Yia-yiá the opportunity for her input. After dinner, the twins announced they would go back to the city and stay at Elena's place. It would be cramped and they would have to share a bed but, as Elena pointed out, it would be less stressful for them.

Maggie went to bed exhausted, but relieved at the temporary reprieve. She was woken just before midnight by the sound of a vehicle in the driveway. Through the louvres at the top of the stairs, she could see Aaron's ute, an enormous vehicle like a life-size Tonka toy with a reflective logo on the side advertising his electrician services. He called his business 'Bright Spark', a misnomer if ever there was one. Having triggered the motion detector lights, Aaron himself stood in the pool of light in the turning circle. He looked up and gave Maggie a childlike wave.

She rushed downstairs and let him in, warning him to be quiet. They went into the kitchen. She closed the dining-room doors and locked them. It was rare for Kristo to wake in the night but if necessary Aaron could make his escape out the back door. 'What are you doing here, Aaron? It's really not a good idea.'

'I just wanted to talk to her.' He looked around hopefully. 'Is there anything to eat?'

'It's practically midnight . . . and anyway, she's not here.'

'Oh. I missed dinner. Sorry.'

Maggie got a cold sausage out of the fridge, sliced open a bread roll, wedged it in and handed it to him.

He took a bite. 'Do you have any tomato sauce? Sorry.'

'If I give you some sauce, will you leave? You don't want Kristo to catch you.' Maggie got the sauce out of the fridge and plonked it in front of him. 'What were you thinking, posting that video online anyway?'

Aaron was a decent boy. It was hard to think of him as anything other than an overgrown child. He was handsome in a chiselled, fit way. Apart from the tribal tattoos he wore like sleeves, he looked like an all-American boy from the fifties with his blond crew cut and muscles.

'I don't know,' he said through a mouthful of sausage, tomato sauce squishing out both sides of the roll. 'Actually, I do. I came home, I was pretty drunk . . . Thea was out . . . I started watching . . . er, never mind. And then . . . I thought . . .'

'Yes, all right. I think I can fill in the blanks myself. Now you have to make things right with Anthea. You don't want her to divorce you, do you?'

He shook his head vehemently, and waited for Maggie to tell him what to do.

'I think you should write a letter. Not an email or a text. A proper letter apologising. A love letter.'

'A letter? Ugh. Can't I just get flowers? Or perfume? She likes perfume.'

'You can do that as well. It only needs to be a short letter. But heartfelt and romantic. Tell her how you feel and how sorry you are.'

He gulped the last of the sausage roll and laboriously licked the sauce off his fingers, getting just as much satisfaction out of that. Maggie couldn't believe how far and wide it had spread, in between his fingers, even traces halfway up his wrist. Finally, he said, 'Could you help me . . . like . . . get started?'

Sighing, Maggie got out some paper and a pen, and put it on the table in front of him. 'Okay, so Dear Anthea, or Thea . . . Dear Thea.'

Aaron stared at the paper as though he'd forgotten how to write. He looked up at her with a tortured expression. Maggie half expected to hear a line of Shakespeare spill poetically from his lips . . . *A rose by any other name* . . .

After a moment he asked, 'Can't I just say "Mate" . . . or even miss that bit out?'

Maggie got up and put the kettle on. It was going to be a long night.

*

Behind the scenes, Rose and Kristo evidently kept in touch because, the next thing Maggie knew, Kristo had latched onto Rose's idea of the three friends revisiting Europe and practically insisted that Maggie must go. In an effort to convince her, he talked up the competencies of his cousin Yannis, who was Maggie's reluctant offsider. Even though he had failed his certification exam, Yannis had high aspirations for himself and he too embraced the idea, knowing he would enjoy an elevated status during Maggie's absence.

Despite wanting to get away, Maggie began to feel she was being got rid of. When she finally agreed to go, Kristo began to tell everyone about her 'adventure', as though he'd dreamed up the whole idea himself. But Maggie wondered privately if a spell in hospital wouldn't be more beneficial than going off with her girlfriends in search of her lost youth. Clearly Kristo preferred the idea that his wife was going on holiday, as opposed to undergoing psychiatric care, and she felt obliged to go along with it.

Nico scowled every time he saw her and persisted in asking why she was going away and where she would go. He was the last person she wanted to know her movements. She made it her business never to be alone with him, despite his constant attempts to orchestrate it. It took all her strength to hide her loathing of him.

Anthea and Elena were unfazed by Maggie's plan. It was only a month. Within minutes of assessing whether her departure would affect them in any way, they were discussing if and when they could join her somewhere on the trip. Normally, Maggie would have agreed. She was inured to the idea that the twins got whatever they wanted, but she knew the minute the girls were involved, the whole enterprise would be derailed by them lobbying for things to be done their way. Rose would hit the roof. Besides, Anthea and Aaron were in counselling and that was the priority right now. And Maggie needed a break from them as much as anything else.

Kristo must have been honest with his mother because, over the next couple of weeks, Maggie noticed Yia-yiá was tearful and anxious, as though Maggie's unravelling had triggered something deep in her.

Yia-yiá and Pappoú had migrated as newlyweds, following his older brother, Georgios, and wife Agnes, to Sydney. They had all worked for another Kytherian, from the same village, who owned a delicatessen. Within two years they had saved enough to set up the fish shop in Marrickville, now the stuff of family legend. By then, Kristo had been born, followed by the other three boys over the next five years. Pappoú and Georgios had manned the front counter and the fryers. Yia-yiá and Agnes were out the back, preparing the potatoes, mixing up the batter, scaling and filleting the fish and minding the children. Face to face with customers, Pappoú and Georgios had continued to improve their English. But Yia-yiá and Agnes only had each other; all their family friends were Greek and, without the time or money for lessons, it took both women years to acquire basic English. Yia-yiá still spoke to her sons almost entirely in Greek and only resorted to English if there was no alternative.

Maggie had often wondered how Yia-yiá had coped with all those babies, the pressure of work and running a household and, on top of that, struggling to understand what was going on around her. But she was young. She had all the boys in her early twenties. That was her lot and she was likely grateful for it. All their friends and family would have worked just as hard; it wasn't as though they were any different. But she would have been perpetually exhausted and there must have been times when she wondered if there was something else – some easier path in life.

Yia-yiá had been elevated by her sons to a legendary status. Her role as the goddess of drudgery did her daughters-in-law a disservice and they all came to resent her for various reasons, even the Greek ones who married with her blessing. Witnessing Maggie's vulnerable state seemed to touch on a truth hidden inside the family mythology.

Kristo wept on the way to the airport, he called Maggie *psichí mou* – my soul – and went on about how much he would miss her. He hadn't showed his affection in this way for years, yet she found herself unmoved by his endearments, as though nothing touched her any more. She remained convinced that everyone simply wanted her to go back to being her old self. Not of ten years or thirty years ago, but a few weeks ago, before they were confronted by her unhappiness.

He wanted to come into the terminal to wave Maggie off, but, fearful of an emotional parting, she insisted that he drop her out the front. They sat in the car, silently watching other vehicles pull in and pop open boots. Passengers spilled out, collected bags. There were embraces and partings. One party waved from the pavement. The other drove away. This level of the airport was the scene of partings, the lower one for joyous reunions; a constant wave of humanity ebbing and flowing across the world. Maggie had no sense of how she would feel on her return. There was nothing but blank space ahead.

'Call me and let me know you've arrived safely,' said Kristo.

'We will arrive safely.' She opened her handbag to check she had her passport for the tenth time. 'But I will text and let you know.'

'You won't do anything silly, will you?' His voice cracked.

'Like jump out of the plane without a parachute?'

He thumped his fist on the steering wheel, giving her a start. 'It's not something to joke about! Okay, I got the message. This is not about me, but I am human. I feel pain too.'

'I'm sorry. I was being flippant. I think I've absorbed so many other people's pain in the last few decades that I've stopped being absorbent.' She leaned over, put her arms around him and kissed his bristly cheek. She whispered in his ear. 'I do love you.'

Kristo nodded miserably. 'I love you too.'

'Please don't get out. I can get my bag myself. You just drive away – I'll be home before you know it.'

She pulled her suitcase from the boot and could feel Kristo's embarrassment radiating from the car, imagining the entire airport had paused to nudge and point at this neglectful husband. Then she walked into the terminal without a backward glance.

As she sat with Rose in the departure lounge, the airport swirled with currents of nervous excitement that amplified Maggie's own anxiety. Announcements urging lost people to come to the gate had a metallic reverberation that made her head throb. Where on earth were all these people? Was there a vortex somewhere in the terminal that sucked unwary travellers into an alternate universe? All she wanted was to be left alone, but right now the best she could hope for was to cram herself into that airline seat, knock back a couple of sleeping tablets and be unconscious for a few sweet hours.

'I think we should have some rules —' began Rose, digging around in the multiple pockets of a daypack she had purchased especially for the trip. 'Where are my tissues? I cannot get on a flight without tissues.'

'Then go and buy some. How about a rule about not asking where things are? That is my chief hate, people asking me where their stuff is,' said Maggie.

'Crisis averted!' Rose pulled a handful of crumpled tissues from the depths of her bag. 'I was thinking more that we ban discussions about how badly we slept and how many times we woke up. Aches and pains. Indigestion . . . um, bloating . . . constipation . . . the effects of gravity —'

'Yes. Okay. I get it.'

Despite Maggie's terse response, Rose pushed on. 'No old-people talk. We need to suck it up. Our young selves danced drunkenly all night and never complained about it.'

'If I agree to all those rules, will you stop talking to me for a while? I just need some quiet time.'

'I can stop speaking to you indefinitely, if you prefer.' Rose gave her a haughty look, then, softening, added, 'Sorry, Magsy – nervous energy. We've still got half an hour before boarding. I'll go for a walk. Give you a break.'

Maggie nodded. She took Rose's hand and held it for a moment. 'Sorry. Thank you.'

'Maggie, I wouldn't have railroaded you into this if I didn't think it was the right thing for you to get away. I will take care of you, I promise.'

Watching Rose stride off down the expanse of glossy linoleum, so confident in her strange harem pants, her mad hair springing off her head like an explosion of silver light, Maggie breathed a sigh of relief. All she needed was a few moments when she didn't have to respond to anyone or pretend to be all right.

When Rose returned from her stroll, she sat down beside Maggie. 'I got herbal tea, some snacky things, chocolate . . . are you okay?'

Maggie nodded. 'What are we doing, Rose? I can't believe that I let you talk me into this. What can we possibly hope to find?'

'Wouldn't you like to find that Adonis you met at that wine festival in Athens? *Man*, he was cute.'

Maggie looked at her in horror. 'I've already got an excess of Greeks in my life, thank you.'

Rose laughed. 'Sorry, bad example.'

'Besides, that Adonis will be a grandfather with a pot belly and an ouzo problem now. What if we find out that nothing is as good as it was in 1978? Where will that leave us?'

'Why are you coming with such a gloomy outlook?' asked Rose.

'Because, as you pointed out, you and Kristo bullied me into it. And I couldn't think of what else to do with myself.'

'Well, brighten up. We need to be open to possibility. That's the thing I remember most. We were open to the world and whatever direction life might take us.'

'Yes. And this is where we ended up. That's how it goes.'

Rose ignored her. 'That's what I want to find . . . that freedom of spirit. I see it as a journey of discovery.'

'You're not going to start singing now, are you?' asked Maggie.

'We are going to sing on this trip. That's non-negotiable.'

'Fine, but no yodelling. I can't bear it when you yodel.'

Rose gave an annoyed sigh. 'Consider it on the list. And I'll sing in my head for the moment.'

'What are you singing? Just so I know.'

Rose closed her eyes for a moment. 'Steppenwolf, baby – "Born to Be Wild".'

Maggie snorted. She watched Rose nodding to the song in her head. 'Okay, start at the beginning.'

Rose counted down, they leaned in, heads touching and began to hum softly together.

Part Two

The Journey

Chapter Six

It was almost five years since Rose had seen Fran in the flesh. She was still elfin, but age had thickened her all over and her face looked slightly wizened, like an apple on the turn.

Since Fran couldn't drive, she made the journey to meet their dawn arrival at Heathrow by public transport. She suggested they all take the shuttle to Paddington and taxi from there, but Maggie wouldn't hear of it. She announced herself exhausted, which seemed incredible given she'd been comatose practically the entire trip. Anyway, Maggie wanted to pay for the cab so that was the end of it.

After the initial excitement of the reunion, there was a sense of anticlimax in the cab. They were all suddenly out of sorts and began to gently bicker. Fran kept insisting that, although her place was small, she wanted them to stay, rather than waste money paying for accommodation.

'We're too old for airbeds and all that,' said Maggie. 'Thanks anyway.'

Rose looked across at her. 'I think saying we're "too old" for anything should be on the banned list.'

'I think the "banned list" should be on the banned list,' Maggie said.

Fran looked anxious. 'What's this list?'

Rose didn't want to squabble. 'It's nothing. Forget it. Anyway, we have a place booked, so we don't even need to have this argument.'

'It's not really an argument,' argued Fran. 'It's a discussion.'

Maggie settled back and closed her eyes. 'I need to be comfortable.'

Check-in wasn't available until midafternoon, so they all went to Fran's place in the meantime. Even by Rose's standards, Fran's place was shabby, with wonky-shaped rooms and traffic noise that surged like a tide in the background. It was cluttered with odd furniture and props left over from various theatrical productions that added a bohemian touch to what would other-wise have seemed squalid. Fran had also acquired a marmalade cat that looked the worse for wear despite its fancy French name.

Fran's plants were a redeeming feature, although there were so many it was starting to look like a greenhouse. Even the light in the room had a green tinge. Every plant, and there were at least a hundred, had a note attached, written in Fran's copper-plate script, with its name and care instructions. These, Fran explained, were for Louis, who had agreed to water them while she was away. Good luck with that, thought Rose. But perhaps she was judging him by Peter's track record.

Rose assumed that their accommodation would be a step up from this, but she wasn't the fussy one. In fact, it was easy to imagine they were still in the seventies here. She had been to two of Fran's other flats, and it occurred to her that Fran had moved so often she never quite settled any more. She'd been here a couple of years but there was still a stack of packing boxes in one corner. Fran began to make tea and toast, then realised she had no milk, having given it all to the cat. And, despite them both insisting black tea was fine, she rushed off down the street to get some.

Rose stood at the window and watched the traffic on the street below. Despite everything that was difficult about London, it had an allure that had never faded, like an adored movie star whose celebrity was undiminished by age. London was the Sophia Loren of cities.

In Sydney, you could breathe sea air and see the horizon from a thousand different vantage points. London had a pulsating energy, this city that millions of people seemed determined to conquer. Great seething masses of people. Rivers of people who poured down escalators like a single entity, long black centipedes of commuters, their bodies pressed tightly into tubes rocketing through the network deep under the city. Here, there were displays of wealth far in excess of anything you would see at home, as well as people sleeping rough, begging outside the railway stations. It was dreary and glorious at the same time. And then there was the weather. It was the last week of May and the sky was dark, rain gusting past the window.

'Rose,' said Maggie from the sofa, 'don't tell Fran about the video thing, you know . . . Anthea . . .'

Rose turned from the window and sat down on the sofa. 'Really? You know she's bonked a few blokes in her time, and shopped around the corner once or twice.'

'What are you talking about?'

'I'm saying, I doubt she'd be shocked by anything of a sexual nature.'

'I just don't want to talk about it any more. I want to forget it and not go over it again. I'm so sick of it. It's finished, anyway.' Maggie put a cushion on the arm of the sofa and laid her head on it like a tired child.

'Fair enough,' said Rose. 'Then you don't mention the restraining-order business.'

'What? I don't know anything about a restraining order.'

Fran rushed in the door with a carton of milk. 'What have I missed? Who's had a restraining order?'

Rose groaned. 'Max. He doesn't *have* a restraining order. He was threatened with one.'

'Oh no! I'm sure it's just a mix up, isn't it?' asked Fran. 'He didn't assault anyone, did he?'

'No, of course not. He was just being a pest. He's not good at reading social cues. He's moved back home to keep Peter company while I'm away. He won't have time for stalking.'

'I don't think you should make light of it, Rose. I've been stalked. It's horrible,' said Maggie, sitting up. '*We* know that Max wouldn't hurt anyone, but his victim doesn't know that.'

'Who stalked you?' asked Rose. 'When was this, recently?'

Maggie looked away. 'As if anyone would stalk me now,' she said evasively.

'Oh, Maggie. It's not a compliment to be stalked,' said Fran.

'How come you've never mentioned it before? Who was it?' asked Rose.

Maggie's expression shut down. 'I'm sorry I brought it up. Forget it.'

'Well, who was it?' Rose repeated.

'No one you know. Just leave it, Rose.'

Rose didn't want to leave it. It was unlike Maggie to be so

secretive, and odd that she'd never mentioned it before. Rose would remember something like that.

'Who was Max bothering anyway?' asked Fran, bringing out the tea on a tray.

'A young woman he went out with a couple times. He really wasn't stalking. She works in the same building and he went to extraordinary lengths to "accidentally" bump into her. And messaged her. Excessively.'

'Stalking and harassment,' said Maggie under her breath.

Rose pressed her lips together and was rewarded with an approving nod from Fran, always the peacemaker. Rose thought it a mystery that, despite being such a good and lovely person, Fran had suffered so many disappointing relationships. She wasn't judgemental enough – too tolerant, always ready to excuse someone's inexcusable behaviour. Rose envisaged a thrift shop of used men, pre-loved, a little worn, frayed at the edges or perhaps no longer suiting or fitting their previous partner. They seemed like a bargain but it didn't take long to realise that there were too many flaws to deal with. It was astonishing that Fran never seemed to give up or become cynical, although lately there had been a weariness in her, a sense of resignation.

'How are you feeling, Maggie?' asked Fran. 'Would you like a lie-down on my bed?'

Maggie sat up straight, smoothed her hair back from her face and flicked it expertly into a knot at her nape. Without the soft frame of hair (these days expensively coloured) her face had a naked, vulnerable look. 'I appreciate your concern, both of you, but I really don't need to be treated like an invalid. There's nothing actually wrong with me, apart from being tired and grumpy.'

'I think that deep down Mags has been very pissed off for a very long time,' offered Rose. 'It was like a subterranean river of discontent running through her. Now it has risen to the surface and flooded her senses and she's pissed off about absolutely everything.'

Fran looked to Maggie for confirmation. 'That fairly much covers it,' admitted Maggie. 'I'll make an effort to be more cheerful.'

'I don't think you should,' said Fran. 'I think you should be completely honest. Let it flow out of your system. You don't have to pretend with us. We're solid. Just lay it on us.'

Rose gave Maggie a sidelong glance. 'Yeah, she's right. You need to stop being polite and spit it out. We can just bitch about you behind your back.'

Fran shook her head seriously. 'Let's all be honest. And not bitch.'

Maggie nodded. She lifted her mug in a salute. 'To our quest, whatever the hell it is.'

Fran and Rose raised their mugs solemnly. 'Our quest.'

The accommodation Rose had booked was a basement flat in a Regency house in Bayswater with a small rear courtyard. Spacious and pleasant, it gained Maggie's full approval. They settled in and walked the surrounding streets to stay awake until a reasonable hour. It was damp with a cool wind and their jackets were only just warm enough. The whole area seemed to be populated by tourist groups, their wheelie suitcases squeaking along the pavements, as though it wasn't really a part of the city but a staging post. They ate in weary silence at a nearby café and went home to bed.

As soon as Rose lay down, she felt wide awake. She kept thinking about Maggie being stalked. In all these years, it would be rare if a month went by without them speaking. They were each other's first responders and their conversations were honest and frank. Rose knew about the intimacies and intricacies of Maggie's life, so how was it possible that she never mentioned a stalker before? Rose had obviously not mentioned the business with Max, but that was an unintentional oversight. Rose was absolutely certain it was a misunderstanding. Then again, did a mother see that side of her son? Mothers make excuses for their sons, hoping they'll eventually live up to their mothers' aspirations. She messaged Max: *Where are you?*

He messaged back: *Y?*

She sent him a kiss. It was futile. She had to trust him. She had to let him suffer the consequences of his actions. And just check up on him now and then. No point in relying on Peter to keep an eye on him.

Peter was able to receive and read messages on his phone but incapable of sending them, so she was quite used to messaging him without expectation of a response. It was, she mused, reflective of their relationship in many ways. She initiated and he considered, pondered, prevaricated, stonewalled and, occasionally, capitulated. He was like a great battleship sunk in the harbour of her life, an obstacle that had to be navigated around.

Fitz, on the other hand, was a prolific communicator. He shared links to articles from *The Guardian*, podcasts, snippets of news, memes, gifs and funny YouTube videos – there were several messages awaiting her attention. They could wait. Everyone could wait. One of the things she wanted to do on this trip was to stop being so responsive to every need that every person thrust at her. She was tempted to send Peter or Max a message to remind them to put the bins out but managed to resist. She turned off her phone to avoid temptation.

After struggling to get to sleep, Rose woke just after midnight feeling as though it was morning. She switched on her lamp and went quietly down the hall to the kitchen, made a cup of tea and brought it back to bed. She was working her way through missives from Fitz when Maggie appeared in the doorway.

Rose put her phone aside. 'Kettle's boiled. Do you want me to get you one?'

Maggie shook her head and disappeared off down the hall. Minutes later, she was back with a steaming mug. 'I'm not used to sleeping alone.'

Rose propped up the pillows on the other side of the bed. 'I'm not going to make a habit of it – just this once.'

Maggie slipped in beside her. They sat sipping their tea and Rose sensed that she needed to be silent, not try to fill the space. It was an effort, but she managed.

After a while Maggie said, 'I felt almost crippled with anxiety today. I woke up just now and started imagining myself falling in front of the Tube or being hit by a cab or a bus . . .'

'What about Uber?'

Maggie gave her a look of disbelief. 'What?'

'Cities are crawling with them and you wouldn't even know. I just wondered if it was a generalised fear of public transport . . . that's all,' she finished lamely.

'No, it's a fear of dying in a strange city and never seeing my family again. I feel exposed and vulnerable.'

'That's because you're usually cocooned in the domestic mayhem of your family life. Now you're out in the world as an individual.'

'I'm not sure I know how to be an individual any more, or want to be one. I'm worried about Kristo and the girls and Yia-yiá and the business.' Maggie's voice was thick with emotion. 'I was lying there sort of scrolling through all these people and their problems in my mind. And leaving the business . . . I feel as though I've left my newborn in the care of a . . . delinquent.'

'Is this your assistant?'

Maggie nodded. 'Yannis.'

'I thought you were trying to get rid of him?'

'I have tried but there's no getting rid of Yannis. I've told Kristo over and over that he's careless and lazy; he doesn't have an aptitude for the work at all. He's Yia-yiá's only nephew. His mother, Theía Agnes, is Yia-yiá's closest friend; they're like sisters. Anyway, the family don't even want to hear about it.'

'It seems ridiculous to have to pay people because they're related to you.'

'It's the way it is and Kristo thinks he's safer behind a computer than out on site, and that is true. He's a fifty-something, grossly overweight man who lives with his mother and his PlayStation. More to the point, he likes the pokies and I don't really trust him.' Maggie sighed. 'I just feel so agitated, I don't know if I can do this. I feel like the house is burning down and I have to rush home and put the fire out.'

'That's because you think you're the only one who can. It's not true. It's going to take some courage, Mags. You need to save yourself first.'

It crossed Rose's mind that Maggie's mental state was actually deteriorating. She was practised at keeping it well hidden. What if these thoughts about buses and taxis were premonitions or a death wish?

'Try and put those worries to sleep for the moment. Close your eyes. I'll keep watch for taxis and whatnot.'

Maggie nodded submissively. She finished her tea in silence, slid down in the bed and closed her eyes. Rose switched off the lamp and lay in the dark listening to the sound of sirens in the distance, wondering what on earth they were doing there.

Rose didn't feel that panic or need to get home. Her life was locked in like a Rubik's cube – you could click the blocks this way or that, but only rearrange what already existed. Perhaps it had always been that way and she just hadn't realised. Apart from becoming more dependent on her, Peter hadn't actually changed much over the years, and she was complicit in his dependence. She had followed her mother's pattern of venerating her husband and infantilising him at the same time. She wondered what a psychologist would make of that. These days she worked around him to get things done without even thinking about it. But they had begun to squabble the way her parents did, and she had to take some responsibility for that friction.

Over breakfast recently, he'd put forward the idea that when he retired, he could train to teach English to foreign students, as Rose did.

'What on earth made you think of that?' Rose asked him.

'You seem to derive satisfaction from it. I can't imagine it's that difficult, especially with my teaching experience.'

'So, let me just clarify that – you think it's easy because I do it?'

'Now you're projecting your own lack of self-regard on to me and imagining an insult where there is none,' he said mildly. He propped the iPad up in front of him and began to scroll through the news, as though the conversation was now over. Or perhaps to avoid the direction it was taking.

'Actually, I think you'd find it very difficult. And you have to write lesson plans. It's interactive. You don't just stand up there and *pontificate*.'

'Rose, you're always urging me to *discuss* things – now I am trying to do just that and you're being combative. I'm simply saying that I don't want to find myself at home, isolated and forced to take up golf, or worse.'

'What's worse than golf?'

He was distracted for a moment by his ritual of systematically compressing the crust around the edge of his toast with the handle of his knife, even though his teeth were in perfect working order. 'I don't know. Gambling?'

'I'm all for you starting something new but not something that involves me in any way. I don't want to ride shotgun for you any more, Peter. We've talked about this so many times.'

He adopted his defeated look then, as though she had now eliminated all possibilities and he would be forced, through no fault of his own, to take up gambling and golf.

Rose wasn't buying it. She'd taught foreign students for twenty years, she was good at it and she knew that he wouldn't be. He was out of touch. He'd only managed to hold his position as long as he had because, beyond his faults and annoying habits, Peter was a brilliant lecturer and a renowned expert on twentieth-century history. In some ways, his age had worked for him. He offered such detailed and vivid narratives, it almost seemed as though he was providing eyewitness accounts.

He was a talented and passionate orator, a raconteur who had a knack for finding unusual connections and parallels that brought the subject matter and the personalities to life. His speciality was the ability to relate historic events to contemporary ones. In person, he was shy and distracted, as if trying to remember where he'd left something or where he should be – which was usually the case. But once on his subject, he lit up and could talk for hours, whether he was being paid or not.

Rose had been in her first year of an Arts degree when she met Peter. She'd come to it late, starting at twenty-four, when most of her contemporaries had already graduated. She'd had enough of waitressing and office temping, singing in pubs and hoping for the big break. She'd also had enough of her volatile on-again off-again relationship with a bass guitarist called Charlie. She'd broken up with him a dozen times, but every time their paths crossed, it was back on again. (All these years later, Charlie in his rock-god leather jeans still featured in her erotic fantasies.) At the time, she had wanted to close that whole chapter of her life and become a serious grown-up.

Peter was the antithesis of Charlie: educated, respected and respectable. She worked hard on her essays for his subject, determined to dazzle her professor, and engaging him in after-lecture conversations. Peter seemed bemused by her enthusiasm, but despite his diffidence (or perhaps because of it) Rose found him complex and fascinating. She invited him to a pub gig where she was singing backup for a band. He didn't show. It wasn't his sort of thing. A clear sign of what was to come. Finally, they went out for dinner, to which he was half an hour late. She threw him into bed at the first opportunity. He was amenable to her attentions and their relationship limped along for a few months – until he realised he needed her.

Rose would soon discover that for all his virtuosity as a lecturer, his writing skills lagged far behind those of his students. His brilliant connections and conclusions were all there in his head but they were impossible for him to articulate onto the page. His spelling was too bewildering for spellcheck and punctuation would be sprinkled as randomly as stardust. If he wrote by hand, he struggled to even separate the letters from each other. It was years before it was properly diagnosed as dysgraphia and he became less self-conscious about it.

He read voraciously and could remember extraordinary amounts of material but his older sister had been his ghostwriter all through school, sticking with him right through university to his PhD. By then, she was married with children, which was difficult enough, but her husband was being transferred to San Francisco and a new helper was needed. Peter could plan his lectures out in his head and dictate them to his sister, or deliver off the cuff, if necessary. But to retain his tenure, he needed to publish papers, and a book was inevitable. Rose was flattered to be asked to assist him. She felt like the chosen one.

Peter was unfazed by the news that Rose was pregnant and took it for granted that he would marry her. In fact, he seemed quite pleased with himself for having accomplished that particular life feat with minimal effort. Rose cried for three days before she adapted to the idea. She'd always wanted to be a mother; it had just happened ahead of schedule. It was a sensible solution and Peter was a good catch. He was decent looking and intelligent. He would be a reliable breadwinner. Her parents were disappointed. She'd been the first in the family to go to university and she'd blown it. She swore that she would finish her degree, but somehow never did.

Under Peter's direction, Rose had ghosted numerous papers and three well-regarded history books. For years, she had longed for her own project, and when she met the artist Inge Bryant, she knew Inge was the subject she had been waiting for. In the sixties, Inge's work had been collected by rock stars. She had lived in the Chelsea hotel in New York for two years and fraternised with such luminaries as Leonard Cohen and Andy Warhol. In a haze of wine and bonhomie, Rose had offered to write Inge's biography. This would be Rose's own work, with her name writ large on the cover.

Rose had been to Melbourne half-a-dozen times and recorded extensive interviews with Inge but still couldn't find the spine of the story. It was a patchwork of anecdotes that changed each time they were told. Inge didn't care that much about the book – perhaps doubted she would live long enough to see it – but liked having an audience and talking about her life. She was now in her eighties and there was less interest in her work. Rose vacillated between feeling the story should be told and Inge's talent and fascinating life acknowledged, and a growing realisation that too much time had passed and, really, no one was interested. Rose had stopped talking about the project, annoyed by scepticism in the blank looks of friends and family.

As she lay in the dark listening to Maggie's soft breathing, Rose wondered if the whole project was really a way for *her* to be acknowledged, for people to recognise that *she* was intelligent and talented. That she was not actually championing Inge, but using her in the same way Rose had been used by Peter. It was a difficult way to get attention and this dawning awareness of her true motives made her doubt if she had a genuine commitment to the project. But she saw herself as a finisher. She was not someone who took up projects and abandoned them. And so it went on. Click click, click – the positions on the cube changed but not the elements.

Rose would not leave Peter for Fitz. She had no plans to give up Fitz. She would not abandon Inge. She would support Max, who was beautiful and intelligent, but had never quite grown up, at least until a capable and patient girlfriend arrived to take over. This was her role in life and she was doomed to play it out to the end. She tried to think of a tune to hum in her head and coax herself to sleep. But there was nothing but the annoying whistle of her tinnitus, which sounded like an old wireless stuck between stations.

When Rose woke, the room was bright with sunlight. It was after eight and Maggie was still asleep, so she went to the kitchen and made them both tea. She put Maggie's on the bedside table and stood at the window watching puffball clouds drift across a blue sky, hoping they hadn't already missed the best part of the day.

Maggie groaned and rolled over. 'Is it morning?'

'Yes. It's morning.'

'Thank God for that. I thought that night would never end.' Maggie pushed herself up against the pillows. 'What do we have to do today?'

Rose turned to look at her. 'Have you looked at the itinerary?'

'I haven't *studied* it . . . okay, no, I haven't looked at it.'

'Why not? Aren't you even curious?' Rose couldn't decide if she was annoyed or not.

Maggie pondered the question. 'No, it seems not. To be honest, I just can't take anything in at the moment. My concentration is shot. I'd actually prefer that you just took care of everything and I'll follow you around.'

Rose sat down on the bed facing her. 'So you're happy to bob along like a cork on the ocean, are you?'

'If you're that ocean, yes. I trust you, Rosie. This whole thing was your idea. I still don't know if there's a point to it. I just needed to get away from my family for a bit. Even if I just lay here for a month, that could be helpful.'

On the bedside table, Maggie's phone pipped with a message and they both watched as a string of texts from Elena ghosted onto the screen in quick succession. Then another pip and a series from Anthea began to pile up.

'Why don't we put our phones on silent?' suggested Rose. 'So you can get a break.'

Maggie's face was expressionless as she scrolled through the messages. 'It seems Aaron made some comments at counselling that the girls have taken exception to.'

'Are both girls going?'

Maggie laughed grimly. 'Can you even imagine? No, Anthea gives Elena a blow-by-blow after the session. Her version, obviously.'

'Mags, it's not your problem. You have no control over it. They can sort it out.'

Maggie flicked the phone to silent and placed it screen-down on the bed. 'That invisible umbilical cord just stretches and stretches through the years, across oceans and skies . . . we can't escape it.'

'Would you have done anything differently, if you'd known that it was a job for life?' asked Rose, sipping her tea.

Maggie sighed. 'I think things would have been different if I'd had another one. The twins got too much attention when they were small. As you know, Kristo wanted to try again, but I really didn't have the strength for it after Kal.'

'Of course you didn't. They were lavished with attention by everyone because of losing Kal. You're a good mum and a good wife and a good daughter-in-law and a good daughter. Jesus, it's a lot, isn't it? Like being chairman of the board for four different corporations.'

'That would be easier,' said Maggie. 'Quite a lot easier.'

'I'm not all those things. Not half as good as you. I just fob everyone off, so things end up going round and round.'

'You've been very good to Pete. And a wonderful mum to your boys,' said Maggie. 'Don't be so hard on yourself.'

Rose had long believed that if you truly wanted to keep a secret, the key was to tell absolutely no one. Resist the urge to ease the burden of guilt. It went against everything in her nature but she had never breathed a word about Fitz to anyone. There was too much at stake. She had no idea how Peter would take it, but she didn't want to put him to the test. The boys would not understand, and it's not as though she deserved understanding. For a moment, she felt an overwhelming desire to clear her conscience, but she was too good a friend to burden Maggie with that right now.

Chapter Seven

In preparation for minding Fran's flat while she was away, Louis arrived at dinnertime with a large suitcase and a carton of Spanish red wine under his arm. Fran had half-hoped that he would make himself available to meet Maggie and Rose, but it was logistically difficult and she didn't want to make a big deal of it. He hadn't taken all that much interest in the arrangements but, as they sat down to dinner, he revealed that it still bothered him that her friends were paying Fran's share of expenses for the trip. He seemed to take it as a personal slight, raising subtle objections as if it were an elaborate plan to make her – and, by association, him – feel inadequate.

'I wouldn't let someone pay for me like that,' he said. 'They might, you know, take advantage, like.'

'What do you mean, "take advantage"?' asked Fran.

'You know, treat you like a second-class citizen or something.'

'Have me carry their bags and mop their brows, you mean? I don't think that's going to happen. Maggie and Rose are both quite well-off, and they want us to go together.'

'I wouldn't want to go to all them different places neither,' Louis countered, coming at it from a new direction. 'I prefer to really get to know a place. I'm more into slow travel. Stay a month or two. That's what Barb does, goes to Spain and does like the Spanish.'

In the past, when Fran had suggested a weekend in Paris or Prague, he was dismissive of these ideas. One of his exasperating habits was to denigrate other people's plans in comparison to his own more expansive imaginary itinerary. He had suggested that, for example, they could go to Africa or South America. He enjoyed arguing the merit of these more ambitious destinations over a mere weekend in Paris, as if he and Fran were the sort of people who had the means to choose one over the other. He wasn't deterred by the fact that none of these plans ever went any further and he never went anywhere. She wondered now, with some irritation, did he even have a passport?

For one discomforting moment, Fran saw him with Rose's more critical eye as he sat hunched over his dinner, his shirt straining at every button, his pectorals like two sandbags resting on a round belly that protruded abruptly from his torso. But his troubled expression touched Fran's heart and she rushed to allay his fears.

'So you think I shouldn't go?' she said, allowing him room to come around to the idea of his own accord. 'It's a bit late to change my mind now.'

'I didn't say that,' he said quickly. 'Nice to go off with your old friends. Nothing wrong with that, is there?' And, after a moment, wistfully, 'What am I gonna do?'

Fran knew now was the time to address that question.

'I haven't seen that much of you recently, Louis. I got the impression you were spending more time with Barbara.'

'Now and then. We've got history, you know that. The kids and everything. She doesn't want me there all the time, though. Hanging around.'

'And if she did, Louis? If she *did* want you around?' Fran didn't want to have this conversation she had so recklessly encouraged but it was too late to scramble out.

'Don't get jealous. I told you from the start me and Barb got on all right.'

'Just be honest with me, Louis,' she said gently.

'You know I don't like —'

'Upsetting people? You're upsetting me by not being honest.' As though sensing she was needed, Gigi leapt onto Fran's lap and made herself comfortable.

'I'm here now. That's what counts, in't? Who knows where the highway of life will take us? Eh? Eh, love?'

Fran almost smiled. *Easy Rider* had been the most profound film that Louis had ever seen. He quoted it often and had the ability to reference it in almost any discussion. Two hippies on Harleys searching for spiritual enlightenment on the highways of America – it expressed everything he believed in. The repression of the ordinary man by the system. Man's desire for freedom. The inevitable crushing of the rebel. It spoke to him in a way that no other film ever had. His belief in life on the metaphorical open road was entirely theoretical. Louis had worked for the same insurance company for twenty-two years, yet he somehow imagined himself as a maverick; a man in search of his own America. Normally Fran humoured him, but not tonight.

'Louis, we can decide where life takes us. You're not a helpless victim of circumstance. And the time will come when you need to make a decision. For both our sakes.' She hesitated, but now she had come this far, asked, 'Can you answer one question for me, honestly?'

'Depends on the question, love.'

'Are you considering going to Malaga with Barbara? Yes or no.'

His blank look revealed the truth but he replied grudgingly, 'Depends.'

Fran told herself that he was the insecure one. He was afraid of ending up alone, that's why he was hedging. In some way, she'd be relieved when he committed whichever way it went; it was this state of limbo that bothered her.

Mr Elcombe wasn't happy about her trip either. She hadn't taken holidays for several years and he must have imagined that she'd lost interest in the whole idea. Fran was confident that she was a valuable employee, not easily replaced, otherwise she never would have risked asking for the time off. Mr Elcombe recognised that she had been pivotal in the shop acquiring a website and the ability to sell books online. He knew that she was patient and kind during long, tedious phone calls from elderly customers, and that she responded to enquiry letters with handwritten replies on shop stationery. These postal transactions were inevitably protracted and she suspected that many of these regulars had need of a penpal. The acquisition of a book was a side issue.

Since Mr Elcombe had neither the desire nor the expertise to use the computer, let alone the patience for letter-writing, he decided to close the shop for the period that Fran was away. When she asked him about Gigi, he looked puzzled. 'Who's Gigi?'

Fran pointed to the cat, spotlit in a patch of sunshine in the front window.

He shrugged. 'The cat is here to do a job. It'll just have to work a bit harder.'

He couldn't know that Fran had been using catch and release traps, setting the mice free outside. Gigi had been redundant for a long time. Fran would have to make sure she was looked after.

It all worked out in the end. Now the cupboards were stocked with cat food for the month, she had left plant and cat care instructions for Louis, and could only hope for the best.

It had never occurred to Fran to go back to the places she had once inhabited. If she set out to revisit everywhere she'd lived in London, it would keep her busy for weeks. But retracing their earlier journey was all part of Rose's master plan and, as a guest on the trip, Fran didn't feel it appropriate to question her decisions, especially at this early stage. And she was curious.

There was a light drizzle as they set off to their first stop in Earl's Court. The B&B on Hogarth Road looked no more or less run-down than when Fran and Rose stayed there. Ragged lace curtains were tugged at odd angles across the windows and a thick crust of dirt adhered to every horizontal surface. Fran got out her camera and took a couple of shots to record the moment.

After barely two minutes of observation, Rose pronounced the experience underwhelming. Maggie, for whom this place meant nothing anyway, suggested they go somewhere dry and get a coffee. But Fran felt the moment warranted more effort and tried to garner some interest. 'I remember we paid thirty pounds a week between us for that room, Rose. With breakfast. Half our wages.'

'That breakfast was dire, as I recall,' said Rose. 'I wonder if old Mrs Whatsit is still living in the kitchen.'

'How old do you think she actually was?' asked Fran.

'We thought she was an old woman but I reckon she'd have been . . . maybe fifty?' said Rose. 'A mere child, in fact.' Her jacket had a rain hood and she pulled it over her head as the drizzle set in. Maggie opened up her umbrella and beckoned Fran to take shelter.

'We used to think she was hilarious the way she would only ever open that door a crack,' said Fran. 'I wonder what her story was.'

'She was probably frightened of you,' suggested Maggie, glancing around. 'Why don't we explore this further in a cosy café?'

'We were insensitive beasts, weren't we?' said Rose, warming to the subject. 'Poor woman probably lost her husband in the war. Lonely war widow forced to let out rooms to obnoxious Australians.'

'I can't even picture her now,' said Fran. 'Don't you think it's strange how people can be a part of your life – you see them every day, they're so vivid and present – and then they're gone. Forever. Like when you're on a train trip and sit opposite someone for hours and their face becomes indelibly imprinted in your mind and you breathe the same air . . . then you never see them again.'

Rose gave her a dubious look. 'Are you saying you miss every person you've ever sat opposite on public transport? You could add them all on Facebook.'

'I know what you mean, Fran,' offered Maggie. 'A better example is when you work with someone you dislike and obsess about them in the middle of the night. Then the person leaves and you never think about them again. The connection is broken and it's as if they never existed.'

'And then, sometime later, you bump into them and are pleased to see them,' said Fran.

Maggie nodded. 'Makes you wonder why we expend so much energy on people we dislike . . . and magnify their faults to a ridiculous degree to justify hating them.'

'Now you've had that insight, what does this mean for Yannis?' asked Rose.

Fran looked at Maggie. 'Who's Yannis?'

'Kristo's cousin. He refers to himself as the Assistant Financial Controller,' said Maggie. 'Anyway, don't get me started on him.'

'Maybe one day in the future when he's out of your life, you'll see him in the street and be like, "Dude! Let's get a beer and catch up",' suggested Rose.

'I doubt that,' said Maggie. 'Now, let's get coffee. Please.'

As they sat in the café with mugs of coffee, Fran watched people hurry past and tried to convey herself back to those first months when she found London exciting and everything wondrous: the queues of double-decker buses like conga lines of giant red playing blocks, the diesel throb of the black cabs, the sudden thrilling glimpses across the skyline to St Paul's or Big Ben. But, try as she might, that enchantment had dissipated years ago. She had changed and so had the city. Now everything was ordinary. Worse than ordinary – dreary. She was tired of London's restless energy. She was exhausted by the constant roar of traffic, jackhammers, leaf blowers and street-cleaning machines, and wondered when it had become so loud. She felt a creeping sense of despair knowing that the time was coming for her to leave simply because she couldn't handle it any more. The only reason she hadn't left yet was that she was afraid and had no idea where to go. Afraid of everything that starting again entailed, and the realisation that she would probably be leaving alone.

'Okay,' began Maggie, sipping her coffee. 'Now that I've confessed to not having looked at the itinerary . . .'

'You want an executive summary, I suppose?' guessed Rose. 'I'm pretty sure I've told you where we are going.'

'I just haven't focused on it until now. So, I'm assuming we couldn't possibly go everywhere we went before – for a start we drove, and now we're going on the train. The first trip took over two months and we've got half that.'

'Correct. The first trip we drove through France and Germany to Berlin and then down through Czechoslovakia – now Czech Republic – to Austria, Hungary, down through what was then Yugoslavia to Greece and then back up through Italy,' recalled Rose. 'This trip, as we have discussed, is the edited highlights.'

'I don't know how we managed all that. We obviously had a lot more energy back then,' said Fran with a laugh.

'I feel tired just thinking about it. In fact, I'm not sure I want to know the detail,' said Maggie.

Rose frowned. 'It's a bit ridiculous, not wanting to know where you're going.'

Maggie shrugged. She stared into her cup for a long minute. 'I don't know why, but coffee doesn't taste of anything any more.'

'Far out!' Rose's chair made a scraping sound as she stood up and marched out the door. Fran and Maggie watched her pace up and down on the pavement, her hands plunged deep into the pockets of her jacket.

'What did I say?' asked Maggie, bewildered. 'She's on a hair-trigger.'

'I think what it is . . .' Fran began carefully, 'I think that Rose wants to try to emulate our younger selves, and that's why —'

'Well, that is completely ridiculous.' Maggie looked out the window and Fran saw her expression soften as she watched Rose trying to get a grip on herself. 'I'm sorry. I went on anti-depressants recently. They obviously haven't fully kicked in yet. I'm really not meaning to be negative.'

'Look, she'll be fine,' said Fran. 'We'll just give her a moment.'

Rose came back inside and sat down, only slightly less grumpy.

Fran got in first. 'Rose, does it really matter? We can just tell Maggie a day ahead. I can imagine it could seem a bit overwhelming . . .'

'Oh, I don't care. It's fine,' said Rose. 'But please just stop complaining.'

'It was just an observation,' said Maggie soothingly.

'If I can give up yodelling, which is an important part of my life, you can give up moaning.'

'Is that a threat?' asked Maggie.

'You better believe it,' said Rose.

Fran wasn't sure where this conversation was going, or even what it was about, but when Maggie laughed, she joined in, and Rose did too. And, for the moment, all was well.

Despite the blustery weather, they all agreed to push on and visit the Battersea flat they had once shared but, before that, Rose wanted to go back to the pub where she'd worked, which wasn't far from the café.

When Fran and Rose first arrived in London, Earl's Court Road seemed wildly exciting with its exotic takeaways and posters advertising magic bus tickets to Greece, Kathmandu, Afghanistan and Morocco – the best-known hippy trails. Places they had never dreamed of going. There was a camaraderie among the restless community of Aussies, Kiwis and South Africans; pilgrims hungry for experiences and a good time. It was no wonder the place ended up with a dubious reputation.

These days Earl's Court was exactly like any other West London shopping strip, lined with clothing franchises, cafés and gastro-pubs. Nothing looked familiar. They walked back and forth searching for a landmark but, on asking in a shop, discovered the Marquis had been pulled down years ago. In its place was a convenience store and a shoe shop.

'It seems incredible,' said Rose, outraged. 'That pub was a hundred and fifty years old! It'd be two hundred years old now.'

'Everything here is two hundred years old, or older. It happens all the time, Rose,' said Fran. 'Don't take it personally.'

'There should be a blue plaque and a heritage order on the building. Rose McLean (née Avery) worked here,' suggested Maggie as she turned away to hail a cab.

'I expect business fell away after I left and it was all downhill from there. I just hate to see history demolished – for this,' said Rose, gesturing dismissively at the nondescript shops that had replaced the pub.

A cab pulled up and Maggie opened the door to get in. 'This is just the beginning, Rosie. You need to pace yourself.'

As the taxi headed down Beaufort Street and onto the Battersea Bridge, Rose bounced back. 'Isn't this fun? Just like the old days.'

'Except we were on the bus,' said Fran. 'Not in a cab. We never took cabs.'

'Really?' asked Rose. 'I remember getting sort of dodgy mini-cabs . . .' As they pulled up outside the Battersea tower block, she fell silent. After a moment she asked, 'Wow. Was it always that ugly?'

Like the Hogarth Road B&B, the building was no more or less neglected than when they had lived there forty years earlier. The pebbledash cladding was just as grubby, the painted railings peeling as they had been then. As the cab drove away, the three of them crowded under the umbrella, dwarfed by the twenty-storey block. Fran had to admit it was much more brutal looking than even she remembered. The architectural style was post-war Eastern Bloc. It looked as though it had been designed by a public servant with a set square. There was another identical building on the estate but not a single tree or shrub to be seen, just cracked and blackened concrete everywhere.

With some trepidation, they walked up the steps only to find the main entry door to the building now needed a card or passcode. Fortunately, a young man was leaving the building and gallantly held the door open for them to enter. The foyer was smaller than Fran remembered.

'I'm having an Alice in Wonderland moment,' remarked Maggie. 'Either we've grown or it's shrunk.'

'Were there always two lifts? I don't remember that,' said Rose as she pressed the lift button. The steel doors opened, she stepped inside and started to laugh.

'What?' asked Maggie, following her. 'Oh no . . . why?!'

'Oh dear,' said Fran, holding her nose. 'I always thought it was just one person who peed in the lift. He's either still here or . . .'

'Or there's another generation of lift-pissers in the building,' said Rose.

It was a relief to escape the stale, acrid odour onto the seventeenth floor. Shared by four flats, the entry doors opened into a small lobby tiled in dark mustard and green, a legacy of its origins as public housing. To the right, a glass door led to the stairwell with views over the rooftops of Battersea to the Thames. To the left was a door that led to the incinerator hatch for rubbish disposal. Rose set off to inspect this and announced it was still in operation. Although she must have used it dozens of times, Fran's strongest memory of this hatch was watching Maggie and Rose shove their hated winter coats down it when they were headed home to Sydney.

Maggie stared wistfully at their old front door. 'Shame we can't get inside. It's probably all been done up now.'

'Wouldn't it be wonderful if you could walk in and find it as you left it . . . if you could walk around your old life and see all the posters still on the walls . . .' said Rose.

'Pink Floyd . . . Siouxsie and the Banshees,' remembered Fran. 'That Queen one from the Hammersmith Odeon would probably be worth a few quid by now.'

'All our old tea cups and chipped plates . . .'

Fran laughed. '. . . still encrusted with food.'

Rose made a face. 'Probably congealed egg. How many eggs did we eat back then?!'

'And risotto from a packet, ugh. Maybe I'd find my grandma's butter knife I left here,' said Maggie.

Rose shook her head in disbelief. 'Who, in God's name, moves to another country with their own butter knife?'

'I do,' said Maggie with a smile. 'Rose, do you remember that night when we'd done the grocery shopping and were laughing about something so much that we dropped a bottle of wine on these tiles?'

'Oh, God. It smashed everywhere. It wasn't funny but we kept laughing like idiots . . . and Fran came out and was really annoyed about the waste of the wine.'

'Wine was such a treat . . .' Maggie's phone began to ring. 'Sorry!' She fumbled in her bag for it and rushed out into the stairwell to take the call.

'It wasn't that,' said Fran, remembering the incident all too well and her sense of being on the periphery. She felt it now, remembering the two of them helpless with laughter, the wine that she had been looking forward to now a dirty puddle and broken glass all over the floor. 'It was you two laughing without me.'

'We weren't laughing about you, sweetie.' Rose began to take photos of the foyer and front door with her phone.

'Rose, don't patronise me, please.'

'I'm not patronising you. You're being super-sensitive. It was forty years ago.'

In light of the journey ahead, Fran felt disturbed by the memory, and Rose's dismissive attitude wasn't helping.

'Sorry, Fran. I'm not meaning to negate whatever you felt.' Rose opened the door to the stairway. 'Come on, let's take the stairs. I cannot get back in that lift.'

Fran hesitated. 'You go. I'll be down in a few minutes.'

Rose looked ready to dissuade her but then turned away and set off down the stairs, and Maggie, still on the phone, followed her.

Alone in the silence of the foyer, Fran tried to calm the ruffling irritation of Rose's impatience. Rose was incapable of simply waiting in the moment to see what might reveal itself. She expected memories to leap out and announce themselves, epiphanies to arrive in a great shaft of light from the heavens without unnecessary delays.

Fran closed her eyes and gently coaxed her thoughts back into that past. She would never again have this opportunity to be right here and focus on that time. She waited, opening herself to the memories, resisting the urge to order them as they tumbled over each other in a confusion of images and sounds.

There was nothing they didn't know about each other in this tiny flat where everything became chaotically communal: clothes, tampons, makeup, perfume. They had lent each other money and shoulders to cry on, and books they loved. It was here that Fran had discovered Doris Lessing, Iris Murdoch, Joan Didion, Margaret Drabble, Beryl Bainbridge – the list went on – a generation of female authors who had entered her life like friends and confidantes.

This flat was full of music. She remembered how Rose had spent a whole day up Tottenham Court Road selecting a hi-fi system that played cassettes and records. She even remembered the first album they bought to play on that stereo was Pink Floyd's *Animals*. From their window, they could see Battersea Power Station, which was featured on the cover, and felt they had some secret inside knowledge. They had become a part of music culture.

She smiled remembering the New Year's Eve party they had here to mark the start of 1979. It was Rose's idea to have a party, even though they didn't have all that many friends. Maggie agreed to invite her cousin and a few select dentists. Rose knew a few people through her pub gigs but Fran wasn't confident that anyone she knew could be counted on to come.

Rose smuggled a bottle of Galliano and one of vodka out of the pub to make Harvey Wallbangers. Fran threaded cocktail onions and cheese cubes onto toothpicks. Maggie made dozens of sausage rolls. It was freezing outside and, with the kerosene heater going all day, the windows streamed with moisture, making the crepe paper streamers limp.

It was after eight when the first knock on the door came, and Rose, who was already quite drunk, threw the door open wide to find Maggie's cousin and his date, Natalie. 'Come in! Come in!' Rose shouted unnecessarily, looking past them for concealed guests. But it was just the two of them.

Fran took their coats, Rose made them a couple of cocktails and Maggie plied them with food. The music was turned up and they filled the tiny living room with their dancing. Rose kept disappearing to check outside the front door, in case there was anyone else lurking out there. There was no one. She ordered them all to dance near the windows, so anyone arriving in the car park below could look up and see how much fun they were having. She flicked the light switch on and off to get a disco vibe happening but Natalie said it made her feel sick and she wanted to go home. And they left.

'Well, this is shit,' said Rose, slamming the door behind them.

Maggie began to laugh. 'No, it's not. We don't need them.' She put her new Supertramp album on the record player and the next thing they were bopping around the living room bellowing 'The Logical Song' at the top of their voices, leaning in to sing together into sausage roll microphones.

Another cocktail or two and the room became unbearably hot. They stripped off to their underwear and leapt about, singing and jumping over the furniture. There was a brief food fight and then, in quick succession, Fran vomited – she'd eaten so much cheese, it looked like fondue – Rose slipped over on a sausage roll and twisted her ankle and a neighbour hammered on the door to complain about the racket. It was barely midnight, the evening was over and the hangovers still to come.

Fran's memories of Maggie and Rose were larger than life, and she began to wonder where she was in all this – an innocent bystander? She saw herself as Nick in *The Great Gatsby*, Stingo in *Sophie's Choice*, the observer–narrator who lived in the shadows of her more interesting and outgoing friends.

It occurred to her in a rush that she hadn't lived in their shadows – quite the opposite. She had lived in their radiant light, and a deep, visceral longing for those days overtook her like nausea. She would give anything to feel, even for a brief moment, that charge of the energy, optimism and lightness she had felt back then, a time when she believed that her life had finally begun. She'd felt free and brave and strong. This flat was her stronghold, Maggie and Rose were her family – the centre of everything. It was as if she had been trying to replicate that experience ever since; trying to find a relationship that would be everything they had been to her. How could she have known that that time would always remain the happiest, least complicated era of her life?

She left the foyer and hurried to the stairwell, almost in tears, feeling she couldn't stand to be there a moment longer. As she descended the stairs, she began to wonder if she had the strength for this trip. It already felt as though it was too testing for her emotionally, being forced to face up to how little she had achieved in her life.

Tomorrow they would be on the Eurostar bound for Paris, a place she had visited only twice, neither with any of the pleasure others seemed to derive from the city. The first time was with Maggie and Rose, a trial run in the Kombi van for the weekend. They had parked in the Bois de Boulogne, believing they were in the countryside outside Paris. They were not aware that the park was a favourite procurement spot for Parisian prostitutes and were frightened by men tapping on the windows in the night. A decade later she had visited with a lover who had marked the occasion by breaking the news that, despite his love for Fran, he had decided to reunite with his wife.

Perhaps this would be her last trip to Paris. It wasn't as though she was going to be more flush with money in the future. Yet she sensed a deepening reluctance for the entire endeavour, already anticipating how she would feel when it was over and she would have to say goodbye to Rose and Maggie. And they would go back to their lives in Sydney and leave her behind. She recognised a response in herself that sometimes sabotaged relationships early on to insure against later pain.

As she walked downstairs, flight after flight, Rose and Maggie's voices echoed further down the stairwell and she felt more alone than ever. Rose called her name. Maggie joined in. Now she heard the familiar strains of an Abba song echoing up the stairwell. As she got closer, she could make out the words they were singing: 'Can you hear the drums, Francesca?'

She laughed and hurried down the stairs, calling, 'Coming! I'm coming!'

Chapter Eight

As they sped past the green fields and picturesque villages of France's countryside at 300 kilometres an hour, Maggie looked across at her travelling companions and had a vivid memory of her first impression of the two awkward Aussie chicks trying to act the part. Wearing floppy muslin dresses, with deep frills around the hems, they could have been mistaken for missionaries – apart from Rose's hair, which looked like a wig thrown on sideways. Even if she hadn't been told, Maggie could have guessed Rose was originally a country girl – there was something in her stride that suggested gumboots. Maggie had liked her immediately. Her energy, good humour and lack of self-consciousness were a charming combination.

The same age as Rose and Fran, Maggie had also been a teen of the sixties, but her sensibilities were still those of her parents' generation, and she remembered being shocked that Rose identified as a feminist, and a radical one at that. Even back then, Rose always had strong opinions. When they'd lived together she used to bang on about unions and socialism and women's lib, insisting everyone read Germaine Greer and Gloria Steinem. Fran had embraced these ideas more readily than Maggie, who found it hard to shake off her conservative upbringing. Back then, she accepted that men were in charge and there was no way they were ever going to let women muscle in on their territory. Forty years later, that was still the case. Maggie's attitudes may have evolved, but it didn't change the reality of the situation. Rose was still fighting the feminist fight, and good luck to her. But then, over the years, Rose had identified with a lot of movements and, depending on the day, had wanted to sing in a band or travel the world. When she met another Aussie who worked as a burlesque dancer in the Monte Carlo Casino, she was ready to sign up for that. It was lucky that Rose had gone home when she did. There was so much more trouble she could have got into.

Later, Maggie had got to know Rose's parents, who had the same refreshing lack of pretension. They were more interested in someone's work ethic than who their family was or had been. After her own family's spectacular fall from grace, Maggie had valued that.

Fran, with her neat black cap of hair and eyeliner that flicked up, cats-eye style, in the corners of her watchful grey eyes, had an innocent kindness about her. It took a while to realise that beneath her calm veneer, she fretted. Fran was trusting, as evidenced by the men who had taken advantage of her over the years, both financially and emotionally. Someone only had to show her some kindness and she was enslaved to them.

Although they were all so different, from the moment Maggie first met Rose and Fran, she felt she could be herself with them; whoever she turned out to be. She hadn't come to London to find herself, but to escape. What she discovered there was purely accidental.

Three months before she set off for London, Maggie could have looked ahead and seen exactly how her life would play out. Her father had encouraged her to go to university and join his accountancy practice. She and her boyfriend Mark were set to marry in a few years when he qualified. His father a well-respected solicitor, Mark was doing law and would join his father's practice. Their family lives mirrored each other and their parents were already chummy, integrated as in-laws.

Mark had been her first serious boyfriend and the only one she had gone all the way with. They would stay at each other's homes and holiday with each other's family, but never sleep in the same room. Sex was covert and took place whenever they found themselves alone in the house, or more often in the back seat of the car when Mark drove her home. It was often uncomfortable and undignified, and she cooperated mainly to stop him bugging her about it. What did they talk about, she wondered now. Did they have a single thing in common?

When she started university, she encountered young people from different worlds. People who lived in share houses and squats, who smoked pot, drank beer and slept around. Maggie realised that she had been sliding into her mother's life, without having ever lived her own, but to extract herself from the situation was unthinkable. She would disappoint everyone.

Her idyllic family life in no way prepared her for what happened next. Halfway through her first year at university, she discovered that her diaphragm had let her down and she was pregnant. The timing could not have been worse. Her father's accountancy practice was under investigation, suspected of promoting tax-evasion schemes to clients. Maggie had worked for him over the summer, shredding documents, never knowing what they were. Her parents had never argued, now they never stopped. Everything buried in their marriage rose to the surface. Everything was in jeopardy. Maggie couldn't bring herself to tell her mother about the pregnancy.

When Mark suggested they get married, Maggie readily agreed. It was the only solution but she felt that her life was over before it had begun. She soon had a call from Mark's mother. 'We need to do everything in the right order,' she said. 'Wedding bells for you two are a few years down the track. I'm going to give you a number. You must ring in the evening after six. Make an appointment.'

The procedure took place in the doctor's surgery without general anaesthetic. Afterwards, Maggie was sent home. The doctor said she was not to contact the surgery again. If things went wrong, she should go to Emergency, and admit nothing or she would be in trouble.

Alone in her bed, towels tucked between her legs, she spent the night writhing in pain from the cramps. She had been instructed that when the foetus came away, it wouldn't be recognisable but she should wrap it up in newspaper and put it out in the bin. She couldn't do it. She wrapped it in a towel, crept out into the garden and buried the bundle under the hedge. She lay on the damp grass and sobbed uncontrollably. From relief or grief, she didn't know.

When she walked back into the kitchen, her mother was there. Maggie's hands were covered in soil, blood had soaked through her sanitary pad and stained the legs of her pyjamas. In one searching glance, Celia put it all together. She took her daughter in her arms and they wept together. Celia cleaned her up, changed the bed and kept watch on her all that night, ready to take her to the hospital if necessary.

In the morning, Celia went to see Mark's mother and told her if they tried to contact her daughter again, she would have them charged. Maggie never saw Mark again. It was shocking how little she missed him. The only thing she did miss was his protective power. She felt safe with him. Right from early adolescence, there was something about her that turned men's heads. She was a magnet for the sleazy comment and men telling her what she needed, openly staring at her breasts. She'd hated it before, and even more so after what she'd been through.

Despite her father's best efforts, the firm was placed in the hands of the receivers and the tax office moved to prosecute. The papers were full of it and, overnight, her father became a pariah and Maggie was out of a job. It was Celia who suggested Maggie take some time out and go overseas for a while.

When she met Rose and Fran, she thought she could learn from them how to be young and carefree again. She realised later that Fran had never been carefree. She was one of those people who made you consider the idea of past lives. Rose made up for Fran's seriousness, bursting with life and energy, a veritable gale of sunshine. Maggie had wanted a piece of that. And here they were, forty years later. They had changed beyond recognition. And not changed at all.

Paris, when they arrived, was cool and windy. Maggie felt little enthusiasm for their time there. It wasn't entirely her low mood – she had been back a few times since their first visit, and the city had lost its sheen for her over the years.

Since neither she nor Rose had felt up to the task of driving in Europe these days, they lacked the flexibility of the earlier trip. Rose must surely realise that it was impossible to emulate it because the essential element was that they'd had no plan, just a spiral-bound map book of Europe and the traveller's bible: Frommer's *Europe on $10 a Day*.

None of them had ever been to Europe and they had no idea what they would find when they crossed the Channel. They bought the VW Kombi from a Kiwi couple at the van mart outside Australia House. It had already lapped the continent a few times and was perfect for them, with one bench seat up the front and a mattress in the back. They bought a pup tent and a folding canvas camp bed for the third person, but when it was raining they had often slept squashed into the van, sardine-style. They did all their cooking on a single-burner gas cooker, mainly rice with vegetables and occasionally some meat. Their few clothes were stuffed in duffel bags under the seats. It was that chaotic trip that gave Maggie back her carefree youth. She got to start adulthood again. It was more fun than she had ever had, before or since. Recapturing that now seemed impossible.

Not having their own transport for this venture limited the possibilities for spontaneity; they were basically stuck in each location until the itinerary moved them on. She needed to make the best of it. She had abdicated all responsibility to Rose, and now she just had to deal with it. Stop complaining in her head and stop trying to control the situation.

That said, Maggie would not have selected the hotel that Rose had booked near the Notre Dame. These days there was no 'out of season' in Paris, especially in this location. The surrounding restaurants would all be expensive tourist fodder. Her room was shabby and so small that almost as soon as she put her suitcase down, she managed to fall over it and hurt her knee. Tall windows looked out onto an atrium courtyard populated by straggly plants searching for more light and sun, but without this dismal view, it would be like a cell.

She lay down on the bed and stared at a faint water stain on the ceiling, the shape of Italy, and pondered the idea that Italy was probably the most common shape for a water stain. Perhaps because water pooled and overflowed, searching for a path to flow along. This, she realised, is what it feels like to think about nothing. She liked it.

It was nice to be alone. The room was relatively quiet. On the other side of the world it was almost midnight and hopefully her family were asleep. The sudden buzzing of her phone indicated otherwise. She had fond memories of the days when global roaming charges were astronomical and no one dared call. These days it was business as usual. It was impossible to actually get away. If she turned her phone off, Kristo would go into panic mode and just start bothering Rose instead.

'Kristo, you don't need to call me every day,' she said gently. 'We can just message. Or not.'

'Are you enjoying yourself, darling?' he asked in honeyed tones. He never called her darling. All these endearments had been nice at first but were now starting to get on her nerves.

'See, that's the sort of question you can text, or even not ask because I don't want to be asked every single day if I'm enjoying myself.' Maggie heaved herself up to a sitting position against the bedhead. The pillows were the synthetic sort she hated. They had to be folded in half to have any substance. 'Is that it? Dear.'

'I'm worried you'll meet a handsome Frenchman and never come home.' Kristo was only half joking. Someone, probably his mother, had put that in his head.

'Kris, I'm an overweight, bad-tempered matron and my hair is falling out. I'm not exactly the temptress you imagine me to be.'

There was a shocked silence at the other end. 'Your hair?'

'It might be stress or just age, I don't know. It's coming out everywhere. I'll probably be bald by the time I get home.'

'Can you get to a doctor? I think you need to see a doctor. Do you want me to come over?'

'How are you going to stop it? Hold it on my head?' She regretted telling him. 'It'll be fine. Don't worry. Everything else all right?'

'There was a big bloody stuff-up with the payroll yesterday. The time sheets were wrong. Yannis sorted it out in the end. Nothing for you to worry about.'

Maggie felt her blood pressure rise like mercury. The time sheets would not be wrong. Yannis's work needed constant checking. He'd obviously stuffed it up and made himself out to be the hero. There was nothing she could do. Her head began to throb but her voice was surprisingly calm. 'If you don't want me to worry, maybe I don't need to know.'

'Anthea is back here again. That counselling doesn't seem to be working. I knew it was a waste of money. That little . . .'

Maggie took a deep breath. 'Aaron needs to move out of the unit, not Anthea. We have a stake in that place. If he takes possession, we won't be able to get him out. Just go around and speak to him, please. But don't touch him. Did you hear that? Don't even shake his hand in case you're tempted to break it.'

'Don't touch him. Got it. Not even a man hug,' he said jovially.

'Okay, I'll call you in a few days. Everything is fine. There's nothing to worry about.'

'I'm lying here in bed. Naked as a baby. Alone. Can you talk to me for a while?'

Maggie snorted. 'No. Talk to yourself.'

'Mag-gie,' he said sulkily. 'Just tell me what you're wearing.'

'Well, obviously that would be a French maid's uniform . . .'

'Yes?' he said brightly.

There was a tap on the door. 'Sorry, Kris. You can take it from there. I have to go.'

Maggie put the phone aside, wriggled off the bed and opened the door.

'We're going out for a walk,' said Rose. 'Stretch the legumes. Are you okay? You look done in. Maybe you should have a nap.'

Maggie agreed she would meet them later. She turned off her phone and got into bed. When she woke, it was dusk. She had slept heavily but been disturbed by flashing nightmares of being pursued by barking dogs and speeding cars. It was like a trailer for an action movie that made no sense. She had no desire to see the full feature.

Despite the pitiful tickle of the shower, she felt revived and in a better frame of mind. She put on some lipstick and mascara and brushed her hair gently.

For a moment, the face reflected in the mirror was her mother's, the same lines beginning to tug at the corners of her mouth. She felt a pang of missing Celia and wondered if a month with her mother in Queensland would have been more beneficial than this, potentially exhausting, trip.

The only good thing to come out of that terrible night all those years ago was the strengthened bond with her mother.

She never told Kristo, or anyone else, about that first pregnancy. Not even Rose or Fran. So when she miscarried her first official pregnancy, Celia was the only one who understood the torment she was feeling. Punished. Guilty. Celia had come and cared for Maggie in the house in Marrickville for a few days.

In a quiet moment when they were alone together, Celia brought up the subject. 'It seems as though we never discussed what happened properly.'

'There was nothing to discuss, really,' Maggie said. 'It was done. I just had to get on with things.'

'I know the termination wasn't your idea, but I hope you don't have regrets.'

Maggie thought about that for a moment. 'If I have any regret, it's that I didn't think for myself and make my own decision.'

'I hope you're not making any connection between this and the first one. Because the two incidents are quite unrelated. It's just bad luck,' said Celia.

'It could be a mechanical failure. Something messed up in there. Or my body rejected the baby, out of . . . I don't know . . . fear of going through that again.'

'Well, you have to keep telling yourself that there is nothing to fear. And next time around, I think you'll be in for a pleasant surprise.'

As it turned out, her mother was right. Twins. It felt like a redemption. The arrival of the girls had a secret significance for Celia and Maggie and they never talked about that night again. Losing Kal was different. He was three weeks old, their loved and welcomed boy, but sadly not for this world. The heartbreak of losing him far outweighed her first and second losses. Even now she and Kristo couldn't talk about it. The grief scarred them deeply in different ways. She would send Kristo a gift from Paris, and Celia too.

When Maggie joined Rose and Fran downstairs, she suggested they walk away from the restaurant area near the Notre Dame, with its tourist menus and spruikers urging customers inside. Better to cross the Seine to Le Marais and find more authentic and better-priced restaurants.

The evening air, crisp and fresh after the stuffy room, lifted her spirits. She reminded herself that they were in Paris. Everyone loves Paris. And while it would be impossible for the city to fulfil every golden promise, it did deliver on so many. It was an unexpected glimpse of the Eiffel Tower sparkling in the night or the rich buttery smell of a patisserie. A café noir, served in a small white cup in a café on the Champs-Élysées. Couples pausing in the street to share a lingering kiss, buskers playing haunting Edith Piaf songs on accordions, and Parisians displaying their effortless *je ne sais quoi* with nothing more than a cunningly knotted scarf. When Maggie tied a scarf like that, it looked as though she was nursing a sore throat or disguising a raddled neck.

As they walked towards Le Marais, Rose talked about a previous visit when she fell down a flight of stairs and, shortly after, bashed her head on one of the heavy metal menu stands that restaurants often put outside on the pavement. Fran laughed dutifully, even though she had probably heard the story before. Maggie was struggling to concentrate. It was as if she constantly needed to push herself out of a fog that surrounded her. It was an effort to connect with anything.

It was early and they found a restaurant that was relatively quiet. The decor was traditional French and it was hard to tell whether the mirrored signs and café furniture were authentic or a convincing reproduction. Their waiter was charming and flirtatious, which cheered them all up. They ordered a bottle of chablis. Fran ordered the steak tartare, Rose, the *salade niçoise*, a perennial favourite, and Maggie got the same. She felt as though they were trying to create a good time, pretending to have fun in Paris, or perhaps that was just a reflection of her mood.

'Maggie, I know you're probably feeling buyer's remorse right now . . .' began Rose.

'No, I'm not. If I'm feeling anything, you'll be the first to know.'

Fran's eyes darted from Maggie to Rose. 'We probably all need to give each other some space.'

'Okay, let's just drift along like flotsam and see where the tide takes us,' said Rose. It was difficult to tell by her tone whether she was being sarcastic or it was a genuine suggestion.

'Rose,' said Fran sternly. 'I don't know why you keep coming back to that. Maggie must regret ever confiding in you.'

'Sorry, Mag. Not intentional. Although, I don't think you're at risk here,' continued Rose. 'No one would throw themselves in the Seine. You'd probably land on a shopping trolley.'

'Let's drop the subject. Permanently,' Fran said firmly.

'It's fine,' Maggie reassured her. 'I know Rose loves her oceanic metaphors. I don't want to take that away from her.'

'Do I?' Rose looked surprised. 'I had no idea my metaphorical repertoire was so limited.'

'What have you got planned for us tomorrow, Rose?' asked Fran.

'I'm not a tour guide, you know. I booked the accommodation and train tickets but that's where it ends. Now we just have to try and have fun.'

All three fell silent and Maggie wondered if this wasn't the greatest challenge of all. Fun was the prerogative of youth. Her expertise lay in organising things for others to enjoy, and then cleaning up afterwards.

Fran had bought a guidebook and, without further dissension, they managed to make some plans, each electing activities for their couple of days in Paris. Maggie wanted to visit Montmartre, preferably early in the morning, to avoid the crowds. Fran was keen to spend at least a couple of hours in the Louvre and visit the legendary English bookshop, Shakespeare and Company, which was near the hotel. Rose suggested they walk from the Louvre through the Jardin des Tuileries to the Place de la Concorde. It was agreed that the second day could be more improvised, perhaps a relaxed lunch and wander around the shops of Le Marais.

It was dark when they left the restaurant. Outside, the street lighting was soft, blurring any distinguishing features. Maggie hesitated. She was normally confident with directions. 'Is this the same entrance we came in? Nothing really looks familiar.'

'I think I remember that patisserie opposite,' offered Fran.

Disoriented, Maggie peered down the street. 'I thought we came from that way. I didn't bring my distance glasses and now my phone is out of charge. Let's walk along and find the street name.'

Rose rifled through her daypack and produced her phone. 'Hang on. I need to find my glasses,' she said, diving back into the depths of her bag.

Maggie found her own reading glasses and put them on.

Fran didn't wear glasses and watched them, evidently mes-merised by this exercise. After a moment she said, 'There's some glasses on your head, Maggie.'

Rose looked up. 'No wonder! They're mine.'

Maggie passed them over. 'Sorry. I must have picked them up off the table by mistake.'

'Okay, all good.' Rose popped her glasses on and held her phone in front of her like a water diviner. 'Hold it – what street was the hotel on?'

'Just get us back to Notre Dame and we'll remember from there,' suggested Maggie.

Rose tapped in their destination and set off down the street with Fran and Maggie following. At the intersection, she stopped dead, staring at her phone. She turned around. 'Oh, the arrow is pointing the other way now.'

'You've got to point the phone in the direction you're going,' said Maggie. 'Not swing it around, confusing the thing.' She took the phone from Rose, put her reading glasses back on and stared at it, turning it this way and that. 'I wish we had a proper map,' she said after a moment. She looked up at the street sign to get her bearings but the white lettering on the blue background, so clear in daylight, was indecipherable in the gloom. 'Can either of you read that sign?'

'So much for the city of bloody lights!' cried Rose.

Maggie hushed her. 'Keep your voice down before you get us arrested.'

Fran was concentrating on the street sign. 'I thought my eye-sight was quite good. It's very indistinct . . . hmm . . . a long name like "Rue Something Something" starting with D or could be O. It's like the optometrist's chart when they switch it to blurry.'

'Let's go back to Mother Google. She knows where we are at all times,' said Rose, taking the phone back from Maggie. 'How do you put the audio on?'

'No idea,' said Maggie. 'It should come on automatically. Just put in the destination again.'

'I'm sorry I'm no help,' said Fran. 'My phone's so old I didn't bother bringing it . . .'

'If we can't get our shit together with two phones, a third one wouldn't help,' said Rose. She fiddled around for a while and finally the audio instructed them to head north-east on Rue Beauregard. 'Dear God, which way is north-east? We'll be here all night.'

'Well, at least we know it starts with a B now,' said Fran helpfully.

A man came towards them, walking briskly with his head down. Maggie stepped out in front of him, '*Pardon, monsieur, où est la Notre Dame?*' Without looking up or breaking his stride, the man pointed back over his shoulder and kept walking.

'I said it was this way, didn't I?' said Rose, marching off ahead of them along the narrow pavement. She was easy to follow; they could see the blue light reflecting off her hair and she was singing 'I Love Paris' – loudly. She was like an out-of-control juke box. Maggie began to wonder if she could spend another day with Rose, let alone more than three weeks.

Back in her room, Maggie found the power converter in her suitcase and plugged in her phone. As it came to life, she stared at the screen with a growing sense of alarm. Three missed calls from Nico. Something must have happened to Kristo. Her hand trembled as she returned the call. It rang over and over and she was about to hang up when Nico answered.

'What's happened?' asked Maggie.

'Nothing's happened. I wanted to speak to you.'

'What? Why? You shouldn't ring me. I've asked you not to do that,' said Maggie, knowing she sounded flustered. She needed to stay in control.

'I need to talk to you. Kristo told me you're unhappy. Is it because of me?'

'Nico, I don't want to have this conversation. It's late and I'm tired.' She desperately wanted to lie down but the power point was under the window so she was tethered there. She tried to marshal her thoughts. The last thing she wanted to do was wind him up.

'Maggie, think about it. I reckon it is. I think it's time to talk to Kristo.'

Maggie's whole body started to tremble. She held on to the window frame for support. She needed to focus, try to second-guess what else he might do, but wine and fatigue were getting in the way. 'Where's Effie? She can't hear you, can she?'

Nico sighed. 'Let me find out.' There was a pause and he called out his wife's name several times. 'No, it's fine.'

'Is she there? Please don't do this.' Her legs felt so weak. She wanted to fall to her knees and beg him but she knew it wouldn't work.

Nico laughed. 'I'm in the car. She's at work.'

He was playing her. She felt like shouting at him, but that would be unwise.

'You know I care about you more than Kristo does.'

Maggie kept her breath quiet and slow. 'Please. Don't do

anything for the moment. Leave everything as it is.' She stopped short of begging.

As often happened, he suddenly capitulated and said he had to go. The line went dead. Maggie felt the bile rise up in her throat. She rushed into the bathroom, dropped to her knees over the toilet and emptied her stomach into the bowl.

Chapter Nine

Rose found Paris as divine as ever, despite the cool, windy weather. There were a few tourists, even this early in the season, but they tended to huddle together, looking like clusters of well-fed crows in their dark puffer jackets. Later in the summer, there would be an infestation of them, roosting in every café and restaurant, screeching down every tiny laneway, defending their territory with selfie sticks. If you were ever going to feel like a real Parisian, now was the time to be here.

The cool snap was unfortunate but Paris was still Paris. Rose loved its grand and generous buildings and narrow cobblestone streets, and thrilled at the sheer ambition of its Napoleonic boulevards. To see the thread of lights swooping up the Champs-Élysées to the Arc de Triomphe and the golden light pouring through the arch at sunset made her heart flutter.

She was fascinated by the secret lives of Parisians. The court-yards and hidden mansions tucked away from prying eyes behind enormous gates and doors. Everywhere she looked there was something of interest. She even admired the indifference that Parisians showed towards tourists, their ability to render these invaders invisible.

Coming out of the restaurant after dinner last night and getting a tiny bit lost was the most fun they'd had so far. They needed more of this crazy random stuff, unexpected incidents to shake them out of the torpor of their boring lives. All three of them were like limpets clinging to the known, to the predictable and comfortable. They'd been trained over the years to steady any rocking boats; never to rock them.

Rose had just woken up when a call came through from Peter, which was highly unusual as he loathed talking on the phone.

'How are you, dear?' he asked. 'Is Paris living up to your usual wildly unrealistic expectations?'

'Exceeding them, actually.' Rose glanced at the time. She'd slept later than she meant to but, with a bit of effort, she could probably get dressed while she was on the phone. There was no such thing as a quick conversation with Peter. She found her earbuds but they looked like her early attempts at macramé, and there was no way to untangle them with one hand.

'This isn't costing a fortune, is it? Roaming and all that?' he asked anxiously.

Rose debated whether it was wise to reveal it was part of her phone plan, in case it encouraged him to call more often but, in the end, honesty prevailed.

'Oh, good,' he said. 'There's a few things I wanted to talk to you about. I've been asked to do a presentation of some sort. Or, actually . . . is it more an interview? Perhaps it is. I need to prepare something, I think. The exact topic's not quite clear.

The woman is a friend of Craig's, you remember him . . . he was a very bright student in my Politics of Western Europe last year. Or perhaps two years ago . . .'

While Peter was warming up, Rose managed to drag her pyjama pants off with her free hand and guide her feet through the leg holes of her undies. She edged them up to her knees, only to discover that they were on backwards, which increased her irritation with Peter. 'Thank you for all that, dear. Can you get to the point, please? I need my *petit déjeuner.*'

'Am I not permitted to telephone my own wife to discuss something of importance? I didn't realise this was a sabbatical *sans* communication. Is that what you're implying?'

'Peter, I know you want me to do something. Just tell me what it is.'

'Well, as I said . . . something needs preparing for this interview. I suppose I need to clarify the topic, but I got the distinct impression that it's up to me . . . so that leaves me the entire twentieth century to choose from. I'd much prefer they specified something . . . even limited it to a particular decade . . .'

Rose decided on the wide-legged knit pants, as they slid on easily. But getting her socks on with one hand proved more difficult than she imagined. Either her legs were getting longer or her arms shorter, but her feet were definitely further away. 'Who are *they*?' she asked. 'I'm not trying to be difficult, Peter. I genuinely have no idea what the heck you're talking about.'

'Well, the friend of Craig. I've got her card here somewhere. Do you want me to look?'

'No. No. Just tell me what you want me to do.' Rose put the phone on speaker and laid it beside her on the bed so she could concentrate on the socks. In less than a week, she had already forgotten how frustrating it was to get information from Peter. 'Anyway, it doesn't matter. I can't help you. I don't have the time. I don't have a laptop. There is literally nothing I can do. You're on your own. Go through the filing cabinet in the sunroom. Every lecture is in there filed under title and dates – just reuse something.'

'It's quite important. I don't know why you had to choose right now to go away when I'm at this crossroad that could go either way. Now I'm stuck . . . and this opportunity will pass me by . . .'

'*What* opportunity?!' Rose picked up the phone, shook it with frustration and flung it back down on the bed. She stood up and tried to calm herself with the Ujjayi breathing they practised in her yoga class and was momentarily distracted by the realisation that this was called the 'ocean breath'. She clearly did have an oceanic connection of some sort.

'The *friend* of Craig's, as I've just explained five times!' said Peter.

With a sigh of deep frustration, Rose sat down to put her shoes on.

'Are you all right?' The voice was thin and reedy, almost ethereal, and her first instinct was to look up. Then she realised she was sitting on Peter.

'Listen,' she said, extracting the phone from under her. 'I can't help you. If you need something specific written, dictate it to Max and he can write it for you. So, plan A, try the filing cabinet and, plan B, ask Max. Peter, it's all in your head.'

'You think I'm imagining it?'

'No, no, no . . . for crying out loud, why are you so literal? You've been lecturing on twentieth-century history for more than thirty years. You know it inside out. If they haven't specified anything, just pick something yourself . . . it's not that difficult!'

'I see what you're driving at,' he said ponderously. 'I think people are a little weary of the world wars. The Cuban missile crisis is probably considered to be more specifically US history now, not as relevant as it once was . . .'

Dear. God. Was he going to now list every major incident of the entire century?! 'Okay, here's another idea. Pick three. Ask Friend-of-Craig's which one she prefers. Done.'

There was a long silence on the other end and finally Peter said sulkily, 'Thanks for your help.'

'My pleasure,' said Rose. They exchanged curt goodbyes and she pushed back a niggling guilt about her indifference to Peter's plight, whatever it was. She couldn't blame him for feeling abandoned.

The hotel dining room was small, only half-a-dozen tables packed in close together. The day outside was dull and overcast but the room was made cheery by bright yellow walls and red-checked table cloths, the air infused with the smell of coffee and warm pastries.

Only two tables were occupied, one by an elderly couple speaking quietly in German and the other by Fran, who looked up with a sweet smile when Rose walked in and said, '*Bonjour!*'

'*Bonjour* to you too!' said Rose, joining her at the table. 'You look fresh and frisky.'

'I'm just so excited to be here.' Fran leaned in close and whispered, 'Everything's so *French*.' She gave a shiver of excitement. Rose gave her a kiss on the cheek, pleased that she was enjoying herself. Fran looked five years younger already. If she kept this up, she'd be back to adolescence in three weeks' time.

They both looked up to see Maggie bump into a chair, knock her hip against a table and apologise to the German couple. She looked so dreadful, the first thing that crossed Rose's mind was getting her to a hospital. Her hair was pulled back and Rose saw with dismay how thin and lank it was. Her face looked swollen and puffy, as though she'd been awake crying all night.

Rose leapt up and took Maggie's arm, helping her into the chair. Fran said she would get them all coffee and croissants and went over to the self-serve coffee machine.

Maggie put her face in her hands, and Rose realised that she had absolutely no idea what to say, which almost never happened. She had run out of soothing comments and was feeling increasingly unequal to the task. She had thought it would simply be a matter of taking Maggie out of her environment and she would come good. Rose knew now that this was magical thinking, something she often subscribed to but seldom admitted. Now she thought that perhaps Kristo should be called. It may even be that he would need to come and get her. Or should Rose be taking her home? There was no way they could leave Maggie to get back to London and on a flight home on her own. And then there was Fran to consider, poor dear.

'Mags, are you all right? You look . . . dreadful,' said Rose.

'I feel okay, actually, just a bit groggy,' said Maggie. She looked around the dining room as if she had no idea where she was.

'Did you sleep badly?' asked Rose.

'I thought we weren't . . .' said Maggie. 'I don't know. I took a sleeping tablet to knock myself out. It felt like I was hovering between sleeping and waking all night.'

'You know, you shouldn't take sleeping tablets when you've been drinking.'

'I wasn't "drinking". You make it sound like I was on a bender.'

Fran came back with the coffee and croissants and sat down. Rose was aware the German couple had paused their conversation to concentrate on eavesdropping.

'Mag, you easily had half that bottle,' whispered Rose. 'Fran and I only had a glass each.'

Maggie stared at her. 'Half a bottle? Big bloody woop!'

'How many tablets did you take? I need to know.'

'Piss off. You're not my doctor, you know,' said Maggie.

'I just want to know all the meds you're on. Just in case something happens. We should all know that about each other,' insisted Rose. 'Fran, you go first.'

Fran looked startled, as though she needed to make something up. 'Ah, glucosamine. Vitamin E?'

Maggie seemed amused by this admission. 'Okay, Rose . . . off you go.'

'Just a statin for cholesterol,' said Rose. 'And I have the occasional joint to sleep.'

'So you're knocking yourself out with pot and taking me to task for having a glass or two of wine?' Maggie paused for Rose's retort. When none was forthcoming, she continued, 'Antidepressants, two types of blood pressure meds, statins for cholesterol . . . what else? No, that's pretty much it. It's pills holding me together. And yes, maybe I shouldn't be having alcohol with antidepressants or sleeping tablets – but what the hell? I don't need you bugging me, Rose!'

The German couple got up and left hurriedly as though the real trouble was about to start. Fran sipped her coffee and watched them leave. 'Well, this is a conversation we never had to have on the last trip,' she observed.

Maggie smiled; her eyes were bloodshot and watery. 'We were so unworldly back then. Do you remember that first time we came to Paris and slept in the van, we went to a restaurant, thinking we were so sophisticated, and the waiter asked if we would like an aperitif?'

Fran smiled. 'And Rose said, "Maybe, what is it?"'

'You didn't know either, Mag. Admit it!' Rose laughed.

'I'd never been offered one before,' said Maggie. 'It was always sherry in our house. We were just kids, so clueless . . . Fran was the only sophisticate back then.'

'Hardly. Mum and Oma might have seemed sophisticated by Australian standards, but only because they were Europeans,' said Fran.

'Educated Europeans, not peasants,' said Rose. 'I remember so clearly coming to your house and thinking it was all so cosmopolitan, with oriental rugs and real paintings on the walls. My parents had faded prints of early Australian artists, McCubbin and that lot, but mainly photos of kittens and puppies and horses that Mum had cut off the top of calendars.'

As they chatted and ate their breakfast, Maggie began to look more relaxed and the flush of her complexion faded. Rose wondered if it was better *not* to talk about Maggie's problems, but distract her away from them. Still, there was one question she had to ask. 'Maggie, be honest – do you want to turn back now, and go home? I haven't talked to Fran about this . . . but . . .'

'That's okay, Rose,' Fran reassured her. 'I understand.'

Maggie looked from one to the other and after a moment said, 'The way I feel right now, I don't want to go home at all.

So, that's a definite no. I want to go on. Just try and be patient with me, Rose.'

Half an hour later they were out in the street in their comfortable walking shoes. Maggie had made a big effort, her hair twisted into a roll, wearing a pair of dangly silver earrings she'd bought in London and fuchsia pink lipstick. She wore a stylish cream wool jacket, and Rose found it reassuring to see her looking more together.

They took the Metro to Anvers and walked up the hill to Montmartre, where they stood at the foot of the Sacré-Cœur Basilica and gazed out across the city. There were layers of dense grey cloud all the way to the horizon that parted occasionally, offering a glimpse of sun and the odd patch of blue, the promise of weather to come.

'Paris looks pretty much like London from this perspective. Overwhelmingly grey,' remarked Fran.

'With more dog poo,' added Maggie, with a quick glance at the soles of her shoes.

This gloomy perspective on everything was getting on Rose's nerves. She'd had thirty-five years of it from Peter, who could always find the downside in any situation, and, before him, her parents. Peter was cautious and it was a way to save himself from disappointment. It wasn't in Maggie's nature to be a pain in the neck, but, so far, she was doing a stellar job, and now Fran was going the same way. Rose knew she could only be patient with this stuff for so long, then she would snap.

The basilica itself was closed, but they wandered around the streets of Montmartre with Rose providing an informed commentary on the fraternity of French artists who had lived there at the turn of the century when it was a bohemian village with vineyards and cheap wine. These days it seemed to be entirely populated by tourists, middle-aged couples and dozens of young Asian women in red-and-blue berets, as though they imagined it was a theme park. While Fran was attentive to the commentary, Maggie wandered along nodding but not really listening, her thoughts clearly elsewhere. From time to time, she checked her phone and seemed relieved by the lack of activity. Rose felt like chucking that phone away and pined for the days when they travelled without any ties to home or the rest of the world. She had loved the idea that no one knew where they were. That was true independence. Complete disconnection.

On that first trip, they couldn't read newspapers or even talk to locals – English speakers were rare. Most cheap restaurants had an old television on a shelf and very often a nonna, dressed in black, sat watching it from the other side of the room. This was their only source of news: a confusion of images in a foreign language that meant very little. Now the problems of the world, and those of their own families, pursued them and it seemed there was no escape. There was no place left on earth that was far enough away.

Given that Montmartre had been Maggie's choice, it was frustrating to Rose that she seemed so uninterested now they were here. Next was Fran's choice – the Louvre. They caught the Metro there but arrived to discover it was closed due to a strike. The Jardin des Tuileries was nearby and the trees were dense with bright new leaves. It was a pleasant walk through the park, although it looked as if the rain could set in at any moment.

'Apart from the Champs-Élysées, this is the only place I distinctly remember from that very first visit,' said Rose. 'I remember I was so impressed by the symmetry of it all.'

'I have no memory of coming here,' said Fran. 'I only remember the main landmarks, like the Eiffel Tower and the Arc de Triomphe.'

'I know people go on about memory loss when you get older,' said Rose, 'but my brain feels like it's actually packed to the rafters with stuff. There's so much archived in there I can never find what I want – when I want it. Then, sometimes, out of the blue, I'll hear a fragment of a conversation with perfect recall from forty years ago.'

'Is it perfect recall?' asked Fran thoughtfully. 'How can you know? Sometimes, I think we've forgotten the context and a "fragment" stands out on its own but it has a different meaning to what was intended at the time.'

Maggie agreed. 'I know what you mean, like something that was meant to be a joke and, years later, feels like an insult.'

'At the risk of bringing down the tone of this philosophical conversation,' said Fran. 'I don't think I've ever told you this, Rose, but I have perfect recall of our first meeting and you farting into Miss Gordon's office.'

Maggie burst out laughing. 'Rose! That's so disgusting! I've never heard about this.'

Rose had no memory of this incident but wasn't surprised. 'Well, you posh girls probably didn't do things like that but I was a bit of a show-off at school.'

'What were you showing off? Your ability to let one rip?' asked Maggie.

'I was really shocked and embarrassed,' said Fran. 'Probably why I've never brought it up before.'

'I had a small repertoire of unladylike habits – burping five-syllable words, that sort of thing,' admitted Rose.

'Oh, yes, I remember that burping now,' said Fran. 'Can you still do it?'

'I'm more focused on repressing my emissions these days.'

Maggie smiled. 'Aren't we all.'

'Rose was a rebel when it was the only cool thing girls could be,' said Fran. 'There were pretty girls who were popular, but Rose was the coolest. She was fearless.'

'Reckless more than fearless,' corrected Rose. She would have liked to be a pretty, popular girl, but was nevertheless pleased by the description. 'I did hold some kind of record for detentions.'

'I didn't envy you that,' said Fran. 'But I envied your refusal to compromise.'

Rose felt unexpectedly furious with herself. 'If my young self could have looked into the future and seen the compromises I've made in my life, she'd throw up. It's been just one compromise after another to make life easy. That's not fearless. It's gutless.'

Fran and Maggie fell silent and she was glad they weren't trying to reassure her. That, at least, was honest. The truth was they too had expected more of her.

Fran linked arms with Rose. 'I know life didn't go quite as you planned. But no one's does, and you have made the best of things. That's brave.'

Maggie nodded. 'You're too hard on yourself, Rose.'

Rose didn't agree but she said nothing.

It started to rain and they found themselves at the Place de la Concorde. It was busy with tourists and traffic, all miniaturised by majestic buildings, extravagant fountains and towering obelisks. In the distance, the Eiffel Tower had all but disappeared into the clouds. It had been a disappointing day and, as they hurried back across the Pont de la Concorde towards the hotel, Rose felt dispirited. Gloomy weather and bitter regret were hardly an auspicious start to the trip.

It was too early for dinner but they had missed lunch, so they bought some pizza slices and a bottle of red wine in the Latin Quarter, and smuggled them into the hotel. They gathered in Maggie's room and sat in a row on the bed, drinking the wine out of their water tumblers and eating the slices of pizza, strings of hot cheese falling onto cardboard trays.

Rose had brought her iPad and they debated what to watch. Rose suggested one of her all-time favourites, *When Harry Met Sally* and Fran, an old-fashioned girl, elected *Breakfast at Tiffany's*. They tossed a coin and eliminated Rose's choice, then Fran's, and settled on Maggie's all-time favourite, *Out of Africa*.

It was like being on school camp, Rose thought, as they tucked themselves into Maggie's bed. The movie was longer than Rose had remembered. Fran, who took up the least space on one side of the bed, was asleep before Meryl Streep had even met Robert Redford. Maggie, sitting in the middle, was gone before the romantic orange-peeling scene, which was her favourite bit. Rose took the iPad from her and soldiered on until it ran out of charge, leaving Meryl alone with her grief in her empty house at the foot of the Ngong Hills.

It was so warm and comfortable in Maggie's bed, Rose was reluctant to go back to her room but it was far too squashy to sleep there. She slipped out of bed and woke Fran, who crept quietly back to her room.

Rose turned off the bedside lamp but, as she was about to leave, Maggie sat upright and stared wildly around the room, not seeming to know where she was. 'It has to be done,' she said in an agitated voice. 'There's not enough of them.' She looked a bit mad with her eye-makeup smeared under her eyes, and still wearing her dangly earrings.

Rose settled her down and tucked her in, murmuring soothingly. She switched off Maggie's phone, ignoring all the messages. She sat on the bed, her body just touching Maggie's, thinking it would help her settle into sleep. That's all she needed – rest and more rest – the poor dear was exhausted to her very core. Rose stayed with her until she began to gently snore.

Back in her room, Rose sat on her bed and wondered how she was going to manage the rest of this trip. She was blessed with a disposition that meant she was mostly upbeat. If she had become slightly more disgruntled in the last few years, it was mainly because Peter grated on her. Sometimes the sight of him walking into the room made her rigid with irritation. However much she tried to combat this tension, it crept back again. And yet she was grateful to him for everything they had together – the house, the boys, their life. But somehow gratitude just wasn't cutting it any more.

She had so much to be grateful for. These friends, this trip, and being here in Paris. As a kid growing up on a farm where nothing of note happened from one year to the next, she couldn't have even imagined she would ever come to Paris. When her parents broke the news that they would move to the city, she'd been beside herself with excitement. She was fourteen years old and desperate to be in the thick of life; Sydney was the most glamorous, beautiful place imaginable.

She and her sister, Chrissy, were living the high life working in the shop after school, selling cigarettes, magazines and newspapers and lottery tickets. They would sit on the bench behind the counter, chewing gum and painting their nails, flirting with the awkward boys from school who hung around. They would tease the boys, chasing them out of the shop and mock wrestling with them on the pavement outside. Sometimes customers complained to her parents and there would be a warning. But she and Chrissy never took that too seriously. Their parents both hated being in the shop, so their jobs were relatively secure.

They were allowed to take home any out-of-date magazines with the covers ripped off and kept a carton full of them in the bedroom they shared. They would lie on their beds reading at night. Rose mainly liked *MAD Magazine* and *Archie* comics. Chris loved *Jackie* and *Seventeen* – she was more romantically inclined. Occasionally they managed to sneak a *Playboy* or *Penthouse* out. These were hidden in the back of the wardrobe to be examined after dark. She and Chrissy both thought it peculiar that people were so interested in photos of women with their tops off, but the articles were highly informative. Rose experimented with taking her top off for small audiences but soon grew bored with that and moved on to the first of a series of boyfriends, most of whom never lasted more than a few weeks.

Fran didn't approve of Rose's 'boy mad' behaviour. She had old-fashioned notions about saving herself for marriage, and wanted a steady, reliable boyfriend. But Rose enjoyed wielding her power and the inevitable dramas that ensued. She was running her own version of *Days of Our Lives*, complete with jealous girlfriends and broken hearts. She enjoyed being the source of intrigue and gossip. Those days were long gone, and probably just as well. It made her laugh to think that working in the newsagents had seemed so glamorous. Back then, Paris was far beyond any dreams she had for herself. Not to be taken for granted.

As she prepared for bed, Rose wondered if she had been over-ambitious with this trip. She was struck by the horrible thought that this well-intentioned adventure could end up costing the three of them their friendship.

Chapter Ten

Fran loved every moment in Paris. The dark, brooding weather and even the museum strike were all part of the experience, although today was definitely more rewarding than yesterday. They managed to spend a few hours in the Musée d'Orsay, followed by a pleasant lunch in Le Marais, with time to mooch around in Shakespeare and Company. The list was all ticked off but in the late afternoon, while Rose and Maggie rested, Fran went out on her own. She wandered along the open-air bookshops, *les bouquinistes*, that lined the pavement beside the Seine, stopping to look at old postcards and maps and the antiquarian books. She leaned on the parapet beside the river to watch the passers-by and wished she had longer here. She could spend whole days doing nothing but this. She would happily become a *flâneur*; someone who wanders around simply observing people.

Standing there beside the Seine, she made a promise to herself that she would return to Paris sometime, alone if necessary. Having these last couple of days to familiarise herself with the city had made her feel more confident about the prospect of a solo trip. She tried to imagine herself going out in the evening alone, stopping at a bar and ordering an aperitif. It was a stretch. Perhaps she needed to learn French first and come for a longer period . . . Could she get a job in a bookshop here? She'd definitely need French for that. But how long would it take to learn the language at her age? How would she afford language classes?

She sighed, recognising that this habit of overthinking an idea until an insurmountable obstacle was reached was a more subtle form of what Louis did. A sneaky way of expanding the project to impossible proportions to avoid making a decision or taking a risk. She needed to hold on to her first thought. She would return and spend more time getting to know this city. That was her promise. And, with that settled, she turned and hurried back towards the hotel. It was almost time to meet Maggie and Rose for their final dinner in Paris. Tomorrow they would catch the early train to Berlin.

Watery light from the window fell across Maggie's face as she slept. Behind her, the countryside rushed past, like time itself, sweeping her forward, asleep or awake. Fran thought that it must be beneficial for her to sleep so much. Rose had made the odd worried comment about Maggie's weight and something about her thinning hair, but she was still a beauty to Fran's eyes. Her face so strong and full of character. Rose, too, barely seemed to age. After so many years, Fran knew she had no objectivity. She could only see the two of them as composites of every phase of their life.

Rose was also oblivious to the passing scenery, completely immersed in a book. Fran couldn't quite see the title and didn't want to disturb her to ask. She was happy enough watching the landscape race past, her thoughts gliding from one subject to another. She had hardly given Louis a single thought in the last couple of days. Right now, she could clearly see that he wasn't central to her life. But how would she feel when she arrived back in London and Maggie and Rose had gone home? She quickly pulled her thoughts from that subject, to the prospect of Berlin.

Fran had strong memories of them driving the Kombi across East Germany along the transit road from Hamburg in the West, to Berlin. Before they made that trip, she had always imagined the country itself was divided by the wall, when, in fact, West Berlin was encircled by it within communist East Germany.

Unaware that vehicles were not permitted to stop on the transit road, they had pulled over to the side and sat on the grass near some woods to boil the billy for tea. Four men in uniform arrived and indicated they would have to move on. Rose put up an argument for at least finishing their tea, without success. Looking back, Fran wondered that they weren't arrested or worse. They really had been very naive, with no concept of the possible repercussions.

They had stayed in a camping ground in West Berlin that was beside the border wall: a huge concrete structure with a roll top that made scaling it from the other side impossible. It was horrible to think that the Death Strip, patrolled by dogs and guards, was hidden behind that wall, but they'd all found it fascinating to be up close with this famous structure.

Apart from the wall, the camp itself was idyllic, surrounded by woods with a lake that had a manned watchtower and barbed-wire fence running across the middle of it. Their camp site was surrounded by large tents furnished with all the comforts of home. Outside each tent was an array of deckchairs, the occupants solid-looking old people exposing their white winter skin to the sun. Some tents had low picket fences and plastic flowers in pots to mark out their territory: camping suburbia.

The Kombi van had an awning attached to one side and at night they would pitch the pup tent beneath this and take turns sleeping in it. It was July, the weather was hot and the evenings long. It was boiling inside the van; they decided to drag the double mattress out and all sleep in the open.

In the site opposite, across a gravel driveway, was a large tent occupied by a group of young men who glanced over each time they passed, spending their time stocking up on beer. The bolder ones called out cheeky greetings in German. Rose was checking them out and rating them out of ten. Maggie was always guarded in these situations; if it wasn't for her resistance, Rose would have invited them over.

As evening fell, the boy tent remained in darkness. The front of the tent was rolled up and Fran could see the boys lolling around inside like young lions. She caught the odd comment, followed by bursts of laughter, and realised the *englische Mädchen* – English girls – were the hot topic. She didn't like the tone of what she heard. Emboldened by beer, they began to call out lyrics in English from pop songs but, as the night wore on, these degenerated into something more threatening.

Rose was the first to get annoyed and was all for going over to confront them. 'How can we sleep with all that going on?'

'Do they really know what they're saying?' asked Fran.

'I'm pretty sure they know what "I wanna fuck you, baby" means,' said Maggie. 'It doesn't necessarily mean they're actually going to try it . . . but . . .'

'Depending how drunk they get. Maybe we should just sleep in the van, to be safe,' suggested Fran.

'Why the hell should we?' Rose dug around the back of the van and got out her hatchet. 'Right, this is what we need.' She looked at her friends' alarmed faces. 'The blunt end, *obviously*.'

Maggie stared at Rose in disbelief. 'Isn't that just going to enrage them? Or kill someone? I think we're better to have a bucket of water to chuck over them if they try anything.'

'Water?' said Rose incredulously. 'That's going to cool them off, not put them off.'

Fran looked around at the neighbouring tents. Everyone was inside now. Most of the tents were dark. She felt a shiver of anxiety that no one would come to their aid. If something happened, people would think it was their own fault, three young women travelling alone. Asking for trouble.

Maggie was getting tetchy. 'What's your plan? Go over and brandish your axe at them? By the way, why bring an axe?'

'It's not an *axe*. It's a hatchet. You can't go camping without one.'

'In the bush. Not here! We're going to end up arrested for carrying a lethal weapon. Anyway, it's too hot to all sleep in the van. And we can't just leave one person outside. We're better to stick together.'

Rose picked up the torch and stalked off towards the woods.

Fran got out her toiletries bag and went off to the ablutions block, pursued by whistles and catcalls as she passed the tent opposite. If she'd been braver, she would have told them off, but she didn't want them to know she spoke German because she'd be stuck in the middle.

She came back to find that Rose had dragged a large dead branch out of the woods.

'We need a camp fire,' announced Rose.

'Won't we get into trouble?' asked Fran.

Rose shrugged. 'Just a small one. It'll be fine.'

There was no one around now and Fran wasn't sure how a fire would help but Rose was determined. Maggie held the torch while Rose, legs planted firmly, swinging from the shoulder, wielded the hatchet with great speed and efficiency, lashing into the branch, to the accompaniment of cheers and shouting from the tent opposite. She chopped it through and then split each piece until it was all kindling, which she propped up teepee-style over a pile of twigs. Maggie lit the fire, and Rose, with a practised flick of the wrist, plunged the hatchet into the ground. Something about this deft movement made the boys' tent fall silent. After a moment, one of them got up and closed the front flap of their tent and they lit a lamp inside.

'There you go,' said Rose. 'I knew a fire would do it. All animals are afraid of fire. It's instinctual. Now, let's get some sleep.'

Fran was entranced by the pale green light pouring into the railway-station lobby of Berlin Hauptbahnhof, a spectacular modern structure of metal and glass. She would have liked to stop and take some photos but, after eight hours on the train, it seemed too much to ask, so she climbed into the taxi without a word.

The accommodation Rose had booked was a room in a hostel on Friedrichshain-Kreuzberg with three single beds. Maggie arched a critical eyebrow but said nothing. Fran was quietly delighted. She loved the idea of sharing a room. It was much closer to the original journey with the three of them bunking in together.

Formerly on the East side of the wall, the room was utilitarian with a communal bathroom down the hall. The only view from their first-floor window was a large industrial construction site. While Rose and Fran got themselves settled, Maggie stood at the window and stared out in silence. Rose threw Fran a questioning look and finally said, 'Missing the world of construction, Mag?'

Maggie turned for a moment with a vague smile, her gaze drawn back to the building site. 'I was thinking how divorced I've become from the daily work of the business. Kristo and I live in quite different worlds now. No wonder we have trouble communicating.'

Unlike Rose, who complained about Peter at any opportunity, Maggie kept complaints about Kristo to herself, so Fran was taken aback by the comment. Especially since Kristo seemed like a big communicator. He loved talking and discussing all sorts of things, even emotions. He wasn't one of those men who sit silently, expecting their wives to do the heavy lifting socially. He was a bit over the top sometimes, but Fran liked him. He was a big personality and besotted with Maggie. It was disheartening to hear that they too were struggling.

The day was fading and they agreed to get a quick meal nearby and an early night, ready for a full day tomorrow. Downstairs, in the hostel bar, a dozen or so young people, mainly men, sat around tables drinking beer, chatting and looking at their phones. They were all dressed similarly in grey and black lightweight outdoor gear. This new breed of backpackers, confident and organised, were the polar opposite of Fran's generation. Beer was the pervading smell in the hostel – that part hadn't changed. Fran felt diminished and aged by their presence and was relieved to push out through the revolving doors into the street. The night air was chilly and they paused to fasten their jackets.

There was a bar and burger place a few doors up and they went in. It was already busy and the music was loud: Earth, Wind & Fire, 'Boogie Wonderland', the song that just kept coming back. Rose grinned and shrugged along to the music as they headed for the only available table. They ordered beers and burgers. It was difficult to talk above the hubbub, which was relaxing in its own way.

Maggie and Rose made short work of the generous burgers, although Fran, with her smaller appetite, struggled to finish hers. Enjoying cold lagers, they started to relax, singing along to 'We Are Family', boogying in their seats, and Fran felt a burst of optimism. They could make this work. They were family. They were sisters. And now they were having fun together.

When the beers were finished and the evening seemed to be coming to a natural end, Maggie went up to the bar and returned with a bottle of red wine and three glasses. Rose refused the offer of wine. Fran agreed to have a glass, only so Maggie wouldn't drink the whole thing on her own. The room was increasingly hot and airless, and red wine was the last thing she felt like right now. Avoiding Rose's frown, Maggie sat back with a full glass in hand, still grooving to the music, enjoying herself. Rose made a comment to Maggie that Fran didn't catch over the music but she could sense where this was going.

Fran leaned over to Rose. 'It's only eight o'clock. We're having a good time. Let's just go with it.'

Rose sighed. 'I thought we agreed on an early night.' But she took the bottle and filled her glass. Maggie smiled. They chinked glasses.

Fran looked around the bar and noticed they were the oldest people there. A group of fresh-faced young women sat at the next table, laughing together and chatting effortlessly over the top of the music. Fran had begun to gaze wistfully at young people. Sometimes, it felt as though she were watching life from the shadows these days.

As the night wore on, attempts at conversation became more exhausting. When the bottle of wine was finished, Maggie bought a single glass of red at the bar. It was as though she would do anything to prolong the evening.

Rose, to her credit, made an effort to keep the mood buoyant, but Fran was relieved when the last drop was gone and they were released out into the street and the fresh night air. They walked back to the hostel in good spirits, Rose humming under her breath, Maggie quiet but seemingly fine. But in the harsh light of the room, Fran noticed Maggie was sluggish, not exactly drunk, but a bit disoriented. She dithered about with her toiletries bag and wandered off to the bathroom in a dazed state.

'That was too much booze for me. I've got a headache now,' said Rose crossly.

Fran gave her a sceptical look. 'Rose, I don't believe you. You've been boasting for years that you've never had a headache in your life. Get your story straight.'

'Well, okay, I can feel one coming on.' Rose massaged her forehead, obviously torn between making a point and maintaining her unblemished record.

'I know you feel we should try to stop Maggie drinking. I just don't know how we can without upsetting her.'

'I don't want to argue about it, Frannie – I enjoy a drink myself. I'm just worried that she's killing herself in plain sight.'

'You're being dramatic, Rose. She just drinks a bit too much. She wants the release . . . that's all. Lots of people do.'

'I don't care about other people drinking themselves to death, I care about her. Especially on all those medications. One or two drinks is fine, but a bottle?'

Fran agreed. 'I just don't know what we can really do.'

'I can't let her do it,' said Rose fiercely. 'I love her too much.'

'I love her too, but —' argued Fran as the door swung open and Maggie reappeared in her cotton robe, having changed in the bathroom.

'Who do you love?' asked Maggie with a smile.

Fran and Rose glanced at each other guiltily.

'You. We were both saying how much we love you,' said Fran, feeling a little silly.

For a moment it seemed as though Maggie's face swelled slightly, then she blinked and said, 'I'll have to go to the bathroom more often.' She didn't look quite herself, her face shiny and naked and her eyes glassy. She took off her earrings, put them on the shelf by the bed. She took various pills out of her handbag and washed them down with a glass of water and got into bed.

They had barely been asleep an hour when Maggie sat up with a shout. Fran got up to see if she was all right. They had left the window blind up and the eerie white light from the building site was reflected in Maggie's eyes. She mumbled something indistinct and slowly lay down again. An hour later, she jerked upright again and struggled to get out of bed. She seemed to be trapped between sleep and waking, murmuring unintelligibly. Fran was about to get up when Maggie collapsed back onto the bed again and began to snore.

'Je-*sus*,' muttered Rose.

'What was she saying?' asked Fran. 'Could you understand her?'

'Speaking in tongues, I think. It's the bloody alcohol and meds.'

'Did you hear that sort of crunching noise?' asked Fran quietly.

'Yeah, what was that? She seems to have gone back to sleep now,' whispered Rose. Within minutes the crunching sound was back, as if Maggie was chewing on a hard-boiled sweet. Rose dragged herself out of bed, swearing under her breath.

'What are you doing? Don't wake her,' said Fran.

Rose bent over Maggie's sleeping form in the dark. She poked around for a minute, picked something up and examined it in the palm of her hand. She got her phone and came to sit on Fran's bed. By the light of the phone, they stared at Rose's palm containing Maggie's mangled silver earring.

Ironically, next morning, Maggie appeared to be the more rested of the three. Fran and Rose had agreed not to mention the turmoil of the night and returned the earring to the bedside shelf. They watched Maggie pick up the earring and inspect it, but she said nothing.

They had breakfast in the hotel dining room and took the U-Bahn to Friedrichstraße to revisit Checkpoint Charlie. None of them had been back to Berlin in the intervening years and the old border entry between West and East was unrecognisable. Once the border had opened and the wall came down, Friedrichstraße, previously the focus of international attention, became just another street in the united city, and Fran found it hard to get her bearings now that the infrastructure of the border crossing had gone. All that remained of that time was the small shed that had been the allied checkpoint. They stood there awkwardly with a few other tourists, looking at this unprepossessing piece of history.

'It's just like a garden shed,' said Rose. 'Actually, I'm pretty sure that one is a fake. It's shabby chic, like a seaside bathing pavilion.'

'I remember it being a bit more utilitarian, and there was another longer shed you walked through and had your ID and bag checked,' remembered Maggie.

'That would have been on the East side,' said Fran. 'There was no need for the Americans to check anything.'

'But, if you recall, they weren't searching for weapons,' said Maggie. 'They were looking for anti-communist material.'

Rose nodded. 'The weapon of the West. I was a card-carrying commie when we came here. I thought I was going to see utopia in action but this Soviet bullshit put me off the whole thing. The way they hunted people and that Death Strip between the two walls where people were shot. What a massive waste of money and human endeavour.'

'I remember we were shocked by East Berlin,' said Fran. 'It looked like the war had finished yesterday, bombed-out buildings and nothing in the shops. Remember we tried to spend some of our East German marks and went into a fruit shop . . .'

'Everything was rotting,' said Rose. 'Disgusting. I keep thinking if they had put the funds they wasted on building and guarding the border wall into making East Germany a decent place to live, things could have been different.'

'Still a hippie at heart, Rose.' Maggie smiled.

'I'm still a socialist. I still believe the government should put the needs of the people ahead of business. That's everything that's wrong with the world right now.'

'Not everything . . .' began Maggie.

Fran quickly interrupted. 'Let's not get into this discussion right now.'

As they wandered away from the checkpoint, Rose said, 'You know, I've just realised something. Coming here and seeing what was really going on was what got me interested in political science and that led to me ending up going to university and —'

Maggie sighed. 'Is this leading back to everything being Peter's fault? Where's that list of banned topics? I need to add something.'

'Sorry. I don't normally go on about it so much. It's not his fault. I just think I could have done something more with my life. Maybe I could have done Peter's job, instead of being tucked away in the engine room doing all the hack work while he got the accolades.'

Fran said nothing. She didn't agree that Rose could have done Peter's job. For a start, he had the staying power that Rose lacked and, despite his difficulties with everyday tasks, he had earned his place in the academic world. Some years ago, Fran had attended one of his public lectures – he was brilliant. All his talents were condensed in this one area and he deserved those accolades, even if he couldn't have achieved them without Rose's support. He didn't appreciate her, or acknowledge her contribution, but that was another matter altogether.

'All I'm saying,' said Rose defensively, 'is I've just realised that that part of my life started here.'

Maggie stopped and looked at her. 'Yes, fine, but what good does it do you? What difference can it possibly make now?'

Fran genuinely felt a headache pushing at her temples and suggested they go across the road to the museum, in the hope of distracting them.

Being among German-speaking people, Fran found her thoughts constantly going back to Oma, remembering her grandmother's dark view of the world, the inhumanity of politics and religions. It was probably just as well that Oma had gone – the re-emergence of right-wing politics would have struck terror into her. It was everything she had feared.

In 1938, Oma had fled Austria for England with her two daughters: Marie was ten and Lena, twelve. By the time the war ended, there was nothing left for them in Austria, and Oma was afraid to go back. She was never convinced that what had happened couldn't happen again. When Lena and her husband, Tom, Fran's father, migrated to Australia in the early fifties, Oma went with them. Fran had no memory of her father, who had returned to England soon after her birth, and she had no real curiosity about him either. Growing up, her mother and Oma were her whole world.

When she was older, Fran began to wonder if the stories that Oma had told her as a child – of servants and balls and visits from royalty – were exaggerated. But when Fran got to know Aunt Marie better, she discovered just how affluent and privileged their lives had been before the war. It was only then that Fran began to fully understand the depth of Oma's losses, and why she had such a yearning for that golden past.

Lena was the more practical one; she had made it clear that romanticising the past was pointless, and painful. She dismissed Oma's stories as *sehnsucht*, an untranslatable word describing a disconsolate pining for the past and a home that no longer exists. Perhaps the word was just as relevant to this trip; a search for something that never really existed. Fran truly hoped that wasn't the case.

On that earlier trip, Fran had gone to the shop in the Tuchlauben district where her family had been jewellers for four generations. The jewellery shop had become a chocolate shop and she felt no real connection with the family's history there, it was so far removed from her experience. Perhaps her attitude had been limited by her own immaturity, because these days she had a different perspective. She had more sense of the layering of memory and time, and realised that Europe was the place where she felt most at home.

As Fran wandered around the Checkpoint Charlie museum, she felt that, in a different frame of mind, it could have been a heartening experience, the resilience of the human spirit and all that. But today, she felt a sense of despair at the desperate measures that East Germans had gone to, attempting to escape by tunnelling, ballooning, jumping – sometimes to their death – or concealed in shopping trolleys and cars. The famous image of the young guard, Conrad Schumann, leaping the barbed-wire fence brought tears to her eyes. The evidence of tens of thousands of Stasi informants spying on their friends and neighbours. Guards shooting their countrymen attempting escape, wanting nothing more than freedom. How were people convinced to betray friends and family in such a vile way in the name of a government?

Fran had never thought of herself as being free. She saw herself as being alone, lonely, unattached and single. All she wanted was to be coupled. But now she thought about the value of being physically free. Free from persecution. Free to think whatever she wanted and go wherever she wanted and speak her mind. It was a good starting point. If she could view her life from a different angle, as someone free from constraints, perhaps she could find a way to embrace that freedom? Rose was right, this was the best chance each of them had to experience a seismic shift. It wasn't going to happen in their daily lives but it could happen on this strange, magical journey. She was torn between being excited by the possibilities and, at the same time, terrified of them.

They took a taxi over to the famous department store KaDeWe, on Tauentzienstraße, for lunch in the sixth-floor food hall. The palatial extravagance of the displays of cheeses and sausages, salads, roasts of meat, platters of lobsters and oysters, piles of exotic fruits and pyramids of chocolates and patisserie were overwhelming. It was hard to know where to start.

Unfazed, Rose led the charge, piling her plate high. Fran took a more cautious approach but she noticed that Maggie, normally enthusiastic about food, was tentative and indecisive. Her plate was still empty while Fran and Rose had paid and were sitting down to eat.

Sensing something was not right, Fran got up from the table and offered to make a selection for her. Maggie handed over her plate with a sigh of relief. 'Just not too much,' she said. 'I'm not all that hungry.'

On their last night in Berlin, Rose put forward the idea that they should go out to a club. Fran and Maggie both flatly refused to even consider it.

'You're a couple of pikers,' Rose railed. 'Come on. Frannie? Just for an hour.'

Fran shook her head. 'I hated clubs even when I was young.'

'That's when people smoked. It'll be cool and edgy. You like that. Come on, guys. We're in Berlin.'

'You know when baby boomers go to cool places, it automatically makes them uncool,' argued Maggie. 'Just by entering a club, we'll tarnish its reputation.'

'Oh, what a load of crap,' said Rose. It took a while, but eventually she accepted that neither of them could be convinced. She put on her jacket and left in a huff.

'Perhaps I should go to keep an eye on her,' suggested Fran with some reluctance.

Maggie shrugged. 'It's up to you. She is a grown woman.'

Unconvinced, Fran grabbed her bag and jacket and hurried after Rose. She took the stairs and, as she reached the first-floor landing, saw Rose exit the lift into the lobby and walk into the hostel bar. Fran hovered unseen outside the door and watched Rose order a beer and take it to a table looking over the street.

'Lose her already?' asked Maggie, looking up from her book in surprise when Fran arrived back in the room a few minutes later.

Fran smiled. 'She's having a beer at the downstairs bar.'

Maggie laughed. 'Did she see you?'

Fran shook her head. 'I feel bad for not going with her but I'm more relieved not to have to go.'

'Oh, Fran. You don't have to do everything Rose wants, you know.'

'I know. Don't tell her I saw her, though. Let's just go along with it.'

Fran didn't hear Rose come in but, next day, couldn't resist asking how it went.

'What happens in Berlin stays in Berlin,' said Rose haughtily and changed the subject.

Chapter Eleven

After the long walk from the station, their suitcases bumping over the cobblestones, followed by having to haul their bags up three flights of stairs, Maggie was very relieved to arrive in their Prague accommodation. Rose had surpassed herself with this booking. On the outskirts of Old Town, it was a spacious three-bedroom flat with high ceilings and double doors between rooms. Maggie opened up the tall casement windows and looked down into the central garden between the adjoining buildings. It was dominated by a pair of huge old beech trees, bright green with new leaves, and populated by a flock of birds with an odd cry, like a trolley with squeaky wheels. Turning from the window, she realised that Rose was waiting eagerly for her approval.

'It's wonderful, Rose,' said Maggie with a smile. 'And so quiet too. Well done.'

Fran agreed and Rose was visibly relieved. Maggie felt guilty and promised herself again that she would curb her complaints, for her own sake as well as theirs.

They decided to rest in their rooms for an hour before they headed out to explore the city.

Maggie lay down on the bed and closed her eyes. Being catapulted from one city to the next was disorienting. Strangely, she had lost any desire to stop, becoming possessed by the urge to keep moving. She had a sense of anticipation for the next place, as though she was searching for somewhere she would feel comfortable and content.

She'd had her phone on silent overnight and deliberately not looked at it. Now she scrolled through the messages, each revealing a new episode in the Dimitratos soap opera. The family had restrained themselves for the first few days after she left but that was now over and every day there was some new tangle to be unravelled. Messaging was such a tedious and laborious way to communicate too, rife with confusion. Yannis was off work sick and Kristo was asking Maggie to check if particular payments had been made. Elena had sent a list of complaints about Yia-yiá's interference in the twins' lives – as if Maggie had any control over that. There was a missed call from the home phone that was most likely Yia-yiá. She was the only one who used it these days. Another missed call from Nico. She needed to manage him somehow until she got her strength back. Then something had to be done. She didn't want to think about that.

She put her phone aside and tried to focus on being here in Prague, a city she had found mysterious and fascinating on that first visit forty years ago. No doubt she would have to endure more history lessons from Rose today. Rose was becoming as bad as Peter. You couldn't offer any opinion on politics or current affairs without Peter making you feel like a goose for your superficial understanding of the world. They were both very knowledgeable and it didn't normally bother Maggie. Perhaps it was less to do with Rose and more that Maggie was off balance at the moment.

But something else had changed. She had completely lost her appetite. It happened in a single moment as she had stood gazing over that smorgasbord in KaDeWe. She had known for months that she ate without noticing or tasting her food, attempting to fill a void, to find some comfort and feel solid within herself. Nothing seemed to satisfy her. Sometimes she would forget what she'd just eaten, no memory of texture or flavour remained. And, much as she resented Rose's accusations, alcohol was the same. It had become impossible to relax without the help of a glass of wine or a vodka, even though it sometimes had the opposite effect, making her tense and anxious. She longed to escape her own skin, even for an hour or two, to shake off the agitation that possessed her. But, in that moment, she had realised that no amount of food would make her feel better. She knew that she needed to make a conscious effort to recalibrate, slow down and try to recapture the pleasure food offered. She didn't feel hungry any more but she felt empty, as though making space for some new connection between belly and brain.

In the late afternoon, they went out into the streets of Old Town Prague. The day was bright but cool. Summer came slow and late to Eastern Europe. The square, with its famous astronomical clock and ornate medieval buildings, was completely packed with other tourists. There was a market selling souvenirs and food. The air smelt of warm cinnamon sugar from the many stalls offering *trdelník*: a sweet pastry tube cooked on long poles over hot embers and filled with chocolate or whipped cream. None of them remembered this confection at all from the previous visit. Some of the stalls sold a dish they did remember: a traditional potato, bacon and cabbage dish called *halušky*. They bought a bowl to share and perched on a bench to watch the crowds. Rose took one spoonful and pulled a face. 'Ugh, it tastes like burnt wallpaper glue.'

Fran tried a few mouthfuls. 'I don't mind it. Smoked bacon is quite strong if you're not used to it.'

'I don't remember the food as being that great,' said Maggie.

'It was under Soviet rule back then,' said Fran. 'I'm sure it has improved. Anyway, this is tourist food, not the best example.'

'I can't believe how many people are here,' said Rose. 'It is a weekend, I suppose. But still.'

On cue, a mob of British lads ran amok in the crowd waving bottles of beer and singing football chants.

'It's cheap flights. You can fly here from the UK for twenty quid,' explained Fran.

Nearby, a dozen or so Italians gathered around a busker with a piano accordion and swayed together as they sang along to 'O Sole Mio' at full volume.

'This part is like any tourist trap. Locals would never set foot here,' said Maggie. 'It's just a shock after it being so quiet when we were here last.'

As they wandered down Karlova Street towards the river, Maggie remembered Prague as a fairytale city populated by unhappy, disheartened citizens, who had stared at them in the streets and ignored them in shops. Shops that had almost nothing to buy; clothes twenty years out of date and food that wasn't far behind. Crossing the border into what was then Czechoslovakia, they'd had to exchange funds into koruna but found nothing to spend it on. Now it was the opposite extreme – the streets lined with souvenir and designer clothes shops.

The famous Charles Bridge, guarded by Gothic statues of saints, spanned the Vltava River connecting Old Town with Lesser Town. Today, there were so many tourists on the bridge, it looked as though there was an exodus taking place. The crowd moved as one body across the pedestrian bridge to the other side, only to turn around and walk back.

They decided it was madness to enter that fray and wandered back to the flat along the quieter back streets to avoid the crush. Rose reminded them about the time they were robbed at the camping ground outside Prague. It had been raining and they had all slept in the van. To make more room, they had packed the tent, camp stretcher and all their food underneath the van. In the morning everything had gone. Rose had insisted the police be called and managed to find an English speaker to interpret. The policeman, who took several hours to arrive, gazed into the distance while the interpreter explained the situation, then he yawned, shrugged, got in his Škoda and left.

'He didn't even ask for a statement, or a list of missing items,' remembered Rose.

'I expect he sent it straight through to Interpol,' said Maggie. 'Too big for the local constabulary to handle. I don't know why you even got the police involved.'

'Bloody annoying, losing our tent like that,' insisted Rose.

'I felt sorry for people having to steal food from us,' said Fran.

Then, as now, Rose had been indignant about the injustice. As far as Maggie and Fran were concerned, it could have been much worse. They could have had the van stolen. Or someone break in while they were in there.

Fran turned to Rose. 'Remember that girl, the one who acted as our interpreter, wanted to buy your jeans?'

Rose laughed. 'I'd forgotten about that. A filthy pair of Levi's. I could have been arrested for jeans trafficking.'

'So funny to think of people buying jeans on the black market. Or smuggling them into the country.' Fran shook her head in disbelief. 'What was that all about?'

'Seems pretty tame compared to what gets smuggled now,' said Maggie.

'They were a symbol of freedom . . .' began Rose, in the lofty tone that Maggie found so annoying.

Maggie sighed. 'Rose, we were there. We all know about it. No need for a lecture.' She turned around in time to see Rose pull a scowling face at Fran. 'I saw that, Rose!'

Rose laughed. She linked arms with Maggie and Fran and they walked along the quiet cobbled laneways together, not quite the laughing girls but at least in step for the moment.

Maggie woke at dawn the next day, dressed quickly and slipped out of the apartment and into the empty streets. Without crowds cluttering the place up, Prague was the fairytale city of old. Every old building was decorated with some mysterious symbol or detail: gargoyles, angels, saints, gold stars and embellishments of flowers. Coded messages from the past to the present, and she wished she had more time to research and interpret them.

She walked through the archway of the tower and onto the Charles Bridge, delighted to find it was empty. A swathe of grey cloud stretched across the pale blue sky like a veil. A flock of birds swooped overhead, turning and spinning along the river, dappled with dawn light. Under her feet, the cobblestones were smooth and burnished by time and she had a sense of finally beginning her journey.

To her left, a weir crossed the river, the water caught in a long seam that continued, smooth as glass, towards another arched bridge. Up the hill on the far side of the bridge were typical Czech-style buildings painted in cream, sienna and terracotta with red roofs, their domes and towers thrown into sharp relief, silhouetted by the sun rising behind them.

She crossed the bridge and walked on up the hill, pausing occasionally to admire the Gothic, baroque and renaissance architecture all around her. As she continued to wander along the winding lanes, molten gold sunlight poured down through the archways towards her. She reached the summit and looked back over the city with its dark domes and sleepy river and saw how beautiful and unchanged it was; much as it had been forty years ago and for centuries before that. A city that had survived so much conflict and hardship, and yet remained as beautiful as ever.

She came to a large square and sat on some steps at the foot of a statue. She looked around her at the old palace and each of the buildings surrounding the square. Years ago, she would have been reading up in her guidebook about the history of these buildings. Now she just wanted to sit with it. As a child, and even later, she would have wanted to draw the buildings as a way of seeing the detail in them. She had once cherished the idea of becoming an architect. It would have been her first choice, ahead of accountancy, which was her father's choice. He didn't believe women were suited to technical careers.

'Architecture is nothing to do with drawing,' he had explained. 'It's engineering. Mathematics. Technical.' She got the idea that it was considered unfeminine. Ironic that she ended up in the construction industry. She had often wondered how she would go as a project manager. The design and building of the house at Bayview had been one of the great pleasures and accomplishments of her life. She had done the original sketches, worked with the architect and supervised the build. She loved every minute of it. Loved seeing it grow and develop, dealing with the trades, solving the problems and watching it all come together. The house was too big for them now, but it would take a lot for her to give it up.

As she walked back down the hill towards the bridge, she felt her spirits lift with a sense of the world opening itself up to her, as it had on that first trip when she'd felt a curiosity and openness. She was annoyed with herself that she put so much energy into finding fault in everything. Over the past few years, she had succumbed to the idea that nothing was as good as it once was, even though she knew that older people only clung stubbornly to this belief because they had forgotten the bad old times.

She stood on the bridge and watched the light on the river. She dug around in her handbag and found a bar of chocolate, broke off a piece and put it in her mouth. She let it sit on her tongue as she watched the city slowly wake up: locals walked briskly to work, a man wandered along with his dog, a couple of school children with violin cases passed her. As the chocolate melted in her mouth, layers of flavour and richness tantalised every tastebud. The light and the sweetness brought a moment of contentment.

She pondered the idea that from the outside she looked like a woman with everything: beautiful daughters, an ambitious husband, an enviable home . . . someone who could buy anything she wanted. What was wrong with her, that it wasn't enough?

It felt as though she was on the verge of finding some clarity, when her phone began to vibrate in her bag. It was Kristo and she took the call.

'What are you up to?' he asked, as though checking up on her.

'Just standing on a bridge, looking over the Vltava River and thinking about —'

'I wish I was standing on a bridge looking at a river instead of drowning in fucking problems.'

Maggie was silent. She felt guilty for not wanting to hear what he had to say.

'Bloody Yannis,' said Kristo. 'You're not going to believe —'

'Kristo, please, I don't want to hear about this. I can't —'

'How does it hurt for you to listen? You're not interested any more? Is that it? Everything is now on my head. You're wandering around looking at rivers while I'm stuck here sorting out everything.'

'Okay, what's happened?' she asked, reluctantly.

'He's only bloody mortgaged Auntie Agnes's house. She didn't know a thing about it. The bank's been sending her letters – of course she gave them to Yannis to read and he told her it was nothing.'

'What's he done with the money?' asked Maggie in dismay.

'He says he's been scammed online. I don't know anything about scamming. Can we get the money back, do you think?'

Maggie sighed. 'I doubt it. We'll look into it when I get back.'

'And don't suggest we fire Yannis because then they'd have no income at all. *Shit!*'

'Can you go and see the bank about the mortgage?'

'Maggie, no. That's the sort of thing you do. Not me. I'll just get mad with them.'

'I don't know why you would. It's not the bank's fault. Anyway, get the documentation and find out what is owing, at least.'

'I don't know why you had to go for so long. I'm having to do everything,' said Kristo plaintively.

'You can sort this out, darling. I have every faith in you.'

There was a silence and he seemed to remember that he was supposed to be on his best behaviour. 'Sorry, baby. I'm just pissed off with everything. And, as usual, Nico has buggered off just when I need help, and dumped me right in it.'

'Where's he gone?' Maggie felt a prickle of discomfort. She glanced around out of habit, even knowing it was completely absurd.

'No idea. Just decided to take a trip. Have a nice holiday some-where. Why now? Hang on.' She waited while he called out, 'Mum! Where did Nico go?'

Maggie could hear Yia-yiá coming closer to the phone, giving a detailed explanation in Greek until Kristo interrupted her. 'Yeah, yeah . . . okay . . . okay. Maggie? Nah, she doesn't know . . .'

'With Effie? Has he gone with Effie?'

'How the hell would I know? I don't keep in touch with her. Oh, Mum says he went off on his own. Left his wife behind. Typical. Why are you so interested, anyhow?'

'I'm not. It just seemed unfortunate that he would choose right now.'

'Yeah, but he was always a selfish piece of . . .' Maggie could hear Yia-yiá scolding him; tough on her boys, she never tolerated them speaking badly of each other.

'Hang on, I just have to go outside . . . Mum, you don't need to follow me . . . stay there . . .'

Maggie heard the glass door to the back deck slide shut.

'It's a long time till you get back, Maggie *mou*,' he said in his mushy voice. 'If you get sick of those girlfriends, can you come home earlier?'

Maggie knew if she got into that discussion, Kristo would start to campaign. She wanted to ask how the twins were, but that too would start a whole new discussion she didn't want to have right now. She said her goodbyes, put the phone away and turned back to the river but the light had changed and her fleeting sense of contentment vanished.

She felt breathless walking back to the flat. Her imagination was working overtime and Agnes's plight had taken a backseat to Nico suddenly going away on his own and being secretive about his destination. Was that coincidental? He did go away from time to time, usually to Bali or somewhere else in Indonesia, but it was unlike him to go alone. Did he know where Maggie was? She stopped dead at the realisation that she had printed Rose's itinerary and stuck it on the fridge for Kristo.

She couldn't get back to the flat fast enough. She hurried up the three flights of stairs and was panting by the time she got inside the door.

It was warm inside the flat, smelling of coffee and fresh bread. Fran and Rose sat at the table having breakfast. Maggie was immensely relieved to see them, as if there was a possibility they might have abandoned her.

'You okay? Someone chasing you?' said Rose, getting up. 'Sit down. I'll get you some coffee. We've got delicious rolls and jam.'

Maggie sat down, still puffed from the exertion of the stairs. 'We need to change our itinerary.'

Rose poured a cup of coffee and placed it in front of Maggie. 'Why, exactly?'

'Not so much the locations. Just the accommodation. Mix it up a bit.'

Fran asked, 'Mix up what with what?'

Maggie tried to sound upbeat. 'You know, be more spontaneous.'

Fran and Rose exchanged puzzled looks.

'There's something very wrong when you're the one advocating spontaneity,' said Rose. 'That's your least-favourite thing. What's going on?'

Maggie had guarded this secret for so long, it had become a part of her. Over the years she had kept it well away from Rose and Fran. For the longest time she'd wanted to pretend that it wasn't happening and talking about it would only make it more real. Had she confided in Rose, she would have been under pressure to bring everything out in the open. Even now, there was a high risk that Rose would take things into her own hands and talk to Kristo. That simply couldn't happen. There wasn't a single person in her life who wouldn't be affected. The family would collapse. The business would collapse. There was no question in her mind that it was partly the burden of this secret that had led to her collapse.

But now she'd gone the wrong way about dealing with this problem. 'Sorry, look, we don't need to change everything. What's our accommodation in Vienna?'

Rose reluctantly scrolled down the screen of her phone and handed it over, as Maggie put her reading glasses on. Thinking furiously, she flicked through the site. 'It says we can cancel for fifty euros. I'll pay that, and we can get a flat like this.' She gestured around cheerfully, ignoring Rose's gaze. 'This sort of thing is perfect.'

Rose and Fran watched her in silence.

'Maggie, tell us what's going on. If you want to change it, fine. But at least explain,' said Rose.

'I will. Just let me think it through. It may be nothing . . .'

'What may be nothing? Are you in danger?' asked Fran. 'Are we in danger?'

'No, of course not. When the time is right, I'll explain everything. Promise.'

Maggie picked up her coffee and gave them both a reassuring smile, but they looked unconvinced.

Chapter Twelve

Rose lay in bed, wide awake. She hadn't enjoyed one single full night's sleep since she'd left Australia. Overstimulated. Strange beds. Too hot. Too cold. Roommates chomping on earrings. Worries about Maggie. Every night there was a different reason with the same result. The worst part was not being able to complain about it. She longed to have a jolly good moan. Her phone lit up with a text.

Fitz: Make it to Vienna?

Rose switched on the bedside lamp, positioned her phone and took a shot of the hotel room replete with gold flocked wallpaper, red velvet curtains and baroque-style furniture. It looked like the set of a Chekhov play. Maggie had clearly spent too much on this accommodation. It was over the top.

Fitz replied with a 'wow' emoticon. Rose found the whole emoticon business tedious. Whenever she felt the urge to use one, she would spend ten minutes trying to decide which expression truly illustrated her point. Was she that tragically sad? Or that boiling mad? Or that stupidly happy? She considered moaning to Fitz about how tired she was but couldn't be bothered. She sent an emoticon of a moon face catching some z's. If only. She switched off the lamp and tried to relax.

Good old Fitzy, he was a decent bloke. He'd been married at one point – no kids, but on friendly terms with his ex. Always a good sign. Unlike Peter, he had a wide variety of interests: played clarinet in a jazz band, was involved with a running group and on the roster of a soup kitchen in the city. Also, unlike Peter, he had mates with whom he periodically sailed or skied or snorkelled – any sport that started with an S, as he sometimes quipped. He had a background in journalism but since that sector had dwindled, he'd reinvented himself as a wordsmith and seemed to have steady work as a ghostwriter and editor for self-publishers.

Part of Fitz's appeal was that he was his own man and, while he was always keen to see Rose, he didn't need her or depend on her. At first she found that confusing, but now it was hard to separate her true affections for him from this refreshing attribute. Was she involved with him simply because he was the opposite of Peter? She certainly trusted his opinions. And she liked him – a lot.

This trip had been constantly pulling her back to the past, bringing up times in her life that she hadn't thought about for years. It had forced her to think about the turning points and why she had taken a particular path. There was a point in her marriage when everything changed and, all these years later, it still unsettled her to think about it.

She had been on her way to drop some documents off to Peter and had stopped to get a takeaway coffee. As she stood waiting at the counter, she gazed idly around the café. A couple sat at a table towards the back, artfully lit by a wash of sunlight from the rear courtyard. First, she saw a couple in love. Then she recognised her husband. It wasn't a movie scene; they weren't clasping hands or blowing kisses. They weren't even touching, but Rose sensed the vibrational energy between them. As though their molecules were drawn to each other by magnetic attraction. Caught in the moment, they probably had no awareness of how transparent their feelings for each other were.

The young woman laughed, arching her slender neck. Peter smiled, his eyes seeming to rest on the curve of her throat. Rose recognised her: Lisa? Liza? Elissa. She'd attended a party they had given, earlier in the year, for Peter's faculty. Rose remembered the way the young woman had glowed around Peter, enthralled by his anecdotes. She remembered that Peter was Elissa's PhD supervisor, so not unusual that they would meet, but the fact that Peter was tucked away in a café off-campus was evidence that something more was going on. The campus was his kingdom. He needed a good reason to stray from it. Staring at them, a number of recent anomalies in Peter's behaviour clunked into place – his cheerfulness for one thing.

A younger Rose would have stormed that love-fest and made a scene but something held her back, some tangled internal debate. Had she seen what she thought she'd seen? Or had she seen nothing but a professor and student sharing coffee? Was she romanticising the woman's neck? Was she simply tapping into the cliché of a professor shagging his PhD student? Was she the victim of her own vivid imagination?

Shaken, she left without her coffee and went straight home. She sat on the back verandah, staring into space, numbly recalibrating all her perceptions of her marriage as stable and predictable and secure. She no longer felt safe.

Elliot was ten years old and Max had just turned six. Rose had been a stay-at-home mum from the outset. She had recently decided to train to teach English as a second language so she could work around the boys' schedules and get out of the house more. She had never sought stability but knew it was vital for the boys. What she had seen was hardly enough to file for divorce and upend the family and their life together.

Peter was a good husband and father in many ways; he brought in a solid income year after year, he wasn't outdoorsy or sporty but he was a kind dad, always willing to talk to the boys and educate them. He could be vague and sometimes pompous but she had great respect for his considered and educated perspective on the world. The prospect of losing him crystallised all his good points in her mind. She had never imagined that Peter could be organised enough to conduct an affair, but now she realised, armed with the right woman, he could leave her. She would become a single mother and Peter a weekend father.

Peter had come home that afternoon, annoyed that she hadn't dropped off the documents he needed. She said she'd forgotten, which she had. There was nothing in her head apart from what she had witnessed. She wanted to demand answers, have it out and release some tension. But the words didn't come. She was afraid to light the fuse.

She waited until they were all together as a family at the dinner table, knowing she would keep a grip on herself in front of the children. 'How are you going with your PhD student?' she asked casually, between ticking the boys off for toying with their food and kicking each other under the table.

'Elissa,' he said and she knew he had been longing to say her name out loud. It had been pent up in him, waiting to be

195

released, like a song. Rose imagined him doodling at his desk, writing their names side by side – *Peter & Elissa* – in his strange, primitive handwriting. That was ridiculous. He was a grown man. 'Fine so far. Clever girl. Industrious.'

'Just remind me of the topic?' She directed her scowl at Max's appalling table manners. 'Max, don't eat with your hands.'

'I'm not sure you need reminding, since I doubt you've ever asked. Why the sudden interest?' Peter finished his meal and crossed his cutlery neatly on the plate.

Rose reached behind her and flicked the kettle on, trained in this task so long ago she never thought about it. 'Well, I'm asking now, and you're being cagey.' Her tone was combative, her grip slipping. 'Boys, if you've finished, you can go play outside for half an hour.'

'Can't we watch TV?' asked Max.

'No, outside!' Rose got up and poured the boiling water into the teapot as the boys chased each other out the kitchen door into the garden.

'Not cagey, simply doubting the sincerity of your interest. Thank you for the tea.' He reached out to take the cup and saucer from her, as though he didn't want her coming too close, then turned his interest to the newspaper in front of him. 'It's a feminist analysis, not something you'd be interested in.'

'Am I not a feminist?' Rose cleared the table and wiped it vigorously, relieved to have something impersonal to argue about.

'Not of the radical bra-burning variety,' he said, without looking up. 'An armchair feminist, perhaps. A fuzzy feminist who enjoys railing against the so-called patriarchy after a few too many wines.' He turned each page and scanned the newspaper thoroughly, pausing occasionally when something interested him.

'Peter, bra-burning was in the mid-sixties, for goodness sake, before I even had boobs. I don't have the time to be an activist, I'm too busy running the household, bringing up our children and working on your . . . *stuff*. If you mean, do I believe that women are equal to men? *Obviously.* You may recall that I started a consciousness-raising group at uni, and I'm quite sure I'd be able to grasp Lisa's thesis.'

'Elissa,' he said, enjoying another opportunity to savour her name. 'Her name's —'

'Yes, I know what her name is,' snapped Rose. Inside she was trembling with rage and indignation. She always felt like slapping him in this superior mood, never more than now. 'How did you become her supervisor? It's hardly your area of expertise.'

'It has its roots in history. *Obviously.* Not just my era but beyond that. She seems very satisfied. I don't know why you're challenging it. Do you know something I don't?'

'That you're screwing her?' The words leapt out of her mouth before she could stop them.

He paused for a moment. 'Rose, that's an unfounded accusation and I'm not going to dignify it with a response.'

'Pleading the fifth amendment? Afraid of incriminating yourself?' She was dizzied by the vision of her marriage slowly toppling over, about to crash and splinter. Why was she pushing it? She couldn't stop.

'Where are the boys?' he asked, glancing around unhurriedly.

'They're in the garden. Just tell me the truth. You owe me that.'

'I have no debt to you, Rose. I did the right thing at the time it was needed and have done it ever since. I'm beyond reproach in that regard.'

The coldness of his comment knocked the breath out of her. 'So the answer is yes?'

His expression, when he finally looked up from the newspaper, was one of mild contempt. 'Think about whether you're in a position to demand "truth", given the scope of the lie you've perpetuated, and the burden that places on me.'

'You promised you'd never bring that up again,' said Rose, suddenly on the brink of tears.

He shrugged philosophically and returned to his newspaper.

Her lack of planning left her nowhere to go, apart from castigating herself in the months to come for not being intellectual enough, letting herself go and not having a neck like a young swan. The discussion was over – his response made that clear. She watched him carefully but found no new evidence. The only comfort was that he didn't want to upend their marriage.

Sometime later she heard that Elissa had been awarded a research grant and gone to live in Chicago or Denver or somewhere suitably far away. Even now, Rose googled her occasionally in the hope that something unpleasant had befallen her but derived no satisfaction from the exercise. The incident had scarred their marriage. It wasn't his straying that eroded her trust so much as the smooth, unruffled way he deflected it back to her and dismissed her enquiry, as though he considered it to be none of her business. Her younger, more impulsive self would have retaliated in some spectacularly destructive way, but the responsibility of parenthood weighed heavily on her. She loved being a mother far more than she ever imagined. She wasn't free to act on her every emotion. And a good thing too. Keeping the family together was the only thing that mattered at that point. She had to keep a lid on it. Make the best of things.

Rose had always thought there would be a great love in her life. Peter was not that love. Neither was Fitz. Bass guitarist Charlie had been her only great passion, but he was never meant to be. The time for finding a soul mate had most likely passed. She'd been busy doing other things. On a bus recently, a young woman had stood up to offer her a seat. Rose had stepped aside for the elderly person she assumed was behind her. It took a moment to dawn that this courtesy was for *her*. She almost wept. It happened so quickly and suddenly, as though she'd gone to bed young and woken up old, like Rip Van Winkle.

Rose looked at her phone. It was nearly midnight. Desperate times. She got up and dug around in her suitcase where she'd hidden the bag of weed she'd bought in the hostel bar in Berlin. There was no balcony, so she'd have to stick her head out the window. She pulled the curtains aside to discover that the windows didn't open. Frustrated, she stamped around the room and would have kicked something if she hadn't learned from bitter experience that she always came off worse.

Then she had an idea.

She thought about a music selection to lift her mood while she patiently untangled her earbuds. She pressed them into her ears, found what she was looking for online and began to sing along to Carole King's *Tapestry* album, every song dear to her heart. She rolled the joint and, sitting cross-legged, pulled the bedcovers over her head to form a tent. It was a bit like being inside a bong. She'd probably only need half the joint. She didn't want to get completely wrecked. Normally, it worked like a charm, partly because she smoked regularly. An occasional joint carried the risk of the opposite effect.

It was cosy under the covers, apart from the smoke making her cough, and she started to feel very mellow. She did make the best of things, and that was partly because she had grown up in a culture of complaint that went against her nature. While they did have some good times singing in the car, most evenings her parents had sat in front of the television bickering with each other and grumbling about the world and those responsible for it not being the way they wanted. The government, politicians, dole bludgers, migrants and corrupt cops all had their role to play.

In the early days, they had drunk flagon wine or beer. Later they migrated to casks, taking turns to get up and squirt a glassful for each other. Rose hated the sound of the liquid jetting into the glass, like someone having a pee. After a few drinks the arguments would start and sometimes they'd go for days pointedly not speaking to each other. Now that he had dementia, her father's defences were down and good cheer leaked out of him all day long. He was unaccountably popular with the staff and residents at the nursing home but still up for a few bouts of contradicting and arguing with his wife.

Rose extinguished the half-smoked joint. It was enough – more than enough. Desperately in need of fresh air, she felt thoroughly stoned and her tinnitus was going berserk, practically drowning out Carole, who wasn't the only one feeling the earth move under her feet right now.

Keeping the cover sealed as tightly as possible, she squeezed her head out and onto the pillow. Now she realised that it wasn't tinnitus but the smoke detector siren. And someone was pounding on the door. She staggered out of bed, but before she could reach the door, a man in uniform opened it and activated the room lights. They stood there gaping at each other and the siren thankfully ceased shrilling.

Rose decided to brave it out. 'Hello, can I help you? I was just asleep.' She pointed to the bed over her shoulder, to indicate where this fiction had taken place.

'Good evening, madam. So were many other guests.' His English was perfect with only a hint of a German accent. He sniffed the air and raised a sceptical eyebrow. 'Has your "cigarette" now been extinguished, madam?'

Rose weighed up the options and decided to cooperate. 'Yes, it has. I'm sorry.'

'Thank you, madam. A charge of one hundred and fifty euros which relates to this incident will appear on your bill when you check out. Have a good night.'

He left, closing the door behind him. Rose turned off the lights, threw herself into bed and fell asleep as her head hit the pillow.

She woke feeling thirsty and famished, dragged herself out of bed and opened the curtains. Finally blue sky and sunshine! Next, breakfast and more breakfast. A walk in the city. Lunch. Maybe a gallery. She had to admit that, so far, this trip was so organised and contained, it lacked that spark or sense of adventure – so unlike their shambolic expedition of the seventies as to be utterly irrelevant. The plans, the bookings, the hotels, the meals in nice restaurants; this was just a tour for old people. Another day, another city. How could it have ever been otherwise?

The buffet breakfast table was laden with tarts and breads, cheeses and cold meats – a dream come true – and Rose piled several plates high and carried them to the table where Fran and Maggie were already seated.

'Did you hear the fire alarm going off last night?' asked Fran, looking at Rose's breakfast selection. 'Bit peckish, Rose?'

'I reckon, what a racket!' said Rose, wolfing down a slice of raspberry tart.

'Probably some idiot smoking in their room,' suggested Maggie.

'Probably,' agreed Rose. 'What an idiot.'

When breakfast was over, she hung around until Maggie and Fran went back up to their rooms, then rushed to the reception desk and asked the young woman on duty to put the smoking fee on her credit card, and not show it on the final bill. Rose's friendly overtures met with a frosty response. No one was amused by the incident.

As agreed, they regrouped in the lobby half an hour later and took the tram into the city centre. Apart from the addition of a few phone shops, Mariahilfer Straße didn't seem to have changed much. That was the beauty of old cities, thought Rose, the history and architecture were preserved and not at the mercy of developers who were constantly pulling buildings down to make room for luxury flats. In Vienna, every public building seemed grander and more extravagant than the last. It was a city punctuated by statues of angels and lions, mythological creatures wrestling with gods, and princes on horseback wearing impractical hats.

When Rose had first walked down Mariahilfer Straße all those years ago, she had thought of Fran's mother, Mrs Fisher, and how at home she would look here among these well-dressed people and elegant shops. Mrs Fisher was long gone now. Fran was only in her thirties when her mother died of some aggressive cancer – Rose couldn't remember which one, and it seemed insensitive and pointless to ask now. It was unfortunate that, after so many years of being single, Mrs Fisher had remarried a few years before she died and it still remained to be seen if Fran would inherit anything when her stepfather died.

Rose's memories of Mrs Fisher were of her intimidating manner and interesting accent. She wore large clip-on gold earrings and high heels; her hair in a chignon at a time when every mother wore her hair short and permed. She ran her own business, which seemed exciting and glamorous, but Fran said her mother complained that her clients had no idea how to display their wares and no taste. It was only then that Rose had become aware there was such a thing as taste, and wondered how to acquire it.

Fran was the only person Rose knew who lived in a flat, which seemed interesting in itself. It was more spacious than she would have expected and it had a particular style, not jumbled bits and pieces. The furnishings, paintings and thick rugs had been chosen with care and attention. The lounge suite was emerald green with a gold stripe in a silky fabric. Rose remembered trying to convince her mother to buy some silky curtains to cultivate a more luxurious mood in the house. Her mother had laughed and said she was happy with their mismatched floral curtains; they only faded anyway. Rose began to suspect that her mother was one of those people with no taste.

Mrs Fisher was often away for days at a time and Rose found it thrilling that during these trips, Fran, at the age of fourteen, would live entirely on her own. The possibilities for misbehaviour seemed limitless but Fran had no imagination in that department. A couple of times they used the phone to call random numbers and give whoever answered cheek, but Fran wasn't much good at that either. She was too polite.

When she was in the house alone, Fran was not allowed to use the stove. Her mother left her large jars of cold vegetables preserved in oil and stewed tomatoes that Fran would eat straight out of the jar. Sometimes there was a bowl containing small pieces of something crumbed that Fran said was sweetbread but tasted more like musty meat than cake – none of which gave Rose much confidence in Austrian cuisine.

Hopefully that would change today, as Rose had booked lunch for them at Café Central, a famous old restaurant in the centre of Vienna that had been operating for a hundred and fifty years. Last century, it had been a political hotbed, with Freud, Trotsky, Stalin and Hitler all being regulars.

When they were here in 1978, she and Maggie and Fran had stood outside the restaurant and gazed in through the window at the palatial interior, too intimidated and cash-strapped to even step inside.

The interior of the restaurant turned out to be even more glorious than Rose remembered. She loved the scale of the sweeping cathedral ceilings and the formality of the waiters flitting about in their black waistcoats and long white aprons. The whiff of old-world glamour.

As they were seated, Fran chatted with the waiter in German, and Rose noticed how different she seemed: less hesitant and reserved; more confident. 'So, here we are. Only took forty years to get in the door,' said Rose as they studied the menu.

'Let's order champagne,' suggested Maggie.

'Are you sure? It's going to be horribly expensive,' said Fran, scanning the menu. 'I wish I could make a contribution.'

Rose agreed with Maggie about the champagne and the two of them would be splitting the bill.

When it arrived, they toasted each other and the trip and then Maggie said, 'I have been thinking.' She hesitated. 'I'm sorry, but this is just not working for me.'

Fran's smile faded. 'The lunch? Or the whole thing?'

'We're just going from one city to another. They're all starting to look the same.'

'You could hardly mistake Vienna for somewhere else,' said Rose.

'Last time we drove all through the countryside in Austria. What I remember are those timber chalets with flower boxes and cows with bells and rolling hills —'

'Alive with the sound of music?' interrupted Rose. 'Unless we want to hire a car, it's pretty difficult to recapture that.'

'I feel as though everything is accelerating – I'm accelerating,' said Maggie. 'As soon as we arrive somewhere I wish we were leaving already. It's the momentum of moving. I can't seem to care about these places. It just seems pointless. I need something more restful.'

'What are you saying, Maggie?' asked Fran. 'You think we should give up?'

'I just can't see the point in what we're doing,' Maggie continued. 'Next thing we'll be in Italy and then we'll be home and wondering what the hell that was all about.'

Rose considered whether she had an objection to giving up. Would she be happier to head off on her own and have less responsibility for making this project work?

'I agree it's not really working,' she said. 'And we're getting on each other's wicks. I was unrealistic, overly optimistic . . . as usual.'

'Oh, Rose. It was a wonderful idea. I've been enjoying it, but I understand . . .' said Fran.

'After that siren went off, I was awake for hours thinking about everything. I'm sorry, but this lunch will be my last hurrah,' said Maggie.

Rose shrugged. 'Okay, if that's what you want.' It was so sudden and final, she felt like bursting into tears.

Maggie gave them both an apologetic smile. 'I can fly from Vienna to Rome, change my flight and go home early.'

'What happened to "I don't want to go home at all" only a few days ago?' asked Rose.

'Kristo needs me there. Looks like Auntie Agnes might lose her house. Nico's gone AWOL. I feel guilty leaving Kris to handle everything.'

'Hang on. Aren't these all other people's problems, the very things you needed a break from?' argued Rose.

'I'm not having a good time, Rose. It's not going anywhere.'

'Maggie, you haven't made any effort to have a good time. You've effectively sabotaged the whole thing, and now you're bailing.'

Fran tapped Rose on the arm. 'Rose. Keep your voice down, people are looking.'

Rose sat back, silently fuming. Hostilities were paused for a few minutes while the waiter took their order. As soon as he had gone, Maggie leaned towards Rose. 'I did not want to do this in the first place. I knew it was pointless —'

'I rest my case,' said Rose. 'Your whole agenda has been to prove it's pointless. You've put all your energy into that, instead of making a modicum of effort to make it work.'

'How can it work? Three old biddies swanning around Europe reminiscing about the past . . . literally a wild goose chase.'

'Why don't we all just calm down a bit and enjoy our champagne?' suggested Fran.

Maggie picked up her champagne and sculled it. 'At least at home I can have a drink without getting the death stare.' She filled her glass and sat glowering at Rose.

'Is that what you really want, Maggie?'

'Why do you need to dramatise everything, for God's sake?'

Fran glanced around, smiling apologetically at other diners. Rose couldn't care less. As it sank in that everything was actually falling apart, she felt desperate to save it. If Maggie left now, there would be no coming back from it, but there wasn't a single thing she could say that hadn't already been said.

'Is that your phone buzzing, Mag?' asked Fran.

Maggie leant down and picked up her handbag off the floor. 'Oh, God. It's the middle of the night at home.' She looked at the caller and went quite pale.

Rose instinctively leaned across to see the caller: Nico.

Maggie put the phone face down on the table, as if she didn't know what to do with it. They watched it pulsate and stop. She slipped it back into her bag and avoided Rose's gaze.

'What's going on, Mag?' asked Rose. 'Why are you looking like that?'

Maggie glanced furtively around the restaurant. 'I think he might be here.'

'Here in the restaurant?' asked Fran in disbelief. 'How could he possibly know we're here?'

'Was it on the itinerary, Rose?' asked Maggie.

'No, I only booked it a couple of days ago. What is going on? Why on earth would he be here?'

Maggie picked up her champagne and attempted a smile. 'I'm being ridiculous. He wouldn't be here. You're right. No one knows we're here. It's fine. Sorry.'

Rose had met Nico many times over the years at various family events. He was a man's man, not interested in anything women had to say. Maggie had occasionally mentioned his rivalry with Kristo, but that seemed to be related to the family business.

'Do you want to talk about it?' Fran asked gently. 'We're just worried about you.'

Maggie paused and took a deep breath. 'It's a long, complicated story. I don't want to ruin this lunch talking about it now.'

'You can always block him,' suggested Rose. 'If you don't want to speak to him. Why —'

Maggie shook her head. 'No. It's fine. Please. Just leave it.'

Rose *hated* leaving things. She wanted things out in the open – most things, not everything. Not her secrets, but certainly other people's. Why was Maggie so rattled? Her speculations were interrupted by the waiter delivering their meals and, for a few minutes, Rose was distracted by a very large Wiener schnitzel. A thought occurred. 'You said you'd been stalked. Is it him?'

Maggie went very still, hunched over her plate. Without looking up, she nodded.

'Shit!' said Rose through a mouthful of schnitzel.

Fran looked horrified. 'Oh, Maggie, how dreadful!'

'Why on earth haven't you mentioned it before? When did it start? Does Kristo know? Obviously not.' Rose laid down her knife and fork and put a comforting hand on Maggie's arm. She wanted to know everything, but Maggie looked so ill, she had to wait. 'I'm sorry, Mag. I'm so sorry, I've been a pain in the arse.'

'No, I'm sorry. I know you've done your best. It's all just overwhelming. Kristo said Nico's gone away somewhere, and so I got it in my head that . . . anyway, I'm just being paranoid.'

'That's why you wanted to change the accommodation?' said Fran.

Maggie nodded. She looked pale.

'We're here for you, Mag. Don't leave us just yet. Please,' said Fran. 'We'll be on our best behaviour.' She shot Rose a meaningful look.

'Yes,' agreed Rose. 'We will. You don't have to tell us anything if you don't want to. Stay a bit longer. Then, if you decide to go, so be it. You can easily fly out of Verona.'

Maggie sat back and thought about this for a long moment. She looked so vulnerable, it was heartbreaking. Finally, she gave a small, silent nod of agreement.

Chapter Thirteen

The tiny shred of optimism Fran had felt when Maggie agreed to push on faltered as they boarded the train from Vienna to Verona. Maggie wasn't the best with early starts and, as they settled into their compartment, she muttered under her breath, 'Eight hours on a train feels like a prison sentence with views.'

Rose was determinedly upbeat. 'Yeah, but with good behaviour you'll be out on parole at the end of the day.'

'And the views through the Alps will be spectacular,' added Fran. 'We'll be in Italy for a late lunch.'

'I know, something to look forward to.' Maggie gave them a wan smile. She folded up her coat against the window, leaned her head on it and closed her eyes.

Rose pursed her lips the way she did when she was forcing herself not to speak, announced she was going to the bathroom and went out, letting the sliding door slam as she stalked off down the corridor. While she was gone, they were joined by another woman of a similar age.

Fran greeted the woman in German and she responded with a greeting and a pleasant smile. Casually well-dressed, she had dark shoulder-length hair and olive skin. She brought with her the faintest hint of honeysuckle, the first sign of summer, and Fran hoped it was a good omen.

A few minutes later, the door slid open and Rose said, 'Maggie, there's an empty compartment next door. You can stretch out on the seat and rest for a while.'

Maggie opened her eyes and looked up.

'Come on,' urged Rose. 'I'll keep you company.'

It was touching to see Rose make such a concerted effort on Maggie's behalf. Fran nodded. 'Yes, you go. I'm fine here with the bags.'

Maggie roused herself, gathered her coat and followed Rose out of the compartment. Left alone, Fran and the woman exchanged smiles. 'Are you British?' asked the woman in German.

'Australian. I live in London now, but originally Australian. And you?'

'Similar situation. I'm Italian but have lived in Munich for many years.'

They lapsed into silence, both looking out the window, although it was barely light and there was nothing to see but grim industrial buildings sliding past.

'My name is Sofia. While your friends are next door, perhaps we can pass the time with a little conversation, if you don't mind conversing in German. But don't feel obliged.'

Fran leapt at the idea of someone new to talk to and agreed readily. Sofia asked where they were headed, and Fran explained the background to the trip.

'It seems a wonderful idea, but I'm not sure how it would work in practice. It wouldn't be easy to travel with friends for an extended time.'

'Are you familiar with Samuel Beckett, the playwright?' asked Fran.

Sofia smiled. 'Of course.'

'It's a bit like being in a Beckett play. We're trapped in the same conversations and, sometimes, the same conflicts we had forty years ago, with only slightly different subjects.'

'So a tragicomedy?' suggested Sofia with a smile.

'Exactly!'

'But instead of "Waiting for Godot", you're searching for him. Or her?'

They both laughed and Fran added, 'I was never a Beckett fan and, to be honest, the whole trip has been exhausting for me. My role is the peacekeeper. I have to be the diplomat, because . . . well, I'm not really in a financial position to do this; I'm here as a guest.'

'I'm sure you add some sweetness to make the combination of flavours more palatable.'

Fran smiled modestly. 'I don't know about that. They are both wonderful friends, something I value more and more – so many people come into our lives and then disappear.'

Sofia agreed. 'It's very easy to get caught up in nostalgia and regret. I've fallen into that trap recently, dwelling on happier times in the past. It's not very helpful.'

Fran knew she too was guilty of this. Constantly drawn back to wondering how things might have been different. She glanced out the window, momentarily lost in thought. The sun had risen and now stretched across undulating green fields dotted with red-roofed chalets.

Sofia explained that her father had died recently and she had decided to retire early and come back to live in the empty family home, which was located in a small village outside Verona. She had come by train this time, to prepare the house for the move in a few days' time.

'Every time I came to Verona to visit my father, I felt very happy and relaxed. So, I thought, why not? The house is probably too large for me but there is room for my children and grandchildren when they visit.'

'What will you do with yourself there?' asked Fran, genuinely interested.

Sofia thought for a moment. 'I'll tell you. I haven't told anyone this yet, but I'm interested in art and ceramics. I'd like to open a small gallery in Verona and sell beautiful pieces – contemporary collectables. Does that seem too crazy?'

'Not at all!'

'I've been so practical and industrious all my life, this seems like exactly the sort of thing my husband and my father, if they were alive, would have thought silly and frivolous.'

'I think beautiful things are good for the soul. It sounds wonderful. I recently met the ceramicist Isabella Manchini. Do you know her?'

'Yes, of course. I love her work.'

'I'd just seen her exhibition at the Tate and she came into the bookshop where I work. She's interested in antiquarian books,' said Fran.

'Antiquarian books? That does sound interesting.'

'Not really. It's sort of sad these days; a dying business. My true passion was for theatre. I somehow thought I'd find a career on the production side but now I'm just a theatre-goer.'

'What a shame you're not here later in the season to see a performance in Arena di Verona. It's not dramatic theatre – mostly opera or sometimes rock concerts – but it's a wonderful experience to enjoy in a Roman colosseum.'

Fran laughed. 'I would not get Maggie or Rose to the opera. Right now, I just want to survive this trip with my sanity intact.'

'I'm sure there will be a new direction for you after this trip. Have courage. This is why they call it the "third age". Being reborn will always be difficult. But this time around, everything has to be our own choice, not that of our parent or partner – or our children.'

'Unfortunately I don't have the excuse of trying to please others. I just haven't planned my life very well,' admitted Fran.

'But don't you think that women of our generation were trained to please others?'

Fran agreed and, as they talked over the next few hours, she found herself opening up to Sofia about her job, Gigi and even the Louis dilemma. And in return, Fran heard more about Sofia's life and what had led to her decision to move back to Italy.

Children ran along the corridor of the train, people walked past with cups of coffee from the dining car, but no one disturbed them. They sat opposite each other, as relaxed as if they were old friends using the opportunity to catch up. And Fran had a moment of regret that, in a few hours, they would part and she would most likely never see this new friend again.

Occasionally, Sofia drew Fran's attention to the passing landscape as it changed from glittering distant lakes to fields with snow-capped mountains in the distance. As the train rushed into a valley pass through the Alps, the view changed again to craggy rock faces, bright-green patches of grass and wildflowers.

They crossed the border into Italy and, when the train

stopped in Bolzano, Rose and Maggie reappeared. 'Sorry for leaving you alone,' said Maggie, sitting down. 'I had the most wonderful sleep. Feel so much better.'

Rose yawned so widely she needed both hands to cover her mouth. 'Maybe we should be taking the night train everywhere. Did we miss anything?'

'Not really,' said Fran, exchanging a smile with Sofia. 'It's been very quiet in here.'

Fran said goodbye to Sofia at Verona Porta Nuova. They embraced and exchanged contact details, and Fran tucked the note into her purse, even though she knew it was pointless.

She joined Maggie and Rose outside the station, where they discussed whether to take a taxi or walk into the city centre. They decided that, despite the suitcases, a walk was desirable, and Fran went back inside the station to use the bathroom. On her return a few minutes later, she noticed Maggie was at the cash machine, and went outside to join Rose, who had been left guarding the three suitcases.

'You are really not going to believe this!' Rose pointed out a white Transit van parked across the street. It had British plates and a handwritten sign taped on the window: *Urgent Sale. Any Offer Considered.* 'She's bought it,' said Rose in disbelief. 'She's bought that heap. What the *fuck*?!'

'What? I've only been gone ten minutes!' said Fran. 'What's she doing now?'

'Getting cash out of the machine for the guy!'

Fran stared at the vehicle across the road. The sliding door was wide open and a young man dressed in a crumpled Manchester

United T-shirt was rapidly stuffing his belongings into a sports bag. As they watched, he closed the door and hurried across the road towards them. He grinned as he passed them. 'Cheers!'

Maggie came out of the station and spoke to the young man for a few minutes. They made an exchange and he dashed off to where the airport shuttle bus was parked and got onboard.

Maggie grabbed her suitcase and said brightly, 'Okay, let's go!'

Fran and Rose followed her across the road in a daze. She opened the sliding door of the van and slung her bag inside. They both did the same and Rose pulled it shut. In the front was a single seat for the driver, and a double for two passengers. The back was almost entirely filled by a mattress, bedding and debris left behind by the previous owner.

Fran climbed into the centre seat and almost gagged at the ripe odour of melted cheese and sweaty sex. Maggie settled herself behind the wheel and put the destination of their B&B into her phone. Rose slammed the passenger door repeatedly, trying to convince it to stay shut. She was surprisingly calm. 'Okay, what is going on? How did this happen?'

As she indicated and pulled out into the street, Maggie explained that the young man and his girlfriend had been travelling for a month. The girlfriend left after an argument and caught the shuttle bus to the airport this morning, to fly back to London. He was desperate to follow her. 'He wanted a thousand euros. I offered him five hundred and he took it. He probably would have just left it somewhere if we hadn't come along.'

Rose was sceptical. 'Sounds like a bit of a story to me. Why would he take half?'

'He could have driven home, instead of being so impatient,' said Fran.

'He said he didn't want to drive all that way on his own.'

'Really? You don't think that's odd?' Rose was interrupted by an angry driver who overtook them, leaning on his horn. She shook her fist at him. '*Bastardo!*'

Maggie's handbag was on the floor. Rose pulled out the registration documents and read them. 'Did you even look at these? The rego expired yesterday!'

Maggie flushed bright red; a film of sweat glowed on her face. 'Rose! Let me concentrate! I'm trying to listen to the GPS.'

Rose and Fran exchanged sidelong glances but remained silent as they continued down the wide streets and crossed the river into a quieter residential area where the GPS confirmed they had reached their destination.

Maggie found a parking space near the *pensione* but it was too difficult to reverse-park the right-hand-drive van into the space. They drove around the block until Fran spotted an easier space in the street behind. Maggie parked and switched off the ignition. The engine gave a series of shudders followed by a long gasp, as though relieved to have made it this far.

As they sat shoulder to shoulder in the front of the van, Fran's expectation was that Maggie would launch into one of her persuasive arguments of earlier days. There was no doubt that she was now back at the helm, which was in itself cause for celebration – despite the strange and surprising turn of events.

Maggie stared out the windscreen for a long minute, then began to bang her forehead on the steering wheel. The horn let out a croak as though in tune with her pain. 'What have I done? Why did I do that? What's wrong with me?' She sat up and stared past Fran to Rose. 'Why the fuck didn't you stop me?!'

Fran opened her mouth to defend Rose but was drowned out by Rose herself shouting, 'Are you kidding me? We didn't even know what was happening! Fran was in the bloody toilet! You have lost it. Completely lost it!'

Fran felt as though she was being teleported back forty years into another stinky van, listening to another shouting match. This was what she had dreaded all along. 'Okay, okay, both of you, calm down! Maggie, please just explain your thinking.'

Maggie put her face in her hands. After a moment, she straightened up and turned to them. 'I just felt *desperate* to escape the bloody timetable. The trains. Dragging ourselves through cities with suitcases like a bunch of middle-aged tourists. We didn't come here to look at the architecture. We came to find something. We haven't even caught a glimpse of it. We've gone out of our way to make sure nothing unexpected ever happens. I saw this and I went for it.'

'Well, this is certainly very unexpected,' said Rose. 'Now we have a clapped-out . . . *shaggin' wagon* that probably won't even make it out of Verona! Now what?'

Fran could feel a headache coming on. 'Rose, please . . . just stop shouting.'

They sat in silence, looking anywhere but at each other. After a while Maggie squinted at the dials and asked, 'Do you think it takes diesel or petrol?'

Rose flipped open the glove box. She took out a filthy ripped handbook and flicked through it. 'Diesel.' She put it back and slammed the lid closed. 'Let's get out of here. It stinks.'

The *pensione* that Maggie had booked was owned by a cheerful, helpful man called Vincenzo, who spoke good English but managed to make himself less understandable by adding an extra vowel to every word. Ordinarily, Rose would have made some cheeky aside, but she took her key and they each went to their rooms without a word being spoken.

It was early afternoon and Fran was keen to go out on her own. She tucked her money belt under her jacket and set off to explore the city. She picked up a complimentary local map and was guided through quiet tree-lined streets to the Ponte Garibaldi and across the bridge, under a bright blue sky, into the centre of Verona.

She had loved the grand sophistication of Vienna, but this smaller city was more her style, with narrow cobbled laneways and café-lined piazzas. She reached the Piazza delle Erbe, busy with market stalls. Some sold fruit and vegetables, fresh fish and hams, and others had belts and handbags made of soft Italian leather. The piazza was surrounded by ancient buildings in yellow ochre, burnt umber and sienna, which reflected the afternoon light. She followed the map down a laneway off the piazza and through a stone archway to view the most famous balcony in the world in the courtyard of Casa di Giulietta.

The courtyard was crowded with a tour group of thirty or so Chinese people, all highly excited, having photographs taken with the bronze statue of Juliet and using their selfie-sticks as pointers. Thankfully, the tour leader soon ushered them out and there was only Fran and a young Asian couple left in the courtyard. Fran turned to smile at them, wondering if they were honeymooners. They smiled back and she asked them if the balcony was as they expected.

The young woman said they had come because it was famous and romantic; they didn't know what to expect. 'Do you think the story of Romeo and Juliet is true?' she asked.

Fran deliberated, like a parent asked about Santa or the tooth fairy. 'I don't really know. Maybe it was inspired by a story that Shakespeare heard. Or someone he knew.'

The couple seemed satisfied with this idea of fiction based on truth. Fran's experience of working in bookshops was that many people were uncomfortable with the idea of a story being a complete fiction, happier to know it was underpinned by truth.

She was struck by the idea that, far-fetched as it was, people wanted to believe this dramatic and tragic tale, proof that romantic love – love worth dying for – does exist. If she had ever believed that, it was a very long time ago. She had been involved in some passionate love affairs but none worth dying for. There was Tony, who went to prison; the writer who turned out to be married; the barrister who became sour and abusive; and many in between. Leading to Louis, the last gasp. He was no Romeo, but perhaps she was guilty of clinging to the fiction of the man she wanted him to be.

She left the courtyard and wandered the streets aimlessly, enjoying being surrounded by the music and rhythm of Italian, a language she had always loved but never learned. She felt more carefree being out on her own. The whole episode with the van was only going to add more stress to the situation. It occurred to her that Verona could be a fitting place to end her trip. It might be perceived as ungrateful for her to leave, but it would be easier for them to carry on in the van without her. Mr Elcombe would be pleased to have her back at work earlier. Louis would probably be glad to have her home, and Gigi certainly would. She could get on a flight in the next couple of days and be in London an hour later. The idea was unexpectedly appealing and she knew that it was the right decision.

Impressed by her decisiveness, she hurried back to the *pensione* to get the deed done. As she turned into their street, Maggie walked out of the laundromat, carrying a pile of linen, and headed down the side street towards where the van was parked. Fran hurried to catch up with her.

'Oh, there you are,' said Maggie. 'We thought you were having a long nap. We're washing everything. There's a couple of sleeping bags, pillows – and we can buy some extra bits tomorrow.'

'Well . . . where are we going?' It seemed a lot had happened in her absence.

'To be decided,' Maggie replied. 'We'll talk about it this evening.'

All the doors of the van were open. The mattress, which took up most of the floorspace, now leaned against the outside of the vehicle. Beside it was a plastic rubbish bag full of discarded clothes and takeaway containers.

Maggie dumped the linen on the front seat. 'I've got some other stuff in the dryer. Should be finished shortly.' She went back to the laundromat and Fran poked her head in the van to talk to Rose, who was sweeping out the plywood floor.

But before Fran had the chance to speak, Rose said, 'There's a box of plates and cutlery there needing washing. Vincenzo said we can use the kitchen off the breakfast room at the top of the stairs.'

Fran didn't say a word. She took the box back to the *pensione* and up the winding staircase to the attic. From the kitchen window, she could see the van on the street below and Rose climbing awkwardly into the back of it with a bucket and mop. An old man stopped and watched, leaning on his walking frame, then walked on. Two young men on a scooter passed and slowed to stare, and Fran had a nice sense of being a part of the place with this unexpected endeavour.

When she next looked up from the sink, Fran noticed that the scooter had stopped further up the street, and the passenger was walking towards the van. The driver's door and sliding door were open on the pavement side. She saw him have a good look inside as he passed, and she was seized by a premonition. She opened the window and shouted Rose's name but it was hopeless. She ran down the stairs and out onto the street in time to hear the throaty sound of the scooter as it took off.

When she reached the van, Rose was singing to herself as she wiped down the walls.

Fran's sprint downstairs had left her panting. 'Rose! Did you see that guy?'

Rose looked up. 'What guy?'

'Did you leave anything in the front? Where's your bag?'

'Tucked under the seat. Why?' Rose turned and stared at the empty space. 'Oh, *shit! Oh, no!*'

'I saw them from upstairs, two guys . . .' began Fran.

Maggie arrived, carrying pillows and towels. 'That's everything.' She caught sight of their expressions. 'What's wrong? What's happened?'

'Both our bags – gone! Stolen,' said Rose.

It took a moment for Maggie to register the catastrophe. She spun around, looking in all directions. 'Did you see who took them?'

'I saw them,' said Fran. 'From upstairs. Two guys on a green scooter. They're long gone.'

Maggie undertook a pointless search under the seats. 'Would you recognise them? Did you get the number plate?'

Fran shook her head and pointed up towards the attic. 'I was right up there.'

'Well, good thing my passport is tucked away in my suitcase,' said Rose.

'Mine too. But my phone was in there. Wallet. Credit cards. Everything else . . .'

Rose nodded. 'Same. Oh, *bugger* . . . the iPad! I was using it on the train. And my glasses too.'

'Okay, let's go back inside and work out what to do,' said Maggie calmly.

They locked up the van and went upstairs, gathering in Fran's room to discuss the options. Rose was all for reporting it to the police. Maggie was against it. 'I can't see the point. We can't identify them. There's no chance of getting our stuff back. And, if they check the van, we'll get fined for having an unregistered vehicle. And they'll probably impound it.'

'Didn't you even look at the papers?' asked Rose.

'I didn't have my glasses on. I'm sorry.'

'Let's not debate that right now,' suggested Fran. 'The chances of getting the stuff back are so low, anyway. I agree with Maggie, it's not worth the bother.'

Vincenzo, when they told him, was sympathetic and unnecessarily apologetic. He offered them the use of his phone and computer to organise for their mobiles to be deactivated and order new cards. By the time all that was complete, it was early evening. Maggie, always the one to think ahead, had fifty euros tucked away with her passport for emergencies. They walked into town, found a small pizzeria and ordered pizzas and a cheap bottle of wine, and sat at a table outside on the piazza.

'The *pensione* is paid for two nights,' said Maggie. 'Vincenzo will probably let us stay until the cards come through, anyway. He feels pretty bad about it.'

'What cards have you got, Fran?' asked Rose. 'How much on them?'

Fran had known this was coming. 'I've just got a cash card. I don't have a credit card.'

'Okay,' said Rose, not to be put off. 'How much money have you got available?'

'In total? All up? About five hundred pounds.'

'That's fine. We can live off your five hundred pounds until the cards come through and pay you back,' said Rose. 'They said a couple of days.'

'If all else fails, we could try and sell the van, I suppose . . .' said Maggie doubtfully.

Rose laughed. 'I think we've got more chance of getting our bags back.'

'We could get money wired from home, I suppose,' said Maggie doubtfully.

'Let's not ask for help from our families unless we're really screwed,' said Rose. 'The whole point is to do this under our own steam. Plus, we'll never live it down.'

Evening fell soft and slow, couples and families wandered by enjoying a leisurely *passeggiata* in the Italian tradition and children played together while their parents caught up with friends. The pizza vanished almost as quickly as it arrived. Maggie gave a satisfied sigh and took a sip of her wine.

'I think food actually tastes better when it's a diminishing resource,' remarked Rose.

'We're hardly going to starve, Rose. You don't seem as upset as I would have expected,' said Fran.

'I'm extremely upset,' said Rose. 'Never mind my stuff – I loved that daypack; all those dinky pockets.'

'Are you really?' asked Fran. 'You both seem relieved. You've been so tied to home. It's like you've only been half here.'

'You never said anything about it before,' said Rose.

'What am I going to say? It's not my place to complain. It's just the way it worked out. Maybe I'm envious. I don't need my phone because no one depends on me.'

'I envy *you*. Peter had Max texting me about this presentation or whatever it is he's doing —'

'You're right,' said Maggie. 'I do feel a bit lighter. It's the first evening I've felt like I can relax, knowing there won't be a load of problems waiting for me at the end of the evening.'

'And not looking over your shoulder all the time, either,' added Rose.

'I was just being silly about that. Too much adrenaline. Hyper-vigilant.'

'Maybe some good will come out of this,' said Fran. 'Look, to be honest, until this happened, I was planning to go home tomorrow or the next day.'

'What?' asked Rose, bewildered. 'Why didn't you say something?'

'I didn't have a chance. I really do appreciate you bringing me and there's been some good moments, but overall it's been stressful. I know that sounds ungrateful . . . I feel very beholden.'

'I'm sorry. I've been so grumpy,' said Maggie.

'I've had the odd moment too,' admitted Rose. 'You should be happy we're dependent on you now, Fran.'

Fran nodded. 'Actually, I do feel better. It feels more equal.'

'So the upshot of this disaster is that it's cheered us all up!' Rose lifted her glass in salute. 'To the unexpected!'

Maggie and Fran chimed glasses and echoed her words.

'I know neither of you subscribe to the idea that everything happens for a reason,' began Fran. 'But what if this did?'

'I was thinking the same thing,' said Maggie. 'This is the closest we've got to our first experience here.'

'With a bit of squabbling thrown in for authenticity,' said Fran with a smile.

Rose grinned. 'Our gift to you.'

'We have somewhere to sleep. All we need is food and petrol,' said Maggie. 'I think we should forget the credit cards and keep travelling.'

'Are you serious? That van will never get out of Verona!' said Rose. 'Did you hear the death rattle coming from under the bonnet?'

Maggie was undeterred. 'Maybe. But I think we should give it a go. We're flying out of Rome in two weeks, right? Let's get our cards sent to the hotel there. If we're really careful, we can live on Fran's cash until then. It's roughly . . . thirteen euros a day each.'

'I'm not sure we even remember how to be that careful,' said Rose.

'Where would we go?' asked Fran.

Maggie shrugged. 'Anywhere. Just head south. If we get stuck, we can get ourselves to Rome somehow.'

Rose was suddenly the cautious one. 'There are so many things that could go wrong with that van —'

'I'm all for it,' interrupted Fran. She glanced across at Rose and smiled. 'And Rose is too.'

Chapter Fourteen

Around town 'the Beast', as it was now known, had been sluggish, the engine spluttering ominously from time to time. It had damage on every panel, warning off other drivers, and the passenger door had a habit of flying open on left-hand turns. But now, apart from the odd hiccup, it roared along the Autostrade towards Bologna, evidently at home on the open road. Maggie was less at home, her foot still trembling nervously on the accelerator.

Bologna was less than two hours from Verona and seemed like a good trial run. Intersections and roundabouts were confusing but, now they were on the Autostrade, it was relatively simple to follow the line of traffic. The slow lane was bumper to bumper with trucks, so she settled in the middle lane and tried to ignore the cars coming up behind her and overtaking at speed. In the back of her mind was the terrifying prospect of the van dying right in the thick of all this traffic.

Since she couldn't drive, Fran had been appointed navigator, in charge of the fold-out map, a role she performed calmly and competently, managing to throw in the occasional encouraging comment. Rose, wearing Maggie's reading glasses, was immersed in a guidebook to camping grounds, and making sure the passenger door stayed closed.

Overnight, life had become analogue, with all its limitations, many of which they had yet to encounter. Maggie's anxiety levels ebbed and flowed. One minute she felt stressed that she was uncontactable, the next, she reasoned that her family were all quite capable of taking care of any situation – and it would be helpful for them to realise that.

It was definitely good to be moving under their own steam. Yesterday, they'd been on a high, rushing to put everything in place for their departure. They stocked up on food and a new pot for the camp stove they'd inherited. They only had one large pot, so their culinary repertoire was limited to rice or couscous with vegetables and meat. There was no means of keeping food cold, so they had to shop each day. Breakfast would be fruit, bread and tea.

Vincenzo had donated extra blankets and pillows, and sent them off to buy a calling card that they could use to make international calls on the phone at the *pensione*. Fran had no need to notify Louis. Rose left a message on Peter's phone, but Maggie had needed to speak to Kristo.

Initially, he was upset about them being robbed, and then he was annoyed that she wasn't going to wait in Verona for her credit card to be delivered, so she could buy a new phone. She had travel insurance, all she had to do was sit tight for a couple of days and everything would be delivered to her. 'Are you trying to run away from us – so we can't even contact you? It's just stupid!'

There was no way to explain this situation to him. 'Kristo, it's only for another couple of weeks —'

'Couple of weeks! Why are you doing this to me?!'

'Please don't shout. I'm doing this for me . . . I need to feel free —'

'Well, you're not free. Why pretend? This is Rose. She's behind it. Giving you stupid ideas. I bet it was her idea to go off air. Have you really lost everything? Or did you throw it in a river?'

'Don't fight with me, Kris. I have my own "stupid" ideas. I don't need help from Rose. No one is forcing me. I'm just trying to make this whole thing work – so it's not a total waste of time.'

'It is a waste of time – and fucking money! I knew that from the start. Everyone said it. Everyone! Here I am, trying to do the right thing. Be the good husband. Now you're pushing me over the edge.'

'Look, I have to go. I'm using a phone card and —' Maggie began.

'A what?! What in the hell is that? Maggie, be reasonable.'

'I have limited minutes on it. I don't want to waste them fighting with you.'

'Okay, fine!' he said and hung up, not realising that he couldn't call back and apologise, as he always did when he calmed down. Not her problem.

It seemed that, for the first time, all three of them were excited and wanted this to work, but Maggie knew it was a game. If it got too hard, they could stop. They still had a safety net that they'd never had in earlier days.

Rose located a camping ground just north of Bologna. Fran guided them off the Autostrade and, using a GPS monotone, through the various turn-offs and roundabouts to the camping ground. The approach to the place was an untidy collection of rural and semi-industrial areas, but the camp itself was pleasant and green, with sites neatly laid out under the shelter of symmetrical rows of trees.

The back of their camp site was delineated by a high hedge and Rose suggested they reverse into it for more privacy. Maggie wanted to avoid reversing altogether, as the van was heavy and visibility was poor. She was not keen on making a public spectacle of herself but agreed to give it a go. The Beast had other ideas, and was determined not to be pigeonholed. To make matters worse, Rose stood beside the van, yelling instructions and drawing unnecessary attention to the exercise.

Maggie's foot started to shake again, and sweat trickled down her back.

'Mags, let's go in frontwards. It really doesn't matter,' suggested Fran.

Maggie wanted to get it right and not have to put up with Rose telling her how it should have been done. But more than that, she wanted to get out of the van. She did a loop around the campground, easily nosed the Beast into the site and switched off the ignition.

Rose popped up at the driver's window. 'What *are* you doing?'

Fran leaned across Maggie and said firmly, 'Rose, just leave it.'

Rose shrugged. She slid open the side door and gazed into the van. 'Oh boy, it's gonna be *tight* tonight.'

'It's much bigger than the Kombi,' said Fran. 'We'll be fine. It'll be cosy.'

Maggie knew Rose was right, it would be tight, but the van was still larger and better organised than the Kombi had been.

Although the mattress took up most of the space, the floor itself was a platform raised above the wheel arches, which allowed for their bags and supplies to be stored underneath. The interior walls had been insulated with plywood and had a few hooks for hanging bits and pieces. It was a conversion put together with some thought, but not much money.

Maggie got out of the van and opened the back doors wide. She kicked off her shoes, crawled onto the bed and lay down. The air was warm and she could feel a patch of sunlight on her bare feet.

'Should we catch the bus into Bologna this afternoon?' suggested Rose, sitting in the doorway.

'You go,' said Maggie. 'I'll stay here. It's really very comfortable. I want to relax.'

Fran got in and lay down beside her. 'Let's just rest for a while. We've done well today. There's no rush. And also, let's be frugal, but not anxious, about the money situation.'

'We can't keep staying in camping grounds,' said Rose. 'This cost ten times what we paid on the last trip. We need to find free places to camp.' She lay down on the bed next to Maggie and began to sing, 'Three old chookies laying in a van, three old chookies laying in a van, if one old chookie should accidentally . . .'

'Fart?' suggested Fran.

'Oh, please, no,' said Maggie, laughing.

'It's what brought us together,' said Fran.

'And keeps us apart,' added Rose.

'Anyway, it needs to rhyme with van,' said Maggie.

'. . . should accidentally . . . something . . .' continued Rose, '. . . there'd be two old chookies laying in the van.'

'That made no sense whatsoever, Rose,' said Fran. 'Let's have some quiet time. I think a restorative nap is in order.'

Maggie drifted off into a dreamless sleep and, when she woke, the sun was low and streaming onto the bed. On her left, Rose snored quietly, and on her right, Fran was curled up like a child. In her groggy state, she was swept back forty years to some intangible feeling of freedom; a time of fresh dawns and the days that unfurled of their own accord, with no sense of time or urgency. A time when they had thought nothing of driving through strange countries, sleeping under the stars and befriending strangers. The feeling passed like a flash of sunlight and she came back to the present with a jolt, wondering when she had become so cautious and careful. Nowadays she viewed everything through a prism of anxiety, obsessed with making sure nothing ever went wrong.

Maggie shuffled forward on her bottom and got out of the van. The light was fading and the camp was busy with arrivals settling in for the night. There was a mix of large luxurious motor homes and older more basic vans – nothing quite as basic as the Beast.

An older couple had pulled into the site next door. They had a Peugeot station wagon and a trailer that popped open to become a neat caravan/tent arrangement. The two of them worked silently and efficiently, well-practised in erecting their accommodation and snapping out their collapsible chairs and table.

Maggie got the stove out from the floor space. She made tea and woke the others. They'd bought some fresh focaccia that morning and pulled it apart to have with cheese and tomatoes and olives. It was a simple meal but Maggie knew the sting of the salt and earthy taste of the oil on the focaccia would fix it in her memory.

When Rose realised that their neighbours were Australian, she urged the couple to come over for a cup of tea. Don and Ann, from Adelaide, were on a three-month tour of Europe, seasoned campers with quick-dry clothes and sturdy walking shoes. Don had a good look inside the Beast. 'Basic but functional. How do you ladies all manage sleeping in there?'

'We'll let you know in the morning,' said Rose with a grimace.

Hands in his pockets, Don bent over and peered under the false floor. 'Very basic. Shame whoever did the conversion didn't make some sliding containers so you could keep things in order. Look at this, Ann.'

Ann came over and conducted her own inspection. 'If you come across some plastic milk crates, they might fit under there, help you get organised.'

'Doubt it,' said Don. 'You want some proper boxes on locking castors and rope handles, so you can —'

'We're happy with the Beast just as she is,' interrupted Rose briskly.

Maggie turned to her in surprise. 'Are we? First I heard of it.'

Fran agreed. 'We want to keep it simple.'

Don invited them over for a tour of their camper trailer, which was like a soft-top caravan with seats that folded into beds and a proper kitchen. He opened cupboards and drawers. Everything was tucked away, ordered to military precision.

'I might come and bunk in with you two tonight,' said Rose with a wink.

Ann gave Rose an odd look but Don laughed. 'We're about to head into town for a look-see and a bite. Why don't you ladies come along with us? You don't want to be dragging the big beastie into the city.'

Next thing, they were all packed into the Peugeot and on the road. It was only fifteen minutes into Bologna and Maggie felt a sense of relief at being a passenger with no responsibilities. Her magnified mirror and makeup had been in her bag, so she had no idea what she looked like, and could only assume disastrous. Her clothes were crushed, face naked, hair tied in a knot, and there was nothing she could do about it.

As they walked into the Piazza Maggiore, the sky overhead was streaked with a lemon and orange sunset. The restaurants clustered around the square buzzed with life; the ancient buildings were a dramatic backdrop to the theatre of the piazza itself. Buskers and backpackers, groups of tourists and young people lounged on the steps of the pale pink basilica.

They wandered into the basilica, gazing up at its soaring arches and vaulted ceilings; towering pillars like great trunks of ancient trees. A choir, perhaps a hundred or more singers, rehearsed a choral piece, nuanced and beautiful, although not something Maggie recognised. She could hear Rose humming under her breath, as though the music trapped in her was desperate to escape. Leaving there, they drifted through the narrow lanes off the main piazza, crowded with restaurants and buzzing with people. Tiny shops sold flowers, fruit and vegetables, sausages and hams. There were giant wheels of Parmigiano-Reggiano on display and delicate pastries and cakes. There was a pleasant familiarity about the place, a vibrancy that Maggie remembered well from all those years ago.

Buying a selection of cheeses, sausages, bread and a six-pack of cold Peroni, they joined the young people sitting on the steps of the basilica. Rose donated her scarf as an improvised table cloth, and the five of them gathered around it. It was almost dark now and floodlights gilded the piazza. Each archway around the square was transformed into a proscenium of golden light.

It transpired that Don was a retired teacher and he and Rose fell into a discussion about education systems. Ann gave Fran a detailed run-down of their travels. Maggie only half listened to both conversations, preferring to watch the activity around them.

A busker set up in the centre of the piazza and began to play 'Hotel California' on a steel guitar. Rose immediately lost all interest in the education system and began to sing along. Maggie recalled how often they sang together on that first trip. The Kombi had no radio and they sang to fill the hours and miles. Rose still had a beautiful voice. To her own surprise, Maggie heard herself join in, and Fran added harmonies. Some Americans sitting nearby began to sing along too, mumbling the words between choruses, but it was Rose's trio who led the song. Encouraged, the busker went on to play 'Heartache Tonight', another song they knew off by heart.

A young couple sitting near them stepped down onto the piazza and began to dance a practised rumba. It was hard not to envy the fluidity of their youthful bodies, the flare of the young woman's hair and the gaze they shared. Maggie had experienced those moments and felt nostalgic for that sensual charge of the slow dance. She felt something rise up in her that she hadn't experienced in a long time. It caught in her throat and stung her eyes. It was a sense of quiet contentment. Everything felt right. When the song finished, Maggie glanced over at Rose and Fran and she knew they, too, had felt a shift.

'You didn't say you were a singing group,' said Don, evidently impressed.

'Nothing formal,' replied Rose. 'Just a happy accident.'

'Songs from our youth,' explained Fran. 'When we had time to learn the lyrics.'

A passer-by threw a two-euro coin onto Rose's scarf and she burst out laughing. 'Wowee! Our first paid gig!'

Fran laughed. 'If we get desperate, we've always got that to fall back on.'

As they stood up to leave, Maggie noticed Rose was staring out into the crowded piazza with an odd expression on her face. 'Hang on,' said Rose. 'Actually, I'll meet you back at the car.' She sounded flustered, and the next moment she rushed off into the crowd. She arrived at the van shortly after the rest of them and when Maggie asked where she'd gone off to, she said it was nothing. 'Just someone I thought I knew.'

On the way back to the camp, it started to rain. Don parked beside the facilities block so everyone could dash in for a relief stop. When they arrived at their site, there were hurried goodbyes with Don and Ann, who would be leaving first thing in the morning. They were driving to Brindisi to catch the ferry and start their tour of the Greek islands.

The belly of the Beast was cold and damp. The cheer of the magical evening quickly evaporated. Maggie hated going to bed without brushing her teeth and spent ten minutes crawling around in the dark with the torch, trying to find her toiletries bag before she finally gave up. There was some jostling over sleeping bags and blankets before they finally all settled down for sleep.

The rain sounded like nails being thrown on the roof and there was a wet dripping sound that was definitely inside the van. Maggie crawled across to the back door and felt around the edges to discover that water was coursing down the inside of the door.

'What is it?' Rose shouted over the noise.

'It's the seal around the door leaking. Just pass me a towel or something thick and I'll jam it in the door,' Maggie shouted back. Something soft landed in her face. She opened the back door, to accompanying screams from Fran and Rose, quickly folded the towel over the doorframe and slammed it shut.

'So this is *la dolce vita . . .*' said Rose, pulling her sleeping bag up to her neck.

Fran got on her knees and felt around under the front seat. 'I think it's time to break this out.'

'What is it? A blunt instrument to finish us off?' asked Rose. 'Hallelujah!'

'No, Rose. It's a cab sav.' Fran paused. 'Oh, no! It's got a cork.'

'I put a corkscrew in the box with the cutlery, but we'd need to open the back doors to get it,' said Rose.

'No, I put that box under the front seat, so it would be easier to get to,' said Maggie. 'Can you climb over the seat, Fran? Take the torch.'

Fran pulled herself up behind the seats, rolled over the top and disappeared. A moment later there was a crow of triumph and her silhouette reappeared clambering back over the seat. She popped opened the bottle, took a swig and handed it to Rose.

Maggie leaned against the back of the seats and tucked the sleeping bag up under her armpits. There was nothing much to see in the darkness. Rain fell steadily on the roof, the wine found its way into her hand, she took a mouthful and felt it go on its own journey.

At the second mouthful, she remembered another night, all those years ago, when they had camped in an olive grove somewhere, Italy or Greece. It was a hot summer's night and they had dragged their bedding out under the olive trees, clearing the ground of twigs and fruit to get comfortable. As they settled down to sleep, the sky was bright with stars and the only sounds were cicadas and crickets.

Maggie had woken in the night with the horrible feeling that someone was pouring water over her. Rose was shouting incoherently and then the headlights of the Kombi came on. The rain was pelting down. They grabbed their sleeping bags and huddled in the van shivering and laughing at their bad luck. It was three in the morning, sleep was impossible, so they had opened a bottle of wine and told ghost stories and sang until dawn. They finally drifted off to sleep when the rain stopped, only to be woken by a herd of curious goats head-butting the side of the Kombi.

'Do you remember that night in the olive grove?' asked Maggie, passing the bottle to Rose.

Rose hooted. 'Oh, God! That was awful! And the bloody goats.'

'But fun too,' remembered Fran. 'Fun to look back on.'

'I don't remember it bothering us all that much at the time,' said Maggie.

'And here we are stuck in a van in the rain, drinking wine in the middle of the night.' Rose laughed. 'Never thought that would happen again. We had a blast this evening, didn't we?'

'Do you think it is too late for us?' asked Maggie, suddenly serious. 'To do what we want with our lives? All I seem to think about is avoiding upsetting people.'

'Your whole family bullies you,' said Rose. 'You never seem to get your own way.'

'Rose, that's a bit harsh,' said Fran. 'Don't start an argument now.'

'And it's not true. I have a say in everything. You're exaggerating.'

'Maybe, but you don't get your own way. You didn't want Kristo's mum to come and live with you. Next thing, she's moved in and you're made to feel guilty.'

'She's not that bad,' said Maggie. 'She has her moments. I have to take responsibility for my role in the situation. Being too compliant. Desperate to please. Not saying what I think. Not being honest. Sex, for example . . .'

'Oh, yes?' said Rose. 'Interesting segue.'

'If I could avoid ever having it again, I'd be delighted. If I fob Kristo off, he gets grumpier by the day and then I think, I might as well get it over with so we can have some peace in the house. We can't discuss it. He takes it super-personally and it turns into an argument.'

'What is it? You just don't fancy him?' asked Rose.

'If I fancied anyone, it would be him. I'm just not interested in sex. I'm never in the mood.'

'It could be menopause, Mags, but it could also be the depression,' suggested Rose. 'It's just you two are out of step right now. For some people, sex is like the WD-40 of their relationship – it smooths things out and gets you through the rough patches.'

Maggie laughed. 'One of your better metaphors, Rosie.'

'When we were young,' remembered Fran, 'we had that idea that to hang on to a guy we had to be "good in bed". We always used to wonder what it meant. We never had the idea that men need to be "good in bed" to please us.'

'Maybe there should be a ranking system, like TripAdvisor. Encourage men to lift their game,' suggested Rose, apparently serious.

'We haven't heard any revelations from you on your favourite topic, Rose,' said Maggie, passing her the bottle. 'Here, have some truth serum.'

'Revelations. Things went off the rails in that department after I found out Peter was banging that PhD student. After that, he never initiated sex. I had to ask. A few years ago, I just stopped asking. And that was it.'

'Oh, Rose! I didn't know that,' said Fran. 'Do you think he's been with anyone else?'

'Peter never tells you anything he doesn't want to. He's on some sort of spectrum, whatever that means. He's very private. I thought that student was the first, but I'm not so sure. There's something about him that women find attractive: that helpless nerdy man-boy thing.'

'You still have a good partnership, despite that. That's something,' said Maggie. 'Hang on. You're not trying to tell us you're celibate?'

There was a long pause, then Rose said, 'No, I'm not. There is someone.'

'You sly dog! I thought you'd been a bit more chirpy,' said Maggie. 'It was around the time you started French classes.'

'There are no French classes,' admitted Rose.

'Is he a good man, Rose?' asked Fran.

'Yes, he's a good man. He and Peter do have one positive thing in common – neither of them try to control me. I've only realised recently why I was so combative in those earlier relationships. I always felt as though I was fighting for my corner.'

Maggie asked Rose if she loved him.

'Not sure I love him, but I like him a lot. So you don't think . . . I don't know . . . badly of me?' asked Rose, uncharacteristically hesitant.

'No, I don't,' confirmed Fran.

'Me neither,' agreed Maggie. 'It's your life, Rose. You deserve to be loved. We all do.'

'Of course we do,' said Rose. 'Thank you.'

The rain began to ease as Maggie snuggled down and tucked the sleeping bag in around her. She tried not to think about the sleeping tablets and the antidepressants that had gone with her bag – coming off them so suddenly could be brutal. Today had been a good day. She would take the night as it came.

Chapter Fifteen

When they left the camping ground next morning, Rose felt obliged to take the wheel. She would have preferred to be in a comfy seat on a train, not having to deal with the fumes and persistent cheesy odour. The night had been rocky. The confined space was going to take some getting used to, but she'd had worse. It could only get better.

Yesterday, it seemed as though Maggie's mood had shifted and they were united in feeling more optimistic about the expedition. Today was completely different. Maggie was very flat and revealed that her antidepressants had been in her stolen handbag. Going off them so suddenly, she could be having withdrawals, but what could they do? Getting a new prescription in Italy would be impossible. They'd have to keep a close eye on her.

Early-morning mist drifted over the ploughed fields beside the Autostrade and Rose thought how nice it would be to remain in the countryside and away from the cities. The immediate problem was that they were headed south without any real plan, and some practical decisions had to be made.

Coming back from Bologna in the car the previous evening, they had vaguely discussed heading south, and perhaps out towards the coast. Don and Ann, who agreed with each other on every topic, had immediately set about dissuading them from that route. 'The whole Adriatic Coast has been destroyed by tourism,' said Ann. 'Hundreds of kilometres of apartments and the beaches covered in millions of deckchairs and umbrellas. You won't like it, I promise.'

Maggie explained that they had two weeks before their flights out of Rome, so plenty of time to explore. Rose thought it would be interesting to see the coast. They didn't have to stay.

'If you go out to the coast, then you'll need to drive across the width of Italy to get to Rome,' said Don. 'The centre is quite mountainous, you know.'

Rose was slightly annoyed by the conversation. 'We're not afraid of a few mountains. We're not helpless little old ladies, you know.' One minute their new friends were trying to help, the next they were taking charge. Despite that, she did feel a bit abandoned seeing the empty site next door this morning. It was nice to think that someone had their backs, even for a short time.

'We can't just keep driving without a clue where we're going,' said Rose. 'Especially on the Autostrade. We'll run out of Italy sooner or later. Or get picked up for driving through the Telepass gates without paying. We've gone from one extreme to the other. From too many plans to not enough.'

Fran opened out the map and inspected it. 'Siena was on our original itinerary. Why not go there? We should get signs when we get to Forli.'

Maggie was quiet. After a moment she agreed with the idea but Rose sensed a reluctance.

'Siena it is, then. *Andiamo* – let's go!' Rose burst into an operatic rendition of 'That's Amore' to cheer everyone up.

'Where did you run off to last night, Rose?' asked Maggie, as though it had been playing on her mind.

Rose kept her eyes on the road, desperately trying to think of a way to avoid this conversation. 'It was nothing, just someone I thought I knew. I told you that.'

'Was it Nico? Is that why you're being evasive?'

'Okay. It was a guy who looked a bit like him. That's all. He wasn't that close, I couldn't really tell, but he was wearing one of those tailored leather jackets Nico likes to wear —' Rose faltered. In the light of day, Rose was more convinced she'd imagined the sighting, feeding into Maggie's paranoia.

'*Shit!* Did he see us?'

'No. He was walking quite fast, just looking around. Alone.'

'And what were you going to do? Confront him? This is exactly why I didn't want you to know about it!' said Maggie.

'It doesn't make any sense,' interrupted Fran. 'It's too much of a coincidence. It's more likely to be Rose's vivid imagination.'

'I agree,' said Rose.

'Was Bologna on the itinerary?' asked Maggie.

'Yes, it was,' said Fran. 'After Verona. Then Siena.'

'We can't go to Siena. Think of somewhere else. We just can't go. Anywhere but there.' Maggie's words tumbled out breathlessly.

'Do you think he's here, following us?' said Fran. 'That feels like something out of a movie.' She hesitated. 'Maggie, I don't think that's real.'

Rose was rattled by the whole conversation. When the sign for *area servizio* came up, she took the exit and pulled into the

Autogrill car park and turned off the ignition. The Beast gave a despairing shudder and fell silent.

'Okay, Maggie, what the hell is going on? You have to tell us.'

Maggie put her face in her hands. 'Not here. I will tell you. Later.'

Rose had never known Maggie to be so secretive and frustrating. At the same time, it was obvious that she was in a very fragile state. 'Let's go in and have a coffee,' suggested Rose.

'I don't want to go in there,' said Maggie quietly. 'I don't want people looking at me.'

Fran and Rose exchanged worried looks. Fran slid her arm around Maggie's shoulder. 'Mags, the way you're feeling now is not real. Your brain is going a bit haywire. But, in a day or two, it will be different. I was on antidepressants for a while, so I know what I'm talking about.'

Maggie nodded, unconvinced.

Fran handed Rose a ten-euro note. 'I'm expecting change – no chocolate bickies.'

'Quite the tyrant now you're in charge, aren't you?' noted Rose.

The Autogrill was straight out of a Jetsons cartoon: 1960s space-age architecture. Inside, it was as fragrant as a nonna's kitchen, with the smell of warm pastries and fresh bread. Rose stood gazing wistfully at the fat focaccia sandwiches of tomatoes, basil and buffalo mozzarella. Pesto pasta. It was too early for lasagna, but chocolate torte? In the end it was just three black coffees as instructed. As she came out, the sight of the van parked between a smart-looking SUV and a sleek Mercedes, in all its ugliness, dirty and misshapen, was sobering, and Rose suddenly felt out of her depth, wondering where on earth this was all going.

Maggie took her coffee with murmured thanks. Rose felt they deserved to have some insight into what was going on, given the constant pressure to change plans. She feared the worst: that Maggie had had an affair with Nico. In which case a nervous breakdown would be fully warranted because that was an incendiary that would blow the Dimitratos family sky high. It needed to be handled delicately. 'Have you got something going on with Nico?' asked Rose. 'Just tell us and get it over with.'

'Rose! She doesn't have to tell us —'

'I know you're not well right now,' Rose continued. 'But at some point we have to make a decision about where to go or where we can't go. So it would be helpful if we knew what's going on. We're your best friends. We're not going to hold anything against you.'

Maggie stared blankly out the windscreen. 'No. Never.'

'Well, that's a good start. You think he's come over here because of you?' asked Rose.

'I don't know. I don't know what I think. Kristo said he's gone away. And if you saw him in Bologna —'

'That was a random sighting . . . it could have been an Italian guy who looked like a Greek guy. So what does it all mean?'

Maggie turned and looked at her. 'If it *was* him, then he has our itinerary.'

Rose didn't know where to start. Was this real or imagined? It made no sense that Nico would fly across the world to trail around after them.

She remembered a recent interaction with him at the Easter lunch that Maggie and Kristo put on every year for family and friends. Maggie would cook for days beforehand and Rose always made a point of arriving when the family got back from church to help with the preparations. They even had a spit barbecue contraption that got wheeled out once a year to cook an entire lamb.

Yia-yiá would be there helping but also pointing out any aspect that wasn't up to her standard. This year, Rose was fed up with it and said, 'Maggie is the best cook I know. Look at this spread!' She gestured towards the huge spinach pies, their filo golden and crackling, and trays of rosemary potatoes and roast vegetables. Rose would have just bought taramasalata at the supermarket, but Maggie made everything from scratch.

Yia-yiá pursed her lips and turned to Maggie. 'What that girl say? I not understand.'

Maggie, one minute drizzling sugar syrup over the baklava, the next, rushing to turn the potatoes in the oven, pretended she hadn't heard the exchange.

'Mrs Dimitratos, you know my name is Rose. I'm Maggie's best friend. And you do understand —'

'Rose, please leave it. You're not helping.' Maggie glanced over her shoulder and Rose noticed her expression change. Nico was leaning in the doorway watching them. Rose dropped the subject, but when she walked past him to take food out to the table, he turned and followed her. 'You should have some respect,' he said. 'You don't speak to our mother like that.'

Rose remembered Nico as a bit of a spunk when he was young, but there was a coldness about him now and he seemed more hostile as the years went on. He was standing so close she could see every follicle in the shadow of his beard. The moment felt both sexual and threatening, and even though there were twenty people in the room, it felt very uncomfortable.

Rose said half-heartedly, 'Just sticking up for Maggie.'

'We can look after Maggie. We don't need your help,' he said. He stood there waiting for a response, perhaps an apology, but Rose had scurried back to the safety of the kitchen.

Now, sitting in the van watching the sun break through the mist across the fields, Rose realised that none of them really knew the truth of each other's lives. They had an occasional peek through the windows but they were not inside those rooms when unforgivable things were said, when hearts were irreparably broken. Wounds inflicted that would never heal. Each of them had their cache of secrets, too painful to reveal. Places they didn't ever want to revisit, Rose included.

'I agree with Maggie. We'll talk about this some other time,' said Fran. 'And, if it's private, then you can keep it that way.'

Maggie sipped her coffee, her eyes looking dead. 'It doesn't matter. We can go to Siena. Anywhere you want. I don't care.'

Fran rubbed Maggie's arm in a motherly way. 'Mag, we're not going to go anywhere you feel uncomfortable. It's not that important.'

'I will tell you. It's a long story.' Maggie's voice was thick with tears. 'I'm just not up to it at the moment. You do whatever you think.'

Rose took the map from Fran and studied it while she drank her coffee. 'We've got plenty of time. We could go down to Naples and then back up to Rome. We don't have to make a decision now. Let's just get off the Autostrade, take the back roads and find a place to camp – and chillax this afternoon.'

Maggie nodded. 'I'm sorry I've been such a liability on this trip.'

'It's fine,' said Fran. 'We wanted to have no plan.'

Rose started up the van. 'Should we just chuck our cups out

the window like everyone else?' she asked, pointing out the litter in the car park.

Fran took the cup from her and put it in a carrier bag. 'I never really trust that you're joking, Rose.'

Rose crunched the van into gear and reversed out of the parking space. 'That's my dry wit for you.'

'Perhaps. But you're a tiny bit crazy too,' said Fran with an indulgent smile.

'You don't know how relieved I am to hear that,' said Rose as she took the entry to the Autostrade and put her foot down.

They took the next exit and headed inland. The cloud lifted and green undulating fields, woods and hills spread out before them. The narrow country roads were almost empty and not so winding as to make driving arduous. Maggie stared silently out the window while Rose and Fran talked in low voices, making navigational decisions as they went. They stopped in a village and bought provisions: sweet strawberries and tart apples.

An hour or so after they left the village, Fran noticed signposts to a lake down a gravel road and suggested they could see if it was suitable to wild camp. They followed the road for a kilometre or so through a forest and came to a picnic area beside a lake with a small, picturesque jetty. They had the place to themselves and Rose parked the van in the trees, tucked away from view. She would be the last to admit that she was a bit uncomfortable about being in an isolated spot. They had bought a good torch but she regretted that they didn't have a trusty hatchet as before.

They opened up the back doors of the van, took out the bedding and draped it over bushes to air out after the damp night. Fran lit the camp stove and boiled water for tea.

The lake was bordered by a narrow beach with round grey pebbles the size of marbles that crunched and rolled underfoot, beyond which was woodlands all around. The weather was warm enough but the lake still chilly. They stripped to their underwear, spread out their towels and lay on the grass in the dappled shade of a tree.

'I haven't missed London for one minute,' said Fran. 'It's sort of good that I'm being pushed out of the city, in a way. It's so hard to make the decision to leave.'

'It's always the decision that's hardest,' said Maggie.

'Decisions are not my forte,' Fran admitted.

Rose was now tired of all the reminiscing and self-recrimination. It was getting them nowhere. The past was dead and gone and she had already wasted too much time wondering what could have been and never would. She felt they were on the cusp of something now. Something precious and full of possibility. She worried that they would end up squandering this opportunity for adventure because they were too afraid to truly embrace it, constantly looking back.

'I think we've done enough wallowing in our past mistakes,' she said. 'The idea of this trip was not to castigate ourselves for not living up to our own expectations, it was to try and remember what they were.'

'Yes. Agreed. And let's stop talking about men altogether,' said Fran.

Maggie rolled over onto her stomach and rested her head on her arms. 'Fran's right. We talk about men way too much. That's something we never did before.'

'We used to talk about imaginary men,' said Rose. 'We were sold up the river by all those movies with happy endings, imagining ourselves as those heroines.' She thought about this for a while. 'I reckon Maggie's alter ego was Grace Kelly in *To Catch a Thief*. I could see you artfully twisting Cary Grant around your little finger.'

Maggie grunted, almost amused.

Fran asked, 'Who's mine, Rose?'

Rose thought for a moment. 'Audrey Hepburn in *Roman Holiday* with Gregory Peck on the back of your scooter, and a cute tiara at the end.'

'You'd be one of Katharine Hepburn's characters,' suggested Fran.

'Nope. Jane Fonda in *Barbarella*. Oh, how I wanted those thigh-high silver boots.'

'Those movies were remnants of the past, even when we watched them,' said Fran. 'And all made by men back then.'

'Or to titillate men, in the case of *Barbarella*,' said Rose.

Maggie seemed to have lost interest in the conversation and withdrawn into herself. In a desperate attempt to distract her from the state she had fallen into, Rose spontaneously leapt to her feet and struck a dramatic pose. 'Rose McLean *is* Barbarella!'

Fran gave a start. 'Rose, you're not very relaxing to be around.'

Maggie looked up with a faint smile, inciting Rose to further excess. She tore off her bra and flung it on the grass.

'Oh God, Rose,' said Maggie. 'You always go too far.'

Fran laughed. 'Do not take your knickers off, please!'

Rose had no plans to go that far. 'Fran Fisher *is* the Black Queen!'

Fran looked nervous. 'Do I have to take my top off?'

'No, that's my domain. You just wear an eye patch.'

'I didn't think to pack an eye patch.'

'Do you remember Barbarella had a top with a see-through section over one boob? How come that never caught on? What I need is a laser gun.' Rose picked up a stick and pointed it at imaginary combatants. 'I can't remember any of the songs, unfortunately.'

'Do I have lines?' asked Fran.

'You say things like "pretty, pretty" but menacingly. Then we fight.'

'Oh no, I'm not fighting you topless, Rose. It's too much.'

Rose launched into a rendition of 'Goldfinger' – the only relevant song she could think of – strutting and posturing until Maggie smiled, despite herself.

'Rose! Rose! Stop!' Fran tossed a sarong at her.

'What?' Rose looked around and realised a car had pulled into the parking area. An elderly couple sat in it, watching her impromptu performance with interest.

'Whoops, busted!' Rose wrapped the sarong around herself, took a bow, and sat down on the grass. She lay low until the elderly couple realised the show was over and drove off.

The evening was warm and they sat on the ground around the stove and cooked dinner together. The vegetable and tuna stew was unceremoniously slopped into bowls, they tore up stale bread and mopped up the sauce, and Rose was surprised at how good it tasted. As the moon rose over the lake, she was aware that, before long, this experience would become a vague memory. It was like a feeling of pre-nostalgia, an odd sadness at the passing of time.

Rose and Fran chatted about where they could go the next

day. Maggie, who had been quiet all evening, had gone back to being distant. Lost in thought, as if she was alone.

'I want to tell you about Nico,' she said, out of the blue.

'You don't have to —' began Fran.

'He has been stalking me for years. I almost can't remember a time when I didn't have to watch out for him.' Maggie didn't look at them but gazed out towards the lake.

'Oh, Maggie,' said Fran, distressed.

Rose felt nothing but fury. 'Years?! Why didn't you ever *say* anything?'

'I have never told anyone. Not a soul. Ever. For a long time I didn't believe it myself. And I knew no one else would believe me.'

'We would have!' insisted Rose. 'Of course we would.'

Maggie turned to her. 'But there's nothing you can do that won't make things worse.'

'Tell us how it started, Mag,' said Fran. 'Tell us whatever you want.'

'It was after we lost Kal. Nico came around to the house one day when I was alone; the girls were at school. I made him coffee and we sat and chatted. He'd never been friendly towards me before; he was always a bit hostile. He seemed genuinely heartbroken for us . . . one minute we were celebrating our beautiful baby boy . . .' Maggie's voice became a whisper and she was silent for a moment. 'We were both a bit teary and emotional. It felt like things would be different between us in the future. When he was leaving, he gave me a hug. I had this wonderful feeling of being cherished and cared for by Kristo's family, for the first time.'

Maggie started to cry. She paused and took a deep breath. 'This hug went on for a bit too long, and I started to feel uncomfortable. As I pulled away, he pulled me to him and kissed me on the lips. I was so shocked. He was holding me really tight . . . and this is what I can't understand. I didn't kiss him back but I didn't push him away either. I let him kiss me! As if he had the right to do that. I didn't want to hurt his feelings. That's all I could think about at the time . . . not *offending* him! Wondering what I'd done to encourage it. How do I explain that? What is wrong with me?!'

'You did nothing wrong, Maggie. That's a completely natural response,' said Fran. 'We've all been there.'

'So it started then?' asked Rose. 'Maggie, that was twenty years ago! I don't understand —'

'I've thought about this a lot. I think he was infatuated with me right from the start. I just didn't see it for what it was . . . I thought he was being competitive with Kristo.'

'He was there with Kristo, that night at Selina's,' remembered Rose.

'I was stupid and weak. I didn't say a thing and he seemed to assume there was some special bond between us. He goes out of his way to catch me alone. He often turns up places, as though he's following me, or knows I'll be there. He's forever making inappropriate comments. I've made it very clear I'm not interested . . . but it's like an obsession for him.'

'He really has a screw loose,' said Fran.

'He does,' said Maggie. 'He enjoys having this power over me. That's why he's been calling me, to scare me. And punish me. He wants to come between me and Kristo.'

'You have to tell Kristo,' said Rose. 'You have to.'

'This is why I've never told you!' said Maggie. 'You don't understand the situation. That comment you made at Easter? He's still talking about that. He told Kristo you were disrespectful to Yia-yiá and shouldn't be invited again. He's manipulative. You can't just blunder in and sort it out.'

'I'm sorry,' said Rose. 'You're right. I didn't realise.'

'I couldn't tell Kristo at the time, and it would be so much worse now that I've hidden it all these years.'

Fran put her arm around Maggie's shoulders. 'Are you afraid of Nico?'

'Of course I'm afraid of him. He's unpredictable. I'm scared of the damage he could do, of losing my family, Kristo, the girls, Yia-yiá. Everyone would blame me. I'd be ostracised. I just can't take that risk.'

Rose could see her point, but felt that Maggie underestimated how loved she was by her family. But in the end it was her decision.

'I don't know what to say, Maggie,' said Fran. 'I just wish we could fix this for you.'

'It's unfixable,' said Maggie wearily. 'Unfixable. All that can happen is it gets worse.'

'I'm not so sure about that,' said Rose. 'We'll think of something.' She helped Maggie to her feet and gave her a hug.

Rose wasn't sure how long she'd been asleep when she woke, feeling cold, and realised that Maggie was gone. She could see the back door had been opened and not closed properly. Maggie had probably gone for a pee.

She crawled over, pushed the door open and looked out to the lake, waiting for Maggie to come back. All was still and quiet, the lake silver in the moonlight. She noticed a shadow, movement on the jetty, then the sound of something heavy falling into the water. Dark ripples ruffled the mirrored surface.

'Fran! Wake up!' Rose scrambled out of the van and sprinted across the grass to the jetty. 'Get the torch!' she screamed. 'Quick!'

As she ran along the jetty, she could see a vortex of bubbles rising to the surface. Without a moment's thought, she jumped into the lake. The chill of the water was shocking. She came to the surface, took a deep breath and dived down, her arms flailing around, frantically searching for a warm body in the cold blackness. In a moment she felt something brush her arm. She grabbed a handful of hair and jerked it towards her. She managed to loop her arms under Maggie's armpits and tried to drag her bodily up to the surface, but her friend struggled against her grip, fighting her off.

The bright light of the torch suddenly appeared above them. Fran was shouting, 'Maggie! Let Rose help you!'

Maggie struck out, trying to swim further into the lake. She was a strong swimmer but Rose quickly grabbed her ankle and pulled hard. Maggie tried to kick her off but Rose kept her grip. She lunged towards Maggie, who pushed her away, but she managed to get an arm across her chest and tuck one hand under her armpit.

As Rose began to paddle back towards the shore, Maggie stopped struggling but her body became a dead weight. Finally, Rose's feet found solid ground and she helped Maggie wade out of the water onto the rocky shore, where Fran stood with the torch, and together they helped Maggie back to the van.

Rose was deeply shocked and confused but she pushed her own emotions down, focusing entirely on Maggie, who said nothing as they pulled off her wet things, dried her and helped her into warm clothes. They got her into bed and tucked her in. No one said a word. Maggie seemed dazed. Fran was crying softly and Rose didn't trust herself to speak.

Only when Maggie was asleep did Rose think to strip off her own wet pyjamas and put on trackpants and a fleece. Fran hung their wet clothes over the bushes to dry out. She lit the stove and made Rose some chamomile tea.

'What just happened?' asked Fran shakily, as they sat down together. 'I can't believe it. Was she awake? Or asleep?'

'She must have had some kind of brain snap,' Rose said with a sob. 'This whole thing has become a complete nightmare. I just want to go home.' She was trembling all over with shock and cold. Fran got a blanket and wrapped it around Rose's shoulders. The tea began to warm and calm her. 'Do you think she told us that story about Nico tonight because she'd already decided . . . or do you think telling it made her realise, you know . . . She kept saying it was unfixable.'

Fran began to cry again. 'I don't know. But I agree, let's go home before something dreadful happens. If you hadn't realised she'd gone . . .'

Rose nodded. 'I know. We nearly lost her, Frannie.'

As Rose lay awake waiting for sleep, that phrase became a constant refrain. She kept going over and over the events of that evening. Almost as disturbing as Maggie going into the lake was the way she had let them put her to bed, like a child, as if she didn't really understand what she had done. What if Rose hadn't noticed she'd gone? How would they have got help? How would she have broken that news to Kristo? How could she and Fran have lived with the consequences? They could have both drowned. Rose tried to calm and comfort herself. All was well. They were all safe now. Maggie was right beside her and sleeping peacefully.

Chapter Sixteen

Fran woke to find the van doors wide open, Rose asleep beside her, and Maggie gone. She sat bolt upright to see Maggie sitting on the grass, peacefully eating an apple and gazing out at the lake.

Rose opened her eyes and looked around in alarm.

'It's okay, she's fine,' said Fran. 'Everything's fine.'

'Jesus, what a night. Puts the earring incident into perspective. Could it even get any worse? We're sticking to the plan, right? Straight to Rome.'

Fran nodded her agreement. She shuffled off the mattress and stepped out into the bright morning. Rose got out behind her. Maggie turned to them with a smile. 'Morning. Beautiful day.'

'So, how are you feeling? After last night,' Rose asked.

Maggie nodded cheerfully. 'Good. Feeling actually really good.'

Fran and Rose exchanged perplexed looks.

'So, what was the story with the midnight swim?' asked Rose.

Maggie's smile faded. 'What? What do you mean?'

'I mean, you tried to drown yourself in the lake.'

Maggie's hand flew to her mouth. She turned to look accusingly at the lake, which continued to sparkle innocently. 'I thought that was a nightmare. It really happened? I don't remember anything clearly . . . it's all sort of fragmented . . .'

'It really happened,' Fran assured her. 'Rose saved your life, Mag.'

'Shit, I thought . . . I'm so sorry. I don't know what to say. That must have been horrible for you. For you both. Thank you.'

'It's okay. We didn't have anything else on last night,' said Rose.

'Well, if it's any consolation, I do feel much better today. Better than I've felt in a while.' Maggie smiled at them both reassuringly. 'I feel . . . lighter.'

Fran couldn't think of what to say. 'That's good, Maggie. Look, we were thinking —'

'Sorry, before we get onto plans,' interrupted Maggie. 'I wondered if you would cut my hair for me? I'm sick of it.'

Fran had no idea what to make of this request. 'Me? I don't have any skills in that area, and we don't have proper scissors.'

'It'll be very simple. Snip. Snip. Take it all off.' As if it was all agreed, Maggie got up and went over to the van.

'I thought we were going to tell her it's all over,' hissed Rose. 'Now she's on a post-suicidal high. Far out. What next?'

Fran watched Maggie disappear inside the van. 'Let's wait and see where this goes.'

Maggie returned a few minutes later with a small pair of scissors, handed them to Fran and sat down on the grass. Fran knelt down behind her. 'I'm not sure about —'

'Just take it all off. I'm done with it,' said Maggie. 'It looks so tatty, and the grey's all coming through.'

'You'll be a platinum blonde like me,' said Rose. Sitting down beside Maggie, she got an apple out of the food box and munched on it noisily.

Maggie laughed. She lifted her hair up with her hands and let it drop, as if saying goodbye.

Fran glanced at Rose for support, but got a helpless shrug in return.

'Are you absolutely sure about this, Mag?'

Maggie nodded and Fran began to nervously lift handfuls of hair and snip them off. She kept on trimming, trying to get it as even as she could. When it was done, it was short and ragged, but could almost pass for an urchin cut. Rose knelt down in front of Maggie to assess the situation. She lifted the hair with her fingers, fluffed it up and sat back on her heels to assess the final effect. 'Holy shit,' she said. 'The cheekbones are back.'

Fran saw Rose was right. Maggie had lost some of the puffiness in her face and the cut looked much better than Fran could have imagined. It brought out the structure of Maggie's face.

Maggie checked out her haircut in the rear-view mirror and was delighted. Although, it seemed to Fran, she was delighted about everything today and it was impossible to know if she had actually turned a corner or would come crashing down to earth any time.

They sat on the grass, ate apples and strawberries for breakfast and discussed their travel plans. 'I don't think we can cope with any more excitement, quite frankly,' said Rose. 'Fran and I think we should head straight to Rome, and call it a day.'

'What would we do with the Beast?' asked Fran.

'We can leave it somewhere with the keys, as far as I'm concerned. Someone will want it for scrap,' said Maggie. 'I know that's what Kristo would want, for me to give up and go home. It's just we've come so far —'

'Maggie,' began Rose. 'I'm still confused about last night . . . you had no idea what you were doing?'

Maggie paused. 'I felt very spaced out yesterday. Nothing seemed real. I remember having a realisation that I was a burden to everyone. I felt certain that everyone would be relieved if I . . . just disappeared. I can only think that I must have unconsciously acted on that belief. I actually thought I could disappear without anyone noticing.' She shrugged apologetically, her expression pained. 'I'm so sorry. I've been in a bad way.'

Fran's throat felt choked. It was hard to get your head around. Even Rose was speechless. Fran leaned over and put her arms around Maggie. Rose took Maggie's hand and held it in hers. There was nothing else to say.

'We don't need to talk about this again,' said Fran. 'Let's try to put it behind us.'

Rose agreed. 'We could stop somewhere else on the way to Rome. On the original trip we went to Rome, Naples and then Brindisi and over to Corfu —'

Maggie held up her hand majestically. 'Corfu. That's where I want to go.'

'What? That is a bloody long drive,' objected Rose.

'It's not that bad,' said Fran, opening up the map. 'If we take the Autostrade, we could be in Brindisi tonight. But the petrol will cut into our funds. Then there's the cost of the ferry. I have no idea what that would be. It could clean us out.'

'We could go to Rome and get our credit cards,' suggested Maggie. 'But it would add a couple of days to the trip.'

'So let's say we get to Corfu, and then what?' asked Rose.

Maggie shrugged. 'I don't know. Isn't that the whole idea?'

'I agree,' said Fran. 'Venturing into the unknown was the objective. Isn't that the place that holds the happiest memories for us? It does for me.'

'What if it's changed so much, it cancels out the good memories we have of it?' asked Rose.

'Who'd have thought that you'd end up being the negative one?' said Maggie. 'Come on. Nothing can cancel out those weeks living on the beach at Agios Papadakis . . .'

'Sitting out on the terrace of the Blue Moon taverna having Greek yoghurt and fruit salad and chocolate for breakfast,' Fran reminded them.

Rose still looked sceptical. 'Well, if we're talking chocolate, I could probably be persuaded.'

'The beach and that turquoise water,' said Maggie. 'I doubt it's changed that much.'

'Yes, all right – you're sounding like a tourist ad now.'

'Let's take a vote. Those in favour?' Maggie raised her hand. Fran voted in favour. She felt a bit sorry for Rose, who had been so upbeat and determined. Her optimistic outlook had taken a battering.

Rose reluctantly lifted her hand. 'Unanimous, I guess. Probably the Beast will have the last word and cark it halfway there.'

'No,' said Fran. 'We will have the last word. We will get there, somehow.'

*

It took an hour to get onto the Autostrada Adriatica, which would take them virtually all the way to Brindisi. Now they were committed, Fran could see that the idea had grown on Rose.

They moved between shadow and sun, as clouds gathered and dispersed, scudding across the sky. They drove past long stretches of green and ploughed fields, clusters of factories and distant villages. They took a break every hour or two and swapped drivers. The slot for the radio was empty, apart from a few loose wires, but Rose got them singing. Her memory for lyrics was faultless and her voice, if anything, was richer and more resonant than Fran remembered. They worked their way through Fleetwood Mac and the Pretenders' hits and were critiqued and directed by Rose. They followed her in an uplifting rendition of 'Hymn to Her'.

'That's our anthem, a hymn to us,' said Fran. 'We're losing things and finding things. We're carrying on . . .'

'And we want more,' agreed Maggie, who was driving. 'It is our song, you're right. All we needed was an anthem!'

'That's who I really wanted to be,' said Rose. 'Chrissie Hynde.'

'So not Barbarella, then?' asked Fran with a smile. 'Make up your mind, Rose.'

'You don't have the fringe to be a Chrissie,' said Maggie. 'You do sound a bit like her, though. Anyway, I remember back then you wanted to be Rula Lenska's character in that show *Rock Follies*.'

Rose laughed out loud. 'Hah! I'd forgotten *Rock Follies*. Her name was Q – I remember we thought having a single-letter name was so cool. And Fran looked a bit like the Julie Covington character.'

Fran glanced over at Rose fondly. 'Ever since I've known you, there have been so many people you've wanted to be, but the only person I ever wanted to be was you.'

She enjoyed watching Rose blush pink. That didn't happen very often. She was almost impossible to embarrass.

'That's nice of you to say, Frannie. I can't imagine why, but feel free to enumerate my admirable qualities.'

'It's mainly just one. That you don't give a fuck. You don't worry about what people think of you. Or whether people like you. I can't imagine how liberating that must be.'

Rose dipped her head in modest acknowledgement. 'Maybe it was all those hours spent reflecting in detention. I was showing off to be popular and everyone thought I was an idiot. At some point, I realised my mistake was *trying* to be liked. It makes no sense. You can never be yourself.' After a moment she added, 'Still, I've made plenty of bigger mistakes since then.'

'Go on then,' said Fran. 'What would you do differently? Be honest.'

'What happens in the Beast stays in the Beast,' Maggie assured her.

'Okay, the truth will come as no surprise – I shouldn't have married Peter. That was the mistake of my life . . .'

'Oh no, Rose, really?' Maggie sounded dismayed. 'He has his faults but he does love you. No marriage is perfect. You've had a good life with him and the boys, and now you have a grandson. You have financial security . . .'

'Do you want an honest appraisal from me? Or just some crap like, "Ohhh, I wish I'd done more sit-ups"?'

'Have you done *any* sit-ups?' asked Maggie.

'I did one back in the eighties, but it hurt,' said Rose. 'I would have preferred a more itinerant life. Meeting crazy people, singing for my supper, writing songs. I wanted to live on the edge:

a few drugs, tattoos, doomed love affairs. But I got pregnant and stuffed it up.'

'As an authority on the doomed love affair, it's all very well in novels and movies,' said Fran. 'It wouldn't be my first choice.'

'And right now, you'd be wishing you had a retirement fund,' added Maggie.

'It's the fact that I've become middle-class, middle-aged and middle-of-the-road that kind of sickens me. Our generation dreamed of peace and freedom, then we got selfish and greedy. We were going to save the world, then did nothing but mess it up. Now we're the generation that moans endlessly about having to treat other people with respect. If I hear that phrase "political correctness gone mad" one more time, I will actually go mad.'

'Okay, Rose, I agree – but getting back to your situation, the fact is that even rock'n'roll chicks end up middle-aged. It's un-avoidable,' Maggie pointed out.

'I've become the sort of person I always despised,' continued Rose. 'I can't put it down to the mistake of getting pregnant. That was a classic case of self-sabotage.'

'You could still have had a singing career,' said Fran. 'After you had Elliot.'

'Seriously? Living with Peter is like having two extra children. I couldn't leave Elliot with him in the evenings without worrying he'd put the baby outside instead of the cat. We couldn't afford sitters. At that stage, Mum and Dad were still getting pissed every night; I didn't trust them.'

Rose pondered the idea for a while. 'I don't like it being my own fault but . . . it's true. I lacked the commitment, and the discipline.'

'We did believe that things would magically happen for us back then,' said Fran. 'That our talent would be "discovered" – you know, like Twiggy or Marianne Faithfull. That was how women became successful. They were discovered by men.'

'Conquered and colonised like a foreign nation,' agreed Rose. 'And how many times did it destroy those women?'

'Would I have married Kristo, if I knew then what I know now? I'm not sure. I saw myself with three or four children, house, garden, dogs. Living in the country. Just the usual things everyone hopes for – apart from Rose. I never wanted to be an accountant. Dad pushed that agenda. I wanted a simple life and ended up with a horribly complicated one.'

'Fifty-nine years on this earth and life's bound to get messy,' said Rose. 'When you say the "country" I think you mean more trees and fewer neighbours. People who do actually live in the country work their butts off to survive – or are poor – or both. There's no geographical shortcut.'

'My life isn't complicated,' said Fran. 'It's empty and boring. And lonely. At least you have people you can subtract from the equation. Additions are harder to arrange. People tell me I'm too fussy, but, if anything, I haven't been fussy enough.'

Maggie nodded. 'We make decisions in the moment that we end up regretting down the track.'

'Oh, my giddy aunt. Let's lighten up. Do you know what I really wish?' asked Rose. 'I wish I'd done more than one sit-up.'

Fran laughed. 'I wish I hadn't plucked my eyebrows when I was young. Who knew they'd come back into fashion?'

'You could get the full Frida tattooed on now if you want,' suggested Rose. 'With sideburns to match.'

'I wish I hadn't spent so much time worrying about my

appearance,' said Maggie. 'Living up to my reputation as the glamorous one. It's made getting old even harder, now I'm losing that battle.'

Rose glanced across at her with a smile. 'You haven't lost the battle yet, baby.'

Maggie laughed out loud. 'In the eye of the beholder, but thank you.'

By early evening, they were lost in industrial car parks, following a confusing array of signs to Porto di Brindisi in search of the ferry terminal. Caught up in the spirit of adventure, it only now occurred to them that the ferries might be booked out for weeks ahead. In any case, they didn't hold out much hope of buying tickets today but, as it turned out, the terminal office was open until late in the evening. The ferry evidently wasn't as popular as it had been before the days of cheap flights, and they managed to get tickets for themselves and the Beast for the midday sailing the next day. They were giddy with relief that things were going their way.

There was a bar in the terminal, but the cost of the tickets meant they were down to their last hundred euros, so there were no funds for dinner or even a celebratory drink. Instead, they sat side by side along the back of the van and ate the last of the apples, carrots and tomatoes for dinner. They used the terminal bathroom for their evening ablutions and found a spot in the parking area between two semitrailers to park the Beast for the night.

While Maggie slept in the back of the van, Fran and Rose sat up front and discussed the money situation, which was now looking grim.

'I think we should just soldier on and, if we really get stuck, I could have Peter send money by Western Union.' Rose paused, thinking about that plan for a few minutes. 'Probably not Peter, but Kristo might be able to do that for us. Or, absolute worst-case scenario, Elliot. Anyway, we'll sort something out.'

'So . . . do you think she's over the worst?' whispered Fran, with a nod towards Maggie. 'She seems fine now. Better than ever. Like she's come through the fire.'

'Bright as a bloody button. I don't know what to say. I'm just relieved.'

'Do you think we should do this?' asked Fran. 'Once we take the ferry, it's a point of no return. It will be much harder to get back.'

'I suppose we could still drive to Rome while she's asleep,' said Rose. 'No. Let's chance it. Oh, Fran, what a horrible mess this trip has been. If I'd had any idea . . . I am such an idiot. I actually thought we would go off and find ourselves, like *Eat Pray Love* – the trilogy. Instead it's been more like *Drink Fight Drown*.'

'Nearly drown,' corrected Fran gently. 'Don't give up hope yet, Rosie. Something good can still come out of it.'

As Fran lay waiting for sleep, her mind drifted back to the conversation with Sofia and how content she had felt during those hours of quiet discussion. It was rare to meet someone so full of energy and interest and curiosity. And refreshing to meet someone new, which so rarely happened these days – and a kindred spirit as well. Fran had promised to get in touch when she got back home. But she knew she wouldn't. It just wasn't her.

The idea of home seemed remote right now. She tried to imagine Louis studying her plant notes, pampering the greenery, and the cat, and generally taking his responsibilities seriously.

It was a struggle to imagine – easier were visions of a starving cat and withered plants.

They woke to a pearlescent dawn illuminating the acres of cracked concrete surrounding them, beyond which, the Adriatic, with its blue horizon, was reassuringly calm.

All three had slept well and were in good spirits. They made use of the bathrooms in the terminal, bought some fresh bread rolls for breakfast and made coffee on the stove.

They were standing beside the van, in the queue waiting to board, when Rose said, 'Is that someone waving at us?' Two people further down the queue were both flapping their arms madly and now walking towards them. 'Oh, how funny. It's Don and Ann!'

'It's the beauties and the Beast!' called Don with a grin, as they approached.

They all embraced like old friends. 'Fancy seeing you here!' said Ann. 'You never mentioned going to the Greek islands.'

'We didn't know,' said Maggie. 'It's a surprise to us too.'

'And you managed to get tickets?' asked Don, seemingly put out. 'Just like that? We booked months ago.'

'That's how we roll,' said Rose. 'Spontaneous.'

Maggie smiled. 'It's lovely to see you again. We only managed pole position at the front because we stayed all night in the car park.'

'I'm not sure that was wise,' said Don with a disapproving frown.

Ann concurred. 'According to our guidebook, Brindisi is dangerous at night.'

'We had no trouble at all, apart from a few truck drivers gawping at us,' said Rose.

'Would you ladies like me to drive the Beast onto the ship for you? It can be a bit hairy getting on the ferry,' offered Don.

He was just being chivalrous, but Rose was unnecessarily abrupt with him. Bristling with indignation, she pointed out that she had been driving for forty years and would be perfectly fine. So it was unfortunate that, distracted by her outrage, she managed to crush half-a-dozen traffic cones boarding the ferry. Fran and Maggie were amused by the squashing of the first cone, but by the fifth, much to Rose's annoyance, they were helpless with laughter.

The sea was calm and the sun warm, making the six-hour trip a relatively pleasant experience. Don redeemed himself by buying a couple of bottles of wine at the bar, and they filled up on the set menu pasta lunch.

By the time the Ionian Islands came into view, it was twilight. Grey wings of cloud floated across a tangerine sunset reflected in the sea. There was something so familiar about the quality of the light, the scattering of islands and rocky outcrops. Fran felt a shiver of anticipation. Everything suddenly felt right – they were meant to be here.

Don and Ann had booked in to a camping ground north of Corfu township. After a brief discussion, Maggie, Fran and Rose agreed that they would take the coast road, following Don and Ann, in the hope that there would be a site available this early in the season.

Both parties made a quick stop at a supermarket on the main road to buy a few provisions. Back in the van, Rose questioned whether this was the right plan.

'Since we don't have a plan, we might as well go with them.

If there's no room in the camp, then we can do something else,' said Maggie.

Rose fired up the Beast. 'The cost of the camp might be an issue for us.'

'Do you think we could borrow a little bit from Don and Ann?' asked Fran, as they set off following the Peugeot.

Maggie wasn't keen. 'Hmm, might be stretching the friendship.'

'I just don't like the way they have sort of adopted us,' said Rose.

Maggie sighed. 'Rose, you are being contrary. They're being friendly and helpful.'

Fran secretly liked the idea that there was someone else looking out for them too.

'That's my point. We don't need help. They think we're three old hens on the loose who need a man to keep an eye on them. I can imagine them going home and telling hygge stories about how they played the good samaritans to these daft old —'

'It's not pronounced hoo-gee, it's hue-gah,' corrected Maggie.

'I doubt they think we're daft or old, given they're older than us. That's *your* perception,' said Fran. 'You're being over-sensitive.'

Rose shrugged and obediently followed the Peugeot through the industrial outskirts of town and into the darkness of the countryside.

'I just think,' said Rose, when everyone had forgotten the conversation, 'we came here to go on *our* journey. Now we're being corralled into someone else's.'

'We can continue on our journey tomorrow, Rose,' said Maggie, wearily.

They were silent for a while, as though hypnotised by the rear lights of the Peugeot up ahead. When they came to a fork in the road, the Peugeot continued along the main road which veered to the right, but Rose swung off to the left.

Maggie grabbed the door handle to stop the door flying open. 'What in hell are you doing, Rose?!'

'I saw a sign back there to Agios Papadakis! I don't want to be dragged around like a bunch of pensioners on a tour. The chooks are going free-range! Yodel-a-ee-he-he-ee, yodel-la-he —'

'Rose! Stop!' shouted Maggie.

'I can't stop *here*, it's dangerous — just wait!' Rose changed gear and put her foot down to tackle the hill ahead.

'Not the van, you nitwit! The *yodelling*! You agreed no yodelling.'

Fran doubled up with silent laughter. 'Really? Why?'

'It's embarrassing; makes me cringe. Look, Rose, we don't have a place to stay. It's late. And what will Don and Ann think?'

'Here's the thing, *ladies*,' said Rose. 'We're never going to see them again! So who gives a flying fuck what they think? They can go on the banned topic list, as far as I'm concerned.'

Fran braced herself for another blow-up, but it didn't come.

'Well, we've lost them now anyway,' said Maggie. 'If we can't find Agios Papadakis, there's plenty of places we can stop until morning.'

The Beast ploughed on into the dark countryside. Apart from the occasional light visible from a distant house, there were no signs of life. No more road signs. It was difficult to know if they were still headed in the right direction but Rose seemed confident and kept driving. After an hour or so, they chugged up a long steep hill, the Beast growling with the strain. When they reached the summit, Maggie suggested they stop to try to work out where they were.

Rose suggested Fran get up on the roof. She might be able to see if there was a village or something nearby.

It was tricky with the van's sloping bonnet. She either had to stand on the driver's seat and try to scramble up, or be given a leg-up. They decided on the latter, joined hands and, with some difficulty, wrested Fran up until she was half on the roof and could pull herself up.

'Just stay still. Don't walk around. And don't fall off,' instructed Rose, unnecessarily.

It was quite pleasant up there with the soft night around her, the sound of insects and chirping cicadas. In the distance beyond, she could see a thread of lights and the moon reflecting off water; a village beside the sea. Getting down off the roof, she slid backwards on her belly while Rose guided her foot to the windowsill and they lifted her down to safety.

Off they went again, down a long twisting road with hairpin bends, another hill and another valley and over the next rise they finally saw the twinkling lights of the village below. They cruised down the hill towards the silken sea beyond.

As they entered the village, the road swung sharply to the right. Rose misjudged and missed the turn and drove straight onto the beach. They all felt the loss of traction as the van slid onto the sand. Rose crunched into reverse, but it only buried the wheels deeper in the sand. She stopped and switched off the engine.

It was almost midnight now. The village was asleep. Their arrival had gone unnoticed. They each got slowly out of the van and stood looking out to the gentle swell of silver sea.

And Rose said softly, 'We're back.'

Chapter Seventeen

As the sun rose, the sky and water were shot through with pink and gold. Maggie sat on the sand watching the changing light. The only sound to be heard was the water rippling gently on the shore. She felt cold and stiff. It had been unbearably hot in the van, and she had dragged her bedding outside sometime during the night. When she lay down in the cool night air, the sand had felt soft. Now it brought back memories of a futon she owned back in the eighties – hard and unyielding.

She pulled off her track top, tiptoed into the water in her T-shirt and undies, and dived under the surface. It was cool and refreshing, stripping the sweat and grime that had accumulated on her skin in the last few days. She pushed her fingers through her hair. It felt good. She felt that sense of lightness again.

As she floated on the surface, watching the golden dawn dissolve into a blue day, all the tension drained from her body. All she could hear was her own breath. Glancing down, she could see silver fish darting beneath the surface of the water.

How strange to find herself back on this beach where, every

night for a month, they had rolled out their sleeping bags and slept under the stars. Young and free, without responsibilities. Those long golden days had remained with her all these years.

Floating peacefully, she was vaguely aware of some commotion in the water, like a large fish thrashing on a hook, or an outboard motor in the distance. It came closer, but before she could find her footing, Rose's distressed face appeared.

There was a beat, then Rose, who was wearing her pyjamas, said, 'Hi!'

Maggie let her feet drop gently to the sandy bottom and stood up. 'Hi.'

Rose stared at her for a moment. 'I was worried . . .'

'Sorry, Rose, I didn't think . . .'

'No, no – it's fine! I was being ridiculous.'

'No, you weren't . . .'

They began to laugh for reasons neither could explain and waded back to the shore together. Two elderly men, one leaning on a walking stick, stood in the street and watched them. Aware she was a sight in her wet T-shirt and underwear, Maggie picked up her sleeping bag and wrapped it around her. She gave the men a friendly wave and called out *'Yassou! Kaliméra!'* She tried to think of another phrase in Greek but nothing appropriate came to mind. The men gave no indication they'd heard her, and were clearly in no hurry to leave.

Rose pulled the side door of the van open, waking Fran, who sat up and stared at them both in their soaking clothes. 'You're keen,' she said. Getting out of the van, she stood on the beach and stretched her arms out wide. 'Best parking spot ever, Rose!'

Rose and Maggie climbed in the back, peeled off their wet things and threw them over into the front seat. They dug around, looking for their clothes. Everything was now mixed up in a tangle.

'Do you think they'll get the police onto us for parking on the beach?' asked Maggie, pulling on her undies.

'More likely send someone with a tractor to tow us off,' said Rose, struggling to get her damp body into a T-shirt. 'Even if someone called the police, I doubt they'd come for a day or two.'

'What the hell? Either my bra has shrunk or my boobs are expanding,' said Maggie, attempting to push her breasts into a black bra.

'That's mine,' said Rose. 'I've been looking for it for days.'

Maggie pulled it off with relief. 'Where's mine, then?'

Rose dived into the mess of clothes among the bedding, pulled out a large-cup bra and gave it a twirl. Maggie snatched it from her and put it on. 'Ah, that's better.'

They set off along the narrow road beside the beach towards the village in search of breakfast. The main part of the village was a straggle of houses with rooms and apartments for holiday rental, and a mini-mart. Last time they were here there were no roads; they'd had to leave the Kombi at the top of the cliff and walk down the rough goat track.

The entire village had consisted of one taverna – the Blue Moon Bar and Restaurant, where they had eaten all their meals, and Rose had worked in the kitchen – and half-a-dozen houses, which were mostly unfinished with steel reinforcing rods sticking out of the roof where a second storey was intended. Now there was a small settlement but it seemed as though whatever affluence had once washed through here had dried up again. Everything looked neglected: paint peeling, black mildew infesting walls. Weeds had grown over discarded building materials, as if the decline had set in before the boom took hold. Or perhaps it never quite reached this quiet corner of the island.

'It was pretty basic when we were here,' remarked Maggie. 'But now it all looks really run-down.'

'At least there isn't a resort here,' said Fran. 'That's one good thing.'

'But look at that,' said Rose. 'The taverna is still here!'

The Blue Moon taverna was still operating and open for breakfast. On the terrace overlooking the beach, the mismatched collection of old vinyl kitchen chairs and wobbly tables had been replaced by uniform plastic tables and chairs. The rickety metal pergola that covered the terrace was now a professionally built timber structure covered in a froth of crimson bougainvillea.

There were a few customers at the tables, drinking coffee or eating breakfast. The two old men they'd seen earlier at the beach sat at a corner table with another elderly man, rotund and voluble with a walrus moustache.

Maggie, Fran and Rose took the table nearest to the beach. After a while, a scowling young woman came out to take their order. They each ordered the same breakfast they had eaten here every day for that month.

Maggie looked around. 'It's still nice. But I liked the way everything was so rough and ready back then.' The plastic table cloth felt sticky. She glanced around for a napkin to wipe it down then decided to let it go.

'The kitchen was certainly rough and ready,' said Rose. 'I wonder what happened to Spyros. He's probably long gone.'

Fran disagreed. 'Not necessarily. We thought he was old back then but he was probably only forty.'

The waitress returned with their order. Maggie realised they'd missed dinner last night and she was starving. The yoghurt was tart and creamy, the fruit was fresh and the coffee thick and grainy – just as she remembered it.

'Wow,' said Rose, licking her spoon. 'This takes me back.'

'We need to make some plans,' said Fran. 'We have about fifty euro left. So, basically, we don't have enough to get to Rome, assuming we're going to fly direct from here. I don't even know what the fares would be.'

Rose shook her head. 'Let's see if we can use a computer later and find out.'

'We've got twelve days,' said Maggie. 'No panic.'

The waitress sauntered out to ask if they wanted anything else. When Rose explained that she had worked there forty years earlier, the girl could not have been less interested.

'We lived here on the beach,' said Maggie, trying to spark her interest. 'We ate here every day. A man called Spyros owned it back then.'

'He's my grandfather,' the girl said unhappily. She nodded towards the table with the three old men. 'The fat one.'

'Really? He probably won't remember us,' said Rose, getting up. The girl shrugged and cleared their dishes as Rose went over to the old men's table and greeted him, '*Kaliméra*, Spyros.'

Spyros turned and nodded amicably. '*Kaliméra*. Something not good?'

'No, all good. You won't remember us. We were here in 1978,' she said. 'The Australians. Rose – I worked here in the kitchen for you.' Rose beckoned Fran and Maggie over.

He looked at them through narrowed eyes. 'Yes . . . yes . . . the "Aussie sheilas"!' He waggled a gnarled finger at Maggie. 'I remember. Is the beautiful one.' His gaze shifted to Fran. 'This one, she's quiet.' His eyes rested on Rose. He frowned. 'This the crazy one.'

Rose grinned, evidently delighted by this description.

'And me, now the fat one!' Spyros said. 'Old one. Eighty-three. I was young man when you here.'

One of the other men at the table made a comment, gesturing towards the van further down the beach. Spyros waved his concerns away. 'Sit. We get tractor later.'

Dismissing his two friends, who got up resentfully and wandered off, Spyros pulled an extra chair over. As the three women sat down, he called to his granddaughter to bring more coffee.

'This Delphine. Is good girl.' He gave her an affectionate pat on the back as she transferred the coffee cups from the tray to the table.

Delphine gave them a weak smile. Maggie thanked her and asked, 'You work here in the summer, Delphine?'

'Not usually. I'm at university in Athens. My mother runs the place now. She comes at the start of summer but my sister just had a baby, so she had to go back to Athens and I had to come instead.'

'So all your friends are having fun in Athens and you're here dealing with the tourists.' Maggie smiled.

Delphine shrugged. 'It's okay. The beach is nice.' She walked slowly back inside, as though she'd rather be anywhere but here.

'So, you come and see me from *Afstralia*!' Spyros grinned. 'Is good. See this place now, very modern, very nice. But is different now. Then, was one taverna. That me. Now is many . . .' He gestured up the hill to the larger, more established village of Palaka.

'Restaurant, club, everything. People come here in the day but in the night is not enough busy. Where you stay?'

'We were going to stay in our van,' said Rose, with a nod towards the Beast.

Spyros shrugged. He pointed to the parking area. 'Put here. Use bathrooms. If you want. No charge.'

'That parking was your vineyard when we were last here,' Fran reminded him. 'There were no cars down here on the beach then.'

'Now cars come here. They need parking. Why stay in van? Is hot. Too many womans. My sister has room in the house. Very cheap.'

'We can't even afford cheap right now,' Rose told him. 'We're broke.'

He looked bewildered. 'You come with no money?'

'We were robbed,' explained Maggie.

He shrugged philosophically. 'You married? Children?'

'Maggie here married a Greek,' offered Rose.

Spyros's face lit up. 'You married Greek man? Is good man?' Maggie nodded. 'Yes, he is a good man.'

'He not here?' he asked with a frown.

'He's at home, working,' said Maggie, and felt herself blush with guilt.

Spyros wanted all the details: how many children they had, the names of the children, what their husbands did. He called Delphine to bring some baklava, which was sticky and stale, and they talked about the past and present, the changes – good and bad – that had arrived in Agios Papadakis in the past decades.

There had been around twenty people sleeping on the beach that summer of '78. Brits, Germans, Americans and Australians:

an international community of travellers. Everyone ate at the Blue Moon. There was no need for a menu. Spyros only cooked one dish each night: either meatballs, moussaka or fish.

After dinner, they would buy wine from him to take down onto the beach. His question was always the same, 'How many peoples?' He would fill a demijohn, encased in a plastic basket, with enough wine to keep them happy but not enough to cause him grief in the early hours with drunken singing or naked running through his vineyard.

It occurred to Maggie that although that time was special for them, for Spyros, every summer brought a new menagerie of young travellers – backpackers and hippies from around the world – all with the same dream of escaping the realities of adulthood for as long as possible. This was his world, and life was hard for him. Between summers there would be no income at all.

'What Greek food you cooking?' Spyros asked Maggie.

Maggie listed them. 'Dolmades, souvlaki, tzatziki, spanakopita, baklava.'

'Delphine, she not good cook. People complaining. You help her in the kitchen. Stay in my sister house. No charge.'

'We're not here very long,' said Maggie. 'I'm not sure how much I can help.'

'Is okay.' He shrugged. 'Maybe you teach her. Or not. My daughter come in . . . hmm . . . maybe one week. Is very good cook.'

'It would be nice to have a room to sleep in,' ventured Fran hopefully.

Maggie felt there was room for negotiation. 'We're really here on holiday, Spyros. It's a lot to give up to work in a kitchen.'

Spyros was unfazed. 'Is very nice room. You have no money.'

'I am a very, very good cook. My baklava . . .'

'Okay. I pay you five euro for the hour *and* the room of my sister.'

Maggie gave it some thought. 'Plus all our meals.'

'Buh, the crazy one eats like man . . .' He then scrutinised Fran, as if assessing her appetite. 'With the little one, is okay.'

'I'll do lunch and dinner service only. Not breakfast,' insisted Maggie.

'Okay, okay, *arketá* – enough. You eat tonight. My guest. Work tomorrow.'

Maggie shook his hand. 'And now we need a tractor.'

Spyros's sister, Mrs Halikiopoulos (immediately nicknamed Mrs Helicopters) was a stout woman dressed in mourning black, with a shock of white hair, who spoke no English. The room, dubbed the Helipad, was spartan as a cell, with whitewashed walls, pale floor tiles and four narrow single beds, one against each wall, but the windows opened wide and looked out to the sea.

The bathroom was basic but clean. The bath had an inbuilt seat, but no hot water. 'I'm just grateful to have a bed and running water. It could have been worse. We might have had to carry buckets from a well,' said Rose.

'I can't believe you still can't flush toilet paper here,' said Maggie. 'They're used to it, I guess.'

'Let's hope no one gets the runs,' said Rose, pulling a face.

Early in the afternoon, Spyros sent a man with a tractor who towed the Beast off the sand. They were able to park it in the yard outside, unpack and settle into their new home. They had cold baths and lay on their beds in the afternoon heat and reassessed the situation.

'In summary, team, good progress,' said Maggie. 'We have a roof over our heads and food in our bellies. If we can get online, maybe we should order another lot of replacement cards?'

'Let's not get them sent here,' said Rose. 'I doubt they have a daily mail delivery.'

'Even if we get thirty hours of work, I don't think that's going to cover our airfares. Besides, it will be in cash. I could get Kristo to wire some money or he could even book our flights to Rome,' suggested Maggie. 'Spyros is bound to know someone who wants the Beast.'

'Good on you for taking the cooking challenge, Mags,' said Fran. 'It got us out of a spot.'

'I'll probably regret it. I've never worked in a restaurant kitchen but I'd like to give it a go.'

'We'll be at your side. It's not going to be just down to you,' Rose reassured her. 'Only having one pair of glasses could be a nuisance. We'll make it work. Hey, do you remember when I worked for Spyros, he gave me three pieces of advice? "Don't wear revealing clothing, don't sleep with the local boys and don't sunbathe nude."'

Maggie laughed. 'I don't think we're at risk this time around.'

'Must have gone right over my head,' admitted Fran. 'I wandered around in a bikini all day – I remember an old woman rushing out of her house with a blanket to cover me. I slept with a very handsome Greek boy from up the hill and sunbathed naked with the Germans.'

Rose shook her head in admiration. 'Bloody Fran, eh? The quiet achiever.'

*

On the way to the Blue Moon that evening, they noticed the mini-mart had a sign in the window offering internet access. Rose and Fran waited outside while Maggie went in and made a voice call on the computer to Kristo. The shop was empty, apart from a teenage boy behind the counter. He was staring at his phone, but his interest was piqued when Kristo began the conversation by shouting, 'Where the fuck are you?! I am out of my fucking mind!'

'Kristo, please. Stop it. And stop swearing. There is no reason for you to be out of your mind. I'm really quite capable —'

'I haven't heard from you in three days. Where are you?!'

'Corfu. It's a long story. We bought a van and —'

'You bought a van!' he squeaked. 'Are you a gypsy now? Or a hippie? Who's there with you? What in the hell is going on?'

'Kristo, stop! You're making things so much worse.'

'What could get worse than my wife going *nuts* and roaming around the world thinking she's a teenager with no responsibilities?'

'Okay, I get it. Right now, I need you to send me some money —'

'What? You just said you were capable. I know what you've been doing, Maggie. Yannis is not as stupid as he looks. He's worked it out. I didn't believe it. He showed me the evidence of what you've been up to. Evidence, Maggie! We need to talk. You need to get back here.'

Maggie felt breathless with panic, wanting nothing more than to get off the call. 'I'm going to go now, Kristo. I can't talk to you like this . . .'

'Okay. Okay. I've calmed down. A bit. I want you to come home now. I've had enough. More than enough. I can't deal with any more.'

Maggie took deep breaths and tried to calm herself. The teenage boy behind the counter had given up any pretence of looking at his phone.

'We've run out of money, and we had the new cards delivered to the hotel in Rome.'

'Well, that was stupid. Why didn't you go to Rome? How in the hell are you living without money?'

Maggie knew this wasn't going to go well. 'I've got a job cooking in a taverna.'

Silence. Then a sob, either laughing or crying, and the line went dead.

Maggie went outside and reported that there would be no funds coming from Kristo at this point. Rose went in to call Peter but there was no answer, so she sent a message to Max.

'I could try Elliot,' Rose said as they walked down to the taverna. 'I've never asked Elliot and Prya for help. I've been trying to give them the impression that I've got my shit together. I don't really want to undo all my good work.'

'Desperate times,' said Maggie unsympathetically. 'If I've got to put up with Kristo bellowing at me, that's no big deal.'

'Why is he bellowing?' asked Fran worriedly.

Maggie brushed off her concern. 'It's just what he does. It doesn't take much. He'll be fine when he calms down. I think.'

'I wish I could do something,' said Fran. 'I don't know how to call Louis from a computer. And I'm not sure he would help, anyway. He wouldn't know how to wire money or anything like that.'

Maggie was only vaguely aware that the sky was streaked with pink and gold. She barely heard the twittering of thousands of swallows swarming in the trees. She regretted calling Kristo.

The Blue Moon was only half full when they got there. Apart from Delphine, there were two boys of about twelve helping with preparations and serving tables. Spyros was enthroned at his corner table, drinking ouzo and handling the financial transactions. He gave them a wave. *'Yiá sas, kalispera!* Sit anywhere, Aussie sheilas!'

The laminated menus were sticky with fingerprints. The plastic cloths on the tables were limp with age. The place was run-down but no more run-down than many others like it. 'Was it always grubby like this?' asked Maggie as they looked over the menu.

Rose nodded. 'There weren't any table cloths or menus but it was clean; probably Delphine being a bit slack with the cleaning. She's only young.'

'I think our standards were lower back then,' said Fran. 'More accepting of squalor.'

Maggie laughed. 'We had the luxury of creating squalor when we were young. Since then, we've spent our days managing other people's and we're less tolerant.'

Maggie ordered the moussaka, which turned out to be lukewarm on the outside and cold in the middle. Fran had the Greek salad, limp but edible. Rose went for the fish of the day, which came encased in a thick batter with lukewarm chips.

'I can see why they're not busy,' whispered Rose. 'I get that the Greeks like their food lukewarm, but cold chips?'

Spyros sent over some baklava, which had the consistency of old newspapers soaked in sticky sugar, probably made in a factory on the mainland. Maggie usually made her own filo, but that was probably impractical here. And at that pay rate, she wasn't planning to make it any harder than it needed to be.

Earlier in the day, Spyros had told them that the kitchen had been completely updated. Once the food service was over, they went to have a proper look at it. That update was a long time ago. Rose said it was much as she remembered it: a large alcove in the back of the restaurant with sink, oven, gas burners, deep fryer and bench for preparation. The only new addition was a microwave. The two boys, Angelos and George, were washing up by hand, no dishwasher. There was no cold room, just three rusting fridges lined up in a makeshift room leading off the kitchen to the yard. The freezer was stacked with foil containers of moussaka and frozen fish. One of Rose's jobs had been grating the cucumbers to make the tzatziki dip fresh every day. These days it was in a bulk container in the fridge. Worse was the disorganisation in the kitchen: open shelves with odd-shaped bowls and pots stacked in teetering piles, and packets of paper serviettes spilling out under benches.

On the walk back to the Helipad, Maggie said, 'This could be a nightmare. Delphine doesn't seem at all cooperative. I have absolutely no idea how to cook for a restaurant.'

'I wouldn't worry about it, Mags. Half the restaurants in the world have no clue. Basically you cook food, hand it out, get money. When I worked there, Spyros did all the cooking and shouting. His wife, Phyllis, pulled it all together. I did the prep and dips, cut up bread and washed up. And flirted with the patrons, obviously.'

'It's not as simple now there's a printed menu,' argued Maggie. 'There's an expectation.'

'We'll be there,' Fran reassured her. 'We're all in this together.'

'Spyros is getting quite the deal, all three of us for five euro an hour,' said Rose. 'You know that's like two dollars fifty an hour each?'

'Plus food and board,' Fran reminded her. 'And we'd be in trouble now without that.'

'Well, let me tell you, the crazy one is going to eat like *two* men.'

Rose had planned to try Peter again, but the shop was closed.

'Next time he's open, let's check airfares to Rome. It must be only an hour or two from here,' said Maggie. 'Maybe not that expensive.'

Rose linked arms with her. 'Mag, let's put our energies into being here, not just trying to escape. It will work out somehow. I'll handle it.'

Maggie agreed. Kristo had rattled her and she wondered exactly what Yannis had found. She had been so careful. It was impossible to imagine Yannis keeping her deception to himself. There would be repercussions. Possibly serious ones.

Fran and Rose were asleep within minutes but Maggie felt restless and unsettled. She got up and went to the open window. Leaning on the sill, she looked out into the night. The village was dark, the night sky alive with stars. The only sounds were crickets, cicadas and the odd bird call, short and sharp. Perhaps owls or night birds out hunting. There was a tall cypress tree beside the house, giving off the fresh smell of pine. She thought about how little they had here, and how much she had at home. She had everything she had ever wanted, apart from time to stop and smell the night.

She felt an unexpected pang of homesickness, wishing Kristo was here with her. Not the shouting, cursing Kristo but the gentle, loving one. The memory of their time in Kythera played in her head like a romantic movie with long walks at sunset, tender kisses and hand-holding. Times that could never be recaptured. They were long gone.

Chapter Eighteen

At breakfast, Spyros's corner table was empty. Rose had talked to Delphine about supplies the evening before and been told that Spyros would go into town first thing in the morning and pick everything up for the next three days. Everything seemed to be running to plan, except that Delphine was nowhere to be found.

A woman they hadn't seen before was running the kitchen. Maggie went in and introduced herself in Greek. The woman said her name was Jocasta and she did not speak English. Remembering the casual staffing arrangements of the past, Rose suggested Maggie ask about Delphine. Jocasta went into a detailed explanation; the only word Rose recognised was *Athena*. Delphine had gone back to Athens? Maggie did her best with the language until she ran out of steam. 'She's gone back to Athens. A boyfriend, I think.'

'We should have seen that coming,' said Rose. 'It might even be easier without her.'

Maggie wasn't so sure. 'I just wish she'd told us, so we could be better prepared.'

Jocasta brought fruit and yoghurt out to the terrace for them. They ate in silence, gazing out across the blue bay.

'The condemned ate a hearty breakfast,' said Maggie, finally.

'I'm not sure you could call yoghurt and fruit "hearty",' said Fran.

'You don't disagree with the condemned part, I notice,' said Rose. 'We'll be fine. The only thing is that when Spyros goes to town for supplies, he's gone for hours. He spends an hour on the shopping and three drinking coffee and catching up with all his buddies.'

Angelos and George turned up, both with backpacks, and stood waiting beside the road. Within minutes they were picked up by a school bus that headed off up the hill.

'So that's them gone too,' said Maggie. 'Not that I was relying on a couple of twelve-year-olds to save us.'

'What's the worst that can happen?' asked Rose. 'We get fired?' She laughed to demonstrate how absurd that was, but neither Fran nor Maggie was amused. Rose felt reasonably relaxed about the job ahead. Both she and Fran had worked as kitchen hands and waited tables, even if it was a few decades ago.

They had barely finished their breakfast when Jocasta came outside and beckoned to them. Dragging themselves away from the glorious morning, they entered the dark realms of the kitchen, where, after a quick tour, Jocasta handed over and went off to her job cleaning holiday flats.

Maggie suggested that the first thing they should do was an audit, so they knew what ingredients they had to work with and didn't get caught out. Since last night, several large iceberg lettuces had appeared in the fridge, probably from Spryos's garden, along with a bucket of fresh tomatoes and figs. There was a vat of olives and two industrial-sized blocks of feta in tubs of brine, and plastic containers of dolmades. Frozen fish and chips, moussaka, pork and beef mince and pastry. No chicken to be found anywhere.

Rose gave Maggie a comforting pat on the back. 'Don't fret. There'll be a dozen for lunch, maximum. That's half the number that come to your place for Easter, and you don't have Yia-yiá running interference.'

It was agreed that Fran would help in the kitchen because Maggie needed the reading glasses for health and safety reasons. Rose would have to take down the orders in her largest printing. There were no credit card facilities to worry about. The cash was kept in a box under the counter.

The first customers to arrive for lunch were a casually, but expensively, dressed couple in their forties, tanned and blond, the type who cruised the islands in their own yacht. They were the sort of people that Rose found intimidating. Meaning to give the impression of professionalism, she bounded out and announced brightly, 'The chicken's off.'

They both looked up in alarm and she realised it sounded like salmonella chicken was the *plat du jour*.

'Not *off* off,' she explained helpfully. 'It's not on the menu.'

'Yes, it is,' said the man, pointing to it seemingly without irony. 'I see it here.' His English was too precise for a first language. He was obviously one of the more pedantic nationalities. Or was he actually trying to be funny?

'We've run out, is what I'm trying to say.' Rose's gaze was drawn to the sea, wishing she was in it, instead of dealing with this character.

'How can you have run out?' asked the woman, lowering her designer sunglasses as she indicated the empty tables. 'We're the first here.'

'Look,' said Rose, with a sigh. 'We don't have chicken. All right? Just pick something else.'

'We'll need a moment to think about it,' the man said smoothly.

Rose nodded, relieved they were all on the same menu now, but when she came back with the bread basket, the table was empty. No great loss. They were the sort of people who would whinge about everything anyway.

The terrace gradually began to fill with customers and Rose rushed back and forth with orders, increasingly flustered. Even though she wrote the orders in large print, her arm wasn't long enough to read it back with any accuracy. Every time she walked into the kitchen, she instantly forgot why she was there. She constantly forgot bread or water and who had ordered what.

No one seemed to mind too much. In fact, a tour group of middle-aged Brits, who had arrived in a minibus, found her antics highly amusing. When she practically ran out to the terrace with a forgotten order, some lark mimed playing the violin while humming a tune that made the whole table erupt with laughter. It was only when they started addressing Rose as Manuel that she realised it was the theme from *Fawlty Towers*. Unamused at first, she got her own back by responding with '¿*Qué?*' every time they asked for something, to uproarious laughter from the group who, when they departed, left a generous tip.

Other patrons were more compassionate: a young French couple with a baby, who were staying locally, helped her pick up cutlery that cascaded off a stack of plates. Three young German backpackers smiled encouragingly and thanked her profusely when she got their order right. She'd set the bar so low at the outset, people became increasingly grateful just to be fed.

Anyway, being front-of-house was preferable to being stuck in the poky, airless kitchen where Fran and Maggie, dripping sweat, worked frantically side by side, chopping, frying and microwaving. Spyros only added to the confusion by arriving in the early afternoon and restocking the kitchen, moving everything around and packing the fridge so densely it was difficult to find anything. It was late afternoon by the time they finished cleaning up. After a quick lunch, it was time to start the prep for dinner. Although Rose's feet felt like steamed puddings, she also felt invigorated, and Fran felt the same. Maggie looked wrung out but, apart from a comment about her creaking knees, made not a single complaint.

In comparison to lunch, the dinner service was easier. Spyros made out the bills, took the payments, chatted to customers and ordered Rose about – he was the ringmaster to Rose's clown act. George and Angelos magically reappeared to help with the clean-up.

Spyros and the boys left around ten. Maggie and Fran got the kitchen back in working order and Rose wiped down all the tables thoroughly, ready for the next day. When they were done, they grabbed some beers and leftovers from the fridge and sat out on the terrace in the cool night air.

'Well, that was not *Masterchef*,' said Maggie. 'But we got through it.'

'We almost operated like a well-oiled machine,' said Fran. 'Nearly nailing it.'

'Oiled being the operative word,' said Rose. 'That kitchen is coated in a thick layer of oil, like it's covered in greasy cling wrap. A fire would be an inferno. Ka-boom!'

'Let's try to not set fire to the place. We don't want to be charged with arson.'

'On top of working illegally,' added Fran. 'And having an unregistered vehicle.'

'We're becoming quite the outlaws,' said Rose happily. She gazed out over the dark sea. 'I think this place is a metaphor for life.'

'Life? Very ambitious,' said Maggie. 'Go on.'

'Out front it's all neat and tidy, and that's all most people see. Behind the scenes, it's one hot friggin' mess.'

Maggie laughed. 'One of your better metaphors, Rosie. Now we're in the thick of the operations side of things, I'm struggling to remember why this place was so idyllic that summer.'

'I've been thinking about that. It wasn't the place, or the summer,' said Fran. 'It was who we were at that time. We've been looking for something that doesn't exist any more: the elusive butterfly of youth.'

'They were our halcyon days . . . we just didn't know it at the time,' agreed Rose.

Maggie nodded. 'You're probably right. And it wasn't "paradise". We never noticed how tough life was for Spyros trying to make enough in the summer season to last the whole year. He was just one character in our self-absorbed story.'

'Yeah,' said Rose. 'But, even though it was a shit fight today, I loved being a part of it. It really took me out of myself. If I ignore my sore back and feet right now, I could almost imagine myself as twenty again. It was a blast.'

'It's not just my back hurting; every part of me aches,' said Maggie. 'But, I know what you're saying. It was a bit of a blast.'

'And when do we ever do this?' asked Fran. 'Sit by the beach and drink beer with our mates at midnight?'

'Midnight!' said Maggie. 'Come on, let's get some sleep.'

As they walked home, Rose told the story of the "off chicken" and being called Manuel, and they laughed until they cried. And then they slept.

The restaurant was now the priority and Rose was forced to stop dithering about the exit plan. First thing in the morning she made a call to Prya, and by that evening, their flights from Corfu to Rome had been booked and cash would be waiting for them at the Western Union office in town, a couple of hours' drive away.

Far from being disapproving about the muddle they had got themselves into, Prya was uncharacteristically excited about the whole adventure. 'I can't wait to hear all about it!' she said. Her enthusiasm and efficiency brought tears to Rose's eyes and she wondered why she had always been so guarded around Prya; always on her best behaviour. They talked about little Austin who, after shuffling around on his bottom for weeks, had finally got to his feet and taken his first steps. Rose promised to visit as soon as she was home.

They had ten days until their departure and with funds waiting for them in town, there was the option of leaving Agios Papadakis. But they voted unanimously, without hesitation, to stay on and see it through.

A routine soon fell into place: an early-morning swim followed by breakfast on the terrace, with just enough time for a cold bath before taking over from Jocasta and getting organised for the lunch service.

The restaurant was busier each day, and regular customers were now on first-name terms. The French couple were Maud and Julien, and their sweet baby, who was the same age as Austin, was called Ezio. It was fun chatting with these new friends and Rose found her memory improving. She was less forgetful and more efficient. The work was still exhausting but they were all getting eight solid hours of sleep every night.

There was no mirror in the Helipad, and the one in the restaurant bathroom had a strange yellow hue, so Rose had no idea how she looked, but noticed that Fran's pasty complexion had a healthier glow and Maggie was also a new, improved version of herself. Her spiky hair suited her and she'd lost some weight but not too much. Even better, Maggie was restored to her cheerful self of earlier days. As each day passed, she became more confident in managing the kitchen and pacing her work. She had found time to make fresh moussaka in the afternoons and added a lemon chicken dish to the menu. Every night there were the regulars and a few more patrons. It was obvious how pleased she was that people were coming there for her cooking.

Ten days passed in a blur. They were due to leave Agios Papadakis on the Sunday, stay the night in Corfu town where they would pick up the cash, and then fly to Rome on Monday morning.

Saturday was their last night and the Blue Moon had a full house for dinner. News of Maggie's cooking had already travelled up the hill to the village of Palaka. Spyros had done his shopping and the fridges bulged with food. Rose's only hope was that they would get through this final service without disgracing themselves and leave on a high note. Angelos and George turned up to help wait tables. Spyros had them on call, and tonight it was all hands on deck.

Rose felt on top of her game. It was fun seeing all the regulars. There was a good buzz and the kitchen was running at peak efficiency. All was well, until the gas burners suddenly went out and everything stopped.

'Ah, is the gas. Is finish,' said Spyros without surprise. He beckoned the boys to come out into the backyard and put another of the giant-sized gas bottles in place. Maggie and Fran were in limbo until the oven and stovetop were back in action. After a few minutes, Spyros came in to report that the spare gas bottle was empty and this was Delphine's fault. He would take the boys to his house to pick up the spare-spare bottle.

The entire service was on hold, dishes half-cooked and going cold. Maggie suggested offering everyone a free drink and putting on some music. Rose went from table to table explaining and apologising. She brought more tzatziki, carrot sticks and pitta bread, and a carafe of retsina for each table. She went through Spyros's limited CD collection, which consisted almost entirely of Demis Roussos, Nana Mouskouri and movie soundtracks by Vangelis; all very patriotic but not conducive to calming a hungry crowd.

Fifteen minutes later, there was no sign of Spyros. The buzz was a hungry one and the crowd was getting restless and irritable.

'Come on, Rose. You're the performer,' urged Fran. 'Go out and do a few numbers.'

Rose gave a squeak. Singing in the car or choir, or even a band, was completely different from standing out there naked and alone. Not literally naked but vocally.

Maggie was busy washing up, preparing for the rush. 'Yeah, Rosie, desperate times. Just distract them. Either sing or get your gear off. Your choice.'

'You can do it,' Fran reassured her. 'This is your time, Rose.'

Terrified as she was, Rose knew she would regret it if she bailed. She could feel herself starting to hyperventilate and forced her breathing to slow down. Bugger the ocean breath. She went behind the bar and poured herself a stiff ouzo. Knocking it back in one made her eyes water and her tongue curl like a cat jettisoning a fur ball. Fran brought her some water and between them they figured out how to switch the sound system over from CD to the microphone that Spyros used for live musicians.

Fran gave her a quick hug. 'Just relax, Rose. You'll never see these people again. Be yourself. You're wonderful.'

Rose's ears were burning with fear. She took a deep breath into her gut, and then another. Something old. Something easy. Just start. Slightly breathless at first, she launched into the first lines of 'Hallelujah', which she had sung countless times with the choir but never like this, a lone voice breaking the silence. There was an encouraging sprinkling of applause at her daring and a few people joined in the chorus. They were willing to be distracted, but not for long.

Feeling more confident, Rose switched it up with 'Dreadlock Holiday', and Fran sidled up to sing harmonies. Rose had been worried that her repertoire would dry up or she might forget the lyrics but the beauty of this gig was that it didn't matter. She could hum, she could fudge, she could screw it up – no one cared. They were just killing time.

By the time she hit the chorus of 'Gypsy', she was channelling Stevie Nicks. All fear was dispelled by an intoxicating sense of freedom as her voice barrelled out into the night beyond the light of the terrace, out to the silver sea. For a big finale, she pulled Fran and Maggie in to sing 'Aquarius'. She and Fran even remembered some of their choreographed moves. It was the song that brought everyone to their feet to dance, clap or drunkenly shout the choruses, partying like it was 1969.

With perfect theatrical timing, Spyros appeared with the boys and walked through the restaurant carrying the full tank, taking all credit for the rapturous applause. Rose wiped her sweaty hands on her apron and took a bow to the calls for an encore, but it was back to work. The gas bottle was installed, food delivered, and Rose spent the rest of the night gracefully accepting compliments. It was a blast beyond blasts.

Everyone had gone and they were ready to close up when a woman walked briskly into the restaurant and introduced herself as Katerina, Spyros's daughter. She spoke good English and they were able to ask about her new grandchild and what had become of Delphine.

'We're very grateful to you for stepping in to help,' she said. 'I didn't know that Delphine had left until I saw her in Athens. I was so angry. I thought she had left her grandfather without help. Of course, there is always someone here who can help out, but not full-time. Thank you.'

Spyros came into the kitchen and bestowed a hug on each of them. '*Efcharistó! Efcharistó! Efcharistó!* You come back again. You can sing, crazy one.'

Katerina calculated how much they were owed and paid them out in cash. Spyros asked what they planned to do with the Beast. He had a van that was smaller and in even worse shape.

'It's not registered, but it's all yours if you want it, Spyros,' Maggie told him. 'I can leave the keys with Mrs Heli . . . your sister tomorrow, when we leave.'

Then they were out in the night. The Beast was gone. The work was done. They had cash in their pockets. They were free. They had everything they needed.

Too wired to sleep, they wandered down to the empty beach. Rose was buzzing, her body tingling; she couldn't stop talking. 'What a night! It was like being in our own musical! And Frannie, gimme five, my little bonsai.' Rose flexed her shoulders and stretched her arms up towards the star-filled sky. Next thing she knew, both hands were planted firmly on the sand, her legs carving a perfect arc through the air.

'Very impressive, Rose.' Fran laughed. 'Didn't know you still had it in you.'

Rose felt she probably had another cartwheel or two in her but decided to leave it at that.

Maggie silently peeled off her cotton dress and her underwear and walked naked into the water. Rose did the same, diving under the surface, rolling around and immersing every pore, rinsing off the oil and sweat of the night. Fran joined them and they floated together, staring up at the explosion of stars in the sky, each silently meditating on this moment.

After some time, they waded out of the water, dried themselves off and pulled their clothes on. It was late but the night was still warm and the gentle lap of the water the only sound. They sat on the sand and watched small fruit bats pass, silhouetted by the light of the moon.

Maggie broke the silence. 'I'm dreading going home.' There was a long silence, followed by a deep sigh. 'I have a confession to make. I've been embezzling the company.'

Rose wasn't sure whether to laugh or not. It was so unlikely. Maggie was a paragon of honesty. 'You're not joking, are you?'

'I've been syphoning off money into a company of which I'm the sole director. Not millions, just a normal salary. A fair amount.'

Rose was confused. 'How can you embezzle your own company?'

'It's not my company. When I started, as you know, I had a job somewhere else and worked in the family business after hours – to help it get going. Then I ended up working there full-time but I've never been paid and I'm not a director.'

'Have you talked to them about it?' asked Fran. 'That seems so unfair.'

'Of course. Whenever I bring it up, the others object that Kristo and I want to double dip, trying to get more than our share . . .'

'But you work in the business,' said Rose. 'You and Kristo are doing the work of two people, not one.'

'That's not the way they see it. It's not about individuals. You look at Spyros's business: family come and go, everyone pitches in to keep it afloat. Kristo and the boys all make good money, they can't see what my problem is. None of them care that I'm trapped, that I don't have choices. Why would they? So I decided to take it, without their permission.'

'Isn't that the definition of a slave?' said Rose. 'Forced to work without payment.'

'I'm stupid for putting up with it all these years. I've got myself in the same position that Mum was in when Dad's firm went bankrupt. No money of my own.'

'All I can say is, good for you – embezzle away,' said Rose. 'Have you got a Swiss bank account or an offshore tax haven in the Cayman Islands?'

Maggie gave a dry laugh. 'Nothing as glamorous as that. The least that will happen is I have to return the money to the company. Worst case, they could prosecute me.'

'Kristo would never let that happen,' Rose reassured her.

Maggie nodded, unconvinced. 'I'm kind of glad that it's out. I'm sick of worrying about it. I was never cut out to be a criminal. I'd love to have a life without secrets. They're exhausting.'

Rose felt something rise up in her. She had kept a secret close to her heart for thirty-five years, and it had never stopped gnawing away at her. She could never be free of the guilt. Each year that passed only made it worse. If she was ever going to share it, now was the time.

'I have a confession too,' Rose said in a rush. 'It's much worse than Maggie's. Much worse because it affects several people's lives. I did something dishonest. And it's no one's fault but mine.' Her voice became a whisper, dreading having to say the words out loud.

'Rose, what is it?' Fran asked.

The words wouldn't come. It felt as though a flood of tears was building. Then the truth burst out of her. 'Elliot is not Peter's son.'

Maggie and Fran were silent and Rose had no idea what they were thinking.

'He's Charlie's, isn't he?' said Maggie finally. 'I have wondered. He's not at all like Peter.'

'Does Peter know?' asked Fran, her voice almost fearful.

'Yes, he does. When Elliot was five and needed blood after that accident on his bike, Peter realised our combined blood types were incompatible with Elliot's. And he asked me the question.'

'Are you sure? Is that accurate?' asked Fran.

'You can't identify a father by blood type,' said Maggie. 'But you can eliminate one.' She paused, and then asked softly, 'Did *you* know, Rose?'

Rose began to cry. 'I wasn't sure . . . I knew it was possible. But when he was born I knew for certain. He was Charlie. No question.' She mopped her face with her T-shirt. It smelled disgusting. 'It was just one slip-up. Peter was being . . . I don't know . . . distant. I wasn't even sure we were going anywhere. I'd had a few drinks – usual pathetic story.'

'And Elliot?' asked Maggie. 'He obviously doesn't know.'

'Here's the thing,' said Rose. 'There's no good time to break that news. Peter doesn't want the boys to know. And I owe Peter a lot for the way he's handled this. He's treated the boys exactly the same. But now that Elliot's got his own child, I feel . . . it's not right. It's been playing on my mind.'

'He should know,' said Maggie. 'It's really his right to know.'

Rose was crying so hard she could hardly speak. 'I don't know . . . yes! Of course it is. But he'll never speak to me again. What about Austin . . . and Prya . . . and Max? I can't do it. I couldn't bear it.'

'What about Charlie? Where's he now?' asked Fran.

Rose wiped her runny nose on her wrist. 'I ran into him earlier in the year. He hadn't been well. Prostate cancer. He'd had the all-clear but I got the feeling it took a lot out of him. I feel guilty about him too.'

Maggie rubbed Rose's back sympathetically. 'Do you think he'd want to know?'

'Yeah, I do. I think he'd be really proud. Elliot is who Charlie could have been with fewer drugs and better parents. Anyway, Peter wants it kept a secret . . . so my hands are tied.'

'Oh, Rose. Peter is just one person affected,' said Fran. 'He doesn't have the last word. In the end, you need to make the right decision for Elliot.'

Rose snuffled unhappily. 'I don't want it to be up to me. I don't want the responsibility.'

Maggie sighed. 'Rose, you have been such a good mother. Marrying Peter was something positive you did for Elliot. I'm going to give you the same advice you gave me. Free yourself from this burden. Talk to Peter about coming clean with the boys. Elliot won't reject you for one mistake. And Max will be fine, I promise. Your boys adore you. They will forgive you. I *know* they will.'

Rose leaned on Maggie's shoulder and sobbed. The time for guilt was over. The time for crying was over. She needed to be strong. She needed to be honest.

As they stood outside the next morning, waiting for the taxi, Rose felt so many conflicting emotions, she didn't dare speak. She felt fear and exhilaration in equal measures. She had never expected to come back here or make the decision that she had made last night. But she was glad they'd come and glad that the time they had spent here, all those years ago, wasn't just a dusty memory. Coming back had given rise to something new – the possibility of a freedom that she found hard to imagine.

Her gaze followed the graceful crescent of the bay. This place was protected by headlands and secluded from the troubles of the world, but the mechanics of living went on just the same. In the last chapter of his life, Spyros was making ends meet, keeping the lights on and the tanks full – most of the time. He was surrounded by his family and people he had known all his life. Every day he sat on the terrace, drinking coffee with his old mates, living proof that there was such a thing as the simple life, and people still came from around the world to experience it for a short time. If there was a metaphor there, it was yet to reveal itself to her.

Soon the taxi would take them to Corfu town, where they would stay the night as tourists, before flying to Rome and home. Anyone who saw them would assume they were three old hens on a cosy holiday, never suspecting that they had met their younger selves, witnessed their lives from a different angle, and were changed in ways even they couldn't yet know.

Part Three

Homecoming

Chapter Nineteen

Rome was a heightened experience for Rose: the food more delicious, the men more handsome, the women more glamorous. She felt a bit stoned and high on life. The trip had reverted to a normal holiday. Armed with their credit cards, they stayed in a luxury hotel – although any hotel would have seemed luxurious after the Helipad, let alone the Beast. They enjoyed hot showers and soft beds, dined in wonderful restaurants, walked the Via Condotti to the Piazza di Spagna and ascended the Spanish Steps. They walked and talked and ate and discussed all that had happened over the past four weeks.

Everything looked quite different from this perspective. Now it seemed as if everything that had happened *needed* to happen. Like an epic tale, each incident had served to propel their story forward. Arguments and mishaps now seemed comedic. And Rose realised the reshaping of this experience had also unwittingly been applied to the first trip. Stressful experiences had been buffed and polished over the years, the true emotions long since forgotten.

Suddenly, though, it was over and they were saying goodbye to Fran, who was on a morning flight back to London. Rose and Maggie hugged her, more than once, and promised to call her as soon as they got home. There was no telling when they would all be together again. As the airport shuttle bus pulled away, Rose saw Fran crumple with grief as she covered her face with her hands.

Rose and Maggie had a few more hours before their flight but both felt flat after Fran had gone, as though her departure marked the end of the trip. They were relieved to finally make their way to the airport and settle in for the long journey ahead.

On the flight home to Sydney, Rose woke from a restless sleep and looked over at Maggie, who had the light on over her seat and was completely engrossed in scribbling notes in an exercise book. Despite being surrounded by hundreds of sleeping strangers, there was a pleasant sense of intimacy in the golden circle of light.

'Writing a book?' asked Rose, leaning over to get a peek.

'Sort of. Just noting all the thoughts I have right now, so I can be clear with myself. Not just ideas, practical application.' She turned to look at Rose. 'Do you know what I realised? I do love being at the centre of the family. I know you dream of flying solo, but that's not for me.'

'Not that long ago you said they were killing you,' Rose reminded her.

'Yes, they were. And they still could. But I'm part of the problem, bending this way and that to keep everyone happy at the expense of my own wellbeing.'

'You're like a sapling that could just snap under pressure,' said Rose. 'Whereas you need to be an oak, immovable. Unshakable. Sheltering but never bending . . .'

'Correct. I need to get clear with myself which battles to fight.'

'Mags, I think you need to be prepared to walk, if need be. Even for a short time. It's not going to be that easy to convince them you're serious, after mopping up everyone's mess for decades. And I still think you have to tell Kristo about Nico.'

Maggie nodded. 'I know. From here on, it's all about coming back from that night at the lake. How about you, Rosie? Made a decision about Peter?'

'If I was only thinking of myself, I'd make the move. But packing Peter in when he's retiring and has nothing but free time ahead seems so lousy. And I am indebted to him. I need to work on accepting him the way he is. He's not going to change.'

Maggie patted her hand. 'See how you feel when you get home. You may feel differently.'

Rose's luggage arrived on the conveyor belt first. She was taking the train to the city. Maggie had emailed Kristo from Rome and was expecting him to pick her up, so they said quick goodbyes in the baggage collection area, promising to meet up soon.

Rose took the train and then a taxi from Central Station. When she arrived in her street, it was lined with a dozen film trucks, their back doors open, revealing rows of neatly packed technical gear. She wheeled her suitcase past an improvised canteen, where crew stood crowded together, deep in discussion over breakfast. Bacon and egg rolls, by the smell in the air.

She stood at her front gate for a long minute. Something definitely had changed. The house and front garden were immaculate. There were two large pots of flowering orchids flanking the front door. As she walked up the path, she saw the verandah had not just been swept, it looked as if it had been washed.

Astonishingly, the timber trim appeared to have had a fresh coat of paint.

The front door was wide open. She walked down the hall, her curiosity growing as she observed that every room was tidy. The living room had been completely rearranged, there were lights on stands and large white reflectors in a semicircle around two expensive-looking armchairs that Rose had never seen before. A couple of paintings, which had been waiting to be hung for a decade, were now up on the wall, perfectly aligned.

At the sound of voices, she turned to see Peter walking down the hall eating a roll and chatting cheerfully to a young woman who walked beside him, carrying a large fishing tackle box. Peter stopped and stared at Rose as though she was the last person he expected to see in her own house.

'Hello, welcome home,' he said. He brushed a kiss on her cheek and turned to the young woman. 'Er, Rose. Paris. My wife.' He waggled the roll in Rose's direction to indicate that she was the wife but, even so, Rose was momentarily confused by the introduction and the realisation that Peter was wearing makeup.

'Nice to meet you, Mrs McLean,' said Paris, extending her hand. 'I'm doing hair and makeup.' She put the tackle box on the kitchen bench. 'Do you mind if I set up here, just for touch ups? I hope that's not in your way.'

'Well, I would like to make a cup of tea,' replied Rose peevishly. Who on earth were these people?

'I'll make you one, Mrs McLean,' said Paris. 'You must be exhausted. Would you like one too, Professor McLean?'

Peter said he would, and Paris beamed at them both, perhaps imagining that they were thrilled to be reunited.

'Peter, what is going on – please?' Rose looked around for somewhere to sit but the sofa had been pushed into a corner against the wall and she didn't like to sit in the strange armchairs.

'It's a long story. Let me explain.' He led her over to the armchairs and gestured for her to take a seat.

Being forced to listen to one of Peter's interminable stories was not what she had planned for this morning. 'Make it a long story short, Peter. I'm not in the mood for one of your long *long* stories.'

'All right. You might remember I was trying to get your assistance with a presentation. Before you disappeared completely. I told you about the friend of Craig's?'

Not this again! It felt as though years had passed since they had that final frustrating conversation in Paris. She'd expected this topic to have disappeared altogether. She nodded.

'Well, I followed your advice, which turned out to be unhelpful. But perhaps you were poorly briefed. Nevertheless, I had a very productive meeting, in what I would call a "seat-of-the-pants" style. And it seems they were impressed.'

Rose had thought a break from Peter might give her more patience, but the opposite had occurred. As he continued in this vein for some minutes, she found herself wondering what waterboarding actually involved, how effective it was, and if you could hire an operative to do it.

'Peter, let's crack on to the present day. You're wearing makeup, there's a film crew outside and all this crap in the living room. Start there.'

He beamed, relieved to have effortlessly reached the punchline. 'I'm going to have my own television show. Technically, not just mine, Max is a co-presenter.'

Absolutely convinced that Peter was confused and had the wrong end of the stick, Rose needed to talk to someone other than him, though preferably not Max – also not a reliable source of information.

'Peter, you're not paying anyone for this, are you?' She had always feared that he might fall victim to some elaborate online scam. It wouldn't need to be all that elaborate.

'Of course not, Rose!' Peter laughed. 'What a ridiculous idea. I'm the one being paid.'

Paris brought two cups of tea and put them on a dinky coffee table between the chairs.

Rose looked up at her. 'Paris, is it possible for you to give me a snapshot of the situation? I've been off air.'

'You better talk to Helena,' she said, gesturing towards a young woman who entered the living room with two crew members. 'She's the producer.'

Rose got up and introduced herself to Helena, who greeted her warmly. 'I can imagine all this must be a bit of a shock, Mrs McLean. It's all moved very quickly, even for us! Let me bring you up to speed. We're a production company called Xylophone Productions, and we make historical documentaries for television. We had secured funding for a series called *Inside the 20th Century* featuring Professor Flanders as the host. Then, three weeks ago, Flanders had some accusations made against him and we couldn't risk proceeding with him. My friend, Craig, suggested his old professor – Peter.'

Rose was not surprised to hear about John Flanders, a long-time colleague and adversary of Peter's, and she could well imagine what the accusations might be. More difficult to imagine was how Peter would go as a television host with his propensity for going into every mind-bendingly tedious detail when he was freed from the constraints of the lecture theatre. Then it dawned on her – they could edit him!

Helena asked if Rose would like to see a segment from the previous day's shoot. Next thing she was sitting in front of a monitor watching Peter and Max, seated in the fancy armchairs, enjoying a chummy father-and-son chat about the origins of the White Australia policy.

Max and Peter both had excellent minds, but there were times when Rose privately thought of them as Dumb and Dumber because they were both so cerebral, lacking any practical commonsense. But here, onscreen, they were in their element. Max looked so fresh-faced and handsome, she felt choked with motherly pride. He was asking intelligent, insightful millennial questions and Peter was his best 'lecturer' self, responding with fascinating snippets and historical background, making sly political jokes and twinkling at the camera.

Rose was dumbstruck. Helena and Peter were clearly waiting for her response. After a moment she shook her head in disbelieving wonder. 'It's brilliant. Absolutely brilliant.'

Helena grinned. 'Aren't they amazing? Peter will be to history what David Attenborough is to nature. He's the right man in the right era. As I'm sure you know, the twentieth century has become so mythologised in the last few years, there's huge interest right now. Older people want a new perspective on events they experienced, and young people are attracted by the cool elements like the sixties and world wars.'

Rose wasn't sure if Helena was implying that world wars were cool, but she let that go.

'It was my idea to involve Max,' said Peter, pleased with himself. 'I needed a student to make it more natural for me.'

Helena and Peter began to discuss the day's shoot and Rose wandered down the hall not knowing where to put herself.

Max bounded in the front door and enveloped her in a bear hug. 'Mumsy! You're back! Did you see us? What did you think?'

'I think . . . look, I'm just trying to catch up, but I think it's fantastic. I don't know what to say. Hang on. Is it all going to be you two chatting in our living room?'

'No, of course not. That's just the opening sequence. Then we're on the road. We're going all over Australia to the locations. It's like we had the convo in the living room and then jumped in the car and went exploring. It's going to take three months to film. It'll be on the ABC next year.'

'What about your job?' asked Rose in dismay.

'I had to resign. This is my job now. Why are you looking like that? I thought you'd be beside yourself, Mum.'

It had taken Max two years to get a permanent position with the Department of Planning and Environment and, in her absence, he had thrown it over for a three-month project. But then again, he radiated a newfound self-confidence. The young woman he'd been accused of stalking worked in the same building, so the further away he was from her, the better. Until now, Max had only revealed his talent for overcomplicating everything, so perhaps this was his chance to shine. His blue eyes clouded with worry, waiting for her response. She opened her arms to him. 'I think it's wonderful, my darling. Well. Done. You!'

His face lit up, as it always did when she bestowed unconditional approval on him. He excused himself, as he was due in a meeting with Helena. Max having meetings . . . The mind boggled. Rose watched him lope down the hallway to the living room and marvelled that all she had to do was go away for a month and her two problem children had magically got their shit together.

There was a lot of activity in the house and nothing for Rose to do but be quiet and stay out of the way. The day passed in slow increments and it was a relief when the film crew finally packed up and departed and she could get into her pyjamas and dressing-gown and order pizza.

She had messaged with Fitz on and off during the day. He was keen to see her and there was some merit in getting out of the house, but conjugating was the last thing on her mind right now. He could wait another day.

By contrast, next day the house was empty. The film crew, the fancy chairs, the equipment and Peter and Max had all gone. It was Sunday, but perhaps they were shooting elsewhere. In any case, it wasn't her problem. All that remained was to pull up stray bits of gaffer tape off the floor and put the furniture back in place. It was a pleasure to stand out the front and see the lawn and garden so groomed, but sadly the pots of orchids had gone as well.

It was nice to have some quiet time to get her bearings and process the fact that some of the more difficult elements in her life had been eliminated. She was no longer Peter's assistant – that was someone else's job now – and he would not be hanging around the house annoying her every day. She no longer had to worry about Max. Involvement with this show was probably what he needed and could quite likely lead to other opportunities.

She called Elliot's mobile and her tummy did an unexpected flip when he picked up. 'Hey, Mum, welcome home! Sounds like you had a real adventure.'

They chatted for a few minutes, catching up, and then Rose said, 'Look, darling, I need to talk to you about something . . .

I don't want to do it on the phone. Do you think we could meet sometime, this week? Just the two of us? It's sort of personal . . .' She could hear how tight and strained her voice sounded.

'Sure, of course. Are you okay, Mum?'

'Absolutely,' she said in a wobbly voice that revealed the opposite.

There was a loaded silence and she knew he was going to ask what it was about.

'It's nothing terrible,' she assured him. 'I haven't got cancer or anything . . .'

'Is it about my father?' he asked.

'What? What do you mean? What are you talking about?'

'Mum, you know what I'm talking about. Charlie.'

Rose was so shocked and confused she couldn't think of how to respond. 'I don't understand . . .' she said in a faint voice.

'I've known for a while. Auntie Chris sent me an email a few months ago. It basically laid out all the evidence. She thought I had a right to know.'

Rose felt a fury rise in her. Bloody Chrissy and her poisonous emails! How she had guessed the truth, Rose had no idea since they had never discussed it. The woman was completely deranged. And didn't even have the guts to actually speak to people.

'She also said Nana was trying to poison Gramps, so I wasn't sure what to believe,' Elliot continued. 'I asked Dad about it when we went to the cabin.'

'What did Dad say?' she asked breathlessly.

'Just what happened. That you two had broken up and got back together. That he knew right from the start. And he was fine about it. He said you guys agreed to keep it to yourselves.

I get that, Mum. I'm fine with it too. Max and I are brothers, but it explains why we're so different.'

Rose perched on the edge of the sofa, hardly daring to breathe. It seemed *impossible* it could be this simple. But this was Elliot's gift – he was pragmatic and fair-minded. He never, ever, felt sorry for himself.

'Oh, darling, I'm so sorry. It's just . . . there never seemed a right time to talk to you about it,' said Rose, tearfully. 'I just feel . . .'

'Mum, don't make it more difficult than it is. I have processed it. I've come to terms with it in my own mind. I didn't want to talk to you until that was done. I asked Dad not to let on I knew. But I thought, since you'd gone on this soul-searching trip, you might want to talk about it when you got back.'

'You're the most emotionally orderly person I know, El. You didn't get that from me. Or Charlie.'

Elliot laughed. 'Yeah, well, I knew you were a bit wild back in the day, Mum, so it all worked out fine, as far as I'm concerned.' He paused, and she heard the emotion in his voice as he said, 'Dad said he was very proud to have me as a son.'

Rose was speechless. That seemed so unlike Peter. But then Peter had told a lie to exonerate her. Had he forgotten her deception? Of course not. He didn't tell that lie for her, he did it for the greater good. He did it for them all. For the family.

'So, Mum . . .'

'Yes, my darling boy?'

'Do you think Charlie would be interested in meeting me?'

'I think he'd love to. I really do,' said Rose, laughing and crying at the same time. 'Just give me some time to break the news to him first.'

She knew there was one last thing she needed to tell him, and braced herself. 'Elliot . . .' She paused to get a grip on her emotions.

'You okay, Mum?'

'I want you to know that I loved Charlie, very much . . . I wish . . . we just couldn't make things work. I'm sorry.'

Elliot was silent. She had no idea what he was thinking but had a terrible feeling he was crying. Finally, he cleared his throat and said softly, 'Thanks, Mum.'

Overwhelmed, Rose changed the subject and they chatted for a few minutes about Austin's progress, then he passed her over to Prya – something that had never happened before.

Rose was convinced that she was on one of Prya's electronic lists as a recurring event: Elliot's Mother. Scheduled and dealt with quickly and efficiently. But now Prya wanted to know how things had panned out in Corfu, and Rose babbled about the Beast and the Blue Moon and the Helipad, overwhelmed with relief and gratitude.

'Oh, that sounds so much fun, Rose!' said Prya, laughing. 'I'm so jealous. I could never do anything like that. We'd like to come over next Sunday, if you're around, and hear all about it. You'll be able to see Austin walking. And we've got some news for you too.'

Rose could guess what that news would be. She knew the minute Austin was walking, they would have scheduled the next one. Even their reproductive organs were running at peak efficiency. She was touched by them wanting to tell her in person, not just over the phone. She invited them for lunch and made a note to pick up some French champagne.

She walked down to Glebe Point Road in a daze, going over and over this unexpected conversation with Elliot, unable to believe that the burden had been lifted from her. It would take some time to get used to, after weighing on her for so long.

She took a bus down to the retirement village to see her mother, a regular Sunday routine. It was difficult to catch the old girl on weekdays – she led a tireless social life and spent more time in the centre's minibus, being ferried to various events, than in her unit.

The unit itself was a pleasant enough place. Given her mother's garish taste, the neutral colour scheme, chosen by a professional, was a blessing. They settled down with a cup of tea, and the macaroons Rose had brought.

'How's Dad doing? Chrissy still making a pest of herself?' Rose wondered if Chrissy had mentioned Charlie to their mother too, but she wasn't going to be the one to bring it up.

'He's much the same. And I've barely heard from Chris. The dust had hardly settled on her divorce and she was on the internet hunting men. Anyway, she's got a new bloke, a cop no less, and he's keeping her busy. She's calmed down a bit. So I'm free to poison your father if I want.'

'She'll probably get him to have you investigated.'

Her mother gave a dismissive grunt. 'My conscience is clear. How did Peter and Max manage without you?'

Rose explained about the television show and her mother rocked with laughter. 'He's full of surprises, old Peter.'

'So I'm discovering,' said Rose.

Her mother gave her a shrewd look. 'Did you make the decision to leave him while you were away?'

'Why do you ask that? I've never said that!'

'Come on, Rose. Wake up to yourself. He's pretty bloody wearing.'

'I thought you liked Peter.'

'Of course I do, but I wouldn't want to be married to him. Why not go off and do your own thing now? There's nothing to hold you there any more, especially if he's got a whole new career. Bloody hell, what more do you need?'

'There's my home of thirty-five years. My family. My husband. What kind of mother are you?'

Her mother took a second macaroon and bit into it. 'An honest one.'

'Now he's not so dependent and won't be around that much; we'll be living separate lives, anyway . . .'

'Rose, marriage is not supposed to be an endurance event. You've always wanted to be your own person. You never planned to get pregnant and married so young. This is your last chance. No good dipping your toe in a puddle. Throw yourself in the deep end. Get yourself a lover and a backpack. Go see the world.'

'I've just got back from seeing the world!' said Rose, feeling under pressure.

'I'm pretty sure you missed a few bits. You're still young; you can do anything you want. Take that voice of yours and do something with it. You don't want to get to my age and kick yourself because you didn't live the life you wanted.'

'So, are you saying that you didn't live the life you wanted?'

'Of course not. But my generation didn't expect that. I was good at science at school, I loved it – still do. I never miss *The Science Show*. Could I have had a career?' She shrugged. 'Bit late to worry about that now. I was a farmer and then a newsagent. They don't write songs about newsagents, you know.'

'Or scientists, for that matter,' said Rose.

'Are you kidding me? How about Coldplay?'

'Coldplay? I had no idea you were a fan, Mum.'

'Old people like Coldplay. That's what killed them.'

The conversation was now going in two opposing directions. Rose picked her preference. 'Killed who, Mum?' she asked, imagining some geriatric genocide she'd missed in the news.

'Coldplay, *obviously*. Anyway, pretty much all songs are about science, because they're about love. Falling in love and falling out of love. The latter being more interesting. Now's your time, Rosie.'

Rose wanted to argue the point on Coldplay but didn't know where to start and her mother seemed better informed on the topic. She watched her mother snaffle the last macaroon and tried to think of a response that didn't require real commitment, so she wouldn't be forced to follow through.

'If you won't do it for yourself, Rose, do it for me. Do it for Granny, who worked herself to death on that bloody farm. You got your beautiful voice from her and all she ever did was sing happy birthday now and then.'

As Rose was leaving, her mother said, 'They were good times we had, singing in the car, weren't they? I miss those days. They seemed like ordinary days at the time. You never know what your happiest moments will be until they're long gone. Don't wait any longer, Rose.'

On the bus back from the retirement village, Rose brimmed with emotion, misty-eyed at the reminder of her lovely Gran who spoke with a smoker's croak in her last years.

She thought about what her mother had said. If she was careful, the money would be adequate once she and Peter sold the house and split their investments. She could get a flat in the area.

The more she thought about it, the less enticing it seemed. Why put herself through all that separation would entail when her situation was really quite tolerable? She was simply being difficult and discontented.

She got off the bus on Glebe Point Road and walked down to Fitz's place. When he opened the door, clearly delighted to see her, she burst into tears. He wrapped his arms around her, drew her inside and shut the door behind them as she sobbed on his chest.

'Is it me?' he asked, guiding her towards the kitchen. 'Or is it you?'

'Me,' she said. 'I'm completely lost.'

'I have missed you,' he said, kissing her while simultaneously removing her jacket. 'I've had champagne on ice waiting for your return.'

'Really?' Rose asked tearfully. 'That's nice.'

He whipped open the fridge with a flourish, extracted a bottle of Veuve and two champagne glasses. He popped the cork, filled the glasses and proposed a toast to her return.

'Now, tell me all about it, every little thing. Perhaps it will all start to make sense,' he suggested cheerfully.

The trip felt like a crushing weight right now. She would tell him some other time, she promised. They chatted about the project he was working on, and she told him about Peter and Max.

Fitz topped up her glass. 'You won't have seen the papers, but there's been a development with your bio project. Inge Bryant died a week ago, which is not good obviously, but . . . I don't remember where you were up to with it?'

Rose shrugged miserably. She didn't know either. She'd almost forgotten the project existed.

'What is good, though,' Fitz continued, 'is there's been quite a resurgence of interest in her work. Typical, isn't it? You have to die to get the recognition you deserve. So it may be worth revisiting for you. It will be so much easier now she's gone.'

It had been a mistake to come here right now. She was looking for an easy exit, for someone to take care of her so she didn't have to be entirely responsible for herself. If she told him she was considering leaving Peter, he would assume it was for him.

It couldn't be for him. It had to be for her.

She allowed him to unbutton her shirt, slip off her cargo pants and lead her to the bedroom. As they made love to 'Highway to Hell' (which had taken on a whole new meaning) she found herself having an out-of-body experience watching them, a couple of middle-aged people looking for some comfort in the world, some stay of execution on old age, some buffer from the indifference of the world. And she felt sad for them both. She was fond of Fitz, but she didn't love him. If she left Peter for him, she would be sabotaging herself all over again. First, she had to experience being free.

Afterwards, they sat up in Fitz's bed and finished their champagne and he said, 'So, I get the feeling that I'm going to become a casualty of your existential crisis.'

'What makes you say that?' asked Rose.

'It's true, isn't it?' He sounded so hurt, she could barely muster a reply.

'It's not forever. I don't want to swap horses mid-stream, I need to get off . . .'

'You want to get into the stream? It could be cold and deep, and a little bit lonely.'

The champagne was making her feel emotional. 'I don't know what I'm doing, so please don't talk me out of it.' She climbed out of bed and pulled her clothes on quickly, suddenly self-conscious. She went around to his side of the bed and sat down facing him. 'I just need some space. And time to sort myself out and clear my head. Please.'

Fitz nodded. He put his arms around her, squeezed her tight and released her. She walked out the door without a backward glance and sobbed uncontrollably all the way to the bus stop.

It was just after five when she got home but the day was over. She showered, slipped into her pyjamas and crawled into bed. She felt ill with fear, magnified by the effects of the champagne. She lay awake for hours, tormented by the decision facing her.

Peter came home at some point and she pretended to be asleep. She drifted off and woke in the early hours. She put on her dressing-gown, went into the kitchen and made tea. She stood at the window and looked out into the garden. There was a bracing chill in the air and a bright moon that lit the garden with a silver fluorescence. The garden was wild and untamed, and she loved it that way. It was so hard to leave and so easy to stay.

She thought back over the last weeks and her mind had already mysteriously interwoven memories of the two trips, forty years apart. When she thought about them singing in the piazza in Bologna, swimming naked in Corfu, sleeping in the van, talking in the dark at the Helipad and singing at the Blue Moon – she could only picture their young selves. There was no sign of three women on the other side of middle age. They had unwittingly shrugged off those perceptions and forgotten all constraints. She realised that the biggest resistance she had to starting a new life was the belief that she was too old to start afresh.

The truth was, she was too old to wait.

Imagining how her life could be, she experienced a sort of euphoria. She felt herself travelling all over the world, these myriad experiences spinning through her mind, faster and faster. She wondered what the heck was in that tea.

Something lifted in her, a weight that she'd been carrying for longer than she could remember. The jittery indecisive feeling she'd had since Corfu subsided and, in its place, a calm certainty.

Rose wrapped her arms around herself and began to sway and sing under her breath. The song that came to her was 'Gypsy' – that would be her anthem. The song rose from deep inside her. She was moving and spinning and dancing, her arms swung wide. She found herself smiling and finished with a deep bow, and she heard distant applause coming down the years, closer and closer, and it was for her. Her alone.

Chapter Twenty

Maggie came down the ramp into the arrivals hall and looked around for Kristo, ready to wave and smile. Instead of Kristo, she saw Nico. He either hadn't seen her or didn't recognise her with the cropped hair, as his gaze swept past her to the other exit door. Without a moment's hesitation, she ducked under the cordon and headed in the opposite direction. She saw the signs for the train and followed them. Anything to get out of the airport. *Where was Kristo?* He had the flight details. He couldn't have sent Nico . . . She had felt quite relaxed coming off the flight, with her plans all in place. Now her heart was racing, her palms sweaty. It was only when she was on the escalator headed down into the station that she dared look behind her, just to be sure.

Safely on the train, her mind whirred. Seeing Nico in the terminal had thoroughly rattled her and she wondered if he had arrived on another flight. In her calmer state over the last week, she had realised that there was no real evidence that Nico had followed her to Europe. The idea was obviously absurd, but she'd been looking over her shoulder for twenty years, trying to second-guess him. It was ingrained in her – which was exactly what he wanted, to be constantly on her mind.

When the train stopped at Central Station, she stood on the platform for a full ten minutes trying to work out how to get home from there. In the end, she boarded another train into the city and took a bus, then a taxi and finally arrived home.

The front door was locked and no one answered the buzzer. She found the hidden key and let herself in. Where on earth was Kristo? He didn't normally work on Saturdays, unless there was a drama on a site somewhere. Perhaps that explained Nico coming to the airport . . . But why not the twins? She walked around the kitchen and living room looking for clues, went upstairs and checked the bedrooms. Mysteriously, even Yia-yiá was missing. She never went out anywhere if she could possibly avoid it.

Maggie walked out onto the back deck and looked over the bay. The flat blue of the winter sky now had a dramatic backdrop of thunderclouds blossoming on the horizon. She heard the thud of distant thunder. White yachts at anchor in the bay bobbed nervously as the breeze quickened. She took a deep breath of fresh sea air and felt it fill her lungs. She realised that there wasn't a single place she had seen on her travels as beautiful as the view from her own house. The breeze ruffled through her hair, and she had an image of herself as a chick emerging from its shell. A fat raindrop fell on the deck and she went back inside and slid the glass door shut.

She heard a car door slam out the front and, a moment later, the front door close. She switched on the coffee machine and turned with a smile to greet Kristo, only to find Nico standing in the doorway. She felt her smile vanish, her greeting falter. 'Why are you here? And since when do you just let yourself into my house?'

'It's not your house. It's my brother's house. I came to the air-port at bloody six in the morning – where were you? I waited for a whole hour.'

'I didn't see you. Where have you been, anyway? Kristo said you were away.'

He smiled. 'Bangkok. Why? Did you miss me? If you'd taken my calls I would have told you myself.'

'I don't need to know where you are. Where's Kristo?'

'He's in the hospital. Heart attack. Everyone's there. I came to get you.'

Maggie gripped the bench for support. Kristo was indestruct-ible. It wasn't possible. Nico was lying. He was lying to get her into his car. Her instinct was not to let him know her suspicions. She needed to find out what was really going on. Kristo's phone sat on the bench. He was never without his phone. She picked it up. There were a dozen missed calls and messages from various people.

'What happened to your hair?' Nico was staring at her, his expression unreadable. She didn't want to read it and could only hope that he was repulsed. After a moment he said, 'It's sexy. You look younger.'

She ignored his comment. 'Is he all right? Which hospital is he in?'

'North Shore. He's okay.' He leaned against the bench and folded his arms, watching her. 'You don't believe me, do you? Call the girls. Anyone.'

Maggie tapped Kristo's code into his phone and pressed Elena's number.

Nico watched her. 'Lets you into his phone, does he? A man with nothing to hide. I'll wait for you in the car.' He walked out of the kitchen and she heard the front door close.

'Mum? Where *are* you? Theíos Nico went to the airport to get you and you didn't arrive.' Elena's voice was husky, on the verge of tears. 'We thought you'd decided not to come home.'

'Ellie, darling, that would never happen. I'm home now. Is Dad okay?'

'He's fine. He's being monitored. It was a shock for him. We've all been so upset and you weren't here. We didn't know what to do.' She began to cry. 'I never thought of you or Dad dying. Ever.'

Maggie wondered privately how someone could get to adult-hood and retain such a childlike view of the world but she said kindly, 'I'm on my way. I'll be there soon.'

Maggie put Kristo's phone in her bag. She locked the front door from the inside and let herself out the side door into the garage. She slipped into her car and pulled the door closed quietly. Out the front, Nico sounded his horn.

Maggie took a deep breath and pressed the door remote. By the time the door rolled up, Nico was standing there, blocking her path, his face dark with anger.

'I'll take you!' he shouted. 'Don't be an idiot.'

She started the car and edged forward. He stepped towards her, his body leaning against the grille of her Audi. Maggie felt the trembling starting in her legs. She sounded the horn. The expression on his face was terrifying. She got Kristo's phone out of her bag. The last thing she wanted to do right now was to call the police. They might not come for hours. She and Nico would be in a stand-off until they arrived. And what could the police do? He would say it was an argument and they'd believe him and leave. Everything would be so much worse. Involving the police could make him more aggressive. She wanted to weep with exhaustion and have someone else take care of this situation. Who else could she call?

While she was distracted, Nico walked back to his car. She felt a wave of relief and eased out of the garage, closing the door behind her with the remote, anxious to get on her way. She watched with dismay as he reversed at high speed and swung his car across the driveway. She was trapped.

He opened the passenger's door and gestured to her to get in. He was barely controlling his rage. She'd seen this many times, but never directed at her. Anything could happen now.

The next-door neighbours, Bob and Alice, might have a view of Nico parked across the driveway, but would probably not be able to see Maggie's car in front of the house. Reluctant as she was to draw them into it, she found Bob's number in Kristo's phone and called. With a sinking feeling, she remembered that they played golf on Saturday afternoons. Still, she waited until it went to voicemail before she disconnected. She was on her own.

Shaking, she jabbed triple zero into the phone. Her request to the operator sounded disjointed, as though she didn't know why she was calling.

Nico got out and approached her car. She hit the button to lock all doors.

He stood beside the driver's window. 'Who are you calling? You stupid bitch. You're just making trouble for me. Making shit up.' He kicked the door, his anger escalating by the minute. 'Get out of the fucking car now!'

The operator asked if she was in immediate danger. Maggie began to say no but all the years of being afraid of Nico, all the game-playing, all the times she caught sight of his malign presence hovering in the shadows, rose up in her and she heard herself saying, 'Yes! Please help me!'

Assured that a patrol car would be with her soon, she disconnected and it was all she could do not to start bawling. She had never felt so alone in her life. He had left her with no choice but to capitulate – or run him down. Now everything was out of her hands.

Nico walked over to the house and tried the front door, further enraged that she had locked up. She couldn't think why he wanted to get inside. Perhaps to get Kristo's tools? Why didn't he just leave, given his plan wasn't working? He was stubborn, that's why. He had to win at any cost.

He paced up and down in front of her car, intermittently coming to tap on the driver's window, demanding she open it and talk to him. Pretending that he had calmed down and was ready to discuss the situation. She ignored him.

She heard the wailing of a siren. She had expected a quieter arrival. Nico turned towards the sound, a look of shocked disbelief on his face. Before he could move away, a patrol car, lights flashing, pulled into the top of the driveway.

Two officers, a man and a woman, got out and came quickly down the driveway towards them. Nico walked up to greet the officers. She could see him smiling and pointing to her car and wondered what story he was making up. Everything felt unreal, as if she was watching the whole thing on television, except there was no way to turn it off. There was no stopping how things unravelled now.

The male officer continued to talk to Nico while the woman came over to Maggie's car. Maggie opened the door and got out. 'That was quick,' she said with a weak smile.

The officer introduced herself as Senior Constable Burke. She asked if Maggie was all right and could she give her version of events.

'I'm okay. My husband's in hospital. I need to get to him,' said Maggie, her voice cracking.

'I understand. This won't take long. We just need to establish what happened here today, then you can go.'

When Maggie gave her details and explained what had occurred, it sounded like a misunderstanding. As if she was being stubborn and difficult. Without the full story, today's episode didn't make any sense.

'Can you tell me specifically why you don't want to go to the hospital with your brother-in-law? Has he been violent towards you in the past?'

Now was the moment. She could tell the truth or fall back on excuses. Everything could go back to the way it was. She knew what Rose would say. *Tell them. Tell them. For God's sake, stand up for yourself!*

'No. Perhaps I overreacted. I am very tired. Sorry to have bothered you. It was probably just a misunderstanding.'

It was obvious that the officer didn't buy this explanation for a minute. She reminded Maggie that the incident would be recorded and it was possible to come to the station and make a statement at a later time. 'If you feel there is the risk of violence, or you feel threatened, you can take out an apprehension order. We can help you with that. Think about it.'

Maggie nodded. All she wanted now was for everyone to leave so she could get to the hospital.

'So I'm guessing you'd still prefer to drive yourself to the hospital?' asked Senior Constable Burke.

Maggie nodded. 'Yes, I would. Most definitely.'

'We'll just move our friend here on, and you can take your time getting there. I'm sure your husband's in good hands.'

Maggie felt like hugging her but it didn't seem quite appropriate.

As the officer walked back towards Nico's car, she stopped and turned to Maggie. 'Take care of yourself, love.'

Maggie gave her a wave and watched the two officers talking seriously to Nico, who was no longer friendly and obliging but aggressive, arguing the point. Nevertheless, he got into his car and, once the patrol car moved out of the driveway, drove away.

There was a thunderclap overhead and splotches of rain landed on the bonnet. She gave herself a moment to sit quietly in the car and gather her thoughts. She'd had the chance to change this situation – why hadn't she taken it? Had she just been weak, not wanting to make a fuss? Then she realised – it wasn't the way she wanted Kristo to find out. Especially when he was in hospital. She had to tell him herself. Just not yet.

Arriving at the hospital, Maggie met Yia-yiá, Elena and Anthea coming down the corridor about to head home, having been there since the previous evening. Anthea was quiet but gave her a long hug. 'We missed you, Mum. And Dad missed you too. What happened to your hair?'

'I just decided to try something different,' said Maggie briskly.

Elena fell on her mother, hugging her tight. 'Oh, we're so glad you're here. We didn't know what to do without you.'

'You didn't need me,' said Maggie brightly. 'Dad needed medical specialists.'

'You make him the stress,' said Yia-yiá grimly.

Maggie gave her a hug. 'It's lovely to see you too, Yia-yiá.'

The twins delivererd a tag-team account of what had happened. Yia-yiá, who was actually the only witness, interrupted and picked up the story. 'He make a sweat on the head. He have pain here.' She patted her shoulder and down the length of her arm. 'I call on the phone. Zero. Zero. Zero. I say my son make attack. And they come.'

Anthea put her arm around her grandmother's shoulders, and Maggie noticed how small and fragile Yia-yiá had become. The experience must have given her a horrible fright.

'Yia-yiá saved him. If he'd been alone, he would have died,' said Anthea, tearfully.

'I'm picking up the general vibe that I'm to blame,' said Maggie.

Anthea glanced at Elena and decided to break ranks. 'No, you're not. You can't be expected to be with Dad every minute.'

Elena nodded her agreement. 'It could have happened on-site. Anywhere.'

'Mum, I need to talk to you,' said Anthea abruptly.

'Now? I need to see Dad. Can it wait?' asked Maggie.

'I've got some news,' she said. 'Dad already knows.'

'She make the baby with *vlákas*,' announced Yia-yiá.

Anthea nodded. 'I'm pregnant.' She watched her mother's face for a response.

'That's wonderful!' said Maggie, giving Anthea a hug. 'Wonderful!'

'Let's wait in the car, Yia-yiá.' Elena linked arms with her grandmother and steered her off down the hall.

'I wanted to tell you myself,' said Anthea. 'I don't know what's going to happen with Aaron. Mum, I'm scared.'

Maggie wrapped her arms around her daughter. 'Don't be. One way or another, it will work out, darling. We'll be here for you. Let's wait until Dad gets home and we'll have a proper celebration.'

Anthea nodded. 'It is exciting, isn't it?'

'Yes,' said Maggie. 'Very, very exciting.'

Sitting up in his hospital bed, Kristo was pleased and relieved to see her; almost apologetic for suffering a heart attack. It wasn't as serious as it seemed, he assured her, but there were two blocked arteries that they would put stents into, either later that day or the next morning. He would come home the day after. Apart from that, he was fine, and would be even better after the operation. She sat on his bed and they held hands.

'Anthea told me her news.'

'Yeah, I thought you'd be happy. Shame Aaron's the father . . .'

'Let's give him a chance, shall we? He's a good boy, really.'

'I like your hair,' he said, running his fingers through it with a smile.

'I thought you preferred it long?'

'I thought I did. Just what I was used to. You have a good head for it.'

'I'd really prefer to be valued for what's in my head,' she said with a smile.

'We've got a lot to talk about, Mag. Serious shit. I don't want to do it here.'

She agreed. 'Let's wait 'til we get home. We can talk about everything.'

She could see that Kristo had been chastened by the failing of his heart; his ego dented and his confidence shaken by this life-threatening event, out of his control. She loved to see this soft, gentle side of him – the vulnerability he only occasionally revealed. She had seen it when the twins were born, and when they lost Kal, and more recently when they parted at the airport. She thought about how different things would be between them if she saw more of that and less of the bluster and bravado.

By the time Maggie brought Kristo home from hospital two days later, Yia-yiá had made enough food to feed the family for months to come, the fridge and freezer stocked with Greek delicacies. They still hadn't talked about anything serious and it was made all the more difficult by Yia-yiá hovering around, constantly bringing him morsels to tempt his appetite. Unusually, Kristo asked his mother to give them some time alone. He had set up Greek TV streaming to the television in her room, so she was more amenable than usual to allowing them some uninterrupted time.

Maggie and Kristo sat together at the kitchen table, drinking coffee and enjoying the winter sun in a quiet companionable way that Maggie couldn't have even imagined a month earlier. Normally Kristo was on his phone, loudly organising teams of people, demanding information and reacting to anything and everything. Now he was subdued, afraid of the effect his reactions could have on his fragile heart.

'I thought you'd left me,' said Kristo. 'I wouldn't blame you.'

'If I was going to leave you, I'd tell you straight out. I would talk to you.'

'There's plenty of things you've been hiding. Stealing from the company, for a start.'

'Kristo, I need my own money. I've tried so many times over the years to convince you and the boys that I need a salary. I felt I had to take matters into my own hands,' said Maggie. 'What are you planning to do? Do the boys know?'

'Nah. I told Yannis I'd fire him if he told them. We need to make it right. I don't know how. You need to work something out.'

'I'm sorry I did it that way. That I didn't tell you,' said Maggie. 'It was wrong.'

Kristo's head dropped to his chest, as though he was being scolded or punished.

'What are you thinking, Kristo? Speak to me.'

He shook his head. 'I feel like I don't know you. You have these secrets . . .'

'I've kept secrets to protect the family. I don't want to keep them any more.'

He raised his eyes to hers accusingly. 'Nico told me he came to pick you up and you called the cops on him. He said you've gone crazy.'

Maggie felt the breath knocked out of her. It was the moment she had dreaded and there was only going to be one shot at this. 'I don't care what he's told you. Nico has been harassing and stalking me for twenty years.'

Kristo shook his head like a maddened bull, gathering himself for an argument.

'And before you start attacking me, Kristo, no, I've never been attracted to him. I don't like him. I've never liked him. In fact, I hate him. I didn't want to destroy the business. Or the family. That's why I didn't tell you.'

His eyes flicked away in disbelief. 'Bullshit. He said —'

'Listen to me! I don't care what he said! Whatever he said is a lie because there is no way he will admit what he's done. Now you have to decide who you believe, Kristo. I'm telling you the truth.'

'He wouldn't do that. He's my brother. It doesn't make any sense. You must have —'

'Encouraged him? So, if I had – which I haven't – would that excuse his behaviour? You just don't want to believe it. He has an obsession with me. Like an addiction.'

Kristo looked at her sceptically. 'So, what? He stares at you or makes comments —'

'You have no idea the countless times I've looked up and seen him, or his car, nearby. At the supermarket, outside the girls' school . . . whenever I had a routine, he made sure that he was there. Watching me. You remember I used to go and have a facial once a month? I turned up one day and they said it had already been paid for – by my brother-in-law. I never went back. He wants me to believe that he's watching me constantly, so he leaves little clues. He calls me and leaves messages. He wants *you* to believe he and I are in a relationship.'

She could see Kristo was shaken. 'So why didn't you tell me? It makes no sense.'

'What am I going to say? "I saw Nico in the supermarket. He paid for my facial. He's following me." There is no way you would have believed me, and you know it. You would have dismissed it as nothing.'

He stared back at her stubbornly but she knew he was listening now.

'And if you don't back me on this, our marriage is on the line. I'm not putting up with it any more. If I have to get a restraining order, I will. Kristo, I'm afraid of him.'

Kristo got up and put his mug in the sink. He stood at the bench and stared out the window silently for a long time. Finally, he said, 'I believe you.'

'You do?' Maggie felt faint with relief. She wanted to burst into tears but held herself in check. There was more work to be done.

He sat down opposite her, his face creased with guilt and remorse. 'I knew he was hot for you right from the start. I saw the way he looked at you. After we got married, I didn't really think about it. He had his own girlfriends, then he married Effie. But one Christmas I saw it again. The girls were still little; about a year after Kal died.' Tears welled in his eyes, as they did whenever Kal's name was mentioned. 'I saw him looking you over . . . and you know what? I thought what a lucky bastard I was, because you were mine. But when you were away, and then he disappeared, and you asked where he was . . . and I found out you were taking money from the company, I put it all together and I thought you were leaving me for him. It was sending me crazy.'

'I knew if I told you, you wouldn't believe me. Or if you did, you'd kill him.'

'I'll tell you what else . . . *shit*!' He shook his head in disbelief. 'He *wanted* me to think that! He left about a week after you did. He deliberately didn't say where he was going . . . I would like to kill him. He's lucky I'm too sick.' He flopped back in his chair defeatedly.

Maggie smiled and put her hand over his. 'You'll be back in the saddle soon, tiger. This is just a setback, not the end of you. I think he sensed we were in trouble and wanted to bring it to a head.'

'We're not in trouble. I'm going to sort this out, Mag. I promise. The end of us would be the end of me. I mean it. I don't want to lose you.'

'There's something else. I've made some decisions.'

He sighed and folded his arms high on his chest, his mouth a stubborn line. 'Yeah? I don't know if I can deal with much more.'

'I want to sell our share in the company. I want us to get out.'

'Nah . . . nope . . . not happening. Because of Nico? I'll just tell him. He can't come in the house. He can't come anywhere near you. I will deal with him, I promise. You know what? If he doesn't back off, we will get a restraining order. I'm dead serious about this.'

'Thank you. You can't even imagine how relieved I am. But, it's not that. The business is too big for us now. It's too stressful. We don't need to be doing this at this time of our lives. We can sell out our share to the boys —'

'What if they don't want to buy it?'

'They will, but we could also sell our share to another party. We can either retire, or we could start something smaller. You and me, just one project at a time. Like when we started.'

'And if I don't agree?' He looked like a man in front of a firing squad.

'You don't have to agree. You can continue as you are . . . but without me in the business. I'm resigning.'

'I don't like ultimatums. You were the one who said they're bad business practice. Now you're doing it.'

'Kristo, I have a job without a salary, or a shareholding. For years I've been asking myself how I let that happen. But how did *you* let that happen? Well, now it's too late. I don't want any of those things any more. The company needs to find a new financial controller – and you'll be paying the best part of a hundred grand a year for one.'

'Any other demands?' asked Kristo irritably. 'Do I have any say at all?'

'Up until now you've had all the say, and you've had everyone's back but mine. I'm not trying to break your balls. I'm trying to even things up.'

'What about Mum?' he said sulkily. 'Does she have to go too?'

Maggie had thought a lot about Yia-yiá over the past few days. She tried to imagine what it must be like to spend almost all your adult life in a country you didn't really understand. Never being able to properly communicate with anyone outside immediate family and a few friends. Never having access to books, or television, or movies. Maggie realised she didn't really know Yia-yiá at all. She only knew the knotty, gnarly, spiky bits that were visible on the surface, but that wasn't all of her. The language barrier would always be there. It wasn't true to say Yia-yiá never complained, because she loved to complain, but she did cope with a lot. All she truly wanted was to see her sons and grandchildren and feed them and be loved by them. That wasn't too much to ask.

'I would like your mother to stay. But there's two conditions.'

Kristo grimaced, clearly worried about what was coming next.

'The first is that I'd like to invite Theía Agnes to come and live with us here too. She can sell her house, pay the bank and whatever she ends up with is a nest egg. We'll look after her. She's your mother's only friend in the world and they should enjoy their last years together.'

Kristo smiled with relief. 'Sure, easy. We can set the other bedroom up for her. Mum will love that. Wait. What's the other condition?'

'Don't let your mother badmouth me. You've encouraged her by ignoring it. If she says something about me, even if it's in Greek and I can't understand it, I want you to step up.

If you hear her criticising me to Theía Agnes, tell her it's not on. It's not fair.'

Kristo did not like to tell his mother off. It didn't feel right to him and he'd do anything to avoid it. He tried pushing back. 'It feels like this is a dictatorship, and you're taking control. Your feminist friends put all these ideas in your head. I have to do what you say or you're going to bugger off.'

'Do you really think respect is a feminist idea? Come on. I've had your back all these years, I want you to have mine now.' Maggie reached across the table and took his hand. 'Kris, when I was away, I nearly drowned. If my friends hadn't saved me, we wouldn't even be having this discussion. You'd be making one hundred per cent of the decisions around here. I'm coming back from that and I have nothing to lose. When I left, I was completely miserable and I couldn't see a way out. Now I do. And things will be better for both of us.'

Kristo was silent for a while. 'Yeah, I get it. We've both had a scare. I guess there is something in that. A message of some sort.'

Maggie got up and went around the table to him. He pushed his chair back and she sat on his lap and cradled his face in her hands. 'We're going to be grandparents. Let's enjoy it, together, the way we never had time to enjoy the girls. Take some time for ourselves. And each other.'

Maggie kissed him tenderly, and as his arms encircled her, she felt that same softening that she had experienced all those years ago.

Kristo nodded slowly. He held her tight and murmured, '*Psichí mou* – my soul. Always.'

Chapter Twenty-one

It was only when she was settled on the train from Stansted that Fran began to look forward to getting home. It was a classic English summer's day, and she pictured her flat awash with sunshine. Gigi would be pleased to see her and, hopefully, Louis would be there to welcome her as promised.

She opened her front door to be met by Gigi squalling, frantic with hunger. The anticipated sunshine had arrived to reveal a month's worth of dust, and many of her plants were half dead from neglect or overwatering. There was no sign of the man himself but evidence of his occupation everywhere: the grubby sheets of the unmade bed, the clothes scattered on the floor and the sink full of dishes. Her fragile good spirits evaporated and she burst into tears.

Fran picked up Gigi and carried her to the kitchen, apologising for all she had suffered. The indignity of starvation. As suspected, all the cat food had gone, and there was nothing to eat for either of them. It broke her heart to leave the distraught cat behind and rush down to the supermarket.

On her return, she felt calmer and more in control as she watched Gigi ravenously attack a bowl of food. She made some tea, the first in her pretty handpainted mug bought at a gallery in Corfu. It seemed impossible that that faraway world of the trip was only hours earlier, now the new reality was taking over. She sat on the sofa and wondered what to do with herself. It felt as though the earth had shifted, or at least her sense of what her life could be and what it was now. She had thought she would come back with answers, but she hadn't.

Gigi jumped up and stretched out on the arm of the sofa. She gave Fran a disdainful glance and sharpened her claws on the velour, knowing she wouldn't be scolded. Fran thought about whether the crimes of plant and cat neglect were sufficient to end a relationship. She couldn't assess that until she knew if Louis was still around, and suddenly realised that this uncertainty was one of the things that made her continue to cling to the relationship.

The front door flew open, announcing Louis's arrival. He seemed genuinely shocked to see her, implying that the itinerary was incorrect. As evidence, he showed her the carrier bags in his possession that contained tins of cat food, wine and snacks. He was preparing for her arrival. Normally, she let his typically defensive responses slip by, not wanting to expose his blustering excuses.

'I didn't change my flight. The itinerary is correct,' she said coolly.

'Let's not worry about that. You're here now. That's what counts. Gimme a hug. Let's be friends. I missed you, kittycat.' He sat down beside her on the sofa, pulled her to him and puckered up for a kiss.

She pulled away and had a proper look at him. 'You look like you've been on your own holiday. You didn't get that tan here.'

'Just a quick trip to Spain to have a look around. Check out the lay of the land. You know how it is.'

Fran extricated herself from his embrace. She went into the kitchen for a jug of water, a damp cloth and a moment to compose herself. She was almost certain the outcome of this conversation would be that she was sleeping alone tonight, and every night thereafter. She began to work her way around the flat, attending to each plant and wiping down the surfaces. 'And what did you discover?'

'It's hot. Really bloody hot. The food is a bit . . . spicy. Loads of people can't speak English.'

Fran had the sense that, even though these were the sorts of things Louis might object to, he was avoiding the real issue. 'But Barbara likes it there, does she?'

He couldn't hide his indignation then. 'You bet. She's shagging some hairy ex-footballer. Day and night they were at it. Could hardly leave each other alone. Didn't know where to look, did I.'

Fran smiled. 'So, she's found a Spanish lover . . .'

'Spanish? He's from Birmingham. She's got this huge flat, three bedrooms and terrace and all. Marble floors and whatnot for less than her rent in Clapham. Anyway, two nights there was enough for me.'

In other words, he would have been happy to relocate if the situation had suited him. But it didn't. 'So what are your plans now?' Fran asked.

'My plans are your plans. What do you say, girl? We throw our lot in with each other?'

'I can't help feeling that I'm second prize, Louis. And, as you can imagine, that's not a nice feeling,' she said in measured tones.

'Of course you're not. It's just I'm married to Barb. I owe it to her and the family to try to make that work. But it's bloody clear she doesn't feel that way.' He made a show of wiping his hands of Barb, and fixed Fran with what he obviously imagined was a beguiling smile. 'My home is here, with you. I've always told you that.'

'Have you told Barbara that?'

'Not yet. I will. She won't care. Come on, stop all that cleaning up. Come over here and have a cuddle with your old man.'

Against her better judgement, Fran did as she was told. Louis gave her a long kiss. He smelt of stale sweat and his face was rough with whiskers. He slipped his hand under her shirt and caressed her breasts and she felt herself weaken. She was under no illusions that Louis loved her, but he was fond of her and that was probably the best she could hope for at this stage. They made love on the sofa, much to Gigi's disgust, and Fran wondered if the cat had more insight into the situation than she did.

Afterwards, Fran had a shower and made the bed up with fresh sheets. Louis picked up all his clothes and packed the washing in a laundry bag and took it off to the laundromat, without being asked. Fran felt a fleeting sense of optimism for the two of them. All it had needed was for him to make up his mind. And even if his mind had been made up for him, wasn't it the same thing in the end? She could almost hear Rose and Maggie both disputing this reasoning. But it was different for them. They had a surplus of people in their lives. She had a deficit and couldn't afford to be careless.

By the time Louis returned from the laundromat, she had the flat back in order and they sat down together with a glass of wine and some crackers and cheese. Louis cheerfully suggested that they go out to the pub for dinner, and Fran was acutely aware of how bleak this first evening would have been on her own. Just her and Gigi. It would be nice to go to the pub together. They might become regulars, and people there would know them as a couple.

'I did miss you, darlin' – a whole month,' Louis told her. 'Just me and that cat.' He and the cat exchanged hostile looks. 'You'll never believe what's happened at work. That young lad from head office who came on as manager while Alan was away is now the full-time claims manager. I couldn't believe my ears when I heard . . .' And on he went, giving her a blow-by-blow of everything that had annoyed him since she left.

Fran tried to take an interest in the machinations of the insurance company, but it was a struggle, and it was hard to believe that he wasn't going to ask her anything about her trip apart from, 'Have a good time, did yer?'

Thoughts of the last month, the places they travelled and conversations, good and bad, crowded her mind like a movie she had just seen that kept pushing its way back into her imagination. Her thoughts wandered back to the Blue Moon, that harrowing trip through Italy, and to Verona and the time she shared with Sofia on the train; those honeysuckle hours.

She wondered where Sofia was now and if she had settled into her father's house. That seemed a difficult task to be faced with: the choice to either overlay your parents' life with yours or discard the remains of their life to establish yourself in their place.

Fran considered whether she could have gone home and lived in the flat after her mother died, although it was never an option, because her stepfather lived there still. She felt her mother's presence would always have inhabited those rooms, watching everything she did, reminding her of her clumsiness, carelessness and lack of social skills.

There was nothing Fran could do that approached her mother's level of competence, and she came to expect that tasks would be snatched from her hands and completed with more efficiency than she could ever hope to achieve. Over time, it made her tentative, hesitant, waiting for the sound of her mother's exasperated exhalation. It was years before she realised that her aversion to food was a desperate attempt to be less visible. Her malnourishment, at that critical time of puberty, was the true cause of her being 'petite'. Rose's friendship had, to some extent, made up for her mother's poor opinion. Being Rose's friend was to be a member of an exclusive club, the unbreakable rule being, in Rose's words, 'not being a dick'. Listening to Louis going on and on about this upstart from head office, this lad – who was likely in his forties – Fran realised that Louis could never qualify for Rose's club. He really was a bit of a dick sometimes.

On Monday morning, Fran and Gigi arrived at the shop to find a handwritten sign on the door stating that the business would be shutting its doors after forty years, as Mr Elcombe was apparently retiring. Fran stood in the street and read this sign over and over but it still said the same thing. The shop was closing, not today, but at the end of the month. It seemed incredible that Mr Elcombe had not said anything to her before she went away, but perhaps he didn't know. Of course he knew. It took him months to plan anything and years to execute it. Even the slightest reorganisation of shelves or creation of new categories was like planning a global summit.

She let herself in and released Gigi, who wandered around the shop checking all her favourite nooks and crannies, stalking the length of the counter and stretching each leg, limbering up for her acrobatic leaps from shelf to shelf.

Mr Elcombe insisted that the front door remain shut, so that they would always hear the bell ding when someone came in. Today, Fran opened it wide and let the precious morning sun inside because it didn't really matter what Mr Elcombe thought any more. She dragged in the inevitable boxes of scruffy books that people dumped at the door, too lazy to walk to the Oxfam shop at the end of the block. She would not even bother sorting them today, just take them down there herself when she closed up.

There had been times when she loved working in this shop. She knew almost every title, and where to find it without recourse to the computer. She enjoyed neatening up the shelves after customers carelessly left books lying here and there. She would open books up and inhale the seductive old-book scent that offered the promise of escape. Sometimes she would read a paragraph aloud to herself and, if it intrigued her, would sit by the gas heater with Gigi on her lap and read through cold rainy days when the shop was quiet and Mr Elcombe far away.

There were other times when a true reader came in and she enjoyed discussing books at a deeper level. She had a particular interest in nineteenth- and twentieth-century British literature and found it so rewarding to share her knowledge. Sometimes younger people who had read Greene or Waugh or Orwell might come in and want something else from the era and she could confidently recommend an author they would enjoy. Just last year, a biography of Anthony Powell had been released and there was something approaching a rush of people looking for a second-hand set of his twelve volume *Dance to the Music of Time*. Fran could discuss the Mitford family at length and made a point of regularly re-reading her first Mitford discovery, *Love in a Cold Climate*, never tiring of Nancy Mitford's bracing wit. Fran had met Jessica Mitford briefly at a book signing in Foyles years ago and, as a result, felt a special connection with the family.

American collectors sometimes came in to look at the antiquarian collection, browsing collectables and first editions. There were no bargains – nothing escaped Mr Elcombe's keen eye and she wasn't permitted to negotiate. Occasionally an aspiring author would request she read their manuscript, somehow imagining that she was part of the publishing world. They were mostly dreadful, only occasionally readable, and it was hard to know how much to encourage these writers in their endeavour, but she did her best to be helpful.

The business was dying; she knew that. They had been forced to join the world of online sales in recent years. Dominated by Amazon, the process was fiercely competitive, and had driven prices down. Mr Elcombe was part of the old world of gentlemen book buyers, and he found it difficult to accept that they had to cast in their lot with the dross online. Since the Oxfam store opened nearby last year, selling books at a nominal rate, even fewer people came into the shop.

She wandered the aisles flicking a dusting wand as though casting a spell over these books. Who knew their destiny now? They would be dispersed into the world, wholesaled to other second-hand booksellers around the country.

If she had the money, she would consider buying the business. Perhaps there was something she could do to save it, if she were in charge. Her only foray into business was another reason she had no savings now. Some years ago, she'd inherited a bit of money from Aunt Marie. At that time Fran was in love with a Turkish man who wanted to open a restaurant. He made her a partner in the business and, with her theatre background, gave her *carte blanche* to style and decorate the space. She never tired of the thrill of entering the restaurant with its brocade wall-hangings, clusters of brightly coloured pendant lights and the spicy amalgam of mint, cumin, cinnamon and oregano in the air, knowing she was instrumental in the creation of this concoction. At first the business was a sizzling success but within a year, things went downhill and suddenly it was closed. Worse than closed – went into receivership. And that was that. But, she reasoned philosophically, if she hadn't blown her inheritance on the restaurant, she would have blown it on the bookshop and probably lost it anyway.

At the ding of the bell, she hurried to the front of the shop to find Mr Elcombe bristling with irritation at the door being left wide open. Now it was closed, Fran had a sense of being cut off from the world outside and she realised with surprise how much she disliked him and would be glad to never have to see him again.

'Ah, we're back from our travels, I see,' he said, flicking through the mail. 'I didn't know whether to expect you in today.'

'I said I would be back today and I am extremely reliable.' Fran smiled to soften her words.

He glanced up, giving her an inquisitive look over his glasses, as if he sensed a change in her attitude.

'I saw the sign,' she said. 'We're closing down?'

He took out his brass letter opener and began to slice each envelope open with a sort of fierceness that Fran found disturbing. 'Yes. Indeed. Difficult times.'

She did feel some empathy for him and his situation, a man born in the first year of the Second World War who had devoted his life to books and reading, confronted by the new world of the twenty-first century. He had three sons, none of whom was interested in the business. It must be dreadfully disappointing in the end to have no one to bequeath his business to, and his decades of experience and knowledge no longer of interest to the world.

'Were you going to tell me that I was losing my job?'

'You'll be needed for a good while yet. Everything needs to be sold off, packed up and dispatched. Of course, once we close the doors, money will be tight. So I may not be able to pay your usual rate. But, I'm sure you understand, in the spirit of the thing, sacrifices must be made.'

Fran felt the breath knocked out of her, and imagined Rose's elbow in her ribs. *Tell him to get stuffed. Go on.* Fran heard herself say, 'I'm already on the minimum wage, Mr Elcombe. I'm not sure that's really legal.'

'Legal?' he countered, in a wounded voice. 'We have a lot of history together. I would have thought loyalty comes into the equation somewhere? You're not the sort to exploit the situation, I wouldn't think.'

Fran was stung by the unfairness of his comments. 'Of course not. I'll do whatever I can, but I also need to pay my rent and look for other work. I'm not that young myself any more . . . Perhaps you could ask some of your contacts in the trade. I'd be prepared to go anywhere.'

He gave a sigh of dissatisfaction at being burdened with her problems. 'All I can do is ask.'

He put the paperknife back on its stand and, picking up the

letters, walked off down to his office, leaving the envelopes scattered on the counter for Fran to dispose of. She imagined herself stalking behind him into the gloom at the back of the shop, holding the paperknife aloft, and . . .

She picked up the discarded envelopes and put them in the box for recycling. Gigi jumped softly onto the counter and offered her arched spine for comfort stroking, her tail held upright like a banner with a kink. Lost in thought, Fran stroked her with strong gentle strokes and whispered, 'You won't be out of a home, my darling. You'll come with me.'

When she told Louis that evening, he looked disconcerted. 'He should be giving you redundancy pay,' he said. 'Not trying to get out of paying you. Bastard.'

Fran sipped her wine but it only added to the dull feeling she had. If anything, the trip had made things worse because she had come back with this fragile sense of possibility, the idea that something magical might occur. Now she felt crushed. 'I don't think there's any hope of that —'

'Take him to court. That's what you've got to do, love.'

'Louis, I have to find a new flat and a new job in the next few months. I don't have the money or the inclination to take anyone to court. We could both live at your place for a while. And if that worked out —'

'I gave up my place months ago. I thought I told you.'

'Months ago? I don't understand. So, where have you been living?'

He looked guilty then, and couldn't meet her eye. 'Well, I was at Barb's for a bit . . .'

'So the reason you offered to mind my place was because Barbara left for Spain and you had nowhere else to live? Louis, please tell me that you weren't getting straight out of my bed and into hers.'

'Don't be like that. I didn't know what I was going to do. Hadn't made me mind up, had I? Now, it's you and me. All good. We'll get a place together. You'll find a new job. Before you know it, we'll be pensioners. We can potter around together. Go on day trips and all that.'

Fran felt ill. It seemed that her whole life had been lead-ing to this point, where the only option left to her was Louis and his self-interested half-truths, until death did them part. She wanted nothing to do with that dreary future and felt a deep sense of despair settle on her. There must be some other possibility.

Louis read the doubt in her eyes. He was eager to please now and even offered to make dinner. Fran cleared the bench for him and placed her new mug well out of reach. While he was banging around in the kitchen, manufacturing a convivial atmosphere, she started up her laptop to check her emails for the first time in a month.

She skimmed through the inbox, deleting as she went. As she sent one from an unfamiliar address to trash, she noticed it was written in German and retrieved it.

Dear Fran,
I very much enjoyed our time together on the train. It seemed fated that we spoke a common language and found ourselves in that confined space together for some hours. It seemed to me that we shared an affinity and there was a

sense that we had known each other for an eternity – perhaps in a past life, although sadly neither of us believe in that idea.

I am living in my father's house now. I couldn't describe it as settled. There is a lot to do and I'm not sure how or where to start. The villa is beautiful, as I told you, with big dark rooms that are cool in summer and a garden full of places to sit and have an aperitif surrounded by the orange grove. But the truth is I feel isolated and lonely. I don't know how to start my life here, all on my own.

You may have forgotten me, and not given me further thought, especially with your extroverted companions and upcoming adventures. But I have thought of our conversation often.

I wonder if you would like to come here and stay with me? Not just for a week but for a good long time. What do you think? Perhaps it is foolish to imagine that you might wish to live in Italy and share a house with someone you barely know. But I do have the feeling that I must take this chance and ask you the question.

You may not be free to come, you may not be willing to take such a risk, but, if the idea appeals to you, let me know. You can bring your belongings, and Gigi is welcome too.

Yours, Sofia

PS Even if you decide it's not for you, there is a retrospective exhibition of Marta Wolfgang's work in Paris in September – perhaps we could go there together? I would be glad to have your company.

The postscript was blurred by Fran's tears. Was it possible? She was afraid to touch the keyboard in case she deleted the email. That was too silly. She had Sofia's email address on a note in her bag. But if this was deleted, would she believe it had existed? It seemed so fragile and beautiful. Like a missive from a future that was beyond her wildest dreams.

'Is there any soy sauce, love?' Louis called from the kitchen.

'In the cupboard. Just open it and have a look.'

In the silence that followed, she rested her fingers lightly, hesitantly, on the keyboard. It felt as though her current life was a powerful magnet pulling her away, dragging her into the kitchen to find the soy sauce, condemning her to this dismal alliance and eternal pottering hell. She braced herself against its power, hunched her full weight over the keyboard and tapped each key, slowly and deliberately. *I will come. I will come very soon.*

And she heard the whoosh as it flew to Italy, to Sofia and to her future life.

Acknowledgements

A big thank you to Jan Wasey and Trish Canny for sharing their memories and travel tales, and to Tess Mallos for consulting on Greek references and Hannah Sandow on German phraseology. Special thanks to Uwe Studtrucker for your support and forty years of friendship, which began on a Greek island in 1978.

Thank you so much to my generous friends for their continued support and constructive criticism on early drafts: Tula Wynyard, Tracey Trinder, Helen Thurloe, Joseph Furolo and Catherine Hersom-Bowens.

Thank you also to the fabulous team at Penguin Random House: Ali Watts, Saskia Adams, Amanda Martin, Nerrilee Weir, Sonja Heijn, Nikki Townsend and Louise Ryan.